A Delicate Truth

A Delicate Truth

JOHN LE CARRÉ

VIKING

VIKING
an imprint of Penguin Canada

Published by the Penguin Group
Penguin Group (Canada), 90 Eglinton Avenue East, Suite 700, Toronto,
Ontario, Canada M4P 2Y3

Penguin Group (USA) Inc., 375 Hudson Street, New York, New York 10014, U.S.A.
Penguin Books Ltd, 80 Strand, London WC2R 0RL, England
Penguin Ireland, 25 St Stephen's Green, Dublin 2, Ireland (a division of Penguin Books Ltd)
Penguin Group (Australia), 707 Collins Street, Melbourne, Victoria 3008, Australia
 (a division of Pearson Australia Group Pty Ltd)
Penguin Books India Pvt Ltd, 11 Community Centre, Panchsheel Park, New Delhi – 110 017,
India
Penguin Group (NZ), 67 Apollo Drive, Rosedale, Auckland 0632, New Zealand
 (a division of Pearson New Zealand Ltd)
Penguin Books (South Africa) (Pty) Ltd, 24 Sturdee Avenue, Rosebank, Johannesburg 2196,
South Africa

Penguin Books Ltd, Registered Offices: 80 Strand, London WC2R 0RL, England

Published in Viking hardcover by Penguin Group (Canada), 2013. Simultaneously published in
the U.S.A. by Viking, a division of Penguin Group (USA).

 2 3 4 5 6 7 8 9 10 (RRD)

Copyright © David Cornwell, 2013

Manufactured in the U.S.A.

Library and Archives Canada Cataloguing in Publication data available upon request to the
publisher.

ISBN: 978-0-670-06716-9
British Library Cataloguing in Publication data available
American Library of Congress Cataloging in Publication data available

Visit the Penguin Canada website at **www.penguin.ca**

Special and corporate bulk purchase rates available; please see **www.penguin.ca/
corporatesales** or call 1-800-810-3104, ext. 2477.

For VJC

No winter shall abate the spring's increase

Donne

If one tells the truth, one is sure, sooner or later, to be found out.

Oscar Wilde

I.

On the second floor of a characterless hotel in the British Crown Colony of Gibraltar, a lithe, agile man in his late fifties restlessly paced his bedroom. His very British features, though pleasant and plainly honourable, indicated a choleric nature brought to the limit of its endurance. A distraught lecturer, you might have thought, observing the bookish forward lean and loping stride and the errant forelock of salt-and-pepper hair that repeatedly had to be disciplined with jerky back-handed shoves of the bony wrist. Certainly it would not have occurred to many people, even in their most fanciful dreams, that he was a middle-ranking British civil servant, hauled from his desk in one of the more prosaic departments of Her Majesty's Foreign and Commonwealth Office to be dispatched on a top-secret mission of acute sensitivity.

His assumed first name, as he insisted on repeating to himself, sometimes half aloud, was Paul and his second – not exactly hard to remember – was Anderson. If he turned on the television set it said *Welcome, Mr Paul Anderson. Why not enjoy a complimentary pre-dinner aperitif in our Lord Nelson's Snug!* The exclamation mark in place of the more appropriate question mark was a source of constant annoyance to the pedant in him. He was wearing the hotel's bathrobe of white towelling and he had been wearing it ever since his incarceration, except when vainly trying to sleep or, once only, slinking upstairs at an unsociable hour to eat alone in a rooftop brasserie washed with the fumes of chlorine from a third-floor swimming pool across the road. Like much else in the room, the bathrobe, too short

I

for his long legs, reeked of stale cigarette smoke and lavender air freshener.

As he paced, he determinedly acted out his feelings to himself without the restraints customary in his official life, his features one moment cramped in honest perplexity, the next glowering in the full-length mirror that was screwed to the tartan wallpaper. Here and there he spoke to himself by way of relief or exhortation. Also half aloud? What was the difference when you were banged up in an empty room with nobody to listen to you but a colour-tinted photograph of our dear young Queen on a brown horse?

On a plastic-topped table lay the remnants of a club sandwich that he had pronounced dead on arrival, and an abandoned bottle of warm Coca-Cola. Though it came hard to him, he had permitted himself no alcohol since he had taken possession of the room. The bed, which he had learned to detest as no other, was large enough for six, but he had only to stretch out on it for his back to give him hell. A radiant crimson counterpane of imitation silk lay over it, and on the counterpane an innocent-looking cellphone which he had been assured was modified to the highest state of encryption and, though he was of little faith in such matters, he could only suppose it was. Each time he passed it, his gaze fixed on it with a mixture of reproach, longing and frustration.

I regret to inform you, Paul, that you will be totally incommunicado, save for operational purposes, throughout your mission, the laborious South African voice of Elliot, his self-designated field commander, is warning him. *Should an unfortunate crisis afflict your fine family during your absence they will pass their concerns to your office's welfare department, whereupon contact with you will be made. Do I make myself clear, Paul?*

You do, Elliot, little by little you do.

Reaching the overlarge picture window at the further end of

the room, he scowled upward through the grimy net curtains at Gibraltar's legendary Rock which, sallow, wrinkled and remote, scowled back at him like an angry dowager. Yet again, out of habit and impatience, he examined his alien wristwatch and compared it with the green numerals on the radio clock beside the bed. The watch was of battered steel with a black dial, a replacement for the gold Cartier presented to him on their twenty-fifth by his beloved wife on the strength of an inheritance from one of her many deceased aunts.

But hang on a minute! *Paul hasn't got a bloody wife!* Paul Anderson has no wife, no daughter. Paul Anderson's a bloody hermit!

'Can't have you wearing *that*, Paul darling, can we now?' a motherly woman his own age is saying to him a lifetime ago in the red-brick suburban villa near Heathrow airport where she and her sisterly colleague are dressing him for the part. 'Not with those nice initials engraved on it, can we? You'd have to say you'd nicked it off of somebody married, wouldn't you, Paul?'

Sharing the joke, determined as ever to be a good chap by his own lights, he looks on while she writes *Paul* on an adhesive label and locks his gold watch away in a cash box with his wedding ring for what she calls *the duration*.

*

How in God's name did I ever get to end up in this hellhole in the first place?

Did I jump or was I pushed? Or was it a bit of both?

Describe, please, in a few well-chosen circuits of the room, the precise circumstances of your unlikely journey from blessed monotony to solitary confinement on a British colonial rock.

*

'So how's your poor dear wife?' asks the not-quite-superannuated ice queen of Personnel Department, now grandly rechristened

3

Human Resources for no reason known to man, having summoned him without a word of explanation to her lofty bower on a Friday evening when all good citizens are hurrying home. The two are old adversaries. If they have anything at all in common, it is the feeling that there are so few of them left.

'Thank you, Audrey, not poor at all, I am pleased to say,' he replies, with the determined levity he affects for such life-threatening encounters. 'Dear but not poor. She remains in full remission. And you? In the pink of health, I trust?'

'So she's leavable,' Audrey suggests, ignoring this kindly enquiry.

'My hat no! In what sense?' – determinedly keeping up the jolly banter.

'In this sense: would four super-secret days abroad in a salubrious climate, just *possibly* running to five, be of any interest to you?'

'They could be of considerable possible interest, thank you, Audrey, as it happens. Our grown-up daughter is living with us at the moment, so the timing could scarcely be better, given that she happens to be a *medical doctor*,' he can't resist adding in his pride, but Audrey remains unimpressed by his daughter's accomplishment.

'I don't know what it's about and I don't have to,' she says, answering a question that he hasn't put to her. 'There's a dynamic young junior minister called Quinn upstairs whom you may have heard of. He'd like to see you immediately. He's a new broom, in case word hasn't reached you in the far wastes of Logistical Contingencies, recently acquired from Defence – hardly a recommendation but there you are.'

What on earth's she on about? Of *course* such news has reached him. He reads his newspapers, doesn't he? He watches *Newsnight*. Fergus Quinn, MP, Fergie to the world, is a Scottish brawler, a self-styled *bête intellectuelle* of the New Labour stable. On television he is vocal, belligerent and alarming. Moreover, he prides himself on being the people's scourge of Whitehall's bureaucracy – a commendable virtue viewed from afar, but scarcely reassuring if you happen to be a Whitehall bureaucrat.

'You mean *now*, this minute, Audrey?'

'That is what I understand him to mean by *immediately*.'

The ministerial anteroom is empty, its staff long departed. The ministerial mahogany door, solid as iron, stands ajar. Knock and wait? Or knock and push? He does a little of both, hears: 'Don't just stand there. Come on in, and close the door behind you.' He enters.

The dynamic young minister's bulk is squeezed into a midnight-blue dinner jacket. He is poised with a cellphone to his ear before a marble fireplace stuffed with red paper foil for flames. As on television, so in the flesh, he is stocky and thick-necked with close-cropped ginger hair and quick, greedy eyes set in a pugilist's face.

Behind him rises a twelve-foot portrait of an eighteenth-century Empire-builder in tights. For a mischievous moment brought on by tension, the comparison between the two such different men is irresistible. Though Quinn strenuously purports to be a man of the people, both have the pout of privileged discontent. Both have their body weight on one leg and the other knee cocked. Is the dynamic young minister about to launch a punitive raid on the hated French? Will he, in the name of New Labour, berate the folly of the howling mob? He does neither, but with a gritty 'Call you later, Brad' for his cellphone, stomps to the door, locks it and swings round.

'They tell me you're a *seasoned member of the Service*, that right?' he says accusingly, in his carefully nurtured Glaswegian accent, after a head-to-toe inspection that seems to confirm his worst fears. '*Cool head*, whatever that means. Twenty years of *kicking around in foreign parts*, according to Human Resources. *Soul of discretion, not easily rattled*. That's quite a write-up. Not that I necessarily believe what I'm told around here.'

'They're very kind,' he replies.

'And you're grounded. Confined to barracks. Out to grass. Your wife's health has kept you back, is that correct, please?'

'But only as of the last few years, Minister' – less than grateful for *out to grass* – 'and for the moment I'm quite at liberty to travel, I'm happy to say.'

'And your present job is –? Remind me, please.'

He is about to do so, emphasizing his many indispensable responsibilities, but the minister impatiently cuts him short:

'All right. Here's my question. Have you had any direct experience of secret intelligence work? You *personally*,' he warns, as if there is another you who is less personal.

'*Direct* in what sense would that be, Minister?'

'Cloak-and-dagger stuff, what d'you think?'

'Only as a consumer, alas. An occasional one. Of the product. Not of the means of obtaining it, if that's your question, Minister.'

'Not even when you were kicking around in those foreign parts that nobody has had the grace to itemize for me?'

'Alas, one's overseas postings tended to be largely economic, commercial or consular,' he explains, resorting to the linguistic archaisms he affects whenever he feels threatened. 'Obviously, from time to time, one had access to the odd secret report – none of it high level, I hasten to say. That, I'm afraid, is the long and short of it.'

But the minister appears momentarily encouraged by this lack of conspiratorial experience, for a smile of something like complacency flits across his broad features.

'But you're a safe pair of hands, right? Untried maybe, but safe, for all that.'

'Well, one likes to think so' – diffidently.

'CT ever come your way?'

'I'm sorry?'

'Counter-terrorism, man! Has it come your way or not?' – spoken as to an idiot.

'I fear not, Minister.'

'But you *care*? Yes?'

'About what exactly, Minister?' – as helpfully as he may.

'The well-being of our nation, for Christ's sake! The safety of our people, wheresoever they may be. Our core values in times of adversity. All right, our *heritage*, if you like' – using the word like an anti-Tory swipe. 'You're not some limp-wristed closet liberal harbouring secret thoughts about terrorists' right to blow the fucking world to pieces, for example.'

'No, Minister, I think I may safely say I am not,' he mumbles.

But the minister, far from sharing his embarrassment, compounds it:

'So then. If I were to tell you that the extremely delicate assignment I have in mind for you involves depriving the terrorist enemy of the means to launch a premeditated assault on our homeland, you would *not* immediately walk away, I take it?'

'To the contrary. I should be – well –'

'You should be *what*?'

'Gratified. Privileged. Proud, in fact. But somewhat surprised, obviously.'

'Surprised by *what*, pray?' – like a man insulted.

'Well, not mine to enquire, Minister, but why me? I'm sure the Office has its fair share of people with the type of experience you're looking for.'

Fergus Quinn, man of the people, swings away to the bay window and, with his chin thrust aggressively forward over his evening tie, and the tie's fixing awkwardly protruding from the cushions of flesh at the back of his neck, contemplates the

7

golden gravel of Horse Guards Parade in the evening sunlight.

'If I were *further* to tell you that for the remainder of your natural life you will not by word or deed or any other means reveal the fact that a certain counter-terror operation was so much as *considered*, let alone executed' – casting round indignantly for a way out of the verbal labyrinth he has talked himself into – 'does that turn you *on* or *off*?'

'Minister, if you consider me the right man, I shall be happy to accept the assignment, whatever it may be. And you have my solemn assurance of permanent and absolute discretion,' he insists, colouring up a bit in his irritation at having his loyalty hauled out and examined before his own eyes.

Shoulders hunched in the best Churchillian mode, Quinn remains framed at the bay window, as if waiting impatiently for the photographers to finish their work.

'There are certain *bridges* that have to be negotiated,' he announces severely to his own reflection. 'There's a certain *green light* that has to be given by some fairly crucial people up and down the road there' – butting his bullish head in the direction of Downing Street. 'When we get it – if we do and not until – you'll be informed. Thereafter, and for such time as I deem appropriate, you will be my eyes and ears on the ground. No sweetening the pill, you understand? None of your Foreign Office obfuscation or persiflage. Not on *my* watch, thank you. You'll give it me *straight*, exactly the way you see it. The cool view, through the eyes of the old pro which I am to believe you to be. Are you hearing me?'

'Perfectly, Minister. I hear you and I understand exactly what you are saying' – his own voice, speaking to him from a distant cloud.

'Have you got any *Pauls* in your family?'

'I'm sorry, Minister?'

'Jesus Christ! It's a simple enough question, isn't it? Is any

8

man in your family named *Paul*? Yes or no. Brother, father, what do I know?'

'None. Not a Paul in sight, I'm afraid.'

'And no *Paulines*? The female version. *Paulette*, or whatever?'

'Definitely none.'

'How about *Anderson*? No Andersons around at all? Maiden name, Anderson?'

'Again, not to my knowledge, Minister.'

'And you're in reasonable nick. Physically. A stiff walk over rugged terrain isn't going to cause you to go faint at the knees in the manner that certain others around here might be afflicted?'

'I walk energetically. And I'm a keen gardener' – from the same distant cloud.

'Wait for a call from a man named Elliot. Elliot will be your first indication.'

'And would Elliot be his surname or given name, I wonder?' he hears himself enquire soothingly, as if of a maniac.

'How the fuck should I know? He's operating in total secrecy under the aegis of an organization best known as Ethical Outcomes. New boys on the block, and up there with the best in the field, I'm assured on expert advice.'

'Forgive me, Minister. What field would that be, exactly?'

'Private defence contractors. Where've you been? Name of the game these days. War's gone corporate, in case you haven't noticed. Standing professional armies are a bust. Top-heavy, under-equipped, one brigadier for every dozen boots on the ground, and cost a mint. Try a couple of years at Defence if you don't believe me.'

'Oh I do, Minister' – startled by this wholesale dismissal of British arms, but anxious to humour the man nonetheless.

'You're trying to flog your house. Right? Harrow or somewhere.'

'Harrow is correct' – now past surprise – 'North Harrow.'

'Cash problems?'

'Oh no, far from it, I'm thankful to say!' he exclaims, grateful to be returned if only momentarily to earth. 'I have a little bit of my own, and my wife has come into a modest inheritance which includes a country property. We plan to sell our present house while the market holds, and live small until we make the move.'

'Elliot will say he wants to buy your house in Harrow. He won't say he's from Ethical or anywhere else. He's seen the ads in the estate agent's window or wherever, looked it over from the outside, likes it, but there are issues he needs to discuss. He'll suggest a place and time to meet. You're to go along with whatever he proposes. That's the way these people work. Any further questions?'

Has he asked any?

'Meantime, you play totally normal man. Not a word to any-one. Not here in the Office, not at home. Is that clearly understood?'

Not understood. Not from Adam. But a wholehearted, mys-tified 'yes' to all of it, and no very clear memory of how he got home that night, after a restorative Friday-evening visit to his Pall Mall club.

*

Bowed over his computer while wife and daughter chatter mer-rily in the next room, Paul Anderson elect searches for Ethical Outcomes. *Do you mean Ethical Outcomes Incorporated of Hous-ton, Texas?* For want of other information, yes, he does.

With our brand-new international team of uniquely qualified geo-political thinkers, we at Ethical offer innovative, insightful, cutting-edge analyses of risk assessment to major corporate and national entities. At Ethical we pride ourselves on our integrity, due diligence, and up-to-the-minute cyber skills. Close protection and hostage negotiators available at immediate notice. Marlon will respond to your personal and confidential inquiries.

Email address and box number also in Houston, Texas. Free-phone number for your personal and confidential enquiries of Marlon. No names of directors, officers, advisors or uniquely qualified geopolitical thinkers. No Elliot, first name or surname. The parent company of Ethical Outcomes is Spencer Hardy Holdings, a multinational corporation whose interests include oil, wheat, timber, beef, property development and not-for-profit initiatives. The same parent company also endows evangelical foundations, faith schools and Bible missions.

For further information about Ethical Outcomes, enter your key-code. Possessing no such key-code, and assailed by a sense of trespass, he abandons his researches.

A week passes. Each morning over breakfast, all day long in the office, each evening when he comes home from work, he plays Totally Normal Man as instructed, and waits for the great call that may or may not come, or come when it's least expected: which is what it does early one morning while his wife is sleeping off her medication and he's pottering in the kitchen in his check shirt and corduroys washing up last night's supper things and telling himself he really must get a hold of that back lawn. The phone rings, he picks it up, gives a cheery 'Good morning' and it's Elliot, who, sure enough, has seen the ads in the estate agent's window and is seriously interested in buying the house.

Except that his name isn't Elliot but *Illiot*, thanks to the South African accent.

*

Is Elliot one of Ethical Outcomes' *brand-new international team of uniquely qualified geopolitical thinkers*? It's possible, though not apparent. In the bare office in a poky side street off Paddington

Street Gardens where the two men sit a mere ninety minutes later, Elliot wears a sober Sunday suit and a striped tie with baby parachutes on it. Cabalistic rings adorn the three fattest fingers of his manicured left hand. He has a shiny cranium, is olive-skinned, pockmarked and disturbingly muscular. His gaze, now quizzing his guest in flirtatious flicks, now slipping sideways at the grimy walls, is colourless. His spoken English is so elaborate you'd think it was being marked for accuracy and pronunciation.

Extracting a nearly new British passport from a drawer, Elliot licks his thumb and flips officiously through its pages.

'Manila, Singapore, Dubai: these are but a few of the fine cities where you have attended statisticians' conferences. Do you understand that, Paul?'

Paul understands that.

'Should a nosy individual sitting next to you on the plane enquire what takes you to Gibraltar, you tell them it's yet another statisticians' conference. After that you tell them to mind their fucking business. Gibraltar does a strong line in Internet gambling, not all of it kosher. The gambling bosses don't like their little people talking out of turn. I must now ask you, Paul, very frankly, please, do you have any concerns whatever regarding your personal cover?'

'Well, maybe just the one concern actually, Elliot, yes, I do,' he admits, after due consideration.

'Name it, Paul. Feel free.'

'It's just that being a Brit – *and* a foreign servant who's been around the halls a bit – entering a prime British territory as a *different* Brit – well, it's a bit' – hunting for a word – 'a bit bloody *iffy*, frankly.'

Elliot's small, circular eyes return to him, staring but not blinking.

'I mean, couldn't I just go as myself and take my chances? We both know I'm going to have to lie low. But *should* it happen that, *contrary* to our best calculations, I *do* bump into someone I know, or someone who knows me, more to the point, then at least I can be who I am. Me, I mean. Instead of –'

'Instead of what exactly, Paul?'

'Well, instead of pretending to be some phoney statistician called Paul Anderson. I mean, who's ever going to believe a cock-and-bull story like that, if they know perfectly well who I am? I mean, honestly, Elliot' – feeling the heat coming into his face and not able to stop it – 'Her Majesty's Government has got a bloody great tri-Services headquarters in Gibraltar. Not to mention a substantial Foreign Office presence and a king-sized listening station. *And* a Special Forces training camp. It only takes one chap we haven't thought of to jump out of the woodwork and embrace me as a long-lost chum and I'm – well, scuppered. And what do I know about statistics, come to that? Bugger all. Don't mean to question your expertise, Elliot. And of course I'll do whatever it takes. Just asking.'

'Is that the complete sum of your anxieties, Paul?' Elliot enquires solicitously.

'Of course. Absolutely. Just making the point.' And wishing he hadn't, but how the hell d'you throw logic out of the window?

Elliot moistens his lips, frowns, and in carefully fractured English replies as follows:

'It is a *fact*, Paul, that nobody in Gibraltar will give a five-dollar fuck who you are for as long as you flash your British passport at them and keep your head below the horizon at all times. However: it's your balls that will be in the direct line of fire, should we strike worst-case scenario, which it is my bounden duty to consider. Let us take the hypothetical case of the operation aborting in a manner not foreseen by its expert planners of whom I pride myself as being one. Was there an inside man? they may ask. And who is this scholarly wanker Anderson who skulked in his hotel room reading books all day and all night? – they will start to wonder. Where is this Anderson to be found, in a colony no bigger than a fucking golf course? If that situation were to arise, I suspect you'd be grateful indeed not to have been the person you are in reality. Happy now, Paul?'

Happy as a sandboy, Elliot. Couldn't be happier. Totally out of my element, whole thing like a dream, but with you all the way. But then, noticing that Elliot looks a bit put out, and fearing that the detailed briefing he is about to receive will kick off on a bad note, he goes for a bit of bonding:

'So where does a highly qualified chap like *you* fit into the scheme of things, if I may ask without being intrusive, Elliot?'

Elliot's voice acquires the sanctimoniousness of the pulpit:

'I sincerely thank you for that question, Paul. I am a man of arms; it is my life. I have fought wars large and small, mostly on the continent of Africa. During these exploits I was fortunate enough to encounter a man whose sources of intelligence are legendary, not to say uncanny. His worldwide contacts speak to him as to no other in the safe knowledge that he will use their information in the furtherance of democratic principles and liberty. *Operation Wildlife*, the details of which I shall now unveil to you, is his personal brainchild.'

And it is Elliot's proud statement that elicits the obvious, if sycophantic, question:

'And may one ask, Elliot, whether this great man has a name?'

'Paul, you are now and for evermore family. I will therefore tell you without restraint that the founder and driving force of Ethical Outcomes is a gentleman whose name, in strictest confidence, is Mr Jay Crispin.'

★

Return to Harrow by black cab.

Elliot says, *From now on, keep all receipts*. Pay off cabbie, keep receipt.

Google Jay Crispin.

Jay is nineteen and lives in Paignton, Devon. She is a waitress.

J. Crispin, Veneer Makers, began life in Shoreditch in 1900.

Jay Crispin auditions for models, actors, musicians and dancers.

But of Jay Crispin, the driving force of Ethical Outcomes and mastermind of *Operation Wildlife*, not a glimpse.

*

Stuck once more at the overlarge window of his hotel prison, the man who must call himself Paul emitted a weary string of mindless obscenities, more in the modern way than his own. *Fuck* – then *double fuck*. Then more *fucks*, loosed off in a bored patter of gunfire aimed at the cellphone on the bed and ending with an appeal – *Ring, you little bugger, ring* – only to discover that somewhere inside or outside his head the same cellphone, no longer mute, was chirruping back at him with its infuriating *diddly-ah, diddly-ah, diddly-ah dee-dah-doh.*

He remained at the window, frozen in disbelief. It's next-door's fat Greek with a beard, singing in the shower. It's those horny lovers upstairs: he's grunting, she's howling, I'm hallucinating.

Then all he wanted in the world was to go to sleep and wake up when it was over. But by then he was at the bed, clutching the encrypted cellphone to his ear but, out of some aberrant sense of security, not speaking.

'Paul? Are you there, Paul? It's me. *Kirsty*, remember?'

Kirsty the part-time minder he'd never set eyes on. Her voice the only thing he knew about her: pert, imperious, and the rest of her imagined. Sometimes he wondered whether he detected a smothered Australian accent – a pair to Elliot's South African. And sometimes he wondered what kind of body the voice might have, and at others whether it had a body at all.

Already he could catch its sharpened tone, its air of portent:

'You still okay up there, Paul?'

'Very much so, Kirsty. You, too, I trust?'

'Ready for some night-birding, owls a speciality?'

It was part of Paul Anderson's fatuous cover that his hobby was ornithology.

'Then here's the update. It's all systems go. Tonight. The *Rosemaria* left harbour bound for Gib five hours ago. *Aladdin* has booked his on-board guests into the Chinese on the Queensway Marina for a big lash-up tonight. He's going to settle his guests in, then slide off on his own. His tryst with *Punter* confirmed for 2330. How's about I pick you up from your hotel at 2100 hours cold? That's 9 p.m. on the dot. Yes?'

'When do I join up with Jeb?'

'As soon as maybe, Paul,' she retorted, with the extra edge in her voice for whenever the name Jeb was mentioned between them. 'It's all arranged. Your friend Jeb will be waiting. You dress for the birds. You do *not* check out. Agreed?'

It had been agreed all of two days ago.

'You bring your passport and your wallet. You pack up your possessions nicely, but you leave them in your room. You hand your room key in at the desk like you're going to be back late. Want to stand on the hotel steps so's you don't have to hang around the lobby and get stared at by the tour groups?'

'Fine. I'll do that. Good idea.'

They'd agreed that, too.

'Look out for a blue Toyota four-by-four, shiny, new. Red sign on the passenger-side windscreen saying CONFERENCE.'

For the third time since he had arrived, she insisted they compare watches, which he considered a needless excursion in these

16

days of quartz, until he realized he'd been doing the same thing with the bedside clock. One hour and fifty-two minutes to go.

She had rung off. He was back in solitary. Is it really me? Yes, it is. It's me the safe pair of hands, and they're sweating.

He peered round him with a prisoner's perplexity, taking stock of the cell that had become his home: the books he had brought with him and hadn't been able to read a line of. Simon Schama on the French Revolution. Montefiore's biography of Jerusalem: by now, in better circumstances, he'd have devoured them both. The handbook of Mediterranean birds they'd forced on him. His eye drifted to his arch-enemy: The Chair That Smelt Of Piss. He'd sat half of last night in it after the bed had ejected him. Sit in it one more time? Treat himself to another watch of *The Dam Busters*? Or might Laurence Olivier's *Henry V* do a better job of persuading the God of Battles to steel his soldier's heart? Or how about another spot of Vatican-censored soft porn to get the old juices flowing?

Yanking open the rickety wardrobe, he fished out Paul Anderson's green wheelie-bag plastered with travel labels and set to work packing into it the junk that made up an itinerant bird-watching statistician's fictional identity. Then he sat on the bed watching the encrypted phone recharge, because he had an unappeasable fear it would run out on him at the crucial moment.

*

In the lift a middle-aged couple in green blazers asked him if he came from Liverpool. Alas, he didn't. Then was he one of the group? Afraid not: what group would that be? But by then his posh voice and eccentric outdoor gear were enough for them and they left him to himself.

Arriving at the ground floor, he stepped into a seething, howling hubbub of humanity. Amid festoons of green ribbon and balloons, a flashing sign proclaimed St Patrick's Day. An accordion was screeching out Irish folk music. Burly men and women in green Guinness bonnets were dancing. A drunken woman with her bonnet askew seized his head, kissed him on the lips and told him he was her lovely boy.

Jostling and apologizing, he fought his way to the hotel steps, where a cluster of guests stood waiting for their cars. He took a deep breath and caught the scents of bay and honey mingled with the oil fumes. Above him, the shrouded stars of a Mediterranean night. He was dressed as he'd been told to dress: stout boots, and don't forget your anorak, Paul, the Med at night gets nippy. And zipped over his heart in the anorak's inside pocket, his super-encrypted cellphone. He could feel its weight on his left nipple – which didn't prevent his fingers from making their own furtive exploration.

A shiny Toyota four-by-four had joined the queue of arriving cars, and yes it was blue and yes there was a red sign saying CONFERENCE on the passenger side of the windscreen. Two white faces up front, the driver male, bespectacled and young. The girl compact and efficient, leaping out like a yachtswoman, hauling back the side door.

'You're Arthur, right?' she yelled in best Australian.

'No, I'm Paul, actually.'

'Oh right, you're Paul! Sorry about that. Arthur's next stop. I'm Kirsty. Great to meet you, Paul. Hop right in!'

Agreed safety formula. Typical over-production, but never mind. He hopped, and was alone on the rear seat. The side door slammed shut and the four-by-four nosed its way between the white gateposts, on to the cobbled road.

'And this here's Hansi,' Kirsty said over the back of her seat. 'Hansi's part of the team. "Ever watchful" – right, Hansi? That's his motto. Want to say hullo to the gentleman, Hansi?'

'Welcome aboard, Paul,' said Ever-Watchful Hansi, without

turning his head. Could be an American voice, could be German. War's gone corporate.

They were driving between high stone walls and he was drinking in every sight and sound at once: the blare of jazz from a passing bar, the obese English couples quaffing tax-free booze at their outdoor tables, the tattoo parlour with its embroidered torso in low-slung jeans, the barber's shop with sixties hairstyles, the bowed old man in a yarmulke wheeling a baby's pram, and the curio shop selling statuettes of greyhounds, flamenco dancers, and Jesus and his disciples.

Kirsty had turned to examine him by the passing lights. Her bony face, freckled from the outback. Short, dark hair tucked into the bush hat. No make-up, and nothing behind the eyes: or nothing for him. The jaw crammed into the crook of her forearm while she gave him the once-over. The body indecipherable under the bulk of a quilted bush jacket.

'Left everything in your room, Paul? Like we told you?'

'All packed up, as you said.'

'Including the bird book?'

'Including it.'

Into a dark side street, washing slung across it. Decrepit shutters, crumbling plaster, graffiti demanding BRITS GO HOME! Back into the blaze of city lights.

'And you didn't check out of your room? By mistake or something?'

'The lobby was chock-a-block. I couldn't have checked out if I'd tried.'

'How about the room key?'

In my bloody pocket. Feeling an idiot, he dropped it into her waiting hand and watched her pass it to Hansi.

'We're doing the tour, right? Elliot says to show you the facts on the ground, so's you have the visual image.'

'Fine.'

'We're heading for Upper Rock, so we're taking in the Queensway Marina on the way. That's the *Rosemaria* out there now. She arrived an hour ago. See it?'

'See it.'

'That's where *Aladdin* always anchors, and those are his personal steps to the dockside. Nobody's allowed to use them except him: he has property interests in the colony. He's still aboard, and his guests are running late, still powdering their noses before they go ashore for their slap-up dinner at the Chinese. Everybody eyeballs the *Rosemaria*, so you can, too. Just keep it relaxed. There's no law says you can't take a relaxed look at a thirty-million-dollar super-yacht.'

Was it the excitement of the chase? Or just the relief of being got out of prison? Or was it the simple prospect of serving his country in a way he'd never dreamed of? Whatever it was, a wave of patriotic fervour swept over him as centuries of British imperial conquest received him. The statues to great admirals and generals, the cannons, redoubts, bastions, the bruised air-raid precaution signs directing our stoical defenders to their nearest shelter, the Gurkha-style warriors standing guard with fixed bayonets outside the Governor's residence, the bobbies in their baggy British uniforms: he was heir to all of it. Even the dismal rows of fish-and-chip shops built into elegant Spanish façades were like a homecoming.

A flash-glimpse of cannons, then of war memorials, one British, one American. Welcome to Ocean Village, hellish canyon of apartment blocks with balconies of blue glass for ocean waves. Enter a private road with gates and a guard-box, no sign of a guard. Below, a forest of white masts, a ceremonial, carpeted landing bay, a row of boutiques and the Chinese restaurant where *Aladdin* has booked his slap-up dinner.

And out to sea in all her splendour, the *Rosemaria*, lit overall with fairy lights. The windows on her middle deck blacked out.

The salon windows translucent. Burly men hovering among the empty tables. Alongside her, at the foot of a gold-plated ship's ladder, a sleek motorboat with two crew in white uniforms waiting to ferry *Aladdin* and his guests ashore.

'*Aladdin* is basically a mixed-race Pole who has taken out Lebanese citizenship,' Elliot is explaining, in the little room in Paddington. '*Aladdin* is the Pole I personally would not touch with a barge, to coin a witticism. *Aladdin* is the most unprincipled fucking merchant of death on the face of this earth bar none, plus also the chosen intimate of the worst dregs of international society. The principal item on his list will be Manpads, I am given to understand.'

Manpads, Elliot?

'Twenty of them at last count. State of the art, very durable, very deadly.'

Allow time for Elliot's bald, superior smile and slippy glance.

'A Manpad is, technically, your man-portable air-defence system, Paul, *Manpad* being what I call an *acronym*. As a weapon known by the same acronym, your Manpad is so lightweight that a kid can handle one. It also happens to be just the item if you are contemplating bringing down an unarmed airliner. Such is the mentality of these murderous shits.'

'But will *Aladdin* have them with him, Elliot, the Manpads? Now? On the night? On board the *Rosemaria*?' he asks, playing the innocent because that's what Elliot seems to like best.

'According to our leader's reliable and exclusive intelligence sources, the Manpads in question are part of a somewhat larger inventory of sale comprising top-of-the-range anti-tanks, rocket-propelleds, and best-brand assault rifles from state arsenals around the known bad world. As in the famous Arabian fairy tale, *Aladdin* has stashed his treasure in the desert, hence the choice of name. He will notify the successful bidder of its whereabouts *when* – and *only* when – he has cut the deal, in this case with none other than *Punter* himself. Ask me what is the purpose of the meeting between *Aladdin* and *Punter* and I will reply that it is in order to set the parameters of the deal, the terms of payment in gold, and the eventual inspection of goods prior to handover.'

★

The Toyota had left the marina and was negotiating a grass roundabout of palm trees and pansies.

'Boys and girls neat and tidy, everyone in place,' Kirsty was reporting in a monotone over her cellphone.

Boys, girls? Where? What have I missed? He must have asked her:

'Two parties of four watchers sitting in the Chinese, waiting for the *Aladdin* party to show up. Two walk-by couples. One tame taxi and two motorcyclists for when he sneaks away from the party,' she recited, as to a child who hasn't been paying attention.

They shared a strained silence. She thinks I'm surplus to requirements. She thinks I'm the Limey know-nothing striped-pants parachuted in to make difficulties.

'So when do I get to meet up with Jeb?' he insisted, not for the first time.

'Your friend Jeb will be ready and waiting for you at the rendezvous as per schedule, like I told you.'

'He's why I'm here,' he said too loud, feeling his gall rising. 'Jeb and his men can't go in without my say-so. That was the understanding from the start.'

'We're aware of that, thank you, Paul, and Elliot's aware of it. The sooner you and your friend Jeb hook up and the two teams are talking, the sooner we can get this thing squared away and go home. Okay?'

He needed Jeb. He needed his own.

The traffic had gone. The trees were shorter here, the sky bigger. He counted off the landmarks. St Bernard's Church. The Mosque of Ibrahim-al-Ibrahim, its minaret lit white. The shrine to Our Lady of Europe. Each of them branded on his memory thanks to mindless leafings through the greasy hotel guidebook. Out to sea, an armada of lighted freighters at anchor. *The seaborne boys will operate out of Ethical's mother ship*, Elliot is saying.

The sky had vanished. This tunnel is not a tunnel. It's a disused mineshaft. It's an air-raid shelter. Crooked girders, sloppy walls of breeze block and rough-cut cliff. Neon strips flying overhead, white road markings keeping pace with them. Festoons of black wiring. A sign saying LOOK OUT FOR FALLING STONES! Potholes, rivulets of brown flood water, an iron doorway leading to God knew where. Has *Punter* passed this way today? Is he hovering behind a doorway with one of his twenty Manpads? Punter's *not just high value, Paul. In the words of Mr Jay Crispin*, Punter *is stratospheric*: Elliot again.

Pillars like the gateway to another world coming at them as they emerge from the belly of the Rock and land on a road cut into the cliff. A hefty wind is rattling the coachwork, a half-moon has appeared at the top of the windscreen and the Toyota is bumping along the nearside verge. Beneath them, lights of coastal settlements. Beyond them, the pitch-black mountains of Spain. And out to sea, the same motionless armada of freight ships.

'Sides only,' Kirsty ordered.

Hansi dowsed the headlights.

'Cut the engine.'

To the furtive mutter of wheels on crumbling tarmac, they rolled forward. Ahead of them, a red pin-light flashed twice, then a third time, closer at hand.

'Stop now.'

They stopped. Kirsty slammed back the side door, letting in a blast of cold wind, and the steady din of engines from the sea. Across the valley, moonlit cloud was curling up the ravines and rolling like gun smoke along the Rock's ridge. A car sped out of the tunnel behind them and raked the hillside with its headlights, leaving a deeper darkness.

'Paul, your *friend's* here.'

Seeing no friend, he slid across to the open door. In front of him, Kirsty was leaning forward, pulling the back of her seat after her as if she couldn't wait to let him out. He started to lower his feet to the ground and heard the scream of insomniac gulls and the zip-zip of crickets. Two gloved hands reached out of the darkness to steady him. Behind them hunched little Jeb with his paint-dappled face glistening inside his pushed-back balaclava, and a lamp like a cyclopic eye stuck to his forehead.

'Good to see you again, Paul. Try these for size, then,' he murmured in his gentle Welsh lilt.

'And jolly good to see *you*, Jeb, I must say,' he answered fervently, accepting the goggles and grasping Jeb's hand in return. It was the Jeb he remembered: compact, calm, nobody's man but his own.

'Hotel okay then, Paul?'

'The absolute bloody pits. How's yours?'

'Come and have a see, man. All mod cons. Tread where I tread. Slow and easy. And if you see a falling stone, be sure and duck, now.'

Was that a joke? He grinned anyway. The Toyota was driving down the hill, job done and goodnight. He put on the goggles and the world turned green. Raindrops, driven on the wind, smashed themselves like insects in front of his eyes. Jeb was wading ahead of him up the hillside, the miner's torch on his forehead lighting the way. There was no track except

24

where he trod. I'm on the grouse moor with my father, scrambling through gorse ten feet high, except that this hillside had no gorse, just stubborn tufts of sand grass that kept dragging at his ankles. Some men you lead, and some men you follow, his father, a retired general, used to say. Well, with Jeb, you follow.

The ground evened out. The wind eased and rose again, the ground with it. He heard the putter of a helicopter overhead. *Mr Crispin will be providing the full American-style coverage*, Elliot had proclaimed, on a note of corporate pride. *Fuller than you will ever be required to know, Paul. Highly sophisticated equipment will be standard for all, plus a Predator drone for observation purposes is by no means beyond his operational budget.*

The climb steeper now, the earth part fallen rock, part wind-blown sand. Now his foot struck a bolt, a bit of steel rod, a sheet-anchor. Once – but Jeb's hand was waiting to point it out to him – a stretch of metal catch-net that he had to clamber over.

'You're going a treat, Paul. And the lizards don't bite you, not in Gib. They call them skinks here, don't ask me why. You're a family man, right?' – and getting a spontaneous 'yes' – 'Who've you got then, Paul? No disrespect.'

'One wife, one daughter,' he replied breathlessly. 'Girl's a medical doctor' – thinking, oh Christ, forgot I was Paul and single, but what the hell? – 'How about you, Jeb?'

'One great wife, one boy, five years old next week. Cracker-jack, same as yours, I expect.'

A car emerged from the tunnel behind them. He made to drop into a crouch, but Jeb was holding him upright with a grip so tight he gasped.

'Nobody can spot us unless we move, see,' he explained in his same comfortable Welsh undertone. 'It's a hundred metres up and pretty steep now, but not a bother for you, I'm sure. A bit of a traverse, then we're home. It's only the three boys and me' – as if there were nothing to be shy of.

And steep it was, with thickets and slipping sand, and another catch-net to negotiate, and Jeb's gloved hand waiting if he stumbled, but he didn't. Suddenly they had arrived. Three men in combat gear and headsets, one of them taller than the rest, were lounging on a tarpaulin, drinking from tin mugs and watching computer screens as if they were watching Saturday-afternoon football.

The hide was built into the steel frame of a catch-net. Its walls were of matted foliage and shrub. Even from a few feet away, and without Jeb to guide him, he might have walked clean past it. The computer screens were fixed at the end of pipe casings. You had to squint into the pipes to see them. A few misty stars glowed in the matted roof. A few strands of moonlight glinted on weaponry of a kind he'd never seen. Four packs of gear were lined up along one wall.

'So this is Paul, lads. Our man from the ministry,' said Jeb beneath the rattle of the wind.

One by one, each man turned, drew off a leather glove, shook his hand too hard and introduced himself.

'Don. Welcome to the Ritz, Paul.'

'Andy.'

'Shorty. Hullo, Paul. Make the climb all right, then?'

Shorty because he's a foot taller than the rest of them: why else? Jeb handing him a mug of tea. Sweet with condensed milk. A lateral arrow-slit was fringed by foliage. The computer pipes were fixed below it, allowing a clear view down the hillside to the coastline and out to sea. To his left the same pitch-black hills of Spain, bigger now, and closer. Jeb lining him up to look at the left-hand screen. A rolling sequence of shots from hidden cameras: the marina, the Chinese restaurant, the fairy-lit *Rosemaria*. Switch to a shaky hand-held shot inside the

Chinese restaurant. The camera at floor level. From the end of a long table in the window bay, an imperious fifty-year-old fat man in a nautical blazer and perfect hair gesticulates to his fellow diners. On his right, a sulky brunette half his age. Bare shoulders, showy breasts, diamond collar and a downturned mouth.

'*Aladdin*'s a twitchy bugger, Paul,' Shorty was confiding. 'First he has a run-in with the head waiter in English because there isn't any lobster. Now his lady friend's getting it in Arabic, and him a Pole. I'm surprised he doesn't give her a thick ear, the way she's carrying on. It's like at home, right, Jeb?'

'Come over here a minute, Paul, please.'

With Jeb's hand on his shoulder to guide him, he made a wide step to the middle screen. Alternating aerial and ground shots. Were they courtesy of the Predator drone that was by no means beyond Mr Crispin's operational budget? Or of the helicopter that he could hear idling overhead? A terrace of white houses, faced with weatherboarding, perched on the cliff's edge. Stone staircases to the beach dividing them. The staircases leading down to a skimpy crescent of sand. A rock beach enclosed by jagged cliff. Orange street lamps. A metalled slip road leading from the terrace to the main coast road. No lights in the windows of the houses. No curtains.

And through the arrow-slit, the same terrace in plain sight.

'It's a tear-down, see, Paul,' Jeb was explaining in his ear. 'A Kuwaiti company's going to put up a casino complex and a mosque. That's why the houses are empty. *Aladdin*, he's a director of the Kuwaiti company. Well now, according to what he's been telling his guests, he's got a confidential meeting with the developer tonight. Very lucrative, it will be. Shaving off the profits for themselves, according to his lady friend. You wouldn't think a man like *Aladdin* would be so leaky, like, but he is.'

'Showing off,' Shorty explained. 'Typical fucking Pole.'

'Is *Punter* already inside the house then?' he asked.

'Let's say, if he is, we haven't spotted him, Paul, put it that way,' Jeb replied in the same steady, deliberately conversational tone. 'Not from the outside, and there's no coverage inside. There hasn't been the opportunity, so we're told. Well, you can't bug twenty houses all in one go, I don't suppose, can you, not even with today's equipment? Maybe he's lying up in one house and sneaking into another for his meeting. We don't know, do we, not yet? It's wait and see and don't go down there till you know who you're taking on, 'specially if you're looking for an al-Qaeda kingpin.'

Memories of Elliot's clotted description of the same elusive figure come sweeping back to him:

I would basically describe Punter *as your jihadist Pimpernel par excellence, Paul, not to say your will-o'-the-wisp. He eschews all means of electronic communication, including cellphones and harmless-seeming emails. It's word of mouth only for* Punter, *and one courier at a time, never the same one twice.*

'He could come at us from anywhere, Paul,' Shorty was explaining, perhaps to wind him up. 'Over the mountains there. Up the Spanish coast by small boat. Or he could walk on the water if he felt like it. Right, Jeb?'

Cursory nod from Jeb. Jeb and Shorty, the tallest and the shortest men in the team: an attraction of opposites.

'*Or* smuggle himself across from Morocco under the noses of the coastguards, right, Jeb? *Or* put on an Armani suit, and fly in Club on a Swiss passport. *Or* charter a private Lear, which is what I'd do, frankly. Having first ordered my special menu in advance from the highly attractive hostess in a mini-skirt. Money to burn, *Punter*'s got, according to our amazing top-of-the-range source, right, Jeb?'

From the seaward side, the pitch-dark terrace was forbidding against the night sky, the beach a blackened no-man's-land of craggy boulders and seething surf.

'How many men in the boat team?' he asked. 'Elliot didn't seem sure.'

'We got him down to eight,' Shorty replied, over Jeb's shoulder. 'Nine when they head back to the mother ship with *Punter*. They hope,' he added drily.

The conspirators will be unarmed, Paul, Elliot was saying. *Such is the degree of trust between a pair of total bastards. No guns, no bodyguards. We tiptoe in, we grab our man, we tiptoe out, we were never there. Jeb's boys push from the land, Ethical pulls from the sea.*

Side by side with Jeb once more, he peered through the arrow-slit at the lighted freighters, then at the middle screen. One freighter lay apart from her companions. A Panamanian flag flapped from her stern. On her deck, shadows flitted among the derricks. An inflatable dinghy dangled over the water, two men aboard. He was still watching them when his encrypted cellphone began cooing its stupid melody. Jeb grabbed it from him, dowsed the sound, handed it back.

'That you, Paul?'

'Paul speaking.'

'This is Nine. All right? Nine. Tell me you hear me.'

And I shall be Nine, the minister is solemnly intoning, like a Biblical prophecy. *I shall not be* Alpha, *which is reserved for our target building. I shall not be* Bravo, *which is reserved for our location. I shall be* Nine, *which is the designated code for your commander, and I shall be communicating with you by specially encrypted cellphone ingeniously linked to your operational team by way of an augmented PRR net, which for your further information stands for Personal Role Radio.*

'I hear you loud and clear, Nine, thank you.'

'And you're in position? Yes? Keep your answers short from now on.'

'I am indeed. Your eyes and ears.'

'All right. Tell me precisely what you can see from where you are.'

'We're looking straight down the slope to the houses. Couldn't be better.'

'Who's there?'

'Jeb, his three men and myself.'

Pause. Muffled male voice off.

The minister again:

'Has anyone any idea why *Aladdin* hasn't left the Chinese yet?'

'They started eating late. He's expected to leave any minute. That's all we've heard.'

'And no *Punter* in sight? You're absolutely sure of that? Yes?'

'Not in sight as yet. I'm sure. Yes.'

'The slightest visual indication, however remote – the smallest clue – possibility of a sighting –'

Pause. Is the augmented PRR breaking up, or is Quinn?

'– I expect you to advise me *immediately*. Understood? We see everything you see, but not so clearly. You have *eyes-on*. Yes?' – already sick of the delay – 'Plain sight, for fuck's sake!'

'Yes, indeed. Plain sight. Eyes-on. I have eyes-on.'

Don has struck up his arm for attention.

In the centre of town a people carrier is nosing its way through night traffic. It has a taxi sign on its roof and a single passenger on the rear seat, and one glance is enough to tell him that the passenger is the corpulent, very animated *Aladdin*, the Pole that Elliot won't touch with a barge. He's holding a cellphone to his ear and, as in the Chinese restaurant, he is gesticulating magisterially with his free hand.

The pursuing camera veers, goes wild. The screen goes blank. The helicopter takes over, pinpoints the people carrier, puts a halo over it. The pursuing ground camera returns. The winking icon of a telephone, top-left corner of the screen. Jeb hands Paul an earpiece. One Polish man talking to another. They are taking it in turns to laugh. *Aladdin*'s left hand performing a puppet show in the rear window of the people carrier. Male Polish merrymaking replaced by disapproving voice of a woman translator:

'*Aladdin* is speaking to brother Josef in Warsaw,' says the woman's voice disdainfully. 'It is vulgar conversation. They are discussing girlfriend of *Aladdin*, this woman he has on boat. Her name is Imelda. *Aladdin* is tired of Imelda. Imelda has too much mouth. He will abandon her. Josef must visit Beirut. *Aladdin* will pay for him to come from Warsaw. If Josef will come to Beirut, *Aladdin* will introduce him to many women who will wish to sleep with him. Now *Aladdin* is on his way to visit special friend. Special *secret* friend. He love this friend very much. She will replace Imelda. She is not gloomy, not bitch, has very beautiful breasts. Maybe he will buy apartment for her in Gibraltar. This is good news for taxes. *Aladdin* will go now. His secret special friend is waiting. She desires him very much. When she opens the door she will be completely naked. *Aladdin* has ordered this. Goodnight, Josef.'

A moment of collective bewilderment, broken by Don:

'He hasn't got fucking *time* to get laid,' he whispered indignantly. 'Not even him.'

Echoed by Andy, equally indignant:

'His cab's turned the wrong way. What the fuck's it gone and done that for?'

'There is *always* time to get laid,' Shorty corrected them firmly. 'If Boris Becker can knock up a bird in a cupboard or whatever, *Aladdin* can get himself laid on his way to sell Manpads to his mate *Punter*. It's only logical.'

This much at least was true: the people carrier, instead of turning right towards the tunnel, had turned left, back into the centre of town.

'He knows we're on him,' Andy muttered in despair. '*Shit*.'

31

'*Or* changed his stupid mind' – Don.

'Hasn't got one, darling. He's a bungalow. It's all down-stairs' – Shorty.

The screen turned grey, then white, then a funereal black.

CONTACT TEMPORARILY LOST

All eyes on Jeb as he murmured gentle Welsh cadences into his chest microphone:

'What have you done with him, Elliot? We thought *Aladdin* was too fat to lose.'

Delay and static over Don's relay. Elliot's querulous South African voice, low and fast:

'There're a couple of apartment blocks with covered car parks down there. Our reading is, he drove into one and came out by a different one. We're searching.'

'So he knows you're on him then' – Jeb – 'That's not helpful, is it, Elliot?'

'Maybe he's aware, maybe it's habit. Kindly get off my bloody back. Right?'

'If we're compromised, we're going home, Elliot. We're not walking into a trap, not if people know we're coming. We've been there, thank you. We're too old for that one.'

Static, but no answer. Jeb again:

'You didn't think to put a tracker on the cab by any chance, did you, Elliot? Maybe he switched vehicles. I've heard of that being done before, once or twice.'

'Go fuck yourself.'

Shorty in his role as Jeb's outraged comrade and defender, pulling off his mouthpiece:

'I'm definitely going to sort Elliot out when this is over,' he announced to the world. 'I'm going to have a nice, reasonable, quiet word with him, and I'm going to shove his stupid South African head up his arse, which is a fact. Aren't I, Jeb?'

'Maybe you are, Shorty,' Jeb said quietly. 'And maybe you're not, too. So shut up, d'you mind?'

*

The screen has come back to life. The night traffic is down to single cars but no halo is hanging over an errant people carrier. The encrypted cellphone is trembling again.

'Can you see something that we can't, Paul?' – accusingly.

'I don't know what you can see, Nine. *Aladdin* was talking to his brother, then he changed direction. Everyone here is mystified.'

'We are, too. You better bloody believe it.'

We? You and who else, exactly? Eight? Ten? Who is it that whispers in your ear? Passes you little notes, for all I know, while you talk to me? Causes you to change tack and start again? Mr Jay Crispin, our corporate warlord and intelligence provider?

'Paul?'

'Yes, Nine.'

'You have eyes-on. Give me a reading, please. *Now.*'

'The issue seems to be whether *Aladdin's* woken up to the fact that he's being followed.' And after a moment's thought: 'Also whether he's visiting a new girlfriend he has apparently installed here instead of keeping his date with *Punter*' – increasingly impressed by his own confidence.

Shuffle. Sounds off. The whisperer at work again. Disconnect.

'Paul?'

'Yes, Nine.'

'Hang on. Wait. Got some people here need to talk to me.'

Paul hangs on. People or person?

'Okay! Matter solved' – Minister Quinn in full voice now – '*Aladdin's* not – repeat *not* – about to screw anybody, man or

33

woman. That's a fact. Is that clear?' – not waiting for an answer. 'The phone call to his brother we just heard was a blind to firm up his date with *Punter* over the open line. The man at the other end was *not* his brother. He was *Punter's* intermediary.' Hiatus for more off-stage advice. 'Okay, his *cut-out*. He was *Aladdin's* cut-out' – settling to the word.

Line dead again. For *more* advice? Or is the Personal Role Radio not quite as augmented as it was cracked up to be?

'Paul?'

'Nine?'

'*Aladdin* was merely telling *Punter* that he's on his way. Giving him a heads-up. We have that direct from source. Kindly pass to Jeb forthwith.'

There was just time to pass to Jeb forthwith before Don's arm shot up again.

'Screen two, skipper. House seven. Seaward-side camera. Light in ground-floor window left.'

'Over here, Paul' – Jeb.

Jeb has dropped into a squat at Don's side. Crouching behind them, he peers between their two heads, unable to make out at first which light he's supposed to be seeing. Lights were dancing in the ground-floor windows, but they were reflections from the anchored fleet. Removing his goggles and stretching his eyes as wide as they'll go, he watches the replay of the ground-floor window of house number seven in close-up.

A spectral pin-light, pointed upward like a candle, moves across the room. It is held by a ghostly white forearm. The inland cameras take up the story. Yes, there's the light again. And the ghostly forearm is tinged orange by the sodium lamps along the slip road.

'He's inside there then, isn't he?' – Don, the first to speak. 'House seven. Ground floor. Flashing a fucking torch because there's no electric.' But he sounds oddly unconvinced.

'It's Ophelia' – Shorty, the scholar. 'In her fucking nightshirt. Going to throw herself into the Med.'

Jeb is standing as upright as the roof of the hide allows. He pulls back his balaclava, making a scarf of it. In the spectral green light, his paint-smeared face is suddenly a generation older.

'Yes, Elliot, we saw it, too. All right, agreed, a human presence. Whose presence, that's another question, I suppose.'

Is the augmented sound system really on the blink? Over a single earpiece he hears Elliot's voice in belligerent mode:

'Jeb? Jeb, I need you. Are you there?'

'Listening, Elliot.'

The South African accent very strong now, very didactic:

'My orders are, as of one minute ago, precisely, to place my team on red alert for immediate embarkation. I am further instructed to pull my surveillance resources out of the town centre and concentrate them on *Alpha*. Approaches to *Alpha* will be covered by static vans. Your detachment will descend and deploy accordingly.'

'Who says we will, Elliot?'

'That is the battle plan. Land and sea units converge. Jesus fuck, Jeb, have you forgotten your fucking orders?'

'You know very well what my orders are, Elliot. They're what they were from the start. Find, fix and finish. We haven't found *Punter*, we've seen a light. We can't fix him till we've found him and we've no PID worth a damn.'

PID? Though he detests initials, enlightenment comes: Positive Identification.

'So there's no finishing and there's no convergence,' Jeb is insisting to Elliot in the same steady tone. 'Not till I agree, there isn't. We're not shooting at each other in the dark, thank you. Confirm you copy me, please. Elliot, did you hear what I just said?'

Still no answer, as Quinn returns in a flurry.

35

'Paul? That light inside house seven. You saw it? You had *eyes-on*?'

'I did. Yes. Eyes-on.'

'Once?'

'I believe I saw it twice, but indistinctly.'

'It's *Punter*. *Punter*'s in there. At this minute. In house seven. That was *Punter* holding a hand torch, crossing the room. You saw his arm. Well, didn't you? You saw it, for Christ's sake. A human arm. We all did.'

'We saw an arm, but the arm is subject to identification, Nine. We're still waiting for *Aladdin* to turn up. He's lost, and there's no indication that he's on his way here.' And catching Jeb's eye: 'We're also waiting for proof that *Punter* is on the premises.'

'Paul?'

'Still here, Nine.'

'We're re-planning. Your job is to keep the houses in plain sight. House seven particularly. That's an order. While we re-plan. Understood?'

'Understood.'

'You see anything out of the ordinary with the naked eye that the cameras may have missed, I need to know instantly.' Fades and returns. 'You're doing an excellent job, Paul. It will not go unnoticed. Tell Jeb. That's an order.'

They're becalmed, but he feels no calm. *Aladdin*'s vanishing act has cast its spell over the hide. Elliot may be repositioning his aerial cameras but they're still scanning the town, homing at random on stray cars and abandoning them. His ground cameras are still offering now the marina, now the entrance to the tunnel, now stretches of empty coast road.

'Come on, you ugly bastard, *show!*' – Don, to the absent *Aladdin*.

'Too busy having it away, randy sod' – Andy, to himself.

Aladdin *is waterproof, Paul*, Elliot is insisting across his desk in

Paddington. *We do not lay one single finger on* Aladdin. *Aladdin is fireproof, he is bulletproof. That is the solemn deal that Mr Crispin has cut with his highly valuable informant, and Mr Crispin's word to an informant is sacred.*

'Skipper' – Don again, this time with both arms up.

A motorcyclist is weaving his way along the metalled service track, flashing his headlight from side to side. No helmet, just a black-and-white keffiyeh flapping round his neck. With his right hand he is steering the bike, while his left holds what appears to be a bag by its throat. Swinging the bag as he goes along, displaying it, showing it off, look at me. Slender, wasp-waisted. The keffiyeh masking the lower part of his face. As he draws level with the centre of the terrace his right hand leaves the handlebars and rises in a revolutionist's salute.

Reaching the end of the service track, he seems all set to join the coast road, heading south. Abruptly he turns north, head thrust forward over the handlebars, keffiyeh streaming behind him and, accelerating, races towards the Spanish border.

But who cares about a hell-bent motorcyclist in a keffiyeh when his black bag sits like a plum pudding in the middle of the metalled track, directly in front of the doorway leading to house number seven?

★

The camera has closed on it. The camera enlarges it. Enlarges it again.

It's a common-or-garden black plastic bag, bound at the throat with twine or raffia. It's a bin bag. It's a bin bag with a football or a human head or a bomb in it. It's the kind of suspicious object which, if you saw it lying around untended at a railway station, you either told someone or you didn't, depending how shy you were.

The cameras were vying with each other to get at it. Aerial

shots followed ground-level close-ups and wide-angle shots of the terrace at giddying speed. Out to sea, the helicopter had dropped low over the mother ship in protection. In the hide, Jeb was urging sweet reason:

'It's a *bag*, Elliot, is what it is' – his Welsh voice at its gentlest and most persistent. 'That's all we know, see. We don't know what's in it, we can't hear it, we can't smell it, can we? There's no green smoke coming out of it, no external wires or aerials that we can see, and I'm sure you can't either. Maybe it's just a kid doing a bit of fly-tipping for his mum . . . No, Elliot, I don't think we'll do that, thank you. I think we'll leave it where it is and let it do whatever it was brought here to do, if you don't mind, and we'll go on waiting till it does it, same as we're waiting for *Aladdin*.'

Is this an electronic silence or a human one?

'It's his weekly washing,' Shorty suggested under his breath.

'No, Elliot, we're not doing that,' said Jeb, his voice much sharper. 'We emphatically are *not* going down to take a closer look inside that bag. We're not going to interfere with that bag in any way, Elliot. That could be exactly what they're waiting for us to do: they want to flush us out in case we're on the premises. Well, we're not on the premises, are we? Not for a teaser like that we're not. Which is another good reason for leaving it put.'

Another fade-out, a longer one.

'We have an *arrangement*, Elliot,' Jeb continued with super-human patience. 'Maybe you've forgotten that. Once the land team has fixed the target, and not before, we'll come down the hill. And your sea team, you'll come in from the sea, and together we'll finish the job. That was the arrangement. You own the sea, we own the land. Well, the bag's on the land, isn't it? And we haven't fixed the target, and I'm not about to see our respective teams going into a dark building from opposite sides,

38

and nobody knowing who's waiting there for us, or isn't. Do I have to repeat that, Elliot?'

'Paul?'

'Yes, Nine.'

'What's your personal take on that bag? Advise me immediately. Do you buy Jeb's arguments or not?'

'Unless you have a better one, Nine, yes I do' – firm but respectful, taking his tone from Jeb's.

'Could be a warning to *Punter* to do a runner. How about that, then? Has anyone thought of that your end?'

'I'm sure they've thought about that very deeply, as I have. However, the bag could equally well be a signal to *Aladdin* to say it's safe, so come on in. Or it could be a signal to stay away. It seems to me pure speculation at best. Too many possibilities altogether, in my view,' he ended boldly, even adding: 'In the circumstances, Jeb's position strikes me as eminently reasonable, I have to say.'

'Don't lecture me. All wait till I return.'

'Of course.'

'And no fucking *of course!*'

The line goes stone dead. No shuffle of breath, no background atmospherics. Just a long silence over the cellphone pressed harder and harder to his ear.

*

'Jesus *fuck!*' – Don, at full force.

Again they are all five huddled at the arrow-slit as a high-sided car with full headlights shoots out of the tunnel and speeds towards the terraces. It's *Aladdin*, in his people carrier, late for his appointment. It's not. It's the blue Toyota four-by-four without its CONFERENCE sign. Veering off the coast road, bumping on to the metalled service track and heading straight for the black bag.

As it approaches, the side door slides back to reveal the

bespectacled Hansi bowed at the wheel and a second figure, undefined but could be Kirsty, stooped in the open doorway, one hand clutching the grab handle for dear life and the other outstretched for the bag. The Toyota's door bangs shut again. Regaining speed, the four-by-four continues north and out of sight. The plum-pudding bag has gone.

First to speak is Jeb, calmer than ever.

'Was that your people I saw just now, Elliot? Picking up the bag at all? Elliot, I need to speak to you, please. Elliot, I think you're hearing me. I need an explanation, please. Elliot?'

'Nine?'

'Yes, Paul.'

'It seems that Elliot's people just picked up the bag' – doing his best to sound as rational as Jeb – 'Nine? Are you there?'

Belatedly, Nine comes back, and he's strident:

'We took the executive decision, for fuck's sake. Someone had to take it, right? Kindly inform Jeb. Now. The decision is set. Taken.'

He is gone again. But Elliot is back at full strength, talking to an off-stage female voice with an Australian accent and triumphantly relating its message to the wider audience:

'The bag contains *provisions*? Thank you, Kirsty. The bag contains *smoked fish* – hear that, Jeb? *Bread. Arab* bread. Thank you, Kirsty. What else do we have in that bag? We have *water. Sparkling water. Punter* likes *sparkling.* We have *chocolate. Milk chocolate.* Hold it there, thank you, Kirsty. Did you happen to catch that, Jeb? The bastard's been in there all the time, and his mates have been feeding him. We're going in, Jeb. I have my orders here in front of me, confirmed.'

'Paul?'

But this is not Minister Quinn alias Nine speaking. This is Jeb's half-blacked face, his eyes whitened like a collier's, except they're palest green. And Jeb's voice, steady as before, appealing to him:

40

'We shouldn't be doing this, Paul. We'll be shooting at ghosts in the dark. Elliot doesn't know the half of it. I think you agree with me.'

'Nine?'

'What the hell is it now? They're going in! What's the problem now, man?'

Jeb staring at him. Shorty staring at him over Jeb's shoulder:

'Nine?'

'What?'

'You asked me to be your eyes and ears, Nine. I can only agree with Jeb. Nothing I've seen or heard warrants going in at this stage.'

Is the silence deliberate or technical? From Jeb, a crisp nod. From Shorty, a twisted smile of derision, whether for Quinn, or Elliot, or just all of it. And from the minister, a delayed blurt:

'The man's in there, for fuck's sake!' Gone again. Comes back. 'Paul, listen to me closely. That's an order. We've seen the man in full Arab garb. So've you. *Punter.* In there. He's got an Arab boy bringing him his food and water. What the hell more does Jeb want?'

'He wants proof, Nine. He says there isn't enough. I have to say, I feel very much the same.'

Another nod from Jeb, more vigorous than the first, again backed by Shorty, then by their remaining comrades. The white eyes of all four men watching him through their balaclavas.

'Nine?'

'Doesn't anybody listen to orders over there?'

'May I speak?'

'Hurry up then!'

He is speaking for the record. He is weighing every word before he speaks it:

'Nine, it's my judgement that by any reasonable standard of analysis we're dealing with a string of unproven assumptions.

41

Jeb and his men here have great experience. Their view is that nothing makes hard sense as it stands. As your eyes and ears on the ground, I have to tell you I share that view.'

Faint voices off, then again the deep, dead silence, until Quinn comes back, shrill and petulant:

'*Punter's* unarmed, for fuck's sake. That was his deal with *Aladdin*. Unarmed and unescorted, one to one. He's a high-value terrorist with a pot of money on his head and a load of priceless intelligence to be got out of him, and he's sitting there for the plucking. *Paul?*'

'Still here, Nine.'

Still here, but looking at the left-hand screen, as they all are. At the stern of the mother ship. At the shadow on her near side. At the inflatable dinghy lying flat on the water. At the eight crouched figures aboard.

'Paul? Give me Jeb. Jeb, are you there? I want you to listen, both of you. Jeb and Paul. Are you both listening?'

They are.

'Listen to me.' They've already said they are but never mind. 'If the sea team grabs the prize and gets him on to the boat and out of territorial waters into the hands of the interrogators while you lot are sitting on your arses up the hill, how d'you think *that's* going to look? Jesus Christ, Jeb, they told me you were picky, but think what's to lose, man!'

On the screen, the inflatable is no longer visible at the mother ship's side. Jeb's battle-painted face inside its scant balaclava is like an ancient war mask.

'Well, not a lot more to say to that, then, is there, Paul, I don't suppose, not now you've said it all?' he says quietly.

But Paul hasn't said it all, or not to his satisfaction. And yet again, somewhat to his surprise, he has the words ready, no fumble, no hesitation.

'With due respect, Nine, there is not, in my judgement, a suf-

42

ficient case for the land team to go in. Or anyone else, for that matter.'

Is this the longest silence of his life? Jeb is crouching on the ground with his back to him, busying himself with a kit-bag. Behind Jeb, his men are already standing. One – he's not sure which – has his head bowed and seems to be praying. Shorty has taken off his gloves and is licking each fingertip in turn. It's as if the minister's message has reached them by other, more occult means.

'Paul?'

'Sir.'

'Kindly note I am *not* the field commander in this situation. Military decisions are the sole province of the senior soldier on the ground, as you are aware. However, I may *recommend*. You will therefore inform Jeb that, on the basis of the operational intelligence before me, I *recommend* but do not *command* that he would be well advised to put *Operation Wildlife* into immediate effect. The decision to do so is of course his own.'

But Jeb, having caught the drift of this message, and preferring not to wait for the rest, has vanished into the dark with his comrades.

*

Now with his night-vision glasses, now without, he peered into the density but saw no more sign of Jeb or his men.

On the first screen the inflatable was closing on the shore. Surf was lapping the camera, black rocks were approaching.

The second screen was dead.

He moved to the third. The camera zoomed in on house seven.

The front door was shut, the windows still uncurtained and unlit. He saw no phantom light held by a shrouded hand. Eight masked men in black were clambering out of the inflatable, one pulling another. Now two of the men were kneeling, training their weapons at a point above the camera. Three more men stole into the camera's lens and disappeared.

A camera switched to the coast road and the terrace, panning across the doors. The door to house seven was open. An armed shadow stood guard beside it. A second armed shadow slipped through it; a third, taller shadow slipped after him: Shorty.

Just in time the camera caught little Jeb with his Welsh miner's wading walk disappearing down the lighted stone staircase to the beach. Above the clatter of the wind came a clicking sound like dominoes collapsing: two sets of clicks, then nothing. He thought he heard a yell but he was listening too hard to know for sure. It was the wind. It was the nightingale. No, it was the owl.

The lights on the steps went out, and after them the orange sodium street lamps along the metalled track. As if by the same hand, the two remaining computer screens went blank.

At first he refused to accept this simple truth. He pulled on his night-vision glasses, took them off, then put them on again and roamed the computers' keyboards, willing the screens back to life. They would not be willed.

A stray engine barked, but it could as well have been a fox as a car or the outboard of an inflatable. On his encrypted cellphone, he pressed '1' for Quinn and got a steady electronic wail. He stepped out of the hide and, standing his full height at last, braced his shoulders to the night air.

A car emerged at speed from the tunnel, cut its headlights and screeched to a halt on the verge of the coast road. For ten minutes, twelve, nothing. Then out of the darkness Kirsty's Australian voice calling his name. And after it, Kirsty herself.

'What on earth happened?' he asked.

She steered him back into the hide.

'Mission accomplished. Everyone ecstatic. Medals all round,' she said.

'What about *Punter*?'

'I said everyone's ecstatic, didn't I?'

'So they got him? They've taken him out to the mother ship?'

'You get the fuck out of here now and you stop asking questions. I'm taking you down to the car, the car takes you to the airport like we planned. The plane's waiting. Everything's in place, everything's hunky-dory. We go *now*.'

'Is Jeb all right? His men? They're okay?'

'Pumped up and happy.'

'What about all this stuff?' – he means the metal boxes and computers.

'This stuff will be gone in three seconds cold just as soon as we get you the fuck out of here. Now move it.'

Already they were stumbling and sliding into the valley, with the sea wind whipping into them and the hum from engines out to sea louder even than the wind itself.

A huge bird – perhaps an eagle – scrambled out of the scrub beneath his feet, screaming its fury.

Once, he fell headlong over a broken catch-net and only the thicket saved him.

Then, just as suddenly, they were standing on the empty coast road, breathless but miraculously unharmed.

The wind had dropped, the rain had ceased. A second car was pulling up beside them. Two men in boots and tracksuits sprang out. With a nod for Kirsty and nothing for himself, they set off at a half-run towards the hillside.

'I'll need the goggles,' she said.

He gave them to her.

'Have you got any papers on you – maps, anything you kept from up there?'

He hadn't.

'It was a triumph. Right? No casualties. We did a great job. All of us. You, too. Right?'

Did he say 'Right' in return? It no longer mattered. Without another glance at him, she was heading off in the wake of the two men.

2.

On a sunny Sunday early in that same spring, a thirty-one-year-old British foreign servant earmarked for great things sat alone at the pavement table of a humble Italian café in London's Soho, steeling himself to perform an act of espionage so outrageous that, if detected, it would cost him his career and his freedom: namely, recovering a tape recording, illicitly made by himself, from the Private Office of a Minister of the Crown whom it was his duty to serve and advise to the best of his considerable ability.

His name was Toby Bell and he was entirely alone in his criminal contemplations. No evil genius controlled him, no paymaster, provocateur or sinister manipulator armed with an attaché case stuffed with hundred-dollar bills was waiting round the corner, no activist in a ski mask. He was in that sense the most feared creature of our contemporary world: a solitary decider. Of a forthcoming clandestine operation on the Crown Colony of Gibraltar he knew nothing: rather, it was this tantalizing ignorance that had brought him to his present pass.

Neither was he in appearance or by nature cut out to be a felon. Even now, premeditating his criminal design, he remained the decent, diligent, tousled, compulsively ambitious, intelligent-looking fellow that his colleagues and employers took him for. He was stocky in build, not particularly handsome, with a shock of unruly brown hair that went haywire as soon as it was brushed. That there was gravitas in him was undeniable. The gifted, state-educated only child of pious artisan parents from the south coast of England who knew no politics but Labour –

47

the father an elder of his local tabernacle, the mother a chubby, happy woman who spoke constantly of Jesus – he had battled his way into the Foreign and Commonwealth Office, first as a clerk, and thence by way of evening classes, language courses, internal examinations and two-day leadership tests, to his present, coveted position. As to the *Toby*, which might by the sound of it set him higher on the English social ladder than his provenance deserved, it derived from nothing more elevated than his father's pride in the holy man Tobias, whose wondrous filial virtues are set down in the ancient scripts.

What had driven Toby's ambition – what drove it still – was something he barely questioned. His schoolfriends had wished only to make money. Let them. Toby, though modesty forbade him to say so in so many words, wished to make a difference – or, as he had put it a little shamefacedly to his examiners, take part in his country's discovery of its true identity in a post-imperial, post-Cold War world. Given his head, he would long ago have swept away Britain's private education system, abolished all vestiges of entitlement and put the monarchy on a bicycle. Yet even while harbouring these seditious thoughts, the striver in him knew that his first aim must be to rise in the system he dreamed of liberating.

And in speech, though he was speaking at this moment to no one but himself? As a natural-born linguist with his father's love of cadence and an almost suffocating awareness of the brand-marks on the English tongue, it was inevitable that he should discreetly shed the last tinges of his Dorset burr in favour of the Middle English affected by those determined not to have their social origins defined for them.

With the alteration in his voice had come an equally subtle change in his choice of clothing. Conscious that any moment now he would be sauntering through the gates of the Foreign Office with every show of being at his managerial ease, he was wearing chinos and an open-necked shirt – and a shape-less black jacket for that bit of off-duty formality.

What was also not apparent to any outward eye was that only two hours previously his live-in girlfriend of three months' standing had walked out of his Islington flat vowing never to see him again. Yet somehow this tragic event had failed to cast him down. If there was a connection between Isabel's departure and the crime he was about to commit, then perhaps it was to be found in his habit of lying awake at all hours brooding on his unshareable preoccupations. True, at intervals throughout the night, they had vaguely discussed the possibility of a separation, but then latterly they often had. He had assumed that when morning came she would as usual change her mind, but this time she stuck to her guns. There had been no screams, no tears. He phoned for a cab, she packed. The cab came, he helped her downstairs with her suitcases. She was worried about her silk suit at the cleaner's. He took the ticket from her and promised to send it on. She was pale. She did not look back, even if she could not resist the final word:

'Let's face it, Toby, you're a bit of a cold fish, aren't you?' – with which she rode away, ostensibly to her sister in Suffolk, though he suspected she might have other irons in the fire, including her recently abandoned husband.

And Toby, equally firm of purpose, had set out on foot for his coffee and croissant in Soho as a prelude to grand larceny. Which is where he now sat, sipping his cappuccino in the morning sun-shine and staring blankly at the passers-by. If I'm such a cold fish, how did I talk myself into this God-awful situation?

For answers to this and allied questions, his mind turned as of habit to Giles Oakley, his enigmatic mentor and self-appointed patron.

★

Berlin.

The neophyte diplomat Bell, Second Secretary (Political), has just arrived at the British Embassy on his first overseas posting. The Iraq War looms. Britain has signed up to it, but denies it has done so. Germany is dithering on the brink. Giles Oakley, the embassy's *éminence grise* – darting, impish Oakley, dyed in all the oceans, as the Germans say – is Toby's section chief. Oakley's job, amid a myriad others less defined: to supervise the flow of British intelligence to German liaison. Toby's: to be his spear-carrier. His German is already good. As ever, he's a fast learner. Oakley takes him under his wing, marches him round the ministries and opens doors for him that would otherwise have remained locked against one of his lowly status. Are Toby and Giles spies? Not at all! They are blue-chip British career diplomats who have found themselves, like many others, at the trading tables of the free world's vast intelligence marketplace.

The only problem is that the further Toby is admitted into these inner councils, the greater his abhorrence of the war about to happen. He rates it illegal, immoral and doomed. His discomfort is compounded by the knowledge that even the most supine of his schoolfriends are out on the street protesting their outrage. So are his parents who, in their Christian socialist decency, believe that the purpose of diplomacy should be to prevent war rather than to promote it. His mother emails him in despair: Tony Blair – once her idol – has betrayed us all. His father, adding his stern Methodist voice, accuses Bush and Blair jointly of the sin of pride and intends to compose a parable about a pair of peacocks who, bewitched by their own reflections, turn into vultures.

Little wonder then that with such voices dinning in his ear beside his own, Toby resents having to sing the war's praises to, of all people, the Germans, even urging them to join the dance. He too voted heart and soul for Tony Blair, and now finds his prime minister's public postures truthless and emetic. And with the launch of *Operation Iraqi Freedom*, he boils over:

The scene is the Oakleys' diplomatic villa in Grunewald. It is midnight as another ball-breaking *Herrenabend* – power dinner for male bores – drags to its close. Toby has acquired a decent crop of German friends in Berlin, but tonight's guests are not among them. A tedious federal minister, a terminally vain titan of Ruhr industry, a Hohenzollern pretender and a quartet of free-loading parliamentarians have finally called for their limousines. Oakley's diplomatic *Ur*-wife, Hermione, having supervised proceedings from the kitchen over a generous gin, has taken herself to bed. In the sitting room, Toby and Giles Oakley rake over the night's takings for any odd scrap of indiscretion.

Abruptly, Toby's self-control hits the buffers:

'So actually screw, sod and fuck the whole bloody thing,' he declares, slamming down his glass of Oakley's very old Calvados.

'The whole bloody thing being *what* exactly?' Oakley, the fifty-five-year-old leprechaun enquires, stretching out his little legs in luxurious ease, which is a thing he does in crisis.

With unshakable urbanity, Oakley hears Toby out, and as impassively delivers himself of his acid, if affectionate, response:

'Go ahead, Toby. Resign. I share your callow personal opinions. No sovereign nation such as ours should be taken to war under false pretences, least of all by a couple of egomaniac zealots without an ounce of history between them. And *certainly* we should not have attempted to persuade other sovereign nations to follow our disgraceful example. So resign away. You're exactly what the *Guardian* needs: another lost voice bleating in the wilderness. If you don't agree with government policy, don't hang around trying to change it. Jump ship. Write the great novel you're always dreaming about.'

But Toby is not to be put down so easily:

'So where the hell do *you* sit, Giles? You were as much against it as I was, you know you were. When fifty-two of our retired ambassadors signed a letter saying it was all a load of bollocks, you heaved a big sigh and told me you wished you were retired too. Do I have to wait till I'm sixty to speak out? Is that what you're trying to tell me? Till I've got my knighthood and my index-linked pension and I'm president of the local golf club? Is that loyalty or just funk, Giles?'

Oakley's Cheshire-cat smile softens as, fingertips together, he delicately formulates his reply:

'Where do I sit, you ask. Why, at the conference table. *Always* at the table. I wheedle, I chip away, I argue, I reason, I cajole, I hope. But I do not expect. I adhere to the hallowed diplomatic doctrine of moderation in all things, and I apply it to the heinous crimes of every nation, including my own. I leave my feelings at the door before I go into the conference room and I *never* walk out in a huff unless I've been instructed to do so. I positively *pride* myself on doing everything by halves. Sometimes – this could well be such a time – I make a cautious démarche to our revered masters. But I *never* try to rebuild the Palace of Westminster in a day. Neither, at the risk of being pompous, should you.'

And while Toby is fumbling for an answer:

'Another thing, while I have you alone, if I may. My beloved wife Hermione tells me, in her capacity as the eyes and ears of Berlin's diplomatic shenanigans, that you are conducting an inappropriate dalliance with the spouse of the Dutch military attaché, she being a notorious tart. True or false?'

Toby's posting to the British Embassy in Madrid, which has unexpectedly discovered a need for a junior attaché with Defence experience, follows a month later.

★

Madrid.

Despite their disparity in age and seniority, Toby and Giles remain in close touch. How much this is due to Oakley's string-pulling behind the scenes, how much to mere accident, Toby can only guess. Certain is that Oakley has taken to Toby in the way that some older diplomats consciously or otherwise foster their favoured young. Intelligence traffic between London and Madrid meanwhile was never brisker or more crucial. Its subject is not any more Saddam Hussein and his elusive weapons of mass destruction but the new generation of jihadists brought into being by the West's assault on what was until then one of the more secular countries in the Middle East – a truth too raw to be admitted by its perpetrators.

Thus the duo continues. In Madrid, Toby – like it or not, and mainly he likes it – becomes a leading player in the intelligence marketplace, commuting weekly to London, where Oakley flits in the middle air between the Queen's spies on one side of the river and the Queen's Foreign Office on the other.

In coded discussions in Whitehall's sealed basement rooms, new rules of engagement with suspected terrorist prisoners are cautiously thrashed out. Improbably, given Toby's rank, he attends. Oakley presides. The word *enhance*, once used to convey spiritual exaltation, has entered the new American dictionary, but its meaning remains wilfully imprecise to the uninitiated, of whom Toby is one. All the same, he has his suspicions. Can these so-called *new* rules in reality be the old barbaric ones, dusted off and reinstated, he wonders? And if he is right, which increasingly he believes he is, what is the moral distinction, if any, between the man who applies the electrodes and the man who sits behind a desk and pretends he doesn't know it's happening, although he knows very well?

But when Toby, nobly struggling to reconcile these questions with his conscience and upbringing, ventures to air them –

purely academically, you understand – to Giles over a cosy dinner at Oakley's club to celebrate Toby's thrilling new appointment on promotion to the British Embassy in Cairo, Oakley, from whom no secrets are hidden, responds with one of his doting smiles and hides himself behind his beloved La Rochefoucauld:

'Hypocrisy is the tribute that vice pays to virtue, dear man. In an imperfect world, I fear it's the best we can manage.'

And Toby smiles back appreciatively at Oakley's wit, and tells himself sternly yet again that he must learn to live with compromise – *dear man* being by now a permanent addition to Oakley's vocabulary, and further evidence, were it needed, of his singular affection for his protégé.

*

Cairo.

Toby Bell is the British Embassy's blue-eyed boy – ask anyone from the ambassador down! A six-month immersion course in Arabic and, blow me, the lad's already halfway to speaking it! Hits it off with Egyptian generals and never once gives vent to his *callow personal opinions* – a phrase that has lodged itself permanently in his consciousness. Goes diligently about the business in which he has almost accidentally acquired expertise; barters intelligence with his Egyptian opposite numbers; and under instruction feeds them names of Egyptian Islamists in London who are plotting against the regime.

At weekends, he enjoys jolly camel rides with debonair military officers and secret policemen and lavish parties with the super-rich in their guarded desert condominiums. And at dawn, after flirting with their glamorous daughters, drives home with car windows closed to keep out the stench of burning plastic and rotting food as the ragged ghosts of children and their shrouded mothers forage for scraps in filthy acres of unsorted rubbish at the city's edge.

And who is the guiding light in London who presides over this pragmatic trade in human destinies, sends cosy personal letters of appreciation to the reigning head of Mubarak's secret police? – none other than Giles Oakley, Foreign Office intelligence broker *extraordinaire* and mandarin at large.

So it's no surprise to anyone, except perhaps young Bell himself, that even while popular unrest throughout Egypt over Hosni Mubarak's persecution of the Muslim Brotherhood is showing signs of erupting into violence four months ahead of the municipal elections, Toby should find himself whisked back to London and yet again promoted ahead of his years, to the post of Private Secretary, minder and confidential counsellor to the newly appointed Junior Minister of State to the Foreign Office, Fergus Quinn, MP, latterly of the Ministry of Defence.

*

'From where I sit, you two are an ideal match,' says Diana, his new Director of Regional Services, as she hacks away manfully at her open tuna sandwich over a dry self-service lunch at the Institute of Contemporary Arts. She is small, pretty and Anglo-Indian and talks in the heroic anachronisms of the Punjabi officers' mess. Her shy smile, however, belies an iron purpose. Somewhere she has a husband and two children, but makes no mention of them in office hours.

'You're both young for your jobs – all right, he's got ten years on you – but both ambitious as all get-out,' she declares, unaware that the description applies equally to herself. 'And don't be fooled by appearances. He's a thug, he beats the working-class drum, but he's also ex-Catholic, ex-communist and New Labour – or what's left of it now that its champion has moved on to richer pastures.'

Pause for a judicious munch.

'Fergus hates ideology and thinks he's invented pragmatism. And of course he hates the Tories, although half the time he's to the right of them. He's got a serious supporters' club in Downing Street, and I don't mean just the big beasts but the courtiers and spinmeisters. Fergus is their boy and they're putting their shirts on him for as long as he runs. Pro-Atlantic to a fault, but if Washington thinks he's the cat's pyjamas, who are we to complain? Eurosceptic, that goes without saying. Doesn't like us flunkies, but what politician does? And watch out for him when he bangs on about the *G-WOT*' – the prevailing in-word for the Global War on Terror. 'It's out of style and I don't need to tell *you* of all people that decent Arabs are getting awfully pissed off with it. He's been told that already. Your job will be the usual. Stick to him like glue and don't let him make any more puddles.'

'*More* puddles, Diana?' Toby asks, already troubled by some fairly loud rumours doing the rounds of the Whitehall gossip mill.

'Ignore totally,' she commands sternly, after another pause for accelerated mastication. 'Judge a politician by what he did or didn't do at Defence, you'd be stringing up half tomorrow's Cabinet.' And finding Toby's eyes still on her: 'Man made a horse's arse of himself and got his wrist smacked. Case totally closed.' And as a final afterthought: 'The only surprising thing is that for once in its life Defence managed to hush up a force-twelve scandal.'

And with that, the loud rumours are officially declared dead and buried – until, in a concluding speech over coffee, Diana elects to exhume them and bury them all over again.

'And just in case anyone should tell you different, both Defence *and* Treasury held a grand-slam internal inquiry with the gloves off, and concluded *unanimously* that Fergus had absolutely no case to answer. At worst, ill advised by his hopeless officials.

Which is good enough for me, and I trust for you. Why are you looking at me like that?'

He isn't looking at her in any way he is aware of, but he is certainly thinking that the lady is protesting too much.

*

Toby Bell, newly anointed Private Secretary to Her Majesty's newly anointed Minister takes up his seals of office. Fergus Quinn, MP, marooned Blairite of the new Gordon Brown era, may not on the face of it be the sort of minister he would have chosen for his master. Born the only child of an old Glaswegian engineering family fallen on hard times, Fergus made an early name for himself in left-wing student politics, leading protest marches, confronting the police and generally getting his photograph in the newspapers. Having graduated in Economics from Edinburgh University, he disappears into the mists of Scottish Labour Party politics. Three years on, somewhat inexplicably, he resurfaces at the John F. Kennedy School of Government at Harvard, where he meets and marries his present wife, a wealthy but troubled Canadian woman. He returns to Scotland, where a safe seat awaits him. The Party spin doctors quickly rate his wife unfit for presentation. An alcohol addiction is rumoured.

Soundings that Toby has taken round the Whitehall bazaar are mixed at best: 'Sucks up a brief quick enough, but watch your arse when he decides to act on it,' advises a bruised Defence Ministry veteran strictly off the record. And from a former assistant called Lucy: 'Very sweet, very charming when he needs to be.' And when he doesn't? Toby asks. 'He's just not *with* us,' she insists, frowning and avoiding his eye. 'He's out there fighting his demons somehow.' But what demons and fighting them how is more than Lucy is willing or able to say.

At first sight, nonetheless, all augurs well.

True, Fergus Quinn is no easy ride, but Toby never expected different. He can be clever, obtuse, petulant, foul-mouthed and dazzlingly considerate in the space of half a day, one minute all over you, the next a brooder who locks himself up with his despatch boxes behind his heavy mahogany door. He is a natural bully and, as advertised, makes no secret of his contempt for civil servants; even those closest to him are not spared his tongue-lashings. But his greatest scorn is reserved for Whitehall's sprawling intelligence octopus, which he holds to be bloated, elitist, self-regarding and in thrall to its own mystique. And this is all the more unfortunate since part of Team Quinn's remit requires it to 'evaluate incoming intelligence materials from all sources and submit recommendations for exploitation by the appropriate services'.

As to the scandal-at-Defence-that-never-was, whenever Toby is tempted to edge alongside it, he bumps up against what feels increasingly like a wall of silence deliberately constructed for his personal benefit: *case closed, mate . . . sorry, old boy, lips sealed . . .* And once, if only from a boastful clerk in Finance Section over a Friday-evening pint in the Sherlock Holmes – *got away with daylight robbery, didn't he?* It takes the unlovable Gregory, seated by chance next to Toby at a tedious Monday focus session of the Staffing and Management Committee, to set his alarm bells ringing at full blast.

Gregory, a large and ponderous man older than his years, is Toby's exact contemporary and supposed rival. But it is a fact known to all that, whenever the two of them are in line for an appointment, it's always Toby who pips Gregory at the post. And so it might have been in the recent race for Private Secretary to the new Junior Minister, except that this time round the rumour mill decreed that there was no proper contest. Gregory had served a two-year secondment to Defence, bringing him into almost daily contact with Quinn, whereas Toby was virgin – which is to say, he brought no such murky baggage from the past.

The focus session drags to its inconclusive end. The room empties. Toby and Gregory remain by tacit agreement at the table. For Toby the moment provides a welcome opportunity to mend fences; Gregory is less sweetly disposed.

'Getting along all right with King Fergie, are we?' he enquires.

'Fine, thanks, Gregory, just fine. A few wrinkles here and there, only to be expected. How's life as Resident Clerk these days? Must be pretty eventful.'

But Gregory is not keen to discuss life as a Resident Clerk, which he regards as a poor second to Private Secretary to the new Minister.

'Well, watch out he doesn't flog the office furniture out the back door is all I can say,' he advises with a humourless smirk.

'Why? Is that his thing? Flogging furniture? He'd have a bit of a problem, humping his new desk down three floors, even him!' Toby replies, determined not to rise.

'And he hasn't signed you up to one of his highly profitable business companies yet?'

'Is that what he did to you?'

'No way, *old sport*' – with improbable geniality – 'not me. I stayed clear. Good men are scarce, I say. Others weren't so fly.'

And here without warning Toby's patience snaps, which in Gregory's company is what it tends to do.

'Actually, what the hell are you trying to tell me, Gregory?' he demands. And when all he gets is Gregory's big, slow grin again: 'If you're warning me – if this is something I should know – then come out with it or go to Human bloody Resources.'

Gregory affects to weigh this suggestion.

'Well, I suppose if it was anything you needed to *know*, old sport, you could always have a quiet word with your guardian angel Giles, couldn't you?'

*

A self-righteous sense of purpose now swept over Toby which, even in retrospect, seated at his rickety coffee table on a sunny pavement in Soho, he could still not wholly justify to himself. Perhaps, he reflected, it was nothing more complicated than a case of pique at being denied a truth owed to him and shared by those around him. And certainly he would have argued that, since Diana had ordered him to stick like glue to his new master and not let him make puddles, he had a right to find out what puddles the man had made in the past. Politicians, in his limited experience of the breed, were repeat offenders. If and when Fergus Quinn offended in the future, it would be Toby who would have to explain why he had let his master off the lead.

As to Gregory's jibe that he should go running to his *guardian angel* Giles Oakley: forget it. If Giles wanted Toby to know something, Giles would tell him. And if Giles didn't, nothing on God's earth was going to make him.

Yet something else, something deeper and more troubling, is driving Toby. It is his master's near-pathological reclusiveness.

What in Heaven's name does a man so seemingly extrovert *do* all day, cloistered alone in his Private Office with classical music booming out and the door locked not only against the outer world but against his very own staff? What's inside those plump, hand-delivered, double-sealed, waxed envelopes that pour in from the little back rooms of Downing Street marked STRICTLY PERSONAL & PRIVATE which Quinn receives, signs for and, having read, returns to the same intractable couriers who brought them?

It's not only Quinn's past I'm being cut out of. It's his present.

*

His first stop is Matti, career spy, drinking pal and former embassy colleague in Madrid. Matti is currently kicking his heels between postings in his Service's headquarters across the river in Vauxhall. Perhaps the enforced inactivity will make him more forthcoming than usual. For arcane reasons – Toby suspects operational – Matti is also a member of the Lansdowne Club off Berkeley Square. They meet for squash. Matti is gangly, bald and bespectacled and has wrists of steel. Toby loses four–one. They shower, sit in the bar overlooking the swimming pool and watch the pretty girls. After a few desultory exchanges, Toby comes to the point:

'So give me the story, Matti, because nobody else will. What went wrong at Defence when my minister was in the saddle?'

Matti does some slow-motion nodding of his long, goatish head:

'Yes, well. There's not a lot I can offer you, is there?' he says moodily. 'Your man went off the reservation, our lot saved his neck and he hasn't forgiven us is about the long and short of it – silly bugger.'

'Saved his neck *how*, for God's sake?'

'Tried to go it alone, didn't he?' says Matti contemptuously.

'Doing what? Who to?'

Matti scratches his bald head and does another 'Yes, well. Not my turf, you see. Not my area.'

'I realize that, Matti. I accept it. It's not my area either. But I'm the bloody man's minder, aren't I?'

'All those bent lobbyists and arms salesmen beavering away at the fault lines between the defence industry and procurement,' Matti complains, as if Toby is familiar with the problem.

But Toby isn't, so he waits for more:

'Licensed, of course. That was half the trouble. Licensed to rip off the Exchequer, bribe officials, offer them all the girls they can eat, holidays in Bali. Licensed to go private, go public, go any way they like, long as they've got a ministerial pass, which they all have.'

'And Quinn had his snout in the trough with the rest of them, you're saying?'

'I'm not saying any bloody thing,' Matti retorts sharply.

'I know that. And I'm not hearing anything either. So Quinn stole. Is that it? All right, not exactly stole, perhaps, but diverted funds to certain projects in which he had an interest. Or his wife did. Or his cousin did. Or his aunt did. Is that it? Got caught, paid back the money, said he was awfully sorry, and the whole thing was swept under the carpet. Am I warm?'

A nubile girl bellyflops into the water to shrieks of laughter.

'There's a creep around called Crispin,' Matti murmurs under the clamour. 'Ever heard of him?'

'No.'

'Well, I haven't either, so I'll thank you to remember that. Crispin. Dodgy bastard. Avoid.'

'Any reason given?'

'Not specific. Our lot used him for a couple of jobs, then dropped him like a hot brick. Supposed to have led your man by the nose while he was Defence. All I know. Could be crap. Now get off my back.'

And with this Matti resumes his brooding contemplation of the pretty girls.

*

And as is often the way of life, from the moment Matti lets the name *Crispin* out of the box, it seems unable to let Toby go.

At a Cabinet Office wine and cheese party, two mandarins talk head to head: '*Whatever happened to that shit Crispin, by the by?*' '*Saw him hanging around the Lords the other day, don't know how he has the gall.*' But on Toby's approach the topic of their conversation turns abruptly to cricket.

At the close of an interministerial conference on intelligence with *frenemy* liaisons, as the current buzzword has it, the name acquires its own initial: *well, let's just hope you people don't do another J. Crispin on us*, snaps a Home Office director at her hated opposite number in Defence.

But is it really just a J? Or is it Jay like Jay Gatsby?

After half a night's googling while Isabel sulks in the bedroom, Toby is none the wiser.

He will try Laura.

★

Laura is a Treasury boffin, fifty years old, sometime Fellow of All Souls, boisterous, brilliant, vast and overflowing with good cheer. When she descended unannounced on the British Embassy in Berlin as leader of a surprise audit team, Giles Oakley had commanded Toby to 'take her out to dinner and charm the knickers off her'. This he had duly done, if not literally; and to such effect that their occasional dinners had continued without Oakley's guidance ever since.

By good fortune, it's Toby's turn. He selects Laura's favourite restaurant off the King's Road. As usual, she has dressed with panache for the event, in a huge, flowing kaftan hung with beads and bangles and a cameo brooch the size of a saucer. Laura loves fish. Toby orders a sea bass baked in salt to share and an expensive Meursault to go with it. In her excitement Laura seizes his hands across the table and shakes them like a child dancing to music.

'*Marvellous*, Toby, darling,' she blurts, 'and high time too,' in a voice that rolls like cannon fire across the restaurant; and then blushes at her own loudness and drops her voice to a genteel murmur.

'So how was Cairo? Did the natives storm the embassy and demand your head on a pike? I'd have been *utterly* terrified. Tell all.'

63

And after Cairo, she must hear about Isabel, because as ever she insists on her rights as Toby's agony aunt:

'*Very* sweet, *very* beautiful, and a ninny,' she rules when she has heard him out. 'Only a ninny marries a painter. As for *you*, you never could tell the difference between brains and beauty, and I suppose that still applies. I'm sure the two of you are perfectly suited,' she concludes, with another hoot of laughter.

'And the secret pulse of our great nation, Laura?' Toby enquires lightly in return, since Laura has no known love life of her own that may be spoken of. 'How are things in the oh-so-hallowed halls of the Treasury these days?'

Laura's generous face lapses into despair, and her voice with it:

'Grim, darling, just appalling. We're clever and nice, but we're understaffed and underpaid and we want the best for our country, which is old-fashioned of us. New Labour loves Big Greed, and Big Greed has *armies* of amoral lawyers and accountants on the make and pays them the earth to make rings round us. We can't compete; they're too big to fail and too big to fight. Now I've depressed you. Good. I'm depressed too,' she says, taking a merry pull at her Meursault.

The fish arrives. Reverent quiet while the waiter takes it off the bone and divides it.

'Darling, *what* a thrill,' breathes Laura.

They tuck in. If Toby is to chance his arm, this is his moment.

'Laura.'

'Darling.'

'Who precisely is J. Crispin when he's at home? And J standing for what? There was some scandal at Defence while Quinn was there. Crispin was mixed up in it. I hear his name all over town, I'm being kept out of the loop and it frightens me. Somebody even described him as Quinn's Svengali.'

Laura studies him with her very bright eyes, looks away, then takes a second look, as if she isn't comfortable with what she's seen there.

'Is this why you asked me to dinner, Toby?'

'Partly.'

'Wholly,' she corrects him, drawing a breath that is nearly a sigh. 'And I think you could have had the decency to tell me that was your fell purpose.'

A pause while they both collect themselves. Laura resumes:

'You're out of the loop for the very good reason that you're not supposed to be in it. Fergus Quinn has been given a fresh start. You're part of it.'

'I'm also his keeper,' he replies defiantly, recovering his courage.

Another deep breath, a hard look, before the eyes turn downward and stay there.

'I'll tell you bits,' she decides finally. 'Not all, but more than I should.'

She sits upright and, like a child in disgrace, talks to her plate.

Quinn walked into a quagmire, she says. Defence was in a state of corporate rot long before he came on the scene. Perhaps Toby knows that already? Toby does. Half its officials didn't know whether they were working for the Queen or the arms industry, and didn't give a hoot as long as their bread was buttered. Perhaps Toby knows that, too? Toby does. He has heard it from Matti, but doesn't let on. She's not making excuses for Fergus. She's saying Crispin was there ahead of him and saw him coming.

Reluctantly, she once more helps herself to Toby's hand, and this time taps it sternly on the table to the rhythm of her words as she scolds him:

'And I'll tell you what you *did*, you evil man' – as if Toby himself is Crispin now – 'you set up your own *spy shop*. Right there inside the ministry. While everyone round you was flogging *arms*, you were peddling raw *intelligence*: straight from the shelf, direct to *buyer*, no stops between. *Unspun, untested, unpasteur-* ized and above all untouched by bureaucratic hands. Which was music to Fergie's ears. Does he still play music in his office?'

'Mostly Bach.'

'And you're Jay like the bird,' she adds, in a flurried answer to his earlier question.

'And Quinn actually *bought from him*? Or his company did?'

Laura takes another pull of her Meursault, shakes her head. Toby tries again:

'Was the stuff any good?'

'It was expensive, so it had to be good, didn't it?'

'What's he *like*, Laura?' Toby insists.

'Your minister?'

'No! Jay Crispin, of course.'

Laura takes a deep breath. Her tone becomes terminal, and even angry:

'Just listen to me, dear, will you? The scandal at Defence is dead, and Jay Crispin is henceforth and forever banished from all ministerial and government premises on pain of death. A strong formal letter has been sent to him to that effect. He will never grace the corridors of Whitehall or Westminster again.' Another breath. 'The inspiring minister whom you have the honour to serve, on the other hand, bruiser though he may be, has embarked on the next stage of his distin- guished career, I *trust* with your help. Now will you please get me my coat?'

After a week of flailing himself with remorse, Toby remains dogged by the same question: *If the scandal at Defence is dead and Crispin will never walk the corridors of Whitehall or Westminster again, then what's the bloody man doing lobbying the House of Lords?*

★

Six weeks roll by. On the surface things continue uneventfully. Toby drafts speeches and Quinn delivers them with conviction, even when there's nothing to be convinced of. Toby stands at Quinn's shoulder at receptions and murmurs the names of foreign dignitaries into his ear as they approach. Quinn greets them as long-lost friends.

But Quinn's continued secretiveness drives not only Toby but the entire ministerial staff to the edge of desperation. He will stalk out of a Whitehall meeting – at the Home Office, the Cabinet Office or Laura's Treasury – ignore his official Rover, hail a cab and disappear without explanation till next day. He will cancel a diplomatic engagement and not inform the diary secretary, his special advisors or even his Private Secretary. The pencilled entries in the diary he keeps on his desk are so cryptic that Toby can decipher them only with Quinn's grudging assistance. One day the diary disappears altogether.

But it's on their trips abroad that Quinn's secretiveness assumes in Toby's eyes a darker hue. Spurning the hospitality offered by local British ambassadors, Quinn the People's Choice prefers to take up residence in grand hotels. When the Foreign Office Accounts Department demurs, Quinn replies that he will pay his own way, which surprises Toby since, like many affluent people, Quinn is notoriously tight.

Or is some secret benefactor perhaps paying Quinn's way for him? Why else would he keep a separate credit card for settling his hotel bills and shield it with his body if Toby chances to come too close?

Meanwhile, Team Quinn is acquiring a household ghost.

*

Brussels.

Returning to their grand hotel at six o'clock in the evening after a long day's haggling with NATO officialdom, Quinn complains

67

of a nauseous headache, cancels his dinner engagement at the British Embassy and retires to his suite. At ten, after heavy soul-searching, Toby decides he must call up to the suite and enquire after his master's welfare. He gets voicemail. A DO NOT DISTURB notice hangs on the ministerial door. After further cogitation he descends to the lobby and shares his concerns with the concierge. Have there been any signs of life from the suite? Has the minister ordered room service, sent down for aspirin or – since Quinn is a notorious hypochondriac – for a doctor?

The concierge is bewildered:

'But Monsieur le Ministre left the hotel in his limousine two hours ago,' he exclaims, in haughty Belgian French.

Now Toby is bewildered. Quinn's *limousine*? He hasn't got one. The only limousine on offer is the ambassador's Rolls, which Toby has cancelled on Quinn's behalf.

Or did Quinn keep his embassy dinner engagement after all? The concierge presumes to correct him. The limousine was not a Rolls-Royce, monsieur. It was a Citroën sedan and the chauffeur was known personally to the concierge.

Then kindly describe to me exactly what took place – pressing twenty euros into the concierge's waiting hand.

'Most willingly, monsieur. The black Citroën pulled up at the front door at the same time as Monsieur le Ministre emerged from the centre lift. One suspects Monsieur le Ministre was advised by telephone of his car's imminent arrival. The two gentlemen greeted each other here in the lobby, got into the car and rode away.'

'You mean a gentleman got *out* of the car to collect him?'

'From the *back* of the black Citroën sedan. He was a passenger, clearly, not a servant.'

'Can you describe the gentleman?'

The concierge baulks.

'Well, was he white?' Toby demands impatiently.

'Completely, monsieur.'

'How old?'

The concierge would guess that the gentleman's age was similar to the minister's.

'Have you seen him before? Is he a regular here?'

'Never, monsieur. I assumed a diplomat, perhaps a colleague.'

'Large, small, what did he look like?'

The concierge again hesitates.

'Like yourself but a little older, and the hair shorter, monsieur.'

'And they spoke what language? Did you hear them talking?'

'English, monsieur. Natural English.'

'Have you any idea where they went? Did you gather where they were going?'

The concierge summons the *chasseur*, a cheeky black Congolese boy in a red uniform with a pillbox hat. The *chasseur* knows exactly where they went:

'To La Pomme du Paradis restaurant close to the palace. Three stars. *Grande gastronomie!*'

So much for Quinn's nauseous headache, thinks Toby.

'How can you be so sure of that?' he demands of the *chasseur*, who is bobbing about in his anxiety to be of help.

'It was the instruction he gave to the driver, monsieur! I heard all!'

'*Who* gave the instruction? To do *what*?'

'The gentleman who collected your minister! He sat down beside the driver and said: "Now one goes to La Pomme du Paradis" just as I was closing the door. His exact words, monsieur!'

Toby turns to the concierge:

'You said the gentleman who collected my minister rode in the back. Now we hear he sat in the front when they drove off. Couldn't the gentleman who collected him have been security?'

69

But it is the little Congolese *chasseur* who holds the floor, and he is not about to relinquish it:

'It was *necessary*, monsieur! Three persons in the back with an elegant lady: that would not be polite!'

A *lady*, thinks Toby, in despair. Don't tell me we've got *that* problem too.

'And what kind of lady are we talking about?' he asks, all jocular, but heart in mouth.

'She was *petite* and very charming, monsieur, a person of distinction.'

'And of what age, would you say?'

The *chasseur* cracks a fearless smile:

'It depends which parts of the lady we are talking about, monsieur,' he replies, and darts off before the concierge's wrath can strike him down.

But next morning, when Toby knocks at the door of the ministerial suite under the pretext of presenting Quinn with a sheaf of flattering British press stories that he has printed off the Internet, it is not the shadow of a young lady or an old one that he glimpses seated at the breakfast table behind the frosted-glass partition to the *salon* as his minister brusquely opens the door to him, grabs the papers and slams the door in his face. It is the shadow of a man: a trim, straight-backed man of average height in a crisp dark suit and tie.

Like yourself but a little older, and the hair shorter, monsieur.

★

Prague.

To the surprise of his staff, Minister Quinn is only too happy to accept the hospitality of the British Embassy in Prague. The ambassadress, a recent Foreign Office conscript from the City of London, is an old buddy of Quinn's from Harvard days. While Fergus was post-gradding in good governance, Stephanie was notching up a Master's in Business Studies. The conference, which takes place in the fabled castle that is Prague's pride, is spread over two days of cocktails, lunches and dinners. Its subject is how to improve intelligence liaison between NATO members formerly under the Soviet maw. By the Friday evening the delegates have departed, but Quinn will stay another night with his old friend and, in Stephanie's words, enjoy 'a small private dinner all for my old schoolmate Fergus', meaning that Toby's presence will not be required.

Toby passes the morning drafting his report on the conference, and the afternoon walking in the Prague hills. In the evening, captivated as ever by the glories of the city, he strolls beside the Vltava, wanders the cobbled streets, enjoys a solitary meal. On returning to the embassy, he chooses for his pleasure the long way past the castle and notices that the lights in the first-floor conference room are still burning.

From the street his view is constricted, and the lower half of each window is frosted. Nonetheless by climbing the hill a few paces and standing on tiptoe, he is able to discern the outline of a male speaker silently holding forth from a lectern on the raised platform. He is of average height. The bearing is erect and the jaw action perfunctory; the demeanour – he cannot say quite why – unmistakably British, perhaps because the hand gestures, while brisk and economic, are in some way inhibited. By the same token Toby has no doubt that English is the language being spoken.

Has Toby made the connection? Not yet. Not quite. His eye is too busy with the audience. It is about twelve strong and comfortably settled in an informal half-circle round the speaker. Only the heads are visible, but Toby has no difficulty in recognizing six of them. Four belong to the deputy chiefs of the Hungarian, Bulgarian, Romanian and Czech military intelligence services, every one of whom, only six hours earlier, professed his undying friendship to Toby before notionally boarding his plane or staff car for the journey home.

The two remaining heads, which are close together and set apart from the rest, are those of Her Majesty's Ambassador to the Czech Republic and her old Harvard chum, Fergus Quinn. Behind them on a trestle table lie the remnants of a lavish buffet that presumably replaced the small dinner all for Fergus.

For five minutes or longer – he will never know – Toby remains on the hillside, ignoring the passing night traffic, staring upward at the lighted windows of the castle, his concentration now fixed on the silhouetted figure at the lectern: on the trim, straight body, the crisp dark suit and the taut, emphatic gestures with which he spells out his rousing message.

But what *is* the mysterious evangelist's message?

And why does it have to be spelt out *here*, rather than in the embassy?

And why does it meet with such conspicuous approval from Her Majesty's minister and Her Majesty's ambassador?

And who above all is the minister's secret sharer, now in Brussels, now in Prague?

*

Berlin.

Having delivered a vacuous speech, written by Toby on demand under the title 'The Third Way: Social Justice and Its European Future', Quinn dines privately at the Adlon Hotel with unnamed guests. Toby, his day's work done, sits chatting in the garden of Café Einstein with his old friends Horst and Monika and their four-year-old daughter, Ella.

In the five years Toby and Horst have known each other, Horst has risen swiftly through the ranks of the German Foreign

Service to a position akin to Toby's. Monika, despite the cares of motherhood, contrives to work three days a week for a human rights group that Toby rates highly. The evening sun is warm, the Berlin air crisp. Horst and Monika speak the north German that Toby is most comfortable with.

'So, Toby' – Horst, sounding not quite as casual as he means to. 'Your Minister Quinn is Karl Marx in reverse, we hear. Who needs the state, when private enterprise will do the job for us? Under your new British socialism, we bureaucrats are redundant, you and I.'

Unsure where Horst is coming from, Toby prevaricates:

'I don't remember putting *that* into his speech,' he says, with a laugh.

'But behind closed doors, that is what he is telling us, is it not?' Horst insists, lowering his voice further. 'And what I am asking you is, Toby, off the record, do you support your Mr Quinn's proposition? It's not improper to have an opinion, surely. As a private person, you are entitled to an off-the-record opinion about a private proposition.'

Ella is crayoning a dinosaur. Monika is assisting her.

'Horst, this is Greek to me,' Toby protests, dropping his voice to match Horst's. '*What* proposition? Made to whom? About what?'

Horst seems undecided, then shrugs.

'Okay. Then I may tell my boss that Minister Quinn's Private Secretary knows nothing? You don't know that your minister and his talented business associate are urging my boss to invest informally in a private corporation that specializes in a certain precious commodity? You don't know that the commodity on offer is supposedly of higher quality than anything available on the open market? I may tell him this officially? Yes, Toby?'

'Tell your boss whatever you like. Officially or otherwise. Then tell me what on earth the commodity is.'

High-grade information, Horst replies.

More commonly known as secret intelligence.

Collected and disseminated in the private sphere only.

Unadulterated.

Untouched by government hands.

And this talented business associate of his? Does he have a name? – Toby, incredulously.

Crispin.

Quite a persuasive fellow, says Horst.

Very English.

*

'*Tobe. A quickie, sir, if I may.*'

Since returning to London, Toby has found himself in an impossible quandary. Officially he knows nothing of his minister's record of mixing private business with official duties, let alone of the scandal at Defence. If Toby goes to his regional director, who expressly forbade him to enquire into such matters, he will be betraying the confidences of Matti and Laura.

And Toby as ever is conflicted. His own ambitions matter to him too. After almost three months as the minister's Private Secretary, he has no desire to compromise whatever bond he has forged with him, tenuous though it is.

He is wrestling with these abstractions when, at four o'clock one afternoon that same week, he receives the familiar summons over the ministerial phone. The mahogany door is for once ajar. He taps, shoves and enters.

'Close it, please. Lock.'

He closes, locks. The minister's manner strikes him as a bit too affable for comfort: and the more so when he rises blithely from his desk and, with an air of schoolboyish conspiracy, steers him to the bay window. The newly installed music system, his pride, is playing Mozart. He lowers the volume but is careful not to dowse it.

'All well with you, Tobe?'

'All fine, thanks.'

'Tobe, I very much fear I'm about to screw up yet another evening for you. Are you game for that?'

'Of course, Minister. If it's necessary' – thinking, Oh Christ, Isabel, theatre, dinner, not another.

'I'm receiving royalty tonight.'

'Literally?'

'Figuratively. But probably a damn sight richer.' Chuckle. 'You help out with the honours, make your mark, go home. How's that?'

'My *mark*, Minister?'

'Circles within circles, Tobe. There's a chance you may be invited aboard a certain very secret ship. I'll say no more.'

Aboard? Invited by *whom*? *What* ship? Under whose captaincy?

'May I know the names of your royal visitors, Minister?'

'Absolutely *not*' – beaming smile of complicity – 'I've spoken to the front gate. Two visitors for the minister at seven. No names, no pack drill. Out by eight thirty, nothing in the book.'

Spoken to the front gate? The man's got half a dozen underlings at his beck and call, all bursting to speak to the front gate for him.

Returning to the anteroom, Toby rallies the reluctant staff. Judy, social secretary, is provided with a ministerial car and dispatched post-haste to Fortnum's to buy two bottles of Dom Pérignon, one jar of foie gras, one smoked salmon pâté, a lemon and assorted crispbreads. She's to use her own credit card and the minister will reimburse. Olivia, the diary secretary, phones the canteen and confirms that two bottles and two jars, contents unstated, can be kept on ice till seven provided it's all right with Security. Grudgingly, it is. The canteen will supply an ice bucket and pepper. Only when all this is achieved may the remaining staff go home.

Alone at his desk, Toby affects to work. At 6.35 he descends to the canteen. At 6.40 he is back in the anteroom spreading foie gras and smoked salmon pâté on crispbread. At 6.55 the minister emerges from his sanctum, inspects the display, approves it and places himself before the anteroom door. Toby stands behind him, on his left side, thus leaving the ministerial right hand free to greet.

'He'll be on the dot. Always is,' Quinn promises. 'So will she, the darling. She may be who she is, but she's got his mindset.'

Sure enough, as Big Ben strikes he hears footsteps approach down the corridor, two pairs, the one strong and slow, the other light and skittish. A man is outstriding a woman. Punctually at the last stroke, a peremptory rap resounds on the anteroom door. Toby starts forward but is too late. The door is thrust open and Jay Crispin enters.

The identification is immediate and definite and so expected as to be anticlimactic. Jay Crispin, in the flesh at last, and high time too. Jay Crispin, who caused an unsung scandal at Defence and will never grace the corridors of Whitehall and Westminster again; who spirited Quinn from the lobby of his grand hotel in Brussels, sat in the front passenger seat of the Citroën sedan that took him to La Pomme du Paradis, breakfasted with him in the ministerial suite and orated from the lectern in Prague: not a ghost, but himself. Just a trim, regular-featured, rather obviously pretty man of no depth: a man, in short, to be seen through at a glance; so why on earth hasn't Quinn seen through him?

And halfway down Crispin's left arm, clinging to it with one bejewelled claw, trips a tiny woman in a pink chiffon dress with matching hat and high-heeled shoes with diamanté buckles.

Age? It depends which parts of the lady we are talking about, mon-sieur.

Quinn reverently takes her hand and ducks his heavy boxer's head over it in a crude half-bow. But Quinn and Crispin are old buddies reunited: see the rugged handshake, the manly shoulder-patting of the Jay-and-Fergus show.

It's Toby's turn to be acknowledged. Quinn lavishly to the fore:

'Maisie, allow me to present my invaluable Private Secretary, *Toby Bell*. Tobe, kindly pay your respects to Mrs Spencer Hardy of Houston, Texas, better known to the world's elite as the one and only *Miss Maisie*.'

A touch like gauze drawn across Toby's palm. A Deep South murmur of 'Why *hullo there, Mr Bell!*' followed by a vampish cry of 'Hey, now listen, Fergus, I'm the only *belle* around here!' to gusts of sycophantic laughter in which Toby obligingly joins.

'And Tobe, meet my old friend Jay Crispin. Old friend since – *when*, for God's sake, Jay?'

'Good to meet you, Toby,' Crispin drawls in upper-end English of the very best sort, taking Toby's hand in a kinsman's grasp and, without releasing it, vouchsafing him the sort of sturdy look that says: We're the men who run the world.

'And good to meet *you*' – omitting the 'sir'.

'And we do *what* here, exactly?' – Crispin, still gripping his hand.

'He's my Private Secretary, Jay! I told you. Bound to me body and soul and assiduous to a fault. Correct, Tobe?'

'Pretty new to the job, aren't we, Toby?' – finally letting his hand go, but keeping the 'we' because they're these two blokish chaps together.

'Three months,' the minister's voice chimes in again excitedly. 'We're twins. Correct, Tobe?'

'And where were we before, may one enquire?' – Crispin, sleek as a cat and about as trustworthy.

'Berlin. Madrid. Cairo,' Toby replies with deliberate carelessness, fully aware that he's supposed to be *making his mark*, and determined not to. 'Wherever I'm sent, really' – *you're too fucking close. Get out of my airspace.*

'Tobe was posted out of Egypt just when Mubarak's little local difficulties started to appear on the horizon, weren't you, Tobe?'

'As it were.'

'See much of the old boy?' – Crispin enquires genially, his face puckering in earnest sympathy.

'On a couple of occasions. From a distance' – *mainly I dealt with his torturers.*

'What do you reckon to his chances? Sits uneasy on his throne, from all one hears. Army a broken reed, Muslim Brotherhood rattling at the bars: I'm not sure I'd like to be in poor Hosni's shoes right now.'

Toby is still hunting for a suitably anodyne reply when Miss Maisie rides to his rescue:

'*Mr Bell*. Colonel Hosni Mubarak is *my friend*. He is America's friend, and he was *put on earth by God to make peace with the Jews*, to fight communism and jihadist terror. Anybody seeking the downfall of Hosni Mubarak in his hour of need is an Iscariot, a liberal and a surrender monkey, Mr Bell.'

'So how about *Berlin*?' Crispin suggests, as if this outburst has not taken place. 'Toby was in *Berlin*, darling. Stationed there. Where we were just days ago. Remember?' – back to Toby – 'what dates are we talking here?'

In a wooden voice, Toby recites for him the dates he was in Berlin.

'What sort of work, actually, or aren't you allowed to say?' – innuendo.

'Jack of all trades, really. Whatever came up,' Toby replies, with assumed casualness.

'But you're straight – not one of *them*?' – tipping Toby the insider's smile. 'You must be, or you wouldn't be here, you'd be the other side of the river' – knowing glance for the one and only Miss Maisie of Houston, Texas.

'Political Section, actually. General duties,' Toby replies in the same wooden voice.

'Well, I'm damned' – turning delightedly to Miss Maisie – 'Darling, the cat's out of the bag. Young Toby here was one of Giles Oakley's bright boys in Berlin during the run-up to *Iraqi Freedom*.'

Boys? Fuck you.

'Do I *know* Mr Oakley?' Miss Maisie enquires, coming closer to give Toby another look.

'No, darling, but you've heard of him. Oakley was the brave chap who led the in-house Foreign Office revolt. Got up the round robin to our Foreign Secretary urging him not to go after Saddam. Did you draft it for him, Toby, or did Oakley and his chums cobble it together all by themselves?'

'I certainly didn't draft anything of the sort, and I've never heard of such a letter, if it ever existed, which I seriously doubt,' the astonished Toby snaps in perfect truth as elsewhere in his mind he grapples, not for the first time, with the enigma that is Giles Oakley.

'Well, jolly good luck to you, anyway,' says Crispin dismissively and, turning to Quinn, leaves Toby to contemplate at his leisure the same straight, suspect back that he glimpsed through the frosted glass of his minister's hotel suite in Brussels, and again through the castle window in Prague.

*

Urgently google Mrs Spencer Hardy of Houston, Texas, widow and sole heiress of the late Spencer K. Hardy III, founder of Spencer Hardy Incorporated, a Texas-based multinational corporation trading in pretty well everything. Under her preferred sobriquet of Miss Maisie voted Republican Benefactress of the Year; Chairperson, the Americans for Christ Legion; Honorary President of a cluster of not-for-profit pro-life and family-value organizations; Chair of the American Institute for Islamic Awareness. And, in what looked almost like a recent add-on: President and CEO of an otherwise undescribed body calling itself Ethical Outcomes Incorporated.

Well, well, he thought: a red-hot evangelist and ethical to boot. Not a given. Not by any means.

*

For days and nights, Toby agonizes over the choices before him. Go running to Diana and tell all? – 'I disobeyed you, Diana. I know what happened at Defence and now it's happening all over again to us.' But what happened at Defence is none of his business, as Diana forcefully informed him. And the Foreign Office has many hellholes earmarked for discontents and whistle-blowers.

Meanwhile, the omens around him are daily multiplying. Whether this is Crispin's work he can only guess, but how else to explain the ostentatious cooling of the minister's attitude towards him? Entering or leaving his Private Office, Quinn now grants him barely a nod. It's no longer *Tobe* but *Toby*, a change he would once have welcomed. Not now. Not since he failed to make his mark and be invited aboard *a certain very secret ship*. Incoming phone calls from Whitehall's heavy hitters that were until now routinely passed through the Private Secretary are rerouted to the minister's desk by way of one of several newly installed direct lines. In addition to the heavily flagged despatch boxes from Downing Street that Quinn alone may handle, there are the sealed black canisters from the US Embassy. One morning a super-strong safe mysteriously appears in the Private Office. The minister alone has the combination to it.

And only last weekend, when Quinn is about to be driven to his country house in his official car, he does not require Toby to pack his briefcase for him with essential papers for his attention. He will do it himself, thank you, Toby, and behind locked doors. And no doubt, when Quinn arrives the other end, he will embrace the rich Canadian alcoholic wife whom his Party's spin doctors have ruled unfit for public presentation, pat his dog and his daughter, and once more lock himself away, and read them.

It therefore comes like an act of divine providence when Giles Oakley, now revealed as the closet author of a round-robin letter to the Foreign Secretary about the insanity of invading Iraq, calls Toby on his BlackBerry with an invitation to dine that same evening:

'Schloss Oakley, 7.45. Wear what you like and stick around afterwards for a Calvados. Is that a yes?'

It is a yes, Giles. It is a yes, even if it means cancelling another pair of theatre tickets.

*

Senior British diplomats who have been restored to their motherland have a way of turning their houses into overseas hirings. Giles and Hermione are no exception. Schloss Oakley, as Giles has determinedly christened it, is a sprawling twenties villa on the outer fringes of Highgate, but it could as well be their residence in Grunewald. Outside, the same imposing gates and immaculate gravel sweep, weed free; inside, the same scratched Chippendale-style furniture, close carpeting and contract Portuguese caterers.

Toby's fellow dinner guests include a counsellor at the German Embassy and his wife, a visiting Swedish ambassador to Ukraine, and a French woman pianist called Fifi and her lover Jacques. Fifi, who is fixated on alpacas, holds the table in thrall. Alpacas are the most considerate beasts on earth. They even produce their young with exquisite tact. She advises Hermione to get herself a pair. Hermione says she would only be jealous of them.

Dinner over, Hermione commands Toby to the kitchen, ostensibly to give a hand with coffee. She is fey, willowy and Irish and speaks in hushed, revelatory gasps while her brown eyes spark to their rhythm.

'This Isabel you're shagging' – poking a forefinger inside his shirt front and tickling his chest hairs with the tip of her lacquered fingernail.

'What about her?'

'Is she married like that Dutch floozie you had in Berlin?'

'Isabel and her husband split up months ago.'

'Is she blonde like the other one?'

'As it happens, yes, she is blonde.'

'I'm blonde. Was your mother blonde at all?'

'For God's sake, Hermione.'

'You know you only go with the married ones because you can give them back when you've finished with them, don't you?'

He knows nothing. Is she telling him he can borrow her too, and give her back to Oakley when he's finished with her? God forbid.

Or was she – a thought that only came to him now as he sipped his coffee at his pavement table in Soho and pursued his sightless contemplation of the passers-by – was she softening him up in advance of her husband's grilling?

*

'Nice chat with Hermione?' Giles asks sociably from his arm-chair, pouring Toby a generous shot of very old Calvados.

The last guests have taken their leave. Hermione has gone to bed. For a moment they are back in Berlin, with Toby about to vent his callow personal opinions and Oakley about to shoot them down in flames.

'Super, as always, thanks, Giles.'

'Did she invite you to Mourne in the summer?'

Mourne, her castle in Ireland, where she is reputed to take her lovers.

'I don't think she did, actually.'

'Snap it up, is my advice. Unspoilt views, decent house, nice bit of water. Shooting, if you're into it, which I'm not.'

'Sounds great.'

'How's love?' – the eternal question, every time they meet.

'Love's fine, thanks.'

'Still Isabel?'

'Just.'

It is Oakley's pleasure to switch topics without warning and expect Toby to catch up. He does so now.

'So, dear man, where in God's name is your nice new master? We seek him here, we seek him there. We tried to get him to come and talk to us the other day. The swine stood us up.'

By *us*, Toby assumes the Joint Intelligence Committee, of which Oakley is some sort of ex-officio member. How this should be is not something Toby asks. Does the man who ran up a seditious joint letter to the Foreign Secretary urging him not to go after Saddam, thereafter earn himself a seat at the Office's most secret councils? – or is he treated, as other rumours have it, as some kind of licensed contrarian, now cautiously admitted, now shut out? Toby has ceased to marvel at the para-doxes of Oakley's life, perhaps because he has ceased to marvel at his own.

'I understand my minister had to go to Washington at short notice,' he replies guardedly.

Guarded because, whatever Foreign Office ethic says, he is still, somehow, the minister's Private Secretary.

'But he didn't take you with him?'

'No, Giles. He didn't. Not this time.'

'He carted you around Europe with him. Why not Washington?'

'That was then. Before he started making his own arrangements without consulting me. He went to Washington alone.'

'You *know* he was alone?'

'No, but I surmise it.'

'You surmise it why? He went without you. That's all you know. To Washington proper, or the Suburb?'

For 'Suburb' read Langley, Virginia, home of the Central Intelligence Agency. Again Toby has to confess he doesn't know.

'Did he treat himself to British Airways First Class in the best traditions of Scottish frugality? Or slum it in Club, poor chap?'

Starting to yield despite himself, Toby takes a breath:

'I assume he travelled by private jet. It's how he went there before.'

'Before being *when* exactly?'

'Last month. Out on the sixteenth, back on the eighteenth. On a Gulfstream. Out of Northolt.'

'*Whose* Gulfstream?'

'It's a guess.'

'But an informed one.'

'All I know for a fact is he was driven to Northolt by private limo. He doesn't trust the Office car pool. He thinks the cars are bugged, probably by you, and that the chauffeurs listen in.'

'The limo being the property of –?'

'A Mrs Spencer Hardy.'

'Of Texas.'

'I believe so.'

'Better known as the mountainously wealthy Miss Maisie, born-again benefactress of America's Republican far right, friend of the Tea Party, scourge of Islam, homosexuals, abortion and, I believe, contraception. Currently residing in Lowndes Square, London SW. One entire side of it.'

'I didn't know that.'

'Oh yes. One of her many residences worldwide. And this is the lady, you tell me, who supplied the limousine to take your nice new master to Northolt airport. I have the right lady?'

'You do, Giles, you do.'

'And in your estimation it was therefore the same lady's Gulfstream that conveyed him to Washington?'

'It's a guess, but yes.'

'You are also aware, no doubt, that Miss Maisie is the protectress of one Jay Crispin, rising star in the ever-growing firmament of private defence contractors?'

'Broadly.'

'Jay Crispin and Miss Maisie recently paid a social call on Fergus Quinn in his Private Office. Were you present for those festivities?'

'Some of them.'

'With what effect?'

'I seem to have blotted my copybook.'

'With Quinn?'

'With all of them. There was talk of asking me aboard. It didn't happen.'

'Consider yourself fortunate. Did Crispin accompany Quinn to Washington in Miss Maisie's Gulfstream, do you suppose?'

'I've no idea.'

'Did the lady herself go?'

'Giles, I just don't *know*. It's all guesswork.'

'Miss Maisie sends her bodyguards to Messrs Huntsman on Savile Row to have them decently dressed. You didn't know that either?'

'Actually, no, I didn't.'

'Then drink some of that Calvados and tell me what you *do* know for a change.'

★

Rescued from the isolation of half-knowledge and suspicions that until now he has been unable to share with a living soul, Toby flops back in his armchair and basks in the luxury of confession. He describes, with growing indignation, his sightings in Prague and Brussels, and recounts Horst's probings in the garden of Café Einstein, until Oakley cuts him short:

'Does the name Bradley Hester sound familiar?'

'I'll say it does!'

'Why the humour?'

'He's the Private Office house pet. The girls adore him. Brad the Music Man, they call him.'

'We're speaking of the same Bradley Hester, I take it: assistant cultural attaché at the US Embassy?'

'Absolutely. Brad and Quinn are fellow music nuts. They've got a project going – transatlantic orchestral exchanges between consenting universities. They go to concerts together.'

'Quinn's diary says so?'

'When last seen. Used to,' Toby replies, still smiling at the recollection of tubby, pink-faced Brad Hester with his signature shabby music case chatting away to the girls in his queeny East Coast drawl while he waits to be admitted to the presence.

But Oakley doesn't warm to this benign image:

'And the purpose of these frequent visits to the Private Office is to discuss musical exchanges, you say.'

'They're written in stone. Brad's the one date of the week that Quinn never breaks.'

'Do you handle the paperwork that results from their discussions?'

'Good Lord, no. Brad takes care of all that. He has people. As far as Quinn's concerned, their project is extramural, not to be done in office hours. To his credit, he's quite particular about it,' Toby ends, slowing down as he meets Oakley's frigid stare.

'And you accept that preposterous notion?'

'I do my best. For want of any other,' Toby says, and grants himself a cautious sip of Calvados while Oakley contemplates the back of his left hand, turning his wedding ring, testing it against the knuckle for looseness.

'You mean you really don't smell a rat when Mr Bradley Hester, Assistant Cultural Attaché, marches in with his music case or whatever he brings? Or you refuse to?'

'I smell rats all the time,' Toby retorts sulkily. 'What's the difference?'

Oakley lets this go. 'Well, Toby, I hate to disillusion you, if that's what I'm doing. Mr Cultural Attaché Hester is not quite the amiable clown you appear determined to take him for. He's a discredited freelance intelligence pedlar of the far-right persuasion, born again, not to his advantage, and grafted on to the Agency's station in London at the behest of a caucus of wealthy American conservative evangelicals convinced that the Central Intelligence Agency is overrun with red-toothed Islamic sympathizers and liberal faggots, a view your nice new master is disposed to share. He is notionally employed by the United States government, but in practice by a fly-by-night company of defence contractors trading under the name of Ethical Outcomes Incorporated, of Texas and elsewhere. The sole shareholder and chief executive officer of this company is Maisie Spencer Hardy. She, however, has devolved her duties to one Jay Crispin, with whom she is having a ball. Jay Crispin, besides being an accomplished gigolo, is the intimate of your distinguished minister, who appears determined to outdo the militarist zeal that informs his late great leader, Brother Blair, though not, it seems, his luckless successor. Should Ethical Outcomes Incorporated ever find itself supplementing the feeble efforts of our national intelligence agencies by mounting a privately funded stealth operation, your friend the Music Man will be tasked with supplying the offshore logistics.'

And while Toby is digesting this, Oakley, as so often, changes direction:

'There's an *Elliot* somewhere in the mix,' he muses. 'Is Elliot a name to you? Elliot? Carelessly dropped? Overheard at the keyhole?'

'I don't listen at keyholes.'

'Of course you do. Albanian-Greek renegade, used to call himself Eglesias, ex-South African Special Forces, killed some chap in a bar in Jo'burg and came to Europe for his health? *That* sort of Elliot? Sure?'

'Sure.'

'*Stormont-Taylor?*' Oakley persists, in the same dreamy tone.

'Of course!' Toby cries in relief. 'Everyone knows Stormont-Taylor. So do you. He's the international lawyer' – effortlessly evoking the strikingly handsome Roy Stormont-Taylor, Queen's Counsel and television idol, with his flowing white mane and too-tight jeans, who three times in the last few months – or is it four? – has, like Bradley Hester, been warmly received by Quinn before being spirited behind the mahogany door.

'And what, so far as you are aware, is Stormont-Taylor's business with your nice new master?'

'Quinn doesn't trust government lawyers, so he consults Stormont-Taylor for an independent opinion.'

'And on what particular matter, do you happen to know, does Quinn consult the bold and beautiful Stormont-Taylor, who happens also to be an intimate of Jay Crispin?'

A fraught silence while Toby asks himself just who is being held to account here – Quinn or himself.

'How the fuck should *I* know?' he demands irritably – to which Oakley offers only a sympathetic 'How indeed?'

The silence returns.

'*So*, Giles,' Toby announces finally, ever the first to break on such occasions.

'So *what*, dear man?'

'*Who* the hell – or *what* the hell – is Jay Crispin in the scheme of things?'

Oakley pulls a sigh and shrugs. When he offers a reply, it comes in grudging fragments:

'Who's *anybody*?' he demands of the world at large, and breaks into grumpy telegramese. 'Third son of a posh Anglo-American family. Best schools. Sandhurst at second attempt. Ten years of bad soldiering. Retirement at forty. We're told voluntary, but one doubts it. Bit of City. Dumped. Bit of spying. Dumped. Sidles up alongside our burgeoning terror industry. Rightly observes that defence contractors are on a roll. Smells the money. Goes for it. Hullo, Ethical Outcomes and Miss Maisie. Crispin *charms* people,' he goes on in puzzled indignation. 'All *sorts* of people, all the time. God alone knows how. Granted, he does a lot of bed. Probably goes in both directions – good luck to him. But bed doesn't last the whole drink through, does it?'

'No, it doesn't,' Toby agrees, his mind darting uncomfortably to Isabel.

'So tell me,' Oakley continues, executing yet another unannounced change of direction. 'What possessed you to spend precious hours of the Queen's time trawling through Legal

Department's archives and pulling out files on such obscure places as Grenada and Diego Garcia?'

'My minister's orders,' Toby retorts, refusing to be surprised any longer either by Oakley's omniscience or his penchant for dealing questions from the bottom of the pack.

'Orders delivered to you personally?'

'Yes. He said I should prepare a paper on their territorial integrity. Without the knowledge of Legal Department or the special advisors. Actually, without the knowledge of anyone' – now that he came to think of it. 'Classify it top secret, bring it to him by Monday 10 a.m. without fail.'

'And you prepared such a paper?'

'At the cost of a weekend, yes.'

'Where is it?'

'Spiked.'

'Meaning?'

'My paper went out on submission, didn't have the traction and was spiked. According to Quinn.'

'Do you mind treating me to a short precis of its contents?'

'It was just a résumé. The alphabet. An undergraduate could do it.'

'Then tell me the alphabet. I've forgotten it.'

'In 1983, following the assassination of Grenada's leftist president, the Americans invaded the island without our say-so. They called the operation *Urgent Fury*. The fury was mainly ours.'

'How come?'

'It was our patch. A former British colony, now a member of the Commonwealth.'

'And the Americans invaded it. Shame on them. Go on.'

'The American spies – your beloved Suburb – had fantasies that Castro was about to use Grenada's airport as a launch pad. It was bullshit. The Brits had helped build the airport and weren't best pleased to be told it was a threat to America's life-blood.'

'And our response, in a word?'

'We told the Americans, please be so good as never to do any-thing like that again on our turf without our permission in advance, or we'll be even more cross.'

'And they told *us*?'

'To go fuck ourselves.'

'And did we?'

'The American point was well taken' – resorting to sarcastic Foreign Office mode. 'Our grip on our Crown territories is so tenuous that the State Department considers it's doing us a favour by acknowledging it. They only do it when it suits them, and in the case of Grenada it didn't suit them.'

'So go fuck ourselves again?'

'Not quite. They rowed back and an entente was hacked out.'

'To what effect, this entente? Go on.'

'In future, if the Americans were going to do something dra-matic on our turf – a special op under the guise of going to the assistance of the oppressed inhabitants, et cetera – they had to ask us nicely first, get our approval in writing, invite us to be part of the action and share the product with us at the end of the day.'

'By product, you mean intelligence.'

'I do, Giles. That's what I mean. Intelligence by another name.'

'And Diego Garcia?'

'Diego Garcia was the template.'

'For what?'

'Oh for God's sake, Giles!'

'I am unencumbered by background knowledge. Kindly tell me exactly what you told your nice new master.'

'Ever since we obligingly depopulated Diego Garcia for them

back in the sixties, the Americans have our permission to use it as a convenience for their blind-eye operations, but only on our terms.'

'The blind eye being in this case a British one, I take it.'

'Yes, Giles. I see I can get nothing past you. Diego Garcia remains a British possession, so it's still a British blind eye. You know *that* much, I trust?'

'Not necessarily.'

It is a principle of Giles when negotiating never to express the smallest satisfaction. Toby has watched him apply it in Berlin. Now he is watching him apply it to Toby.

'Did Quinn discuss the finer aspects of your paper with you?'

'There weren't any.'

'Come. It would only be courteous. What about the application of the Grenada experience to more substantial British possessions?'

Toby shakes his head.

'So he didn't discuss with you, even in the broadest brush, the rights and wrongs of an American intrusion into British Crown territory? On the basis of what you had unearthed for him?'

'Not even.'

A stage pause, of Oakley's making.

'Does your paper point a moral?'

'It limps to a conclusion, if that's what you mean.'

'Which is?'

'That any unilateral action by the Americans on British-owned territory would have to have a British fig leaf for cover. Otherwise, it would be no go.'

'Thank you, Toby. So what or who, I wonder, in your personal judgement, sparked this enquiry?'

'Honestly, Giles, I've no idea.'

Oakley raises his eyes to Heaven, lowers them, sighs:

'Toby. Dear man. A busy minister of the Crown does *not*

instruct his gifted young Private Secretary to burrow his way through dry-as-dust archives in search of *precedent* without first sharing his game plan with said underling.'

'This one fucking well *does!*'

And there you have Giles Oakley, the consummate poker player. He springs to his feet, tops up Toby's Calvados, sits back and declares himself content.

'So tell me' – all-confiding now that they are at ease with each other again – 'what on *earth* does one make of your nice new master's bizarre request of the Office's hard-pressed Human Resources Department?'

And when Toby protests yet again – but meekly this time because, after all, they are so relaxed – that he hasn't a clue what Oakley is talking about, he is rewarded with a satisfied chuckle.

'For a *low flyer*, Toby! Come! He's looking for a *low flyer* by yesterday. You *must* know that! He's got half our resourceful humanoids standing on their heads, looking for the right fellow. They've been calling round the houses, asking for recommendations.'

Low flyer?

For a fleeting moment Toby's mind wrestles with the spectre of a daredevil pilot gearing up to fly under the radar of one of Britain's vanishing protectorates. And he must have said something of this, because Giles almost laughs aloud and vows it's the best thing he's heard in months.

'*Low* as opposed to *high*, dear man! A reliable has-been from the ranks of our own dear Service! Job qualifications: an appropriately lacklustre record, his future behind him. An honest-to-God Foreign Service dobbin, no frills, one shot left in his locker before retirement. You in twenty-eight years' time or whatever it is,' he ends teasingly.

So that's it, thinks Toby, trying his best to share Giles's little joke. He's telling me, in the gentlest possible way, that Fergus

Quinn, not content with cutting me out of the loop, is actively seeking my replacement: and not just any replacement, but a has-been who will be so scared of losing his pension that he will bend whichever way he is ordered by his nice new master.

*

The two men stand side by side on the doorstep, waiting in the moonlight for Toby's cab. Toby has never seen Oakley's face more earnest – or more vulnerable. The playfulness in his voice, the little grace notes, are gone, replaced by a note of urgent warning:

'Whatever they're plotting, Toby, you are *not* to join it. You hear something, you take note, you text me on the cellphone number you already have. Marginally that will be more secure than email. Say you've been jilted by your girlfriend and need to weep on my shoulder, or some such nonsense.' And as if he hasn't made his point strongly enough: 'You do *not* on any account become part of it, Toby. You agree to nothing, you sign nothing. You do *not* become an accessory in any way.'

'But accessory to *what*, Giles, for pity's sake?'

'If I knew, you'd be the last person I'd tell. Crispin looked you over and mercifully didn't care for what he saw. I repeat: count yourself lucky you didn't pass the test. If it had gone the other way, God alone knows where you might have ended up.'

The cab arrives. Extraordinarily, Oakley holds out his hand. Toby takes it and discovers that it is damp with sweat. He releases it and climbs into the cab. Oakley taps on the window. Toby lowers it.

'It's all prepaid,' Oakley blurts. 'Just give him a pound tip. Don't pay twice, whatever you do, dear man.'

*

'*A quickie, Master Toby, sir, of your goodness.*'

Somehow, a whole week has passed. Isabel's resentment at

Toby's neglect has erupted into sullen fury. His apologies – abject, but distracted – have further incensed her. Quinn has shown himself equally intractable, now fawning on Toby for no good reason, now cutting him dead, now vanishing without explanation for an entire day and leaving him to pick up the pieces.

And on the Thursday in the lunch hour, a strangled call from Matti:

'That game of squash we never had.'

'What about it?'

'It didn't happen.'

'I thought we'd already agreed that.'

'Just checking,' said Matti, and rang off.

Now it's ten o'clock in the morning of yet another Friday and the familiar summons Toby has been dreading has rung out over the internal phone.

Is the Champion of the Working Classes about to pack him off to Fortnum's for more Dom Pérignon? Or is he shaping up to tell him that, appreciative as he is of Toby's talents, he proposes to replace him with a *low flyer* and wants to give Toby the weekend to recover from the shock?

The big mahogany door ajar as before. Enter, close, and – anticipating Quinn's command – lock. Quinn at his desk, looking like ministerial thunder. His officious voice, the one he uses for gravitas on *Newsnight*. The Glaswegian accent all but forgotten:

'I fear I am about to interfere with your plans for a mini-break with your significant other, Toby,' he announces, managing to imply that Toby has only himself to blame. 'Is that going to cause you major problems?'

'None at all, Minister,' Toby replies, mentally saying goodbye to a brief getaway in Dublin, and probably to Isabel as well.

'I happen to be under considerable pressure to hold an extremely secret meeting here tomorrow. In this very room. A meeting of the highest national importance.'

'You wish me to attend it, Minister?'

'Far from it. On no account may you attend, thank you. You're not cleared; your presence is in no way desirable. Don't take that personally. However, once again I wish your assistance in making the advance preparations. No champagne this time, alas. No foie gras either.'

'I understand.'

'I doubt it. However, for the meeting that has been thrust upon me, certain exceptional security measures require to be taken. I wish you, as my Private Secretary, to take them for me.'

'Of course.'

'You sound puzzled. Why?'

'Not *puzzled*, Minister. It's just – if your meeting is so secret, why does it have to be held in this room at all? Why not outside the Office altogether? Or in the soundproof room upstairs?'

Quinn jerks up his heavy head, scenting insubordination, then consents to answer:

'Because my very insistent visitor – visitors *plural*, actually – are in a position to call the shots, and it is my bounden duty as minister to deliver. Are you up for it, or do I look for someone else?'

'Entirely up for it, Minister.'

'Very well. You know, I take it, a certain side door leading into this building from Horse Guards? For the tradesmen and non-classified deliveries? A green metal door with bars in front of it?'

Toby knows the door but, not being what the Man of the People calls a tradesman, hasn't had occasion to use it.

'You know the ground-floor corridor that leads to it? Beneath us now, as we stand here? Two floors down?' – losing patience – 'As you come in by the main doors, for God's sake, on the right-hand side of the lobby. You pass it every day. Yes?'

Yes, he knows the corridor, too.

'Tomorrow morning, Saturday, my guests – my *visitors*, all right? – whatever they want to call themselves' – the note of resentment now becoming a refrain – 'will arrive at that side entrance in two parties. Separately. One after the other. In short order. Still with me?'

'Still with you, Minister.'

'I'm glad. From 11.45 to 13.45 hours precisely – for those two hours *only*, got it? – that side entrance will be *unmanned*. No member of security staff will be on duty for those *one hundred and twenty minutes*. All video cameras and other security devices covering that side entrance, *and* the route from that side entrance to this room, will be rendered *inert*. Deactivated. Switched off. For those two hours only. I've fixed it all personally. You don't have to do anything on that front, so don't even try. Now follow me closely.'

The minister raises a squat, muscular palm to Toby's face and demonstratively tweaks the little finger with the thumb and index finger of the other hand:

'On your arrival tomorrow morning at 10 a.m. you go straight to Security Department and confirm that my instruction to vacate and unlock the side entrance and turn off *all* surveillance systems has been duly noted and is about to be complied with.'

Ring finger. The gold ring very thick, with the cross of St Andrew embossed in bold blue.

'At 11.50 a.m. you proceed to the external side entrance by way of Horse Guards and enter the building by means of the said door, which has been unlocked in accordance with my instructions to Security Department. You then advance along the ground-floor corridor, establishing en route that the corridor and the rear staircase leading up from it are in no way occupied or obstructed. Still with me?'

Middle finger:

'You then make your way at your usual pace and, acting as my personal guinea pig, proceed by way of the rear staircase and adjoining landing – don't skip or pause for a pee or anything, just *walk* – to this very room where we are now standing. You then confirm with Security, by internal telephone, that your journey has passed undetected. I've squared them, so again don't do anything beyond what I've told you to do. That's an order.'

Toby wakes to discover he is the beneficiary of his master's election-winning smile:

'So then, Toby. Tell me I've ruined your weekend for you, the way they've ruined mine.'

'Not at all, Minister.'

'But?'

'Well, one question.'

'Many as you like. Fire away.'

Actually he has two.

'If I may ask, Minister, where will you be? You personally. While I am taking' – he hesitates – 'taking these precautions.'

The electoral smile widens.

'Let's say, minding my own fucking business, shall we?'

'Minding your own business until you arrive, Minister?'

'My timing will be impeccable, thank you. Any more?'

'Well, I was wondering, perhaps gratuitously: how will your parties get out again? You said the systems will be deactivated for two hours. If your second party is arriving in short order and the system is reactivated at 13.45, that leaves you not much more than ninety-odd minutes for your meeting.'

'Ninety minutes will hack it easy. Don't give it a thought' – the smile by now radiant.

'You're absolutely sure of that?' Toby urges, seized by a need to extend the conversation.

'Of *course* I'm bloody sure. Dinna *fash* yersel'! Couple of handshakes all round and we're home free.'

*

It is the lunch hour of the same day before Toby Bell feels able to slip away from his desk, hasten down Clive Steps and take up a position beneath a spreading London plane tree on the edge of St James's Park as a prelude to composing his emergency text to Oakley's cellphone.

During the time since Quinn has served him with his bizarre instructions, he has mentally drafted any number of versions. But rumour has it that Office security staff keep a watch on personal communications emanating from inside the building, and Toby has no wish to excite their curiosity.

The plane tree is an old friend. Set on a rise, it stands a stone's throw from Birdcage Walk and the War Memorial. A hundred yards on, and the bay windows of the Foreign Office frown sternly down on him, but the passing world of storks, mallards, tourists and mums with prams deprives them of their menace.

His eye and hand are dead steady as he holds his BlackBerry before him. So is his mind. It is a truth that puzzles Toby as much as it impresses his employers that he is immune to crisis. Isabel may be mercilessly dissecting his shortcomings: she did so in spades last night. Police cars and fire engines may be howling in the street, smoke pouring out of adjoining houses, the enraged populace on the march: they did all that and more in Cairo. But crisis, once it strikes, is Toby's element, and it has struck now.

Say you've been jilted by your girlfriend and need to weep on my shoulder, or some such nonsense.

Natural decency dictates he will not take Isabel's name in vain. *Louisa* comes to mind. Has he had a Louisa? A hasty roll call assures him he has not. Then he will have her now: *Giles. Louisa just walked out on me. Desperately need your urgent advice. Can we speak soonest? Bell.*

Press 'send'.

He does, and glances at the illustrious bay windows of the Foreign Office with their layers of net curtain. Is Oakley sitting up there even now, munching a sandwich at his desk? Or is he locked in some underground fastness with the Joint Intelligence Committee? Or ensconced in the Travellers Club with his fellow mandarins, redrawing the world over a leisurely lunch? Wherever you are, just for God's sake read my message soonest and get back to me, because my nice new master is going off his head.

*

Seven interminable hours have passed, and still not a peep out of Oakley. In the living room of his first-floor flat in Islington, Toby sits at his desk pretending to work while Isabel potters ominously in the kitchen. At his left elbow lies his BlackBerry, at his right the house telephone, and in front of him a draft paper Quinn has commissioned on opportunities for private–public partnerships in the Gulf. In theory, he is revising it. In reality, he is mentally tracking Oakley through every possible version of his day and willing him to respond. He has re-sent his message twice: once as soon as he was clear of the Office, and again as he emerged from Angel underground station before he arrived home. Why he should have regarded his own flat as an insecure launch pad for text messages to Oakley he can't imagine, but he did. The same inhibitions guide him now, when he decides that, importunate though it may be, the time has come to try Oakley at his home.

'Just popping out to get us a bottle of red,' he tells Isabel through the open kitchen door, and makes it to the hallway before she can reply that there's a perfectly good bottle of red in the stores cupboard.

In the street, it is pouring with rain and he has not thought to provide himself with a raincoat. Fifty yards along the pavement, an arched alley leads to a disused foundry. He dives into it and from its shelter dials the Oakley residence.

'Who the hell's this, for God's sake?'

Hermione, outraged. Has he woken her? At *this* hour?

'It's Toby Bell, Hermione. I'm really sorry to trouble you, but something a bit urgent's come up, and I wondered whether I could have a quick word with Giles.'

'Well, I'm afraid you *can't* have a quick word with Giles, or a slow one, for that matter, Toby. As I suspect you're thoroughly aware.'

'It's just work, Hermione. Something urgent's cropped up,' he repeated.

'All right, play your little games. Giles is in Doha, and don't pretend you didn't know. They packed him off at crack of dawn for a conference that's supposed to have blown up. Are you coming round to see me or not?'

'*They?* Which *they?*'

'What's it to you? He's gone, hasn't he?'

'How long will he be gone for? Did they say?'

'Long enough for what you're after, that's for sure. We've no live-in servants any more. I expect you knew that too, didn't you?'

Doha: three hours ahead. Brutally, he rings off. To hell with her. In Doha they eat late, so it's still the dinner hour for delegates and princelings. Huddled in the alleyway, he gets through to the Foreign Office resident clerk and hears the ponderous voice of Gregory, unsuccessful contender for his job.

'Gregory, hullo. I have to get in touch with Giles Oakley rather urgently. He's been rushed to Doha for a conference and for some reason he's not picking up his messages. It's a personal thing. Can you get word to him for me?'

'If it's personal? Tricky, I'm afraid, old sport.'

Don't go there. Stay calm:

'Do you happen to know if he's staying with the ambassador?'

'Up to him. Maybe he prefers big, expensive hotels like you and Fergus.'

Exert Herculean restraint:

'Well, kindly give me the number of the residence anyway, will you? Please, Gregory?'

'I can give you the *embassy*. They'll have to put you through. Sorry about that, old sport.'

Delay, which Toby perceives as deliberate, while Gregory hunts for the number. He dials it and gets a laborious female voice telling him, first in Arabic and then in English, that if he wishes to apply for a visa he should present himself in person at the British Consulate between the following hours and be prepared for a long delay. If he wishes to contact the ambassador or a member of the ambassador's household, he should leave his message *now*.

He leaves it:

'This is for Giles Oakley, currently attending the Doha Conference.' Breath. 'Giles, I sent you several messages, but you don't seem to have picked them up. I'm having serious personal problems, and I need your help as soon as possible. Please call me any time of day or night, either on this line or, if you prefer, on my home number.'

Returning to his flat, he realizes too late that he has forgotten to buy the bottle of red wine that he went out to get. Isabel notices, but says nothing.

*

Somehow, morning has broken. Isabel lies asleep beside him, but he knows that one careless move on his part and they will either quarrel or make love. In the night they have done both, but this has not prevented Toby from keeping his BlackBerry at his bedside and checking it for messages on the grounds that he is on call.

Neither have his thought processes been idle during this time, and the conclusion they have reached is that he will give Oakley until ten o'clock this morning, when he is pledged to perform the antics required of him by his minister. If by that time Oakley has not responded to his messages he will take the executive decision: one so drastic that at first glance he recoils at the prospect, then cautiously tiptoes back to take a second look.

And what does he see in his mind's eye, lying in wait for him in the deep right-hand drawer of his very own desk in the ministerial anteroom? Covered in mildew, verdigris and, if only in his imagination, mouse droppings?

A Cold War-era, pre-digital, industrial-sized tape recorder – an apparatus so ancient and lumbering, so redundant in our age of miniaturized technology as to be an offence to the contemporary soul: for which reason, if for no other, Toby has repeatedly requested its removal on the grounds that if any minister wished for a secret recording of a conversation in his Private Office, the devices available to him were so discreet and varied that he would be spoiled for choice.

But thus far – providentially or otherwise – his pleas have gone unanswered.

And the switch that operates this monster? Pull out the drawer above, hunt around with your right hand, and there it is: a sharp, hostile nipple mounted on a brown Bakelite half-cup, up for off, down for record.

*

0850 hours. Nothing from Oakley.

Toby likes a good breakfast but this Saturday morning doesn't feel peckish. Isabel is an actress and therefore doesn't touch breakfast, but she is in conciliatory mode and wishes to sit with him for friendship and watch him eat his boiled egg. Rather than precipitate another row, he boils one and eats it for her. He finds her mood suspect. On any past Saturday morning when he has announced he must pop into the office to clear up a bit of work, she has remained demonstratively in bed. This morning – although by rights they should be enjoying their weekend, sampling the delights of Dublin – she is all sweetness and understanding.

The day is sunny so he thinks he will leave early and walk it. Isabel says a walk is just what he needs. For the first time ever, she accompanies him to the front door, where she bestows a fond kiss on him, then stands watching him down the stairs. Is she telling him she loves him, or waiting till the coast is clear?

★

0952 hours. Still nothing from Oakley.

Having maintained a vigil over his BlackBerry while marching at exaggerated speed through the sparsely populated London streets, Toby starts his countdown to Birdcage Walk by way of The Mall and, adjusting his pace to that of the sightseers, advances on the green side door with metal bars in front of it.

He tests the handle. The green door yields.

He turns his back on the door and with studied casualness takes in Horse Guards, the London Eye, a group of wordless Japanese schoolchildren and – in a last, desperate appeal – the spreading London plane tree from whose shade he had yesterday dispatched the first of his unanswered messages to Oakley.

A last forlorn glance at his BlackBerry tells him that his appeal remains unheeded. He switches it off and consigns it to the darkness of an inner pocket.

★

Having performed the ludicrous manoeuvres required of him by his minister, Toby arrives in the anteroom to the Private Office and confirms by internal telephone with the bemused security guards that he has successfully escaped their attention.

'You were solid glass, Mr Bell, sir. I saw straight through you. Have a nice weekend.'

'You too, and thanks a bundle.'

Poised over his desk, he is emboldened by a surge of indignation. Giles, you're forcing me to do this.

The desk is supposedly prestigious: a kneehole-style reproduction antique with a tooled-leather worktop.

Seating himself in the chair before it, he leans forward and eases open the voluminous bottom right-hand drawer.

If there is a part of him that is still praying that his requests of Works Department have miraculously been answered during the night, let it pray no more. Like a rusting engine of war on a forgotten battlefield, the ancient tape recorder lies where she has lain for decades, waiting for the call that will never come: except that today it has. In place of voice activation, she boasts a timing device similar to the one on the microwave in his flat. Her aged spools are bare. But two giant tapes in dust-caked cellophane packets lie ready for duty on the shelf above her.

Up for off. Down for record.

And wait for tomorrow when I come and get you, if I'm not already in prison.

*

And tomorrow had finally come, and Isabel had gone. It was today, an unseasonably sunny spring Sunday, and church bells were summoning the sinners of Soho to repentance, and Toby Bell, bachelor of three hours' standing, was still seated at his pavement table over his third – or was it fifth? – coffee of the morning, steeling himself to commit the irrevocable act of felony that he had been planning and dreading all night: to wit, retrace his steps to the ministerial anteroom, collect the tape and spirit it out of the Foreign Office under the noses of the security guards in the manner of the vilest spy.

He still had a choice. He had worked that out, too, in the long, wild reaches of the night. For as long as he sat at this tin table, he could argue that nothing untoward had happened. No security officer in his right mind would consider checking out an age-old tape recorder mouldering in the bottom of his desk drawer. And in the distant possibility that the tape *was* discovered, well, he had his answer ready: in the stressful run-up to an ultra-secret meeting of immense national importance, Minister Quinn had remembered the existence of a covert audio system and instructed Toby to activate it. Later, with his head full of affairs of state, Quinn would deny that he had given such an order. Well, an aberration of that kind, for those who knew the man, would by no means be out of character; and for those who remembered the tribulations of Richard Nixon, all too familiar.

Toby peered round for the pretty waitress and, through the café doorway, saw her leaning over the counter, flirting with the waiter.

She gave him a lovely smile and came trotting out to him, still flirting.

Seven pounds, please. He gave her ten.

He stood on the kerb, watching the happy world brush past him.

Turn left for the Foreign Office, I'm on my way to prison. Turn right to Islington, I go home to a blessedly empty flat. But already, in the brightness of the morning, he was striding purposefully down Whitehall.

'Back again, Mr Bell? They must be running you ragged,' said the senior guard, who liked a chat.

But the younger ones only glowered at their screens.

The mahogany door was closed, but don't trust anything: Quinn may have snuck in early or, for all Toby knew, been in there all night, hunkered down with Jay Crispin, Roy Stormont-Taylor and Mr Music Brad.

He banged on the door, called 'Minister?' – banged again. No answer.

He strode to his desk, yanked open the bottom drawer and to his horror saw a pin-light burning. *Christ Almighty: if anybody had spotted it!*

He wound back the tape, coaxed it from its housing, returned switch and timer to their previous settings. With the tape wedged under his armpit he set out on his return journey, not forgetting a wave of 'Cheerio' to the older guard and a 'fuck you' nod of authority to the younger ones.

*

It is only minutes later, but already a calm of sleep has descended over Toby, and for a while he is standing still and everything is passing him by. When he wakes, he is in the Tottenham Court Road, eying the windows of second-hand electronics dealers and trying to decide which of them is the least likely to remember a thirty-something bloke in a baggy black jacket and chinos who wanted to buy a clapped-out second-hand family-sized tape recorder for cash.

And somewhere along the way he must have stopped at a cashpoint, bought himself a copy of the day's *Observer*, and also a carrier bag with a Union Jack on it, because the tape is nestling inside the bag between the pages of the newspaper.

And probably he has already dropped in on two or three shops before he lucked out with Aziz, who has this brother in Hamburg whose line of business is shipping scrap electronic equipment to Lagos by the container load. Old fridges, computers, radios and clapped-out giant tape recorders: this brother can't get enough of them, which is how Aziz comes to be keeping this pile of old stuff in his back room for his brother to collect.

And it is also how Toby, by a miracle of luck and persistence, becomes the owner of a replica of the Cold War-era tape recorder in the bottom right-hand drawer of his desk, except that this version was coloured a sleek pearl-grey and came in its original box which, as Aziz regretfully explained, made it a collector's item and therefore ten quid more, plus I'm afraid it's got to be another sixteen for the adaptor if you're going to wire it up to anything.

Manhandling his booty into the street, Toby was accosted by a sad old woman who had mislaid her bus pass. Discovering he had no loose change, he astonished her with a five-pound note.

Entering his flat, he was brought to a dead halt by Isabel's scent. The bedroom door was ajar. Nervously he pushed it open, then the door to the bathroom.

It's all right. It's just her scent. Jesus. You never know.

He tried wiring up the tape recorder on the kitchen table but the flex was too short. He uncoupled an extension lead from the living room and attached it.

Grunting and whimpering, the great Hebbelian Wheel of Life began to turn.

*

You know what you are, don't you? You're a bloody little drama queen.

No titles, no credits. No soothing introductory music. Just the minister's unopposed, complacent assertion, delivered to the beat of his bespoke suede boots by Lobb at a thousand pounds a foot, as he advances across the Private Office, presumably to his desk.

You're a drama queen, you understand? D'you even know what a drama queen is? You don't. Well, that's because you're pig-ignorant, isn't it?

Who the hell's he talking to? Did I come in too late? Did I set the timer wrong?

108

Or is Quinn addressing his Jack Russell bitch Pippa, an election accessory that he sometimes brings in to amuse the girls?

Or has he paused in front of the gilt-framed looking-glass and he's giving himself the New Labour mirror test, and soliloquizing while he does it?

Preparatory honking of ministerial throat. It's Quinn's habit to clear his throat before a meeting, then wash his mouth with Listerine with his loo door open. Evidently, the drama queen – whoever he or she is – is being berated *in absentia*, and probably in the mirror.

Squeak of leather as he lowers himself into his executive throne, ordered from Harrods on the same day he took office, along with new blue carpet and a clutch of encrypted phones.

Unidentified scratching sounds from desk area. Probably tinkering with the four empty red ministerial despatch boxes he insists on keeping at his elbow, as opposed to the full ones Toby isn't allowed to open.

Yes. Well. Good of you to come, anyway. Sorry to fuck up your weekend. Sorry you fucked up mine as a matter of fact, but you don't give a shit about that, do you? How've you been? Lady wife in good form? Glad to hear it. And the little brats all well? Give them a kick up the arse from me.

Footsteps approaching, faint but getting louder. Party the first is arriving.

The footsteps have passed through the unmanned, unlocked side entrance, traversed unmonitored corridors, scaled staircases, without pausing to pee: all just as Toby did yesterday in his role of ministerial guinea pig. The footsteps approaching the anteroom. One pair only. Hard soles. Leisured, nothing stealthy. These are not young feet.

And they're not Crispin's feet either. Crispin marches as to war. These are peaceful feet. They are feet that take their time, they're a man's and – why does Toby think he knows this, but he does – they're a stranger's. They belong to someone he hasn't met.

At the door to the anteroom they hesitate but don't knock. These feet have been instructed not to knock. They cross the anteroom, passing – oh, mother! – within two feet of Toby's desk and the recorder grinding away inside it with its pin-light on.

Will the feet hear it? Apparently they won't. Or if they do, they make nothing of it.

The feet advance. The feet enter the presence without knocking, presumably because that too is what they've been told to do. Toby waits for the squeak of the ministerial chair, doesn't hear it. He is briefly assailed by a dreadful thought: what if the visitor, like cultural attaché Hester, has brought his own music?

Heart in mouth, he waits. No music, just Quinn's offhand voice:

'You weren't stopped? Nobody questioned you? Bothered you?'

It's minister to inferior, and they already know each other. It's minister to Toby on an off day.

'At no stage was I bothered or in any way molested, Minister. Everything went like clockwork, I'm glad to say. Another fault-free round.'

Another? When was the last fault-free round? And what's with the equestrian reference? Toby has no time to linger.

'Sorry about screwing up your weekend,' Quinn is saying, in a familiar refrain. 'Not of my doing, I can assure you. Case of first-night wobblies on the part of our intrepid friend.'

'It's of no consequence whatever, Minister, I assure you. I had no plans beyond clearing out my attic, a promise I am only too happy to defer.'

Humour. Not appreciated.

'You saw Elliot, then. That went off all right. He filled you in. Yes?'

'Insofar as Elliot was able to fill me in, Minister, I'm sure he did.'

'It's called need-to-know. What did you make of him?' – not waiting for an answer. 'Good bloke on a dark night, they tell me.'

'I shall be happy to take your word for it.'

Elliot, Toby is remembering, *Albanian-Greek renegade . . . ex-South African Special Forces . . . killed some chap in a bar . . . came to Europe for his health.*

But by now the scenting British animal in Toby has parsed the visitor's voice, and hence its owner. It is self-assured, middle to upper class, literate and non-combative. But what surprises him is its cheeriness. It's the notion that its owner is having fun.

The minister again, imperious:

'And you're *Paul,* right? That's understood. Some sort of conference academic. Elliot's got it all worked out.'

'Minister, a large part of me has been Paul Anderson since our last conversation, and it shall remain Paul Anderson until my task is complete.'

'Elliot tell you why you're here today?'

'I'm to shake the hand of the leader of our small British token force, and I'm to be your red telephone.'

'That your own, is it?' – Quinn, after a beat.

'My own what, Minister?'

'Your own *expression,* for Heaven's sake. *Red telephone?* Out of your own head. You made it up? Yes or no?'

'If it's not too frivolous.'

'It's bang on the button, as it happens. I might even use it.'

'I should be flattered.'

Disconnect resumes.

'These Special Forces types are inclined to get a bit uppity.' Quinn, a statement for the world. 'Want everything cut, dried and legalled before they'll get out of bed in the morning. Same problem all across the country, if you want my view. Wife still doing all right, is she?'

'In the circumstances, splendidly, thank you, Minister. And never a word of complaint, I may say.'

'Yeah, well, women. What they're good at, isn't it? They know how to deal with that stuff.'

'Indeed they do, Minister. Indeed they do.'

Which is the cue for the arrival of party the second: another single pair of footsteps. They are lightweight, heel to toe and purposeful. On the point of casting them as Crispin's, Toby finds himself quickly corrected:

'Jeb, sir,' they announce, coming to a smart halt.

*

Is this the drama queen who has fucked up Quinn's weekend? Whether he is or not, with Jeb's arrival a different Fergus Quinn takes the stage. Gone the sulky lethargy and in place of it enter the raunchy, straight-from-the-shoulder Glaswegian Man of the People that his electorate falls for every time.

'*Jeb!* Good man. Really, really great. Very proud *indeed*. Let me say first that we're *fully* appreciative of your concerns, right? And we're here to solve them any which way we can. I'll do the easy bit first. Jeb, this is Paul, okay? Paul, meet Jeb. You see each other. You see *me*. I see you both. Jeb, you're standing in the Minister's Private Office, *my* office. I am a minister of the Crown. Paul, you're an established senior foreign servant of long experience. Do me a favour and confirm that for Jeb here.'

'Confirmed to the hilt, Minister. And honoured to meet you, Jeb' – to a rustle of shaking hands.

'Jeb, you will have seen me on television, going the rounds of my constituency, performing at Question Time in the House of Commons and all that.'

112

Wait your turn, Quinn. Jeb's a man who thinks before he answers.

'Well now, I *have* visited your website, as a matter of fact. Very impressive, too.'

Is this a Welsh voice? It assuredly is: the Welsh lilt with all its cadences in place.

'And I in turn have read enough of your record, Jeb, to tell you straight off that I admire and respect you, *and* your men, plus I'm *totally* confident you'll all do a really, really fine job. Now then: the countdown's already begun, and very understandably and *rightly*, you and your men wish to be one hundred per cent assured of the British chain of command and control. You have last-minute worries you need to get off your chest: *absolutely* understood. So do I.' Joke. 'Now. Let me address a couple of niggles that have reached me and see where we stand, right?'

Quinn is pacing, his voice darting in and out of the steam-age microphones hidden in the wooden panelling of his office as he swishes past them:

'Paul here will be your man on the spot. That's for starters. Plus it's what you've been asking for, right? It is not proper *or* desirable that I, as a Foreign Office minister, give direct military orders to a man in the field, but you, at your own request, will have your own official-unofficial Foreign Office advisor, Paul here, *at* your elbow, to assist and advise. When Paul conveys a command to you, it will be a command that comes from the top. It will be a command that bears the *imprimatur* – signature, that is – of certain people over *there*.'

Is he pointing at Downing Street as he says this? The slur of a body movement suggests he is.

'I'll put it this way, Jeb. This *little red fellow* sitting here connects me directly with those certain people. Got it? Well, Paul here will be *our* red telephone.'

Not for the first time in Toby's experience, Fergus Quinn has brazenly stolen a man's line without attribution. Is he waiting for applause and not getting it? Or is it something in Jeb's expression that sets him going? Either way, his patience snaps:

'For Christ's *sake*, Jeb. Look at you! You've *got* your guarantees. You've got *Paul* here. You've got your green light, and here we are with the bloody clock ticking. What are we actually *talking* about?'

But Jeb's voice displays no such disquiet under fire:

'Only I tried to have a word with Mr Crispin about it, see,' he explains, in his comforting Welsh rhythm. 'But he didn't seem to want to listen. Too busy. Said I should sort it out with Elliot, him being the designated operational commander.'

'What the hell's wrong with Elliot? They tell me he's absolutely top of the range. First rate.'

'Well, nothing really. Except Ethical's sort of a new brand to us, like. Plus we're operating on the basis of Ethical's intelligence. So naturally we thought we'd better come to you, well, for reassurance, like. Only it's no bother for Crispin's boys, is it? Them being American and exceptional, which is why they were chosen, I suppose. Big money on the table if the operation is successful, plus the international courts can't lay a finger on them. But my boys are British, aren't they? So am I. We're soldiers, not mercenaries. And we don't fancy sitting in prison in The Hague for an indeterminate period of time accused of participating in an act of extraordinary rendition, do we? Plus we've been struck off regimental books for reasons of deniability. The regiment can wash its hands of us any time it wants if the operation comes unstuck. Common criminals, we'd be, not soldiers at all, according to our way of thinking.'

★

Here Toby, who until now had kept his eyes closed the better to visualize the scene, wound back the tape and played the same passage again, then, leaping to his feet, grabbed a kitchen notebook with Isabel's scrawls all over it, tore off the top few pages and scribbled down such abbreviations as *extr/rendition, US exceptnls* and *no int./justice.*

★

'All done, Jeb?' Quinn is asking, in a tone of saintly tolerance. 'No more where that came from?'

'Well, we do have a couple of supplementaries, like, since you ask, Minister. Compensation in the worst contingency is one. Medevac for if we're wounded is another. We can't stay lying there, can we? We'd be embarrassing either way, dead or wounded. What happens to our wives and dependants, like? That's another one, now we're not regiment any more till we're reinstated. I said I'd ask, even if it was a bit on the academic side,' he ends, on a note that to Toby's ear is too concessive by half.

'Not academic at all, Jeb,' Quinn protests expansively. 'Quite the reverse, if I may say so! Let me make this very clear' – the Glaswegian Man of the People's accent taking convenient wing as Quinn enters his hectoring salesman's mode – 'the legal headache you describe has been thought through at the very highest level and *totally* discounted. Thrown out of court. Literally.'

By whom? By Roy Stormont-Taylor, the charismatic television lawyer, on one of his many social visits to the Private Office?

'And I'll tell you *why* it's been thrown out, if you want to know, Jeb, which you very rightly do, if I may say so. Because *no British team will be taking part in an act of extraordinary rendition.* Period. The British team will be based on precious British soil. Solely. You will be *protecting* British shores. Furthermore, this government is on record, at *all* levels, as refuting *any* suggestion of involvement in extraordinary rendition *whatsoever*, past, present or future. It is a practice that we abhor and condemn

115

unconditionally. What an American team does is *entirely* its own affair.'

In Toby's racing imagination the minister here casts Jeb a glower of immense import, then shakes his brawler's gingery head in frustration as if to say: if only his lips weren't sealed.

'Your remit, Jeb, is – repeat – to capture or otherwise neutralize with minimum force an HVT' – hasty translation, presumably for Paul's benefit – 'High-value Target, right? – target, not terrorist, though in this case the two happen to be one and the same – with a very large price *on* his head who has been unwise enough to intrude himself *on to* British territory' – hitting the prepositions, a sure sign to Toby's ear of his insecurity. 'Of necessity, you will be there incognito, undeclared to the local authorities, *in* accordance with the tightest possible security. As will Paul. You will achieve your aim by approaching your HVT from the landward side only, at the same time as your non-British sister force approaches from the sea, albeit in British territorial waters, whatever the Spanish may say to the contrary. Should this non-British seaborne team, *of* its own volition, elect to abstract or exfiltrate that target and remove him from the jurisdiction – i.e. *out* of British territorial waters – neither you personally, nor any member of your team, will be complicit *in* that act. To recapitulate' – and incidentally wear down – 'you are a *landborne protection force* exercising its duty of *defending sovereign British territory* in a totally *legal and legitimate manner* under international law, and you have no further responsibility whatever for the outcome of the operation, be you clad in military uniform or civilian attire. I am quoting directly a *legal opinion* passed down to me by arguably the best and most qualified international lawyer in the land.'

Re-enter, in Toby's imagination, the bold and beautiful Roy Stormont-Taylor, QC, whose advice according to Giles Oakley is startlingly free of official caution.

'So what I'm saying, Jeb, *is*' – the Glaswegian accent now positively priestly – 'here we are, with the countdown to D-Day already ringing in our ears – *you* as the Queen's soldier, *me* as the Queen's minister, and Paul here, shall we say – yes, Paul?'

'*Your red telephone?*' Paul offers helpfully.

'So what I'm saying *is*, Jeb: keep your feet squarely planted on that precious bit of British rock, leave the rest to Elliot and his boys, and you're in legal clover. You were defending sovereign British territory, you were assisting in the apprehension of a known criminal, as were others. What happens to the said criminal once he's been removed from British territory – *and* British territorial waters – is no concern of yours, nor should it be. *Ever.*'

⋆

Toby switched off the recorder.

'British *rock*?' he whispered aloud, head in hands.

With a capital R or a small one, please?

Listen again in horrified disbelief.

Then a third time as he again scribbled feverishly on Isabel's shopping pad.

Rock. Hold it there.

That precious bit of British Rock to keep your feet squarely planted on: more precious by far than Grenada, where the ties to Britain were so flimsy that American troops could barge in without so much as ringing the doorbell.

There was but one Rock in the world that met these stringent qualifications, and the notion that it was on the point of becoming the scene of an extraordinary rendition mounted by discharged British soldiers out of uniform and American mercenaries who were legally inviolate was so monstrous, so incendiary, that for a while Toby, for all the Foreign Office instruction he had received in measured, non-judgemental responses at all times, could only stare stupidly at the kitchen wall before listening to whatever was left.

★

'So have we any more questions where those came from, or are we done?' Quinn is enquiring genially.

In his imagination, Toby, like Jeb, is looking at the raised eyebrows and grim-set half-smile that tell you that the minister, courteous though he is, has reached the limit of his allotted time and yours.

Is Jeb deterred? Not in Toby's book, he isn't. Jeb's a soldier, and knows an order when he hears one. Jeb knows when he's had his say and can't say more. Jeb knows the countdown has begun and there's a job to do. Only now do the *sirs* come:

He is grateful for the minister's time, sir.

He is grateful for the *legal opinion* of the best and most qualified international lawyer in the land, sir.

He will pass Quinn's message back to his men. He can't speak for them, but thinks they will feel better about the operation, sir.

His last words fill Toby with dread:

'And very nice to have met you too, Paul. See you on the night, as they say.'

And Paul, whoever *he* is – such a patently *low flyer*, now that the afterthought presents itself to Toby's raging mind – what's *he* doing, or rather *not* doing, while the minister throws his magic dust in Jeb's eyes?

I'm your red telephone, silent till rung.

★

Expecting to hear little more from the tape than departing footsteps, Toby is again jerked to attention. The footsteps fade, the door closes and is locked. Squelch of Lobb shoes advancing on desk.

118

'Jay?'

Has Crispin been there all this time? Hiding in a cupboard, ear to the keyhole?

No. The minister is talking to him on one of his several direct lines. His voice is fond, almost obsequious.

'We're *there*, Jay. Bit of nitpicking, as had to be expected. Roy's formula went down a treat . . . Absolutely *not*, old boy! I didn't offer it, he didn't ask for it. If he *had* asked, I'd have said, "Sorry, mate, not my business. If you feel you've a claim, take it up with Jay" . . . probably fancies himself a cut above you bounty-hunters . . .' A sudden outburst, part anger, part relief: 'And if there's one thing in the world I can't stand, it's being preached at by a fucking Welsh dwarf!'

Laughter, distantly echoed over the phone. Change of subject. Ministerial *yeses* and *of courses*:

'. . . and Maisie's all right with that, is she? Still on side, no headaches? Atta girl . . .'

Long silence. Quinn again, but with a submissive fall in the voice:

'Well, I suppose if that's what Brad's people want, that's what they must have, no question . . . all right, yes, fourish . . . the wood, or Brad's place? . . . the wood suits me a lot better, to be frank, more private . . . No, no, thanks, no limo. I'll grab a common black cab. See you fourish.'

*

Toby sat on the edge of his bed. On the sheets, traces of their final loveless coupling. On the BlackBerry beside him, the text of his last message to Oakley sent an hour ago: *love life shattered vital we talk soonest, Toby.*

Change sheets.

Clear bathroom of Isabel's detritus.

Wash up last night's supper dishes.

Pour rest of red Burgundy down sink.

Repeat after me: *countdown's already begun . . . here we are with the bloody clock ticking . . . see you on the night, as they say, Paul.*

Which night? Last night? Tomorrow night?

And still no message.

Make omelette. Leave half.

Switch on *Newsnight*, encounter one of God's little ironies. Roy Stormont-Taylor, Queen's Counsel, the silkiest silk in the business, in striped shirt and white open-necked collar, is pontificating on the essential differences between law and justice.

Take aspirin. Lie on bed.

And at some point, unknown to himself, he must have dozed off, because the shriek of a text message on his BlackBerry woke him like a fire alarm:

Urge you forget lady permanently.

No signature.

Text back, furiously and impulsively: *No way. Too bloody important. Vital we discuss soonest. Bell.*

*

All life has ceased.

After the headlong sprint, the sudden, endless, fruitless wait.

To sit all day long at his kneehole desk in the ministerial anteroom.

To work methodically through his emails, take phone calls, make them, barely recognizing his own voice. *Giles, where in God's name are you?*

At night, when he should be celebrating bachelorhood regained, to lie awake longing for Isabel's chatter and the solace of their carnality. To listen to the sounds of carefree passers-by in the street below his window and pray to be one of them; to envy the shadows in the curtained windows opposite.

And once – is it night one or two? – to be woken from a

half-sleep to the absurdly melodious strains of a male choir declaring itself – as if for Toby's ears alone – *'impatient for the coming fight as we wait the morning's light'*. Convinced he is going mad, he scrambles to the window and sees below him a ring of ghostly men in green, bearing lanterns. And he remembers belatedly that it's St Patrick's Day and they are singing 'A Soldier's Song' and Islington has a thriving Irish population: which in turn sends his mind skimming back to Hermione.

Try calling her again? No way.

As to Quinn, the minister has providentially embarked on one of his unexplained absences, this time an extended one. Providentially? – or ominously? Only once does he offer any sign of life: a mid-afternoon phone call to Toby's cellphone. His voice has a metallic echo, as if it is speaking from a bare cell. Its tone verges on the hysterical:

'Is that you?'

'It is indeed, Minister. Bell. What can I do for you?'

'Just tell me who's been trying to get hold of me, that's all. Serious people, not riff-raff.'

'Well, to be frank, Minister, nobody very much. The lines have been strangely quiet' – which is no less than the truth.

'What do you mean, "strangely"? Strangely how? What's strange? There's nothing strange going on, hear me?'

'I wasn't suggesting there was, Minister. Just that the silence is – unusual?'

'Well, keep it that way.'

As to Giles Oakley, unwavering object of Toby's despair, he is being equally elusive. First, according to Victoria, his assistant, he is still in Doha. Then he is in conference all day and possibly all night as well, and may on no account be disturbed. And when Toby asks whether the conference is in London or Doha, she replies tartly that she is not authorized to supply details.

'Well, did you tell him it was urgent, Victoria?'

'Of course I bloody did.'

'And what did he say?'

'That urgency is not synonymous with importance,' she replies haughtily, no doubt quoting her master word for word.

It is another twenty-four hours before she calls him on the internal line, this time all sweetness and light:

'Giles is at Defence right now. He'd love to talk to you but it's likely to drag on a bit. Could you possibly meet him at the foot of the Ministry's steps at half seven, take a stroll along the Embankment and enjoy the sun?'

Toby could.

*

'And you heard all this how?' Oakley enquired conversationally.

They were strolling along the Embankment. Chattering girls in skirts flounced past them arm in arm. The evening traffic was a stampede. But Toby was hearing nothing but his own too-strident voice and Oakley's relaxed interjections. He had tried to look him in the eye and failed. The famous Oakley pebble jaw was set tight.

'Let's just say I picked it up in bits,' Toby said impatiently. 'What does it matter? A file Quinn left lying about. Things I overheard him whispering on the phone. You *instructed* me to tell you if I heard anything, Giles. Now I'm telling you!'

'I instructed you *when*, exactly, dear man?'

'At your own house. Schloss Oakley. After a dinner discussing alpacas. Remember? You asked me to stick around for a Calvados. I did. Giles, what the fuck *is* this?'

'Odd. I have no memory of any such conversation. If it took place, which I dispute, then it was surely private, alcohol-induced and not in any circumstance for quotation.'

'Giles!'

122

But this was Oakley's official voice, speaking for the record; and Oakley's official face, not a muscle moving.

'The further suggestion that your minister, who I understand to have spent a relaxing and well-deserved weekend in his recently acquired Cotswold mansion in the company of close friends, was engaged in promoting a hare-brained covert operation on the shores of a sovereign British colony – *wait!* – is both slanderous and disloyal. I suggest you abandon it.'

'Giles. I don't believe I'm hearing this. *Giles!*'

Grabbing Oakley's arm, he drew him into a recess in the railing. Oakley looked down icily at Toby's hand; and then, with his own, gently removed it.

'You are mistaken, Toby. Were such an operation to have occurred, do you not imagine that our intelligence services, ever alert to the danger of private armies going off the reservation, would have advised me? They did *not* so advise me, therefore it has manifestly not occurred.'

'You mean the spies don't *know*? Or are deliberately looking the other way?' – thoughts of Matti's phone call – 'What *are* you telling me, Giles?'

Oakley had found a spot for his forearms and was straining forward as if to relish the bustling river scene. But his voice remained as lifeless as if he were reading from a position paper:

'I am telling you, with all the emphasis at my command, that there's nothing for you to know. There *was* nothing to know, and there will *never* be anything to know, outside the fantasies of your heat-oppressed brain. Keep it for your novel, and get on with your career.'

'*Giles,*' Toby pleaded, as if in a dream. But Oakley's features, cost him what it might, remained rigidly, almost passionately, in denial.

'Giles *what*?' he demanded irritably.

'This isn't my *heat-oppressed brain* talking to you. Listen:

123

Jeb. Paul. Elliot. Brad. Ethical Outcomes. The Rock. Paul's in our very own Foreign Office. He's a member in good standing. Our colleague. He's got a sick wife. He's a *low flyer*. Check the leave-of-absence roster and you've got him nailed. Jeb's *Welsh*. His team comes from our own Special Forces. They've been struck off the regimental roll in order to be deniable. The Brits push from the land, Crispin and his mercenaries pull from the sea with a little help from Brad Hester, graciously financed by Miss Maisie and legalled by Roy Stormont-Taylor.'

In a silence made deeper by the clatter round him, Oakley went on smiling fixedly at the river.

'And all this you have from fag ends of conversation you weren't supposed to overhear, but did? Misrouted files with stickers and caveats all over them that just *happened* to come your way. Men bound together in conspiracy who just *happened* to reveal their plans to you in careless conversation. How very resourceful you are, Toby. I seem to remember your telling me you didn't listen at keyholes. For a moment, I had the very vivid feeling you had been present at the meeting. *Don't*,' he commanded, and for a moment, neither man spoke.

'Listen to me, dear man,' he resumed, in an altogether softer tone. 'Whatever information you imagine you possess – hysterical, anecdotal, electronic, don't tell me – destroy it before it destroys you. Every day, all across Whitehall, idiotic plans are aired and abandoned. Please, for your own future, accept that this was another.'

Had the lapidary voice faltered? What with the bustling shadows of pedestrians, the passing lights and din of river traffic, Toby could not be sure.

*

Alone in the kitchen of his Islington flat, Toby first played the analogue tapes on his replica recorder, at the same time making a digital recording. He transferred the digital recording to his desktop, then to a memory stick for back-up. Then buried the recording as deep in the desktop as it would go, while aware that if the technicians ever got their hooks on it nothing was going to be buried deep enough and the only thing to do in that unhappy eventuality was to smash the hard drive with a hammer and distribute the fragments over a wide area. With a strip of industrial-quality masking tape conveniently left behind by an odd-job man, he pasted the memory stick behind a foxed photograph of his maternal grandparents on their wedding day which hung in the darkest corner of the hallway, next to the coat hooks, and tenderly consigned it to them for safekeeping. How to dispose of the original tape? Wiping it clean wasn't enough. Having cut it into small pieces, he set fire to them in the sink, nearly setting fire to the kitchen in the process, then flushed what remained down the sink disposal unit.

His posting to Beirut followed five days later.

3.

The sensational arrival of Kit and Suzanna Probyn in the remote North Cornish village of St Pirran did not at first receive the ecstatic welcome that it merited. The weather was foul and the village of a mood to match: a dank February day of dripping sea-mist, and every footstep clanking down the village street like a judgement. Then at evening around pub time, the disturbing news: the gyppos were back. A camper – new, most likely stolen – with an upcountry registration and curtains in the side windows had been sighted by young John Treglowan from his father's tractor as he drove his cows to milking:

'They was up there, bold as brass, on Manor parkland, the exact same spot they was last time, proud of that clump of old pines.'

Any brightly coloured washing on the line then, John?

'In this weather? Not even gyppos.'

Children at all, John?

'None as I did see, but most likely they was hid away till they knowed the coast was clear.'

Horses then?

'No horses,' John Treglowan conceded. 'Not yet.'

And still only the one camper, then?

'You wait till tomorrow, and we'll have half a dozen of the buggers, see if we don't.'

They duly waited.

And come the following evening were still waiting. A dog had been spotted, but not a gyppo dog, or not to look at, it being a plump yellow Labrador accompanied by a big-striding bloke in a broad mackintosh hat and one of those Driza-Bone raincoats down to his ankles. And the bloke didn't look any more gyppo than the dog did – with the result that John Treglowan and his two brothers, who had been spoiling to go up there and have a quiet word with them, same as last time, were restrained.

Which was as well, because next morning the camper with its curtains and upcountry registration and yellow Labrador in the back rolled up at the post-office mini-market, and a nicer spoken pair of retired foreigners you couldn't wish to ask for, according to the postmistress – foreigner being anyone who had the ill taste to come from east of the Tamar river. She didn't go as far as to declare they were 'gentry' but there was a clear hint of quality in her description.

But that don't solve the question, do it?

Not by a long way, it don't.

Don't begin to.

Because what right has anyone to go camping up the Manor in the first place? Who's given them permission then? The commander's bone-headed trustees over to Bodmin? Or those shark lawyers up in London? And how about if they're paying *rent* then? What would that mean? It would mean another bloody caravan site, and us with two already and can't fill them, not even when 'tis season.

But as to asking the trespassers themselves: well, that wouldn't be proper now, would it?

It wasn't till the camper appeared at Ben Painter's garage, which does a line in do-it-yourself hardware, and a tall, angular, cheery fellow in his sixties jumped out, that speculation came to an abrupt halt:

'Now, sir. Would you be Ben, by any chance?' he begins, leaning forward and downward, Ben being eighty years old and five feet tall on a good day.

'I'm Ben,' Ben concedes.

'Well, I'm *Kit*. And what I need, Ben, is a pair of man-sized metal-cutters. Sort of chaps that'll snip through an iron bar *this size*,' he explained, making a ring of his finger and thumb.

'You off to prison then?' Ben enquires.

'Well, not just at this *moment*, Ben, thank you,' replies the same Kit, with a raucous *hah!* of a laugh. 'There's this giant padlock on the stable door, you see. A real *thug* of a chap, all rusted up and no key in sight. There's a place on the key board where it *used* to hang, but it's not hanging there any more. And believe you me, there's *nothing* more stupid than an empty key-hook,' he asserts heartily.

'The stable door down the *Manor*, you was talking about then, was it?' says Ben, after prolonged reflection.

'The very one,' Kit agrees.

'Should be full of empty bottles, that stable should, knowing the commander.'

'Highly likely. And I hope *very* shortly to be picking up the deposit on them.'

Ben reflects on this too. 'Deposit's not allowed no more, deposit isn't.'

'Well now, I suppose it isn't. So what I'll *really* be doing is running them down to the bottle bank for recycling, won't I?' says Kit patiently.

But this doesn't satisfy Ben either:

'Only I don't think I should be doing that, should I?' he objects, after another age. 'Not now you've told me what it's *for*. Not the Manor. I'd be aiding and abetting. Not unless you own the bloody place.'

To which Kit, with evident reluctance because he doesn't want to make old Ben look silly, explains that while he personally doesn't own the Manor, his dear wife Suzanna does.

'She's the late commander's *niece*, you see, Ben. Spent her absolute happiest childhood years here. Nobody else in the family wanted to take the place on, so the trustees decided to let us have a go.'

Ben absorbs this.

'She a Cardew, then, is she? Your wife?'

'Well, she *was*, Ben. She's a Probyn now. Been a Probyn for thirty-three glorious years, I'm proud to say.'

'She Suzanna, then? Suzanna Cardew as rode the hunt when she were nine year old? Got out in front of the Master, had to have her horse hauled back by the Field Master.'

'That sounds like Suzanna.'

'Well I'm buggered,' says Ben.

A couple of days later an official letter arrived at the post office that put paid to any lingering suspicions. It was addressed not to any old Probyn but to *Sir Christopher Probyn*, who, according to John Treglowan, who'd looked him up on the Internet, had been some sort of ambassador or commissioner, was it, to a bunch of islands in the Caribbean that was still supposed to be British, and had a medal to show for it too.

*

And from that day on, Kit and Suzanna, as they insisted on being called, could do no wrong, even if the levellers in the village would have wished it different. Where the commander in his later years was remembered as a lonely, misanthropic drunk, the Manor's new incumbents threw themselves on village life with such zest and goodwill as even the sourest couldn't deny. It didn't matter that Kit was practically rebuilding the Manor single-handed: come Fridays, he'd be down at Community House with an apron round his waist, serving suppers at Seniors' Stake-Nite and staying for the washing-up. And Suzanna, who they say is ill but you wouldn't know it, like as not helping out with the Busy Bees or sorting church accounts with Vicar after the treasurer went and died, or down Primary School for the Sure

Starters' concert, or up Church Hall to help set up for Farmers' Market, or delivering deprived city kids to their country hosts for a week's holiday away from the Smoke, or running somebody's wife to the Treliske in Truro to see her sick husband. And stuck-up? – forget it, she was just like you and me, ladyship or not.

Or if Kit was out shopping and spotted you across the street, it was a pound to a penny he'd be bounding towards you between the traffic with his arm up, needing to know how your daughter was enjoying her gap year or how your wife was doing after her dad passed away – warm-hearted to a fault, he was, no side to him either, and never forgets a name. As for Emily, their daughter, who's a doctor up in London, though you wouldn't think it to look at her: *well*, whenever *she* came down she brought the sunshine with her, ask John Treglowan, who goes into a swoon every time he sees her, dreaming up all the aches and pains he hasn't got, just to have her cure them for him! Well, a cat may look at a queen, they do say.

So it came as no surprise to anybody, except possibly Kit himself, when Sir Christopher Probyn of the Manor was paid the unprecedented, the unique honour, of becoming the first non-Cornishman ever to be elected Official Opener and Lord of Misrule for Master Bailey's Annual Fayre, held by ancient rite in Bailey's Meadow in the village of St Pirran on the first Sunday after Easter.

★

'Funky but not over the top is Mrs Marlow's advice,' said Suzanna, busying herself in front of the cheval mirror and talking through the open doorway to Kit's dressing room. 'We're to preserve our dignity, whatever *that's* supposed to mean.'

'So not my grass skirt,' Kit called back in disappointment. 'Still, Mrs Marlow knows best,' he added resignedly, Mrs Marlow being their elderly, part-time housekeeper, inherited from the commander.

'And remember you're not just today's *Opener*,' Suzanna warned, giving a last affirmative tug at her stock. 'You're Master of Misrule too. They'll expect you to be funny. But not *too* funny. And none of your blue jokes. There'll be Methodists present.'

The dressing room was the one part of the Manor Kit had vowed never to lay his do-it-yourself fingers on. He loved its faded Victorian wallpaper, the clunky antique writing desk set in its own alcove, the worn sash window looking out over the orchard. And today, oh gladness, the aged pear and apple trees were in blossom, thanks to some timely pruning by Mrs Marlow's husband, Albert.

Not that Kit had just stepped into the commander's shoes. He had added bits of himself too. On the fruitwood tallboy stood a statuette of the victorious Duke of Wellington gloating over a crouching Napoleon in a sulk: bought in a Paris flea market on Kit's first foreign tour. On the wall hung a print of a Cossack musketeer shoving a pike down the throat of an Ottoman janissary: Ankara, First Secretary, Commercial.

Yanking open his wardrobe in search of whatever was funky but not over the top, he let his eye wander over other relics of his diplomatic past.

My black morning coat and spongebag trousers? They'd think I was a bloody undertaker.

Dinner tails? Head waiter. And in this heat daft, for the day against all prediction had dawned cloudless and radiant. He gave an ecstatic bellow:

'*Eureka!*'

'You're not in the *bath*, are you, Probyn?'

'Drowning, waving, the lot!'

A yellowing straw boater from his Cambridge years has

caught his eye and, hanging beneath it, a striped blazer of the same period: perfect for my Brideshead look. An ancient pair of white ducks will complete the ensemble. And for that touch of foppery, his antique walking stick with scrolled silver handle, a recent acquisition. With knighthood, he had discovered a harmless thing about walking sticks. No trip to London was complete without a visit to the emporium of Mr James Smith of New Oxford Street. And finally – whoopee! – the fluorescent socks that Emily had given him for Christmas.

'Em? Where is that girl? Emily, I require your best teddy bear immediately!'

'Out running with Sheba,' Suzanna reminded him from the bedroom.

Sheba, their yellow Labrador. Shared their last posting with them.

He returned to the wardrobe. To set off the fluorescent socks he would risk the orange suede loafers he'd bought in Bodmin at a summer sale. He tried them on and let out a yip. What the hell? He'd be out of them by tea time. He selected an outrageous tie, squeezed himself into the blazer, clapped on the boater at a rakish angle and did his Brideshead voice:

'I say, Suki, darling, do ya happen to remember where I put m' bally speech notes?' – posing hand on hip in the doorway like all the best dandies. Then stopped, and lowered his arms to his sides in awe. 'Mother of pearl. Suki, darling. Hallelujah!'

Suzanna was standing before the cheval mirror, scrutinizing herself over her shoulder. She was wearing her late aunt's black riding habit and boots, and the white lace blouse with its stock for a collar. She had pulled her strict grey hair into a bun and fixed it with a silver comb. On top of it she had set a shiny black topper that should have been ridiculous but to Kit was utterly disarming. The clothes fitted her, the period fitted her, the topper fitted her. She was a handsome, sixty-year-old

Cornishwoman of her time, and the time was a hundred years ago. Best of all, you'd think she'd never had a day's illness in her life.

Pretending to be unsure whether it was permitted to advance further, Kit made a show of hovering in the doorway.

'You *are* going to enjoy it, aren't you, Kit?' Suzanna said severely into the mirror. 'I don't want to think of you going through the motions just to please me.'

'Of *course* I'm going to enjoy it, darling. It'll be a hoot.'

And he meant it. If it would have made old Suki happy, he'd have put on a tutu and jumped out of a cake. They'd lived *his* life and now they would live hers, if it killed him. Taking her hand, he raised it reverently to his lips, then lifted it aloft as if he were about to dance a minuet with her before escorting her across the dust sheets, down the staircase to the hall, where Mrs Marlow stood clutching two posies of fresh violets, Master Bailey's flower of choice, one each.

And standing tall beside her, dressed in Chaplinesque rags, safety pins and battered bowler hat, their peerless daughter, Emily, recently returned to life after a disastrous love affair.

'You all right there, Mum?' she asked briskly. 'Got your make-me-betters?'

Sparing Suzanna a reply, Kit gives a reassuring pat to his blazer pocket.

'And the squeezer, for in case?'

Pats the other pocket.

'Nervous, Dad?'

'Terrified.'

'So you should be.'

The Manor gates stand open. Kit has pressure-washed the stone lions on the gateposts for the occasion. Costumed pleasure-seekers are already drifting up Market Street. Emily spots the local doctor and his wife, and nimbly attaches herself to them, leaving her parents to process alone, Kit comically doffing his straw boater to left and right and Suzanna managing a sporting shot at the royal wave as they confer their praises in their separate ways:

'Gosh, Peggy darling, that's so absolutely *charming*! Wherever did you get such lovely satin from?' Suzanna exclaims to the postmistress.

'Well fuck me, Billy. Who else have you got under there?' murmurs Kit, *sotto voce*, into the ear of portly Mr Olds, the butcher, who has come as a turbanned Arab prince.

In the gardens of the cottages, daffodils, tulips, forsythia and peach blossom raise their heads to the blue sky. From the church tower flies the black-and-white flag of Cornwall. A bevy of equestrian children in hard hats comes trotting down the street, escorted by the redoubtable Polly from the Granary Riding School. The festivities are too much for the lead pony and it shies, but Polly is on hand to grab the bridle. Suzanna consoles the pony, then its rider. Kit takes Suzanna's arm and feels her heart beating as she presses his hand lovingly against her ribs.

It's here and now, Kit thinks, as the elation rises in him. The jostling crowds, the palominos cavorting in the meadows, the sheep safely grazing on the hillside, even the new bungalows that deface the lower slopes of Bailey's Hill: if this isn't the land they have loved and served for so long, where is? And all right, it's Merrie bloody England, it's Laura bloody Ashley, it's ale and pasties and yo-ho for Cornwall, and tomorrow morning all these nice, sweet people will be back at each other's throats, screwing each other's wives and doing all the stuff the rest of the world does. But right now it's their National Day, and who's an ex-diplomat of all people to complain if the wrapping is prettier than what's inside?

At a trestle table stands Jack Painter, red-headed son of Ben from the garage, in braces and a Stetson. Beside him sits a girl in a fairy dress with wings, selling tickets at four pounds a shot.

'You're *free*, Kit, dammit!' Jack cries boisterously. 'You're the bloody Opener, man, same as Suzanna!'

But Kit in his exultation will have none of it:

'I am *not* free, thank you, Jack Painter! I am *extremely* expensive. And so is my dear wife,' he retorts and, happy man that he is, slaps down a ten-pound note and drops the two pounds change into the animal-welfare box.

A hay cart awaits them. A beribboned ladder is lashed against it. Suzanna grips it with one hand, her riding skirts in the other, and with Kit's help ascends. Willing arms reach out to receive her. She waits for her breathing to calm down. It does. She smiles. Harry Tregenza, The Builder You Can Trust and celebrated rogue, wears an executioner's mask and brandishes a silver-painted wooden scythe. He is flanked by his wife wearing bunny ears. Next to them stands this year's Bailey Queen, bursting out of her corsage. Tipping his boater, Kit plants chivalrous kisses on the cheeks of both women and inhales from each the same waft of jasmine scent.

An ancient hurdy-gurdy is playing 'Daisy, Daisy, give me your answer, do'. Smiling energetically, he waits for the din to subside. It doesn't. He flaps an arm for silence, smiles harder. In vain. From an inside pocket of his blazer he extracts the speech notes that Suzanna has nobly typed for him, and waves them. A steam engine emits a truculent shriek. He mimes a theatrical sigh, appeals to the heavens for sympathy, then to the crowd beneath him, but the din refuses to let up.

He goes for it.

First he must bawl out what he amusingly calls the Church Notices, though they concern such non-ecclesiastical matters as toilets, parking and baby-changing. Does anyone hear him? Judging by the faces of the listeners hanging around the foot of the hay cart, they don't. He names our selfless volunteers who have laboured night and day to make the miracle happen, and invites them to identify themselves. He might as well be reading out the names of the Glorious Dead. The hurdy-gurdy has gone back to the beginning. *You're Master of Misrule too. They'll expect you to be funny.* A quick check of Suki: no bad signs. And Emily, his beloved Em: tall and watchful, standing, as ever, a little apart from the pack.

'And lastly, my friends, before I step down – though I'd better be jolly careful when I do!' – zero response – 'it's my pleasure, and my very happy duty, to urge you to spend your hard-earned money *unwisely*, flirt *recklessly* with one another's wives' – wished he hadn't said that – 'drink, eat and revel the day away. So *hip hip*' – tearing off his boater and thrusting it in the air – '*hip hip!*'

Suzanna raises her topper to join his boater. The Builder You Wouldn't Trust Further Than You Could Throw Him can't raise his executioner's mask, so punches the air with his clenched fist in an unintended communist salute. A long-delayed *Hooray!* tears through the loudspeakers like an electrical fault. To murmurs of 'Good on you, my handsome!' and 'Proper job, my robin!', Kit clambers gratefully down the ladder, lets his walking stick fall to the ground and reaches up to take hold of Suzanna by the hips.

'Bloody wonderful, Dad!' Emily declares, appearing at Kit's side with the walking stick. 'Want a sit-down, Mum, or *flog on?*' – using a family expression.

Suzanna, as ever, wants to flog on.

★

The royal tour of Our Opener and His Lady Wife begins. First, inspect shire horses. Suzanna the born country girl chats to them, strokes and pats their rumps without inhibition. Kit makes a show of admiring their brasses. Home-grown vegetables in their Sunday best. Cauliflowers that the locals call broccoli: bigger than footballs, washed clean as a pin. Home-made breads, cheeses and honey.

Sample piccalilli: tasteless but keep grinning. Smoked salmon pâté excellent. Urge Suki to buy some. She does. Linger over Gardening Club's floral celebration. Suzanna knows every flower by its first name. Bump into MacIntyres, two of life's dissatisfied customers. Ex-tea-planter George keeps a loaded rifle at his bedside for the day the masses assemble at his gates. His wife, Lydia, bores for the village. Advance on them with outstretched arms:

'George! Lydia! Darlings! *Marvellous!* Super dinner at your house the other night, really one of those evenings. Our turn next time!'

Move gratefully to our bygone threshing machines and steam engines. Suzanna undaunted by stampede of children dressed as anything from Batman to Osama. Kit yells at Gerry Pertwee, village Romeo, squatting up on his tractor in Red Indian headdress:

'For the umpteenth time, Gerry, when are you going to mow our bloody paddock?' And to Suzanna, aside: 'Damned if I'll pay the bugger fifteen quid an hour when the going rate's twelve.'

Suzanna waylaid by Marjory, rich divorcee on the prowl. Marjory has set her sights on the dilapidated greenhouses in the walled garden of the Manor for her Orchid Club, but Suzanna suspects it's Kit she's set her sights on. Kit the diplomat rides to the rescue:

'Suki darling, hate to interrupt – Marjory, you're looking extremely dishy, if I may say so – small drama, darling. You alone have the power to solve.'

Cyril, church warden and lead tenor in the choir, lives with mother, banned from unsupervised contact with schoolchildren; Harold, drunk dentist, early retirement, pretty thatched cottage off the Bodmin road, one son in rehab, wife in the bin.

Kit greets them all lavishly, sets course for Arts and Crafts Expo, Suki's brainchild.

Marquee a haven of quiet. Admire amateur watercolours. Forget the quality, endeavour is all. Proceed to other end of marquee, descend grassy knoll.

Straw boater cutting ridge in forehead. Suede loafers giving him hell as predicted. Emily at edge of frame, keeping a quiet eye on Suzanna.

Enter roped-off enclosure of our Rustic Crafts section.

*

Does Kit feel a first *chill* on entering here, a *presence*, an *intimation*? Does he hell: he's in Eden, and he intends to remain there. He's experiencing one of those rare sensations of pure pleasure when everything seems to have come right. He's gazing with unbounded love on his wife in her riding rig and topper. He's thinking of Emily, and how even a month ago she was still inconsolable, and today she's right back on her feet and ready to take on the world.

And while his thoughts are contentedly drifting in this way, so is his gaze, which has fixed itself on the furthest limits of the enclosure and, seemingly of its own accord, on the figure of a man.

A hunched man.

A *small* hunched man.

Whether permanently hunched or merely at that moment hunched is thus far unknown. The man is hunched, and he is either squatting or sitting on the tailgate of his traveller's van. Oblivious to the midday heat, he is wearing a shiny, full-length, brown leather coat with the collar up. And for a hat, a broad-brimmed affair, also of leather, with a shallow crown and a bow at the front, less a cowboy's hat than a Puritan's.

The features, what Kit can make of them in the shadow of

the brim, are emphatically those of a small white male in middle life.

Emphatically?

Why the emphasis suddenly?

What was so *emphatic* about him?

Nothing.

The fellow was exotic, true. And small. In burly company, the small stand out. That doesn't make him special. It simply makes you notice him.

A tinker was Kit's first determinedly light-hearted thought: whenever did he last see a real *tinker?* Romania fifteen years back, when he was doing a stint in Bucharest. He may actually have turned to Suzanna to suggest this. Or perhaps he only thought of turning to her, because by now he had transferred his interest to the fellow's utility van, which was not only his workplace but his humble home – witness the Primus stove, bunk bed and rows of pots and cooking implements mingling with the craftsman's pliers, gimlets and hammers; and on one wall, desiccated animal skins that presumably served him as carpets when, his day's work done, he gratefully closed his door on the world. But everything so orderly and shipshape that you felt its owner could put his hand to any part of it blindfold. He was that kind of little fellow. Adept. Foot-sure.

But positive, irrevocable recognition at this stage? Certainly not.

There was the creeping, insidious intimation.

There was a coming together of certain fragments of recollection that shuffled themselves around like pieces in a kaleidoscope until they formed a pattern, vague at first, then – but only by degrees – disturbing.

There was a belated acknowledgement, sounded deep down by the inner man – then gradually, fearfully, and with a sinking heart, accepted by the outer one.

There was also a walking away, physically, though the details remained fuzzy in Kit's later memory. Chubby Philip Peplow, hedge-fund manager and second-homer, seems to have barged into the picture, attended by his newest squeeze, a six-foot model clad in Pierrot tights. Even with a gale-force storm shaping in his head, Kit didn't lose his eye for a pretty girl. And it was the six-foot girl in tights who did the talking. *Would Kit and Suzanna like to swing by for drinks tonight? It would be fab, open house, seven onwards, come as you are, barbie if it doesn't piss with rain.* To which Kit, overdoing it a bit to compensate for his confused state of mind, heard himself say something like: *we'd absolutely love to, six-foot girl, but we've got the entire Chain Gang coming to dinner, for our sins –* 'Chain Gang' being Kit and Suzanna's home-made term for local dignitaries with a weakness for aldermanic regalia.

Peplow and squeeze then depart and Kit goes back to admiring the tinker's wares, if that's what he's been doing, with the part of his head that still refuses to admit the inadmissible. Suzanna is standing right beside him, also admiring them. He suspects, but isn't sure, that she's been admiring them before he has. Admiring, after all, was what they were there to do: admire, move on before you get bogged down, then do some more admiring.

Except that this time they weren't moving on. They were standing side by side and admiring, but also recognizing – *Kit* recognizing, that is – that the man wasn't a tinker at all, and never had been. And why the devil he had ever rushed to cast him as a tinker was anyone's guess.

The fellow was a bloody *saddler*, for Christ's sake! What's the matter with me? He makes saddles, blast him, bridles! Briefcases! Satchels! Purses, wallets, ladies' handbags, coasters! Not pots and pans at all, he never had! Everything *around* the man was in leather. He was a leather man advertising his product. He was modelling it. The tailgate of his van was his *catwalk*.

All of which Kit had until this moment failed to accept, just as he had failed to accept the totally obvious lettering, hand-daubed in gold print on the van's side, proclaiming JEB'S LEATHERCRAFT to anyone who had eyes to see it, from fifty, more like a hundred, paces. And beneath it, in smaller letters admittedly but equally legible, the injunction *Buy From Van*. No phone number, no address, email or otherwise, no surname. Just Jeb and buy from his van. Terse, to the point, unambiguous.

But why had Kit's otherwise fairly well-regulated instincts gone into anarchic, totally irrational denial? And why did the name Jeb, now that he consented to acknowledge it, strike him as the most outrageous, the most irresponsible breach of the Official Secrets Act that had ever crossed his desk?

★

Yet it did. Kit's whole body said it did. His feet said it did. They had gone numb inside his badly fitting loafers. His old Cambridge blazer said it did. It was clinging to his back. In the middle of a heatwave, cold sweat had soaked its way clean through his cotton shirt. Was he in present or past time? It was the same shirt, the same sweat, the same heat in both places: here and now on Bailey's Meadow to the thump of the hurdy-gurdy, or on a Mediterranean hillside at dead of night to the throb of engines out to sea.

And how do two confiding, darting, brown eyes manage to grow old and wrinkled and lose their lightness of being in the ridiculously short space of three years? For the head had lifted, and not just halfway but all the way back, till the brim of the leather hat cocked itself, leaving the harrowed, bony face beneath it in *plain sight* – a turn of phrase he suddenly couldn't get rid of – gaunt cheekbones, resolute jaw, and the brow, too, which was etched by the same web of fine lines that had collected themselves at the corners of his eyes and mouth, drawing them downward in some kind of permanent dismay.

And the eyes themselves, formerly so quick and knowing, seemed to have lost their mobility, because once they had settled on Kit, they showed no sign of shifting but stayed there, fixed on him, so that the only way either man was ever going to break free of the other was if Kit did the breaking; which he duly achieved, but only by turning his whole head to Suzanna and saying, *Well, darling, here we are, what a day, eh, what a day!* – or something equally fatuous, but also sufficiently untypical of him for a frown of puzzlement to pass across Suzanna's flushed face.

And this frown has not quite disappeared when he hears the soft Welsh voice he is praying uselessly not to hear:

'Well, Paul. Quite a coincidence, I will say. Not what either of us was led to expect, was it?'

But though the words came smashing into Kit's head like so many bullets, Jeb must in reality have spoken them quietly, because Suzanna – either thanks to the imperfections of the little hearing aids she wore under her hair, or to the persistent boom-boom of the fairground – failed to pick them up, preferring to manifest an exaggerated interest in a large handbag with an adjustable shoulder strap. She was peering at Jeb over her bunch of Bailey violets and she was smiling a bit too hard at him and being a bit too sweet and condescending altogether for Kit's taste, which was actually her shyness at work, but didn't look like it.

'Now you're Jeb himself, are you? The real thing.'

What the hell does she mean, *real* thing? thought Kit, suddenly outraged. Real as compared to *what*?

'You're not a substitute or a stand-in or anything?' she went on, exactly as if Kit had put her up to explaining her interest in the fellow.

And Jeb for his part was taking her question very seriously:

'Well now, I wasn't *christened* Jeb, I'll admit that,' he replied, directing his gaze away from Kit at last and bestowing it on Suzanna with the same steadfastness. Adding with a loquacity that cut straight to Kit's heart: 'But the name they gave me was such a mouthful, frankly, that I decided to do some essential surgery on it. Put it that way.'

But Suzanna was in her asking mode:

'And where on *earth* did you find such *marvellous* leather, Jeb? It's perfectly *beautiful*.'

At which Kit, whose mind by now had switched to diplomatic autopilot, announced that he too had been bursting to ask the same question:

'Yes, indeed, where *did* you get your splendid leather from, Jeb?'

And there follows a moment where Jeb considers his questioners in turn as if deciding which of them to favour. He settles on Suzanna:

'Yes, well now, it's actually *Russian reindeer* hide, madam,' he explains, with what to Kit is by now an unbearable deference, as he takes down an animal skin from the wall and spreads it lovingly on his lap. 'Recovered from the wreck of a Danish brigantine that went down in Plymouth Sound in 1786, they tell me. She was on her way from St Petersburg to Genoa, you see, sheltering from the south-westerly gales. Well, we all know about *them*, don't we, down these parts?' – giving the skin a consoling stroke with one tanned little hand – 'not that the leather minded, did you? Couple of hundred years of seawater were just what you liked,' he went on quaintly, as if to a pet. 'The minerals in the wrapping may have helped too, I dare say.'

But Kit knew that if Jeb was delivering his homily to Suzanna, it was Kit he was talking to, Kit's bewilderment and frustration and anxiety he was playing on, and – yes, his fear too – galloping fear – though of what precisely he had yet to work out.

143

'And you do this for a *living*, do you, Jeb?' Suzanna was demanding, overtired and sounding dogmatic in consequence. 'Full time? You're not just *moonlighting* or *two-jobbing* or studying on the side? This isn't a *hobby*, it's your *life*. That's what *I* want to know.'

Jeb needed to think deeply about these large questions. His small brown eyes turned to Kit for help, dwelt on him, then turned away, disappointed. Finally he heaved a sigh and shook his head like a man at odds with himself.

'Well, I *suppose* I did have a couple of alternatives, now I come to think of it,' he conceded. 'Martial arts? Well, these days they're all at it, aren't they? Close protection, I suppose,' he suggested after another long stare at Kit. 'Walking rich kids to school in the mornings. Walking them home evening time. Good money in it, they say. But *leather* now' – giving the hide another consoling caress – 'I've always fancied a good-quality leather, same as my dad. Nothing like it, I say. But is it my *life*? Well, life's what you're left with, really' – with yet another stare at Kit, a harder one.

*

Suddenly everything had speeded up, everything was heading for disaster. Suzanna's eyes had turned warning-bright. Fierce dabs of colour had appeared on her cheeks. She was sifting through the men's wallets at an unhealthy speed on the specious grounds that Kit had a birthday coming up. He had, but not till October. When he reminded her of this, she gave an over-hearty laugh and promised that, if she decided to buy one, she would keep it secret in her bottom drawer.

'The *stitching* now, Jeb, is it *hand* or is it *machine*?' she blurted, forgetting all about Kit's birthday and grabbing impulsively at the shoulder bag that she had first picked up.

'Hand, ma'am.'

'And that's the *asking* price, is it, sixty pounds? It seems an *awful* lot.'

Jeb turned to Kit:

'Best I can do, I'm afraid, Paul,' he said. 'Quite a struggle for some of us, not having an index-linked pension and similar.'

Was it hatred that Kit was seeing in Jeb's eyes? Anger? Despair? And what was Jeb seeing in Kit's eyes? Mystification? Or the mute appeal not to call him Paul again in Suzanna's hearing? But Suzanna, whatever she'd heard or hadn't, had heard enough:

'Well then, I'll have it,' she declared. 'It'll be just right for my shopping in Bodmin, won't it, Kit? It's roomy and it's got sensible compartments. Look, it's even got a little side pocket for my credit card. I think sixty pounds is actually jolly reasonable. Don't you, Kit? Of course you do!'

Saying which, she performed an act so improbable, so provocative, that it momentarily banished all other preoccupations. She placed her own perfectly serviceable handbag on the table and, as a prelude to digging in it for her money, removed her top hat and shoved it at Jeb to hold. If she'd untied the buttons on her blouse, she could not, in Kit's inflamed perception, have been more explicit.

'Look here, *I'll* pay for this, don't be bloody silly,' he protested, startling not only Suzanna but himself with his vehemence. And to Jeb, who alone appeared unperturbed: '*Cash*, I take it? You deal in cash only' – like an accusation – 'no cheques or cards or any of the aids to nature?'

Aids to nature? – what the hell is he blathering about? With fingers that seemed to have joined themselves together at the tips, he picked three twenty-pound notes from his wallet and plonked them on the table:

'There you are, darling. Present for you. Your Easter egg, one week late. Slot the old bag inside the new one. Of *course* it'll go. Here' – doing it for her, none too gently. 'Thanks, Jeb. Terrific find. Terrific that you came. Make sure we see you here next year, now.'

Why didn't the bloody man pick up the money? Why didn't he smile, nod, say thanks or cheers – *do* something, like any normal human being, instead of sitting down again and poking at the money with his skinny index finger as if he thought it was fake, or not enough, or dishonourably earned, or whatever the hell he was thinking, back out of sight again under his Puritan hat? And why did Suzanna, by now feverish, stand there grinning idiotically down at him, instead of responding to Kit's sharp tug at her arm?

'That's your other name then, is it, Paul?' Jeb was enquiring in his calm Welsh voice. '*Probyn?* The one they blasted over the loudspeaker, then. That's you?'

'Yes, indeed. But it's my dear wife here who's the driving force in these things. I just tag along,' Kit added, reaching out to retrieve her topper and finding it was still rigid in Jeb's hand.

'We met, didn't we, Paul?' Jeb said, gazing up at him with an expression that seemed to combine pain and accusation in equal measure. 'Three years back. Between a rock and a hard place, as they say.' And when Kit's gaze darted downward to escape his unflinching stare, there was Jeb's iron little hand holding the top hat by its brim, so tightly that the nail of his thumb was white. 'Yes, Paul? You were my *red telephone.*'

Moved to near-desperation by the sight of Emily, appearing out of nowhere as usual to hover at her mother's side, Kit summoned the last of the fake conviction left to him:

'Got the wrong chap there, Jeb. Happens to us all. I look at you, and I don't recognize you from Adam' – meeting Jeb's unrelenting stare. '*Red telephone* not a concept to me, I'm afraid. *Paul?* – total mystery. But there we are.'

And still somehow keeping up the smile, and even contriving an apologetic laugh as he turned to Suzanna:

'Darling, we mustn't linger. Your weavers and potters will never forgive you. Jeb, good to meet you. Very instructive listening. Just sorry about the misunderstanding. My wife's topper, Jeb. Not for sale, old boy. Antique value.'

'Wait.'

Jeb's hand had relinquished the topper and risen to the parting of his leather overcoat. Kit moved to place himself in front of Suzanna. But the only deadly weapon that emerged in Jeb's hand was a blue-backed notebook.

'Forgot to give you your receipt, didn't I?' he explained, tut-tutting at his own stupidity. 'That VAT man would shoot me dead, he would.'

Spreading the notebook on his knee, he selected a page, made sure the carbon was in place and wrote between the lines with a brown military pencil. And when he had finished – and it must have been quite an exhaustive receipt, reckoned by the time it took to write it – he tore off the page, folded it and placed it carefully inside Suzanna's new shoulder bag.

*

In the diplomatic world that had until recently claimed Kit and Suzanna as its loyal citizens, a social duty was a social duty.

The weavers had clubbed together to build themselves an old-world handloom? Suzanna must have the loom demonstrated to her, and Kit must buy a square of handwoven cloth, insisting it would be just the thing to keep his computer from wandering all over his desk: never mind this asinine comment made no sense to anyone, least of all to Emily who, never far away, was chatting to a trio of small children. At the pottery stall, Kit takes a turn at the wheel and makes a hash of it, while Suzanna smiles benignly on his endeavours.

Only when these last rites have been performed do Our Opener and His Lady Wife bid their farewells and by silent consent take the footpath that leads under the old railway bridge, along the stream and up to the side entrance to the Manor.

Suzanna had removed her topper. Kit needed to carry it for her. Then he remembered his boater and took that off too, laying the hats brim to brim and carrying them awkwardly at his side, together with his dandy's silver-handled walking stick. With his other hand he was holding Suzanna's arm. Emily started to come after them, then thought better of it, calling through cupped hands that she'd see them back at the Manor. It wasn't till they had entered the seclusion of the railway bridge that Suzanna swung round to face her husband.

'Who on earth was *that man*? The one you said you didn't know. *Jeb*. The leather man.'

'Absolutely *nobody* I know,' Kit replied firmly, in answer to the question he had been dreading. 'He's a total no-go area, I'm afraid. Sorry.'

'He called you Paul.'

'He did, and he should be prosecuted for it. I hope he bloody well will be.'

'*Are* you Paul? *Were* you Paul? Why won't you answer me, Kit?'

'I can't, that's why. Darling, you've got to drop this. It's not going to lead anywhere. It can't.'

'For security reasons?'

'Yes.'

'You told him you'd never been anyone's red telephone.'

'Yes. I did.'

'But you have. That time you went away on a hush-hush mission, somewhere warm, and came back with scratches all over your legs. Emily was staying with us while she studied for her tropical-diseases qualification. She wanted you to have a tetanus injection. You refused.'

'I wasn't supposed to tell you even that much.'

'But you did. So it's no good trying to untell it now. You were going off to be the Office's *red telephone*, and you wouldn't say how long or where it was, except it was warm. We were impressed. We drank to you: "Here's to our red telephone." That happened, didn't it? You're not going to deny that? And you came back scratched and said you'd fallen into a bush.'

'I had. I did. A bush. It was true.'

And when this failed to appease her:

'All right, Suki. All right. Listen. I was Paul. I was his red telephone. Yes, I was. Three years ago. And we were comrades-in-arms. It was the best thing I ever did in my entire career, and that's all I'm going to tell you ever. The poor chap's gone completely to pieces. I hardly recognized him.'

'He looked a good man, Kit.'

'He's more than that. He's a thoroughly decent, brave chap. Or was. I'd no quarrel with him. Quite the reverse. He was my – *keeper*,' he said, in a moment of unwelcome honesty.

'But you denied him all the same.'

'I had to. No choice. Man was out of court. Whole operation was – well, *beyond* top secret.'

He had thought the worst was over, but that was to reckon without Suzanna's grip.

'What I *don't* understand at *all*, Kit, is this. If *Jeb* knew you were lying, and *you* knew you were lying, why did you have to lie to him at all? Or were you just lying for me and Emily?'

She had done it, whatever *it* was. Seizing upon anger as his excuse, he emitted a gruff 'I think I'll just go and have it out with him, if you don't mind' and the next thing he knew, he had thrust the hats into her arms and was storming back along the towpath with his walking stick and, ignoring the ancient DANGER notice, clattering over the rickety footbridge and through a spinney of birches to the lower end of Bailey's Meadow; then over a stile into a pool of mud and fast up the hillside, only to see below him the Arts and Crafts marquee half collapsed and the exhibitors, with more energy than they'd shown all day, dismantling tents, stands and trestle tables and slinging them into their vans: and there among the vans, the space, the very space, which only half an hour earlier Jeb's van had occupied and now occupied no more.

Which didn't for a second prevent Kit from loping down the slope with his arms waving in false jocularity:

'Jeb! Jeb! Where the hell's Jeb? Anyone seen *Jeb* at all, the leather chap? Gone off before I could pay him, silly ass – bunch of his money in my pocket! Well, do *you* know where Jeb's gone? And you don't either?' – in a string of vain appeals as he scoured the line of vans and trucks.

But all he got for an answer were kindly smiles and shakes of the head: no, Kit, sorry, nobody knows where Jeb's gone, or where he lives for that matter, or what his other name is, come to think of it, Jeb's a loner, civil enough but not by any means what you'd call chatty – laughter. One exhibitor thought she'd seen him over to Coverack Fair a couple of weeks back; another said she remembered him from St Austell last year. But nobody had a surname for him, nobody had a phone number, or even a number plate. Most likely he'd done what other traders do, they said: spotted the ad, bought his trading ticket at the gate, parked, traded and moved on.

'Lost someone, have you, Dad?'

Emily, right beside him – girl's a bloody genie. Must have been gossiping with the stable girls behind the horseboxes.

'Yes. I have actually, darling. Jeb, the leather-maker chap. The one your mum bought a bag from.'

'What does he want?'

'Nothing. I do' – confusion overcoming him – 'I owe him money.'

'You paid him. Sixty quid. In twenties.'

'Yes, well, this was for something else' – shiftily, avoiding her eye. 'Settlement of an old debt. Different thing entirely' – then, babbling something about needing to 'have a word with Mum', barged his way back along the path and through the walled garden to the kitchen, where Suzanna, with Mrs Marlow's help, was chopping vegetables in preparation for this evening's dinner for the Chain Gang. She ignored him, so he sought sanctuary in the dining room.

'Think I'll just buff up the silver,' he announced, loud enough for her to hear and do something about him if she wanted.

But she didn't, so never mind. Yesterday he had done a great job of polishing the commander's collection of antique silver – the Paul Storr candlesticks, the Hester Bateman salts, and the silver corvette complete with decommissioning pennant presented by the officers and crew of his last command. Bestowing a cheerless flap of the silver cloth on each, he poured himself a large Scotch, stomped upstairs and sat at the desk in his dressing room as a preliminary to performing his next chore of the evening: seating cards.

In the normal way, these cards were a source of quiet gratification to him, since they were his official calling cards left over from his last foreign posting. It was his little habit to look on surreptitiously as one or other of his dinner guests turned over the card, ran a finger across the embossed lettering and read the magic words: *Sir Christopher Probyn, High Commissioner of Her Majesty the Queen.* Tonight he anticipated no such pleasure. Nevertheless, with the guest list before him and a whisky at his elbow, he went diligently – perhaps too diligently – to work.

'That chap Jeb's gone, by the way,' he announced in a deliberately offhand voice, sensing Suzanna's presence behind him in the doorway. 'Upped sticks. Nobody knows who he is or what he is or anything else about him, poor man. All very painful. Very upsetting.'

Expecting a conciliatory touch or kindly word, he paused in

his labours, only to have Jeb's shoulder bag land with a thump on the desk in front of him.

'Look inside, Kit.'

Tilting the open bag irritably towards him, he groped around until he felt the tightly folded page of lined notepaper on which Jeb had written his receipt. Clumsily, he opened it, and with the same shaky hand held it under the desk lamp:

> To one innocent dead woman .... *nothing.*
> To one innocent dead child .... *nothing.*
> To one soldier who did his duty ....*disgrace.*
> To Paul .... *one knighthood.*

Kit read it, then stared at it – no longer as a document but as an object of disgust. Then he flattened it on the desk among the place cards, and studied it again in case he had missed something, but he hadn't.

'Simply not true,' he pronounced firmly. 'The man's obviously sick.'

Then he put his face in his hands and rolled it about, and after a while whispered, 'Dear God.'

*

And who was Master Bailey when he was at home, if he ever was?

An honest Cornish son of our village, if you listened to the believers, a farmer's boy unjustly hanged for stealing sheep on Easter Day for the pleasure of a wicked Assize judge over to Bodmin.

Except Master Bailey, he was never really hanged, or not to death he wasn't, not according to the famous Bailey Parchment in the church vestry. The villagers were so incensed by the unjust verdict that they cut him down at dead of night, they did, and resuscitated him with best applejack. And seven days on, young Master Bailey, he did take his father's horse and rode over to Bodmin, and with one sweep of his scythe he did chop the head clean off of that same wicked judge, and good luck to him, my dove – or so they do tell you.

All drivel, according to Kit the amateur historian who, in a few idle hours, had amused himself by researching the story: sentimental Victorian hogwash of the worst sort, not a scrap of supporting evidence in local archives.

The fact remained that for the last however many years, come rain or shine, peace or war, the good people of St Pirran had joined together to celebrate an act of extrajudicial killing.

*

The same night, lying in wakeful estrangement beside his sleeping wife and assailed by feelings of indignation, self-doubt and honest concern for an erstwhile companion-at-arms who, for whatever reason, had fallen so low, Kit deliberated his next move.

The night had not ended with the dinner party: how could it? After their spat in the dressing room, Kit and Suzanna barely had time to change before the Chain Gang's cars were rolling punctually up the drive. But Suzanna had left him in no doubt that hostilities would be resumed later.

Emily, no friend of formal functions at the best of times, had bowed out for the evening: some shindig in the church hall she thought she might look in on, and anyway, she didn't have to be back in London till tomorrow evening.

At the dinner table, sharpened by the knowledge that his world was falling round his ears, Kit had performed superbly if erratically, dazzling the Lady Mayor to his right and the Lady Alderman to his left with set pieces about the life and travails of a Queen's representative in a Caribbean paradise:

'My accolade? Absolute fluke! Nothing whatever to do with merit. Parade-horse job. Her Maj was in the region and took it into her head to drop in on our local premier. It was my parish, so bingo, I get a K for being in the right place at the right time. And *you*, darling' – grabbing his water glass by mistake and raising it to Suzanna down the line of the commander's Paul Storr candlesticks – 'became the lovely Lady P, which is how I've always thought of you anyway.'

But even while he makes this desperate protestation, it's Suzanna's voice, not his own, that he is hearing:

All I want to know is, Kit: did an innocent woman and child die, and were we packed off to the Caribbean to shut you up, and is that poor soldier right?

And sure enough, no sooner has Mrs Marlow gone home and the last of the Chain Gang's cars departed, there Suzanna is, standing stock-still in the hall waiting for his answer.

And Kit must have been unconsciously composing it all through dinner, because out it pours like a Foreign Office spokesman's official statement – and probably, to Suzanna's ear, about as believable:

'Here is my final word on the subject, Suki. It's as much as I'm allowed to tell you, and probably a great deal more.' Has he used this line before? 'The *top-secret* operation in which I was privileged to be involved was afterwards described to me by its planners – at the *highest* level – as a *certified, bloodless* victory over some *very bad men*.' A note of misplaced irony enters his voice which he tries in vain to stop: 'And for all I know, *yes*, maybe my modest role in the operation was what secured our posting, since the same people were kind enough to say I had done a pretty decent job, but unfortunately a medal would be too conspicuous. *However*, that was *not* the reason given to me by Personnel when the posting was offered to me – *a reward for lifelong service* was how they sold it to me, not that I needed much selling – any more than you did, as I recall' – pardonable dig. '*Were* the Personnel people – or Human Resources or whatever the hell they call themselves these days – aware of my role in a certain enormously delicate operation? I very much doubt it. My guess is, they didn't even know the very little you know.'

Has he persuaded her? When Suzanna looks like this, anything can be going on. He becomes strident – always a mistake:

'Look, darling, at the end of the day, who are you actually going to *believe*? Me and the top brass at the Foreign Office? Or some very sad ex-soldier down on his luck?'

She takes his question seriously. Weighs it. Her face locked against him, yes; but also blotchy, resolute, breaking his heart with its unbending rectitude, the face of a woman who got the best law degree of her year and never used it, but is using it now; the face of a woman who has looked death in the eye through a string of medical ordeals, and her only outward concern: how will Kit manage without her?

'Did you *ask* them – these planners – whether it was bloodless?'

'Of course I didn't.'

'Why not?'

'Because with people like that you don't challenge their integrity.'

'So they volunteered it. In as many words? "The operation was bloodless" – just like that?'

'Yes.'

'Why?'

'To reassure me, I assume.'

'Or to deceive you.'

'Suzanna, that is not worthy of you!'

Or not worthy of me? he wonders abjectly, first storming off to his dressing room in a huff, then sneaking unnoticed into his side of the bed where hour after hour he peers miserably into the half-darkness while Suzanna sleeps her motionless, medi-cated sleep: until at some point in the interminable dawn, he discovers that an unconscious mental process has delivered him a seemingly spontaneous decision.

*

Rolling silently off the bed and creeping across the corridor, Kit threw on a pair of flannels and a sports jacket, detached his cell-phone from its charger and dropped it into his jacket pocket. Pausing at the door to Emily's bedroom for sounds of waking, and hearing none, he tiptoed down the back staircase to the kitchen to make himself a pot of coffee, an essential prerequisite for putting his master plan into effect: only to hear his daughter's voice addressing him from the open doorway leading to the orchard.

'Got a spare mug on you, Dad?'

Emily, back from her morning run with Sheba.

At any other time, Kit would have relished a cosy chat with her: just not on this particular morning, though he was quick to sit himself opposite her at the pine table. As he did so, he caught sight of the purpose in her face and knew she had turned back from her run when she spotted the kitchen lights on her way up Bailey's Hill.

'Mind telling me what's going on exactly, Dad?' she enquired crisply, every bit her mother's child.

'Going on?' – lame smile. 'Why should anything be *going on*? Your mum's asleep. I'm having a coffee.'

But nobody fobs off Emily. Not these days. Not after that scoundrel Bernard two-timed her.

'What happened at Bailey's yesterday?' she demanded. 'At the leather stall. You knew the man but you wouldn't acknowledge him. He called you Paul and left some foul note in Mum's hand-bag.'

Kit had long abandoned his attempts to penetrate the near-telepathic communications between his wife and daughter.

'Yes, well, I'm afraid that's not something you and I are able to discuss,' he replied loftily, avoiding her eye.

'And you're not able to discuss it with Mum either. Right?'

'Yes, it *is* right, Em, as it happens. And I'm not enjoying it any more than she is. Unfortunately, it's a matter of considerable official secrecy. As your mother is aware. And accepts. As perhaps you should.'

'My patients tell me their secrets. I don't go handing them around. What makes you think Mum will hand yours around? She's silent as the grave. A bit more silent than you are sometimes.'

Time to mount his high horse:

'Because these are *state* secrets, Emily. Not mine and not your mother's. They were entrusted to *me* and no one else. The *only* people I can share them with are the people who know them already. Which makes it, I have to say, *rather* a lonely business.'

And on this fine note of self-pity, he rose, kissed her on the head, stalked off across the stable yard to his improvised office, locked the door and opened up his computer:

Marlon will respond to your personal and confidential inquiries.

*

With Sheba riding proudly in the back of the nearly new Land Rover that he had acquired in exchange for his aged camper, Kit drives purposefully up Bailey's Hill until he arrives by design at a deserted lay-by with a Celtic cross and a view of the morning mist rising in the valley. His first call is foredoomed, as he intends it to be, but Service ethic and some sense of self-protection requires him to make it. Dialling the Foreign Office switchboard, he gets a determined woman who requires him to repeat his name clearly and slowly. He does, and throws in his knighthood for good measure. After a delay so long that he would be justified in ringing off, she informs him that the erstwhile minister Mr Fergus Quinn has not been at his post for three years – a thing Kit well knows but this doesn't stop him from asking – and that she has no number for him and no authority to pass messages. Would Sir Christopher – *finally*, thank you! – care to be connected with the resident clerk? No thank you, Sir Christopher would not, with the clear implication that a resident clerk wouldn't match up to the level of security involved.

Well, I tried, and it's on record. Now for the tricky bit.

Extracting the piece of paper on which he had written down Marlon's telephone number, he touches it into his cellphone, turns the volume to maximum because his hearing's going a bit, and swiftly, for fear of hesitation, presses green. Listening tensely to the number ringing out, he remembers too late what time of day it is in Houston, and has a vision of a bleary Marlon groping for his bedside phone. Instead, he gets the sincere voice of a Texan matron:

'We *thank* you for calling Ethical Outcomes. Remember: at Ethical, *your* safety comes *first!*'

Then a blast of martial music, and the all-American voice of Marlon on parade:

'Hullo! This is *Marlon*. Kindly be advised that your inquiry will *always* be treated in the strictest confidence in accordance with Ethical's principles of integrity and discretion. I'm sorry: there's nobody around just now to take your personal and private call. But if you would care to leave a simple message of no more than two minutes in duration, your confidential consultant will get right back to you. After the signal, please.'

Has Kit prepared his simple message of no more than two minutes in duration? During the long night, he evidently has:

'This is *Paul* and I need to speak to *Elliot*. Elliot, this is Paul, from three years ago. Something pretty unpleasant has cropped up, not of my making, I may say. I need to talk to you urgently, obviously not on my home number. You've got my personal cellphone number, it's the same old one as before, not encrypted, of course. Let's fix a date to meet as soon as possible. If you can't make it, perhaps you'd put me in touch with somebody I'm authorized to talk to. I mean by that somebody who knows the background and can fill in some rather disturbing blanks. I look forward to hearing from you very soon. Thank you. Paul.'

With a sense of a tricky job well done in under two minutes, he rings off and sets out along a pony track with Sheba at his heels. But after a couple of hundred yards his sense of achievement deserts him. How long will he have to wait before anyone calls back? And, above all, *where* will he wait? In St Pirran there's no cellphone signal – you can be on Orange, Vodafone or whatever. If he goes home now, all he'll be thinking of will be how to get out again. Obviously, in due course he will be offering his womenfolk some unclassified account of what he's achieved – but not until he's achieved it.

So the question is: is there a middle way, a stopgap cover story that will keep him within range of Marlon but out of range of his women? Answer: the tedious solicitor in Truro he recently engaged to sort out various piddling family trusts. Suppose, for argument's sake, something has cropped up: a knotty legal matter that needs to be thrashed out in a hurry? And suppose Kit in the rush of events has completely forgotten all about the appointment till now? It plays. Next move, call Suzanna, which will take nerve, but he's ready for her.

Summoning Sheba, he returns to the Land Rover, slots his cellphone into its housing, switches on the ignition and is

159

startled by the deafening shriek of an incoming call on maximum sound.

'Is that Kit Probyn?' a male voice blurts.

'This is Probyn. Who's that?' – hastily adjusting the volume.

'My name's Jay Crispin from Ethical. Heard marvellous things about you. Elliot's off the radar at the moment, a-chasing the deer, as we say. How's about I stand in for him?'

Within seconds, as it seems to him, the thing is settled: they will meet. And not tomorrow but tonight. No beating about the bush, no umming and ahhing. A forthright British voice, educated, one of us, and not in the least defensive, which of itself speaks volumes. The kind of man that in other circumstances it would be a pleasure to get to know – all of which he duly reported to Suzanna in suitably coded terms while they hurriedly dressed him in time to catch the ten forty-one from Bodmin Parkway station:

'And you'll be *strong*, Kit,' Suzanna urged him, embracing him with all the power in her frail body. 'It's not that you're weak. You're not. It's that you're kind and trusting and loyal. Well, Jeb was loyal too. You said he was. Didn't you?'

Did he? Probably he did. But then, as he reminded her sagely, people do change, darling, even the best of us, you know. And some of us go clean off the rails.

'And you'll ask your Mister Big, whoever he is, straight out: "Was poor Jeb telling the truth and did an innocent woman and her child die?" I don't want to know what it's about. I know I never shall. But if what Jeb wrote on that beastly receipt is true, and that's why we got the Caribbean, we must face up to it. We can't live a lie, however much we might like to. Can we, darling? Or *I* can't,' she added, as an afterthought.

And from Emily, more baldly, as they pulled into the station forecourt:

'Whatever it is, Dad, Mum's going to need proper answers.'

'*Well, so am I!*' he had snapped back at her in a moment of angry pain that he instantly regretted.

*

The Connaught Hotel in the West End of London was not an establishment that had come Kit's way but, seated alone amid the bustle of waiters in the post-modern splendour of its lounge, he rather wished it had; for in that case he would not have chosen the elderly country suit and cracked brown shoes that he had snatched from his wardrobe.

'If my plane's late, just tell 'em you're waiting for me, and they'll look after you,' Crispin had said, without troubling to mention where his plane was coming from.

And sure enough, when Kit murmured Crispin's name to the black-suited major-domo poised like a great conductor at his lectern, the fellow had actually smiled:

'Come a long way today, have we, Sir Christopher? Well, Cornwall, that *is* a long way. What may I tempt you with, compliments of Mr Crispin?'

'Pot of tea, and I'll pay for it myself. Cash,' Kit had retorted stiffly, determined to retain his independence.

But a cup of tea is not something the Connaught gives up lightly. To obtain one, Kit must settle for the Chic & Shock Afternoon Tea and look on helplessly while a waiter brings cakes, scones and cucumber sandwiches at thirty-five pounds plus tip.

He waits.

Several potential Crispins enter, ignore him, join others or are joined by them. From the strong, masterful voice he has heard on the telephone, he instinctively looks for the man to match it: big-shouldered perhaps, bags of confidence, a good stride. He remembers Elliot's glowing eulogy of his employer. He wonders to himself in nervous jest what earthly form such powers of leadership and charisma will take. And he is not entirely disappointed when an elegant forty-something man of medium height, wearing a well-cut grey pinstripe suit, sits himself quietly down beside him, takes his hand and murmurs, 'I rather think I'm your man.'

And the recognition, if such it could be called, is immediate. Jay Crispin is as English and smooth as his voice. He is clean-shaven and, with his groomed, swept-back head of healthy hair and smile of quiet assurance, what Kit's parents would have called clean-limbed.

'Kit, I'm just so very sorry that this should have happened,' the perfectly tuned voice declares, with a sincerity that cuts straight to Kit's heart. 'What a bloody awful time you've had. My God, what are you drinking – not *tea*!' And as a waiter glides to their side: 'You're a whisky man. They do a pretty decent Macallan here. Take all this stuff away, will you, Luigi? And bring us a couple of the eighteen-year-olds. Make 'em big 'uns. Ice? – no ice. Soda and water on the side.' And as the waiter departs: 'And look here, thanks a million for making the trip. I'm just so *terribly* sorry you had to make it at all.'

*

Now Kit would never admit that he was attracted to Jay Crispin, or that his judgement was in any way undermined by the man's compelling charm. From the outset, he would insist, he had harboured the gravest suspicions about the fellow, and kept them going throughout the meeting.

'And life in darkest Cornwall suits you all right, does it?' Crispin asked conversationally while they waited for their drinks to arrive. 'You don't pine for the bright lights? Personally, I'd be talking to the dicky birds after a couple of weeks. But that's my problem, they tell me. Incurable workaholic. No powers of self-entertainment.' And after this little confidence: 'And Suzanna on the mend, I gather?' – dropping the perfect voice for intimacy.

'*Vastly* better, thank you, vastly. Country life is what she loves,' Kit replied awkwardly, but what else is he supposed to say when the man asks? And gruffly, in an effort to turn the conversation round:

'So where are *you* actually based? Here in London or – well, Houston, I suppose?'

'Oh my God, London, where else? Only place to be, if you want my view – apart from North Cornwall, obviously.'

The waiter was back. Hiatus while he poured out the drinks to Crispin's specification.

'Cashews, bits?' Crispin asked Kit solicitously. 'Or something a bit more substantial after your travels?'

'Thank you, I'm doing very well' – keeping his guard up.

'Shoot away, then,' said Crispin when the waiter had left.

Kit shot. And Crispin listened, his handsome face puckered in concentration, his neat head wisely nodding to imply he was familiar with the story; even that he'd heard it before.

'And then, the same evening, there was *this*, you see,' Kit protested and, drawing a damp brown envelope from the recesses of his country suit, passed Crispin the piece of flimsy lined paper that Jeb had torn from his pad. 'Take a look at *that*, if you will,' he added, for extra portent – and watched Crispin's manicured hand take it over, noting the double cuffs of cream silk and the gold engraved links; watched him lean back and, holding the paper in both hands, scrutinize it with the calm of an antiquarian examining it for watermarks.

Well, did he look guilty, darling? Did he look shocked? Well, he must have looked something!

But Crispin, so far as Kit could make out, didn't look anything. The regular features didn't flinch, there was no violent trembling of the hands: just a forlorn shake of the trim head, accompanied by the officer-class voice.

'Well, you poor chap is all I can say, Kit. You absolute poor chap. What a truly bloody awful situation. And your poor Suzanna too. Ghastly. What *she* must be going through, God alone knows. I mean, she's the one who *really* took the flak. Quite apart from not knowing why or where it's coming from, and knowing she can't ask. What a little shit. Forgive me. *Christ!*' he said vehemently under his breath, suppressing some stab of inner pain.

'And she *really* needs to get a straight answer,' Kit insisted, determined to stick to his guns. 'However bad it is, she's *got* to know what happened. So have I. She's taken it into her head that our posting to the Caribbean was a way of shutting me up. She even – totally unintentionally – seems to have infected our daughter with the same idea. So not a very *pleasant* insinuation, as you can imagine' – cautiously encouraged by Crispin's sympathetic nod – 'not a very *happy* way to go into retirement: reckoning you've done a decent job for your country, then discovering it was all a charade to cover up a – well – *murder*, not to put too fine an edge on it' – pausing for a waiter to bustle past pushing a trolley bearing a birthday cake with a single candle sparking on it. 'Then throw in the fact that a first-class soldier has had his *whole life* trashed for him, or may have done. That's not the sort of thing Suzanna takes lightly, seeing she tends to care rather more about other people than she does about herself. So what I'm saying is: no beating around the bush, we need to have the facts. Yes or no. Straight out. Both of us. *All* of us. Anyone would. Sorry about that.'

Sorry how? Sorry to hear his voice slither out of control and feel the colour surge to his face? Not sorry at all. His dander was up at last, and so it should be. Suki would be cheering him on. So would Em. And the sight of this fellow Jay Crispin, smugly nodding away with his pretty head of wavy hair, would have infuriated them quite as much as it was starting to infuriate *him*.

'Plus I'm the villain of the piece,' Crispin suggested nobly, in the tone of a man assembling the case against him. 'I'm the bad guy who set the whole thing up, hired a bunch of cheap mercs, conned Langley and our own Special Forces into providing support-in-aid and presided over one of the great operational fuck-ups of all time. That right? Plus I delegated the job to a useless field commander who lost his rag and let his men shoot the hell out of an innocent mother and her child. Does that about cover it, or is there anything else I did that I haven't mentioned?'

'Now look here, I didn't say *any* of that –'

'No, Kit, you don't have to. Jeb said it, and you believe it. You don't have to sweeten it. I've lived with it for three years, and I can live with it for another three' – all without a hint of self-pity, or none that reached Kit's ear. 'And Jeb's not the only one, to be fair on him. In my line of country we get 'em all: chaps with post-traumatic stress disorder, real or imagined, resentment about gratuities, pensions, fantasizing about themselves, re-inventing their life stories, and rushing to a lawyer if they're not muzzled in time. But this little bastard is in a class of his own, believe you me.' A forbearing sigh, another sad shake of the head. 'Done *great* work in his day, Jeb, none better. Which only makes it worse. Plausible as the day is long. Heart-breaking letters to his MP, the Ministry of Defence, you name it. *The poison dwarf*, we call him at head office. Well, never mind.' Another sigh, this one near silent. 'And you're absolutely sure the meeting was coincidence? He didn't track you down somehow?'

'Pure coincidence,' Kit insisted, with more certainty than he was beginning to feel.

'Did your local newspaper or radio down in Cornwall announce that Sir Christopher and Lady Probyn would be gracing the platform, by any chance?'

'May have done.'

'Maybe that's your clue.'

'No way,' Kit retorted adamantly. 'Jeb didn't know my name until he showed up at the Fayre and put two and two together' – glad to keep up the indignation.

'So no pictures of you anywhere?'

'None that came *our* way. And if there had been, Mrs Marlow would have told us. Our housekeeper,' he declared stoutly. And for extra certainty: 'And if she *did* miss something, the whole village would be telling her.'

The waiter wanted to know whether they would like the same again. Kit said he wouldn't. Crispin said they would and Kit didn't argue.

'Want to hear something about our line of work at all, Kit?' Crispin asked, when they were alone again.

'Not sure I should, really. Not my business.'

'Well, I think you should. You did a great job in the Foreign Office, no question. You worked your backside off for the Queen, earned your pension and your K. But as a first-rate civil servant you were an *enabler* – all right, a bloody good one. You were never a *player*. Not what we might call a hunter-gatherer in the corporate jungle. Were you? Admit it.'

'Don't think I know where you're leading,' Kit growled.

'I'm talking *incentive*,' Crispin explained patiently. 'I'm talking about what drives the average Joe Bloggs to get out of bed in the morning: money, filthy lucre, dosh. And in my business – never yours – who gets a piece of the cake when an operation is as successful as *Wildlife* was. And the sort of resentments that are aroused. To the point where chaps like Jeb think they're owed half the Bank of England.'

'You seem to have forgotten that Jeb was *army*,' Kit broke in hotly. '*British* army. He also had a bit of a *thing* about bounty-hunters, as he happened to inform me during our time together. Tolerated them, but that was as much as he could manage. He was proud of being the Queen's soldier, and that was enough for him. Made the very point, I'm afraid. Sorry about that' – getting hotter still.

Crispin was gently nodding to himself, like a man whose worst fears have been confirmed.

'Oh dear. Oh Jeb. Oh boy. He actually *said* that, did he? God-a-mercy!' He collected himself. 'The Queen's soldier doesn't hold with mercenaries, but wants a mega-slice of the bounty-hunters' cake? I love it. Well done, Jeb. Hypocrisy hits new depths. And when he doesn't get what he wants, he turns round and shits all over Ethical's doorstep. What a two-faced little' – but for reasons of delicacy he preferred to leave the sentence unfinished.

And again Kit refused to be deterred:

'Now look here, all that's beside the point. I haven't got my answer, have I? Nor has Suzanna.'

'To *what*, exactly, old boy?' Crispin asked, still struggling to overcome whatever demons were assailing him.

'The answer I came for, damn it. Yes or no? Forget rewards, bounty, all that stuff. Total red herring. My question is, one: was the operation bloodless or was it not? Was *anybody killed*? And if so, who were they? Never mind about innocent or guilty: *were they killed*? And *two*' – no longer quite the master of his arithmetic, but persisting nonetheless – 'was a *woman* killed? And was her *child* killed? Or *any* child, for that matter? Suzanna has a right to know. So've I. And we both need to know what to tell our daughter, because Emily was there too. At the Fayre. Heard him. Heard things that she shouldn't have done. From Jeb. Not her fault that she heard them but she did. I'm not sure how much, but enough.' And as a mitigating afterthought, because his parting words to Emily at the railway station still shamed him: 'Earwigging, probably. I don't blame her. She's a doctor. She's observant. She needs to know things. Part of her job.'

Crispin appeared surprised, even a little hurt, to discover that such questions should still be out there on the table. But he elected to answer them anyway:

'Let's just take a look at *your* case first, Kit, shall we?' he suggested kindly. 'D'you honestly think the dear old FO would have given you that posting – that *honour* – if there'd been blood all over the Rock? Not to mention *Punter* singing his heart out to his interrogators at an undisclosed location?'

'Could have done,' Kit said obstinately, ignoring the outsider's hated use of *FO*. 'To keep me quiet. Get me out of the firing line. Stop me from blabbing. The Foreign Office has done worse things in its time. Suzanna thinks they could, anyway. So do I.'

'Then watch my lips.'

From under furrowed brows, Kit was doing just that.

'Kit. There was zero – repeat: zero – loss of life. Want me to say it again? Not *one* drop of blood, not anyone's. No dead babies, no dead mothers. Convinced now? Or do I have to ask the concierge to bring a Bible?'

⋆

The walk from the Connaught to Pall Mall on that balmy spring evening was for Kit less a pleasure than a sad celebration. Jeb, poor fellow, was obviously very damaged goods indeed. Kit's heart went out to him: a former comrade, a brave ex-soldier who had given in to feelings of avarice and injustice. Well, he'd known a better man than that, a man to respect, a man to follow. Should their paths happen to cross again – which God forbid, but should they – he would not withhold the hand of friendship. As to their chance meeting at Bailey's Fayre, he had no time for Crispin's base suspicions. It was sheer coincidence, and that was that. The greatest actor on earth couldn't have faked that ravaged face as it stared up at him from the tailgate of the van. Jeb might be psychotic, he might be suffering from post-traumatic stress disorder or any of the other big words we throw around so easily these days. But to Kit he would remain the Jeb who had led him to the high point of his career, and nothing was ever going to take that away, period.

And it was with this determinedly honed formulation in his head that he stepped into a side street and called Suzanna, a thing he had been dying to do, but also in some indefinable way dreading, ever since he had left the Connaught.

'Things are *really* good, Suki' – picking his words carefully because, as Emily had unkindly pointed out, Suzanna was if anything more security conscious than he was. 'We're dealing with a very sick chap who's tragically lost his way in life and can't tell truth from fiction, okay?' He tried again. 'Nobody – repeat: *nobody* – got hurt in the accident. Suki? Are you there?'

Oh Christ, she's crying. She's not. Suki never cries.

'Suki, darling, there was *no accident*. None plural. It's *all right*. No *child* left behind. Or mother. Our friend from the Fayre is *deluded*. He's a poor, brave chap, he's got mental problems, he's got money problems, and he's all muddled up in his head. I've had it straight from the top man.'

'Kit?'

'What is it, darling? Tell me. Please. Suzanna?'

'I'm all right, Kit. I was just a bit tired and low. I'm better now.'

Still not weeping? Suki? Not on your life. Not old Suki. Never. He had been intending to call Emily next, but on reflection: best give it a rest till tomorrow.

*

In his club, it was the watering hour. Old buddies greeted him, bought him a jar, he bought one back. Kidneys and bacon at the long table, coffee and port in the library to make a proper night of it. The lift out of service, but he negotiated the four flights with ease and groped his way down the long corridor to his bedroom without knocking over any bloody fire extinguishers. But he had to run his hand up and down the wall to find the light switch that kept eluding him, and while he was groping he noticed there was a lot of fresh air in the room. Had the previous occupant, in flagrant contradiction of club rules, been smoking and left the window open to conceal the evidence? If so, Kit was minded to write a stiff letter to the secretary.

And when eventually he did find the switch, and put on the light, there on a Rexine-covered armchair beneath the open window, wearing a smart dark-blue blazer with a triangle of white handkerchief in the top pocket, sat Jeb.

4.

The brown A4 envelope landed face upwards on the doormat of
Toby Bell's flat in Islington at twenty past three on a Saturday
morning, shortly after his return from a rewarding but stressful
tour at the British Embassy in Beirut. Immediately on security
alert, he grabbed a hand torch from his bedside and tiptoed
warily along the corridor to the sound of softly retreating footsteps down the stairs and the closing of the front door.

The envelope was of the thick, oily variety, and unfranked.
The words PRIVATE & CONFIDENTIAL were written in large
inked capitals in the top-left corner. The address *T. Bell, Esquire,
Flat 2*, was done in a cursive, English-looking hand he didn't
recognize. The back flap was double sealed with sticky tape,
the torn-off ends of which were folded round to the front. No
sender's name was offered, and if the antiquated *Esquire*, spelt
out in full, was intended to reassure him, it had the opposite
effect. The contents of the envelope appeared to be flat – so
technically a letter, not a package. But Toby knew from his
training that devices don't have to be bulky to blow your hands
off.

There was no great mystery about how a letter could be
delivered to his first-floor flat at such an hour. At weekends the
front door to the house was often left unlocked all night. Steeling himself, he picked up the envelope and, holding it at arm's
length, took it to the kitchen. After examining it under the overhead light, he cut into the side of it with a kitchen knife and
discovered a second envelope addressed in the same hand:
ATTENTION OF T. BELL, ESQ. *ONLY.*

This interior envelope too was sealed with sticky tape. Inside it were two tightly written sheets of headed blue notepaper, undated.

As from:
The Manor,
St Pirran,
Bodmin,
Cornwall

My dear Bell,

Forgive this cloak-and-dagger missive, and the furtive manner of its delivery. My researches inform me that three years ago you were Private Secretary to a certain junior minister. If I tell you that we have a mutual acquaintance by the name of Paul, you will guess the nature of my concern and appreciate why I am not at liberty to expand in writing.

The situation in which I find myself is so acute that I have no option but to appeal to your natural human instincts and solicit your complete discretion. I am asking you for a personal meeting at your earliest possible convenience, here in the obscurity of North Cornwall rather than in London, on any day of your choosing. No prior warning, whether by email, telephone or the public post, is necessary, or advisable.

Our house is presently under renovation, but we have ample room to accommodate you. I am delivering this at the start of the weekend in the hope that it may expedite your visit.

Yours sincerely,

Christopher (Kit) Probyn.

PS Sketch map and How to Reach Us attached. C.P.

PPS Obtained your address from a former colleague under a pretext. C.P.

As Toby read this, a kind of magisterial calm descended over him, of fulfilment, and of vindication. For three years he had waited for just such a sign, and now here it was, lying before him on the kitchen table. Even in the worst times in Beirut – amid bomb scares, kidnap fears, curfews, assassinations and clandestine meetings with unpredictable militia chiefs – he had never once ceased to wrestle with the mystery of the Operation That Never Was, and Giles Oakley's inexplicable U-turn. The decision of Fergus Quinn, MP, white hope of the powers-that-be in Downing Street, announced just days after Toby was whisked off to Beirut, to step down from politics and accept the post of Defence Procurement Consultant to one of the Emirates, had provided fodder for the weekend gossip writers, but produced nothing of substance.

Still in his dressing gown, Toby hurried to his desktop. Christopher (Kit) Probyn, born 1950, educated Marlborough College and Caius, Cambridge, second-class honours in Mathematics and Biology, rated one tight paragraph in *Who's Who*. Married to Suzanna née Cardew, one daughter. Served in Paris, Bucharest, Ankara, Vienna, then various home-based appointments before becoming High Commissioner to a pattern of Caribbean islands.

Knighted *en poste* by the Queen, retired one year ago.

With this harmless entry, the floodgates of recognition were flung wide open.

Yes, Sir Christopher, we do indeed have a mutual acquaintance by the name of Paul!

And yes, Kit, I really do guess the nature of your concern and appreciate why you are not at liberty to expand in writing!

And I'm not at all surprised that no email, telephone or public post is necessary or advisable. Because Paul is Kit, and Kit is Paul! And between you, you make one low flyer and one red telephone, and you are appealing to my natural human instincts. Well, Kit – well, Paul – you will not appeal in vain.

★

As a single man in London, Toby had made a point of never owning a car. It took him ten infuriating minutes to extract a railway timetable from the Web, and another ten to arrange a self-drive from Bodmin Parkway station. By midday he was sitting in the buffet section watching the rolling fields of the West Country stutter past so slowly that he despaired of arriving at his destination before nightfall. By late afternoon nevertheless, he was driving an overlarge saloon with a slipping clutch and bad steering through narrow lanes so overhung with foliage that they resembled tunnels pierced with strands of sunlight. Soon he was picking up the promised landmarks: a ford, a hairpin bend, a solitary phone box, a cul-de-sac sign, and finally a milestone saying ST PIRRAN CH'TOWN 2 MILES.

He descended a steep hill and passed between fields of corn and rape bordered by granite hedges. A cluster of farm cottages rose up at him, then a sprawl of modern bungalows, then a stubby granite church and a village street; and at the end of the street on its own small rise, the Manor, an ugly nineteenth-century yeoman's farmhouse with a pillared porch and a pair of outsized iron gates and two pompous gateposts mounted with stone lions.

Toby did not slow down on this first pass. He was Beirut Man, accustomed to collecting all available information in advance of an encounter. Selecting an unmetalled track that offered a traverse of the hillside, he was soon able to look down on a jumble of pitched slate roofs with ladders laid across them, a row of dilapidated greenhouses and a stables with a clock tower and no clock. And in the stable yard, a cement mixer and a heap of sand. *The house is presently under renovation, but we have ample room to accommodate you.*

His reconnaissance complete, he drove back to the village high street and, by way of a short, pitted drive, drew up at the Manor porch. Finding no bell but a brass knocker, he gave it a resounding whack and heard a dog barking and sounds of ferocious hammering from the depths of the house. The door flew open and a small, intrepid-looking woman in her sixties sternly examined him with her sharp blue eyes. From her side, a mud-caked yellow Labrador did the same.

'My name's Toby Bell. I wondered if I might have a word with Sir Christopher,' he said, upon which her gaunt face at once relaxed into a warm, rather beautiful smile.

'But of *course* you're Toby Bell! D'you know, for a moment I really thought you were too young for the part? I'm *so* sorry. That's the problem with being a hundred years old. *He's here, darling! It's Toby Bell.* Where *is* the man? Kitchen probably. He's arguing with an old bread oven. *Kit, stop banging for once and come, darling!* I bought him a pair of those plastic earmuff things but he won't wear them. Sheer male obstinacy. Sheba, say hullo to Toby. You don't mind being Toby, do you? I'm Suzanna. *Nicely*, Sheba! Oh dear, she needs a wash.'

The hammering stopped. The mud-caked Labrador nuzzled Toby's thigh. Following Suzanna's gaze, he peered down an ill-lit flagstone corridor.

'That really him, darling? Sure you've got the right chap? Can't be too careful, you know. Might be the new plumber.'

An inward leap of recognition: after three years of waiting, Toby was hearing the voice of the true Paul.

'Of *course* he's the right chap, darling!' Suzanna was calling back. 'And he's absolutely *dying* for a shower and a stiff drink after his journey, aren't you, Toby?'

'Good trip, Toby? Found your way and everything? Directions didn't lead you astray?'

'Absolutely fine! Your directions were impressively accurate,' Toby called, equally heartily, down the empty passage.

'Give me thirty seconds to wash my hands and get these boots off and I'll be with you.'

Torrent of tap water, honk, gurgle of pipes. The true Paul's measured footsteps approaching over flagstones. And finally the man himself, first in silhouette, then in worker's overalls and ancient gym-shoes, drying his hands on a tea cloth before grasping Toby's in a double grip.

'Bloody good of you to come,' he said fervently. 'Can't tell you what it means to us. We've been absolutely worried sick, haven't we, darling?'

But before Suzanna could confirm this, a tall, slender woman in her late twenties with dark hair and wide Italian eyes had appeared as if from nowhere and was standing at Kit's side. And since she seemed more interested in taking a look at Toby than greeting him, his first assumption was that she was some kind of house servant, perhaps an au pair.

'Hi. I'm Emily. Daughter of the house,' she said curtly, reaching past her father to give his hand a perfunctory shake, but with no accompanying smile.

'Brought your toothbrush?' Kit was asking. 'Good man! In the car? You fetch your things, I'll show you up to your room. And darling, you'll rustle up some boys' supper for us, will you? The fellow must be starving after his travels. One of Mrs Marlow's pies will do him a power.'

*

The main staircase was work in progress, so they were using the old servants' staircase. The paint on the wall *should* be dry, but best not touch it, Kit said. The women had

176

disappeared. From a scullery, sounds of Sheba getting her wash.

'Em's a medic,' Kit volunteered as they climbed, his voice echoing up and down the stairwell. 'Qualified at Bart's. Top of her year, bless her. Tends the poor and needy of the East End, lucky devils. Dicky floorboard here, so watch your step.'

They had reached a landing with a row of doors. Kit threw open the middle one. Dormer windows gave on to a walled garden. A single bed was neatly turned down. On a writing table lay foolscap paper and ballpoint pens.

'Scotch in the library as soon as you've powdered your nose,' Kit announced from the doorway. 'Stroll before supper if you're up for it. Easier to talk when the girls aren't around,' he added awkwardly. 'And watch out for the shower: it's a bit of a hot number.'

Entering the bathroom and about to undress, Toby was startled to hear a blare of angry voices coming through the door. He stepped back into the bedroom to see Emily in tracksuit and sneakers, balancing a remote control in her hand, standing over the television, running through the channels.

'I thought I'd better check that it worked,' she explained over her shoulder, making no effort to lower the sound. 'We're in a foreign posting here. Nobody's allowed to hear what anyone is saying to anyone else. Plus walls have ears and we haven't got any carpets.'

The television still blaring, she came a stride closer.

'Are you here instead of *Jeb*?' she demanded, straight into his face.

'Who?'

'*Jeb*. J–E–B.'

'No. No, I'm not.'

'Do you *know* Jeb?'

'No. I don't.'

'Well, Dad does. It's his big secret. Except Jeb calls him Paul.

177

He was supposed to be here last Wednesday. He didn't show. You're in his bed, actually,' she added, still regarding him with her brown gaze.

On the television, a quiz-show host was whipping up a furore.

'I don't know a Jeb, and I've never met a Jeb in my life,' Toby replied in a carefully measured voice. 'I'm Toby Bell, and I'm Foreign Office.' And as a calculated afterthought, 'But I'm also a private person, whatever that means.'

'So which are you being now?'

'A private person. Your family's guest.'

'But you still don't know Jeb?'

'Not as a private person, nor as a Foreign Service official do I know a Jeb. I thought I made that clear.'

'So why've you come?'

'Your father needs to talk to me. He hasn't yet said why.'

Her tone eased, but only a little:

'My mother's discreet unto death. She's also ill and doesn't respond well to stress, which is unfortunate because there's a lot of it about. So what I'm wondering is, are you here to make things worse or better? Or don't you know that either?'

'I'm afraid I don't.'

'Does the Foreign Office know you're here?'

'No.'

'But on Monday, it will.'

'I don't think you should presume that at all.'

'Why not?'

'Because first I need to listen to your father.'

Howls of jubilation from the television set as somebody wins a million pounds.

'You talk to my father tonight and leave in the morning. Is that the plan?'

'Assuming we've done our business by then.'

'It's St Pirran's turn for Matins. My parents will be on church

178

parade at ten. Dad's a sidesman or a beadle or something. If you say your goodbyes before they leave for church, you could stay behind and we could compare notes.'

'So far as we can, I'd be happy to.'

'What does that mean?'

'If your father wants to talk confidentially, then I have to respect his confidence.'

'What about if I want to talk confidentially?'

'Then I would respect your confidence too.'

'Ten o'clock then.'

'Ten o'clock.'

Kit was standing in the hall, clutching a spare anorak: 'Mind if we do whisky later? Spot of weather coming up.'

*

They tramped through the drenched walled garden, Kit flourishing an old ash walking stick, Sheba at his heels and Toby struggling after them in a pair of borrowed wellingtons that were too big for him. They followed a towpath lined with bluebells and crossed a rickety bridge marked DANGER. A granite stile gave on to the open hillside. As they climbed, a west wind blew fine rain into their faces. There was a bench on the hilltop, but it was too wet to sit on, so they stood partly facing each other, eyes half closed against the rain.

'All right up here?' Kit asked, meaning, presumably: do you mind standing here in the rain?

'Of course. Love it,' Toby said politely, and there was a hiatus in which Kit seemed to screw up his courage, then plunge.

'*Operation Wildlife*,' he barked. 'Roaring success, we were told. Drinks all round. Knighthoods for me, promotion for you – what?'

And waited, scowling.

'I'm sorry,' Toby said.

'What for?'

'I've never heard of *Operation Wildlife*.'

Kit was staring at him, the affability draining from his face. '*Wildlife*, for Christ's sake, man! Hugely secret operation! Public-private enterprise to kidnap a high-value terrorist' – and when Toby still gave no sign of recognition: 'Look here. If you're going to deny you ever heard of it, why the devil did you come down here?'

Then stood there glowering, with the rain running down his face, waiting for Toby's answer.

'I know you were Paul,' Toby said, in the same measured tone he had employed with Emily. 'But I'd never heard of *Operation Wildlife* until you mentioned it just now. I never saw any papers relating to *Wildlife*. I never attended meetings. Quinn kept me out of the loop.'

'But you were his Private Secretary, for Christ's sake!'

'Yes. For Christ's sake, I was his Private Secretary.'

'How about Elliot? You heard of *Elliot*?'

'Only indirectly.'

'*Crispin?*'

'Yes, I've heard of Crispin,' Toby conceded, in the same level tone. 'I've even met him. And I've heard of Ethical Outcomes, if that's any help.'

'*Jeb?* How about Jeb? Heard of *Jeb?*'

'Jeb is also a name to me. But *Wildlife* isn't, and I'm still waiting to know why you asked me to come here.'

If this was supposed to mollify Kit, it had the opposite effect. Jabbing his stick at the dip directly below them, he roared above the wind:

'I'll tell you why you're here. That's where Jeb parked his bloody van! Down there! Tyre marks till the cows trampled them. *Jeb*. Leader of our gallant British detachment. The chap they chucked on the scrapheap for telling them the truth. Down on his uppers. And you had no part in any of it, I suppose?'

180

'None whatever,' Toby replied.

'Then *maybe* you'll tell me,' Kit suggested, his rage abating slightly, 'before one or other of us goes mad, or we *both* do: how come you *don't* know what *Operation Wildlife* was about, whereas you *do* know Paul and Jeb and the rest of them *despite* the fact that your own minister kept you out of the loop, *which I personally find bloody hard to believe?*'

Delivering his simple answer, Toby was surprised to discover that he had undergone no crisis of the soul, only an agreeable sense of catharsis:

'Because I tape-recorded your meeting with the minister. The one where you said you were his red telephone.'

Kit took a while to absorb this:

'Why the hell would Quinn do that? I never saw a man so jumpy. Tape his own secret meeting? Why?'

'He didn't tape it. I did.'

'Who for?'

'Nobody.'

Kit was having trouble making himself believe this:

'Nobody *told* you to do it? You did it absolutely on your own. Secretly? With nobody's permission?'

'Correct.'

'What an absolutely bloody filthy thing to do.'

'Yes. Wasn't it?' Toby agreed.

In single file they returned to the house, Kit stomping ahead with Sheba and Toby trailing at a respectful distance.

★

Heads down, they sat at the long pine table drinking Kit's best Burgundy and eating Mrs Marlow's steak-and-kidney pie while Sheba watched covetously from her basket. It was beyond Kit's powers to neglect his duties as a host, and Toby, whatever his faults might be, was his guest.

'Don't envy you bloody Beirut, I will say,' he said stiffly, replenishing Toby's glass.

But when, in a spirit of reciprocity, Toby enquired after Kit's tour of the Caribbean, he was curtly warned off:

'Not a good subject in this house, I'm afraid. Bit of a sore point.'

After which, they had to make do with Foreign Office chit-chat – who the big guns were these days, and whether Washington might finally come back to the Office, or be given to another outsider. But Kit very quickly lost patience and soon they were scurrying across the stable yard in pouring rain, Kit leading the way with a torch as they skirted piles of sand and granite setts. Then the sweet smell of hay as they passed empty horseboxes on their way to the old saddle room, with its brick walls, high, arched windows, and iron Victorian fireplace, ready laid.

And on an old linen press that did duty as a sofa-table, a wad of A4 paper, a pack of best bitter beer and a bottle of J&B, unbroached – all set ready, Toby assumed, not in honour of himself, but of Jeb, the guest who hadn't come.

Kit had dropped into a crouch and was holding a match to the fire.

'We've got a thing here called Bailey's Fayre,' he said into the fireplace, poking with his long forefinger at the flames. 'It's supposed to go back to God knows when. Load of balls.' And after puffing vigorously at the kindling: 'I'm about to break every bloody rule I ever believed in, in case you didn't know.'

'Well, that makes two of us, doesn't it?' Toby replied.

And some kind of complicity was born.

*

Toby is a good listener, and for a couple of hours he has barely spoken except to offer the odd murmured word of sympathy.

Kit has described his recruitment by Fergus Quinn, and his

briefing by Elliot. He has flown to Gibraltar as Paul Anderson, paced his hated hotel room, huddled on the hillside with Jeb, Shorty, Andy and Don, and provided his own ear- and eye-witness account of *Operation Wildlife* and its supposedly glorious conclusion.

He has described the Fayre: scrupulously monitoring himself as he goes along, catching himself out on this or that small point and correcting himself, then carrying on.

He has described with determined dispassion, though it comes hard to him, the discovery of Jeb's handwritten receipt, and its impact upon Suzanna, then himself. He has yanked open a drawer of his desk and with a brusque 'take a look for your-self', pressed on him the flimsy piece of lined paper.

He has described with thinly disguised revulsion his meeting with Jay Crispin at the Connaught, and his reassuring phone call to Suzanna that in retrospect seems to cause him more pain than any other single episode.

And now he is describing his encounter with Jeb at the club.

'How the hell did he know you were staying there?' Toby interrupted in subdued bewilderment, at which a kind of joy briefly suffused Kit's harrowed features.

'Bugger stalked me,' he said proudly. 'Don't ask me how. All the way from here to London. Saw me board the train in Bod-min, rode on it himself. Stalked me to the Connaught, stalked me to my club. *Stealth*,' he added in marvel, as if stealth were a brand-new concept to him.

★

The club bedroom boasts a school bedstead, a washbasin with a towel no bigger than a pocket handkerchief and a two-bar elec-tric fire that used to be coin-operated until an historic decision by the committee ruled that the cost of heating be included in the nightly charge. The shower is an up-ended coffin of white plastic crammed into a cupboard. Kit has successfully found the light switch but not yet closed the bedroom door behind him. Wordless, he watches Jeb get up from his chair, advance across the floor to him, pick the room key out of his hand, lock the door with it, drop it into the pocket of his smart blazer, and return to his seat beneath the open window.

Jeb orders Kit to switch off the overhead light. Kit obeys. Now the only light source is the glow of London's orange night sky through the window. Jeb asks Kit for his cellphone. Kit mutely hands it over. Unbothered by the half-darkness, Jeb removes the battery, then the SIM card as deftly as if he were stripping down a gun, and tosses the pieces on to the bed.

'Take your jacket off, please, Paul. How drunk are you?'

Kit manages 'not very'. The *Paul* discomforts him but he takes his jacket off anyway.

'Have a shower if you like, Paul. Just leave the door open.'

Kit doesn't like, but ducks his head into the washbasin and sluices water on to his face, then rubs his face and hair with the towel in an effort to rub himself sober, but he is becoming more sober by the second anyway. A mind under siege can do a lot of things at once, and Kit's is doing most of them. He is making a last-ditch effort to persuade himself that Jay Crispin was telling the truth and Jeb is the barking psychopath with the gift of the gab that Crispin said he was. The bureaucrat in him assesses his best course of action on this unproven assumption. Should he humour Jeb, offer him sympathy, medical help? Or should he – fat chance – lull him into complacency and wrest the key from him? Or failing that, make a mad dash for the open window and the fire escape? All this over urgently transmitted messages of love and abject apology to Suzanna, and requests to Emily for advice on the handling of the mentally sick and potentially vio-lent patient.

Jeb's first question is the more alarming for its placidity:

'What did Crispin tell you about me, Paul, back there in the Connaught Hotel?'

To which Kit mumbles something to the effect that Crispin merely confirmed that *Operation Wildlife* was an unqualified success, an intelligence coup of exceptional value, and bloodless:

'Everything it was trumped up to be, in fact. *More*' – cavalierly adding – 'despite that foul message you wrote on your so-called receipt for my wife's handbag.'

Jeb stares at Kit without expression, as if he has misheard. He whispers something to himself that Kit can't catch. Then there follows a moment which Kit, for all his determined objectivity, seems at a loss to describe in comprehensible terms. Somehow Jeb has crossed the bit of threadbare carpet that separates him from Kit. And Kit, with no memory of how he got there, finds himself jammed up against the door with one arm behind his back and one of Jeb's hands holding him by the throat, and Jeb is talking into his face and encouraging Kit's replies with smacks of his head against the doorpost.

Kit stoically recounts what happened next:

'*Bang.* Head against the doorpost. Red sky at night. "What were you getting out of it, Paul?" What d'you mean? I say. "Money, what d'you think I mean?" Not a bloody bean, I told him. You've got the wrong man. *Bang.* "What was your share of the bounty, Paul?" *Bang.* Didn't have a bloody share, I told him, and take your hands off me. *Bang.* I was angry with him by then. He'd got my arm in this bloody horrible twist. If you go on doing that, I said, you'll break my fucking arm, and neither of us will be any the wiser. I've told you everything I know, so leave me alone.'

Kit's voice lifts in pleased surprise:

'And he did, dammit! Just like that. Left me alone. Took a long look at me, stood back and watched me slide down the wall in a heap. Then helped me to my feet again like a bloody Samaritan.'

Which was what Kit called the turning point: when Jeb went back to his chair and sat in it like a beaten boxer. But now Kit becomes the Samaritan. He doesn't like the way Jeb is heaving and shaking:

'Sort of sobbing noise coming out of him. Lot of choking. *Well*' – indignantly – 'if your wife's been ill half her life, and your daughter's a bloody doctor, you don't just sit there gawping, do you? You *do* something.'

So Kit's first question of Jeb, after they have sat in their separate corners for a while, is whether there's anything Kit can get for him, his idea being – though he keeps the thought to himself – that *in extremis* he'll track down old Em, as he insists on calling her, and get her to phone through a prescription to the nearest all-night chemist. But Jeb's only response is to shake his head, get up, walk across the room, pour himself a toothglass of water from the washbasin, offer it to Kit, drink some himself, and sit down again in his corner.

Then after a while – could have been minutes, says Kit, but neither of them's going anywhere so far as he knows – Jeb asks, in a hazy sort of voice, whether there's any food about. It's not that he's actually hungry as such, he explains – bit of pride kicking in here, according to Kit – it's for fuel purposes.

Kit regrets he has no food with him, but offers to pop downstairs and see if he can rustle something up with the night porter. Jeb receives this suggestion with another prolonged silence:

'Seemed a bit *out of it*, poor chap. Gave me the impression he'd lost his train of thought and was having a spot of trouble getting it back. Know the feeling well.'

But in due course, good soldier that he is, Jeb braces himself, and digs in his pocket and hands over the bedroom key. Kit gets up from the bed and puts on his jacket.

'Cheese all right?'

Cheese will be fine, says Jeb. But plain mousetrap, he can't handle blue. Kit thinks that's all he's got to say, but he's mistaken. Jeb needs to make a mission statement before Kit goes off to find cheese:

'It was one big load of lies, see, Paul,' he explains, just as Kit is preparing to go downstairs. '*Punter* was never in Gibraltar. It was all made up, see. And *Aladdin*, well, he was never going to meet him, not in those houses or anywhere else, was he?'

Kit is wise enough to say nothing.

'They conned him. Ethical did. Conned that minister of yours, Mr Fergus Quinn. Jay Crispin, the great one-man private-intelligence service. They led Quinn up the garden path and over the edge, same as where he led us, didn't he? Nobody wants to admit they handed over a couple of million dollars in a suitcase for a load of old cobblers, well do they?'

Kit supposes not.

Jeb's face has gone back into darkness and he is either silently laughing or – only Kit's guess – silently weeping. Kit dithers at the door, not wanting to leave him, but not wanting to fuss over him either.

Jeb's shoulders settle. Kit decides it's all right to go downstairs.

*

Returned from his foray in the bowels of the club, Kit heaves the bedside table to the middle of the floor and sets a chair either side of it. He lays out a knife, bread, butter, Cheddar cheese and two pint bottles of beer and a jar of Branston Pickle that the night porter insisted on including in exchange for his twenty-pound tip.

The bread is white and pre-sliced in anticipation of tomorrow's breakfast. With a slice laid flat on his palm, Jeb spreads butter, adds the cheese and trims it till it tessellates on the bread.

Then he spoons pickle on top, takes up another slice of bread and makes a sandwich and cuts it methodically into quarters. Regarding such precision as unnatural in a Special Forces soldier, Kit puts it down to Jeb's troubled state of mind and busies himself with the beer.

'So down the hill we go to the terrace then, don't we?' Jeb resumes, when he's taken the edge off his appetite. 'No point in not, really, is there? Well, we had our reservations, naturally. Fix, find and finish? Well, maybe we hadn't begun, what with Andy having done a job with Elliot way back, and not possessing a high opinion of him, frankly, not of his abilities, and not of the intelligence at his disposal either. Source *Sapphire* her name was, according to Elliot at the pre-operational briefing.'

'What briefing was that then, Jeb?' Kit interrupts, momentarily resentful that he wasn't invited.

'The briefing in Algeciras, Paul,' Jeb replies patiently. 'Pre-op. Just across the bay from Gibraltar. Just before we're to get ourselves into position on the hillside. In a big room above a Spanish restaurant, it was, and us all pretending to be a business conference. And Elliot up there on the platform, telling us how it's going to be, and his ragtag team of American freebooters sitting there in the front row, not talking to us because we're regular and Brits. Source *Sapphire* says this, source *Sapphire* says that. Or Elliot says she does. It's all according to *Sapphire*, and she's right there with *Aladdin* on the fancy yacht. She's *Aladdin*'s mistress and I don't know what else she isn't, all the pillow talk she's hearing. Reading his emails over his shoulder, listening to his phone calls in bed, sneaking up on deck and telling it all to her *real* boyfriend back in Beirut, who passes it on to Mr Crispin at Ethical, and Bob's your uncle, like.'

He loses the thread, finds it, and resumes:

'Except Bob isn't anybody's uncle, is he? Not Bob. Maybe as far as Ethical is concerned, he is. But not for our own British intelligence. Because British intelligence won't buy into the operation, will it? Same as the regiment won't – or nearly won't. The regiment doesn't like the smell of it – who would? But it doesn't like missing out either. And it doesn't like political pressure. So it's a good old British compromise: a deniable toe in the water but not the whole foot. And me and the boys, we're the toe, like. And Jeb here will be in charge because good old Jeb's the steady one. Maybe a bit on the pernickety side, but with those daredevil mercs around, all the better for it. *Granny* Jeb, they used to call me. Not that I minded, if it meant not taking unnecessary risks.'

Jeb takes a sip of his beer, closes his eyes, and plunges quickly on.

'House number seven it's supposed to be. Well, we thought: let's take six and eight too while we're about it, one house per man and me the back-up, it's all a bit daft anyway, what with Elliot at the controls there. All a bit Mickey Mouse, frankly, half the equipment not working the way it ought, what's the difference? There's no way they'd teach you that in training, is there? But the targets weren't going to be armed, were they? Not according to Elliot's brilliant intelligence. Plus we only wanted one of them, and the other we can't touch. So go into the three houses simultaneously for the surprise, we say, and do a room-by-room. Catch your man, make sure he's the right man, bundle him over the balcony to the shore party, keeping your feet at all times planted firmly on the Rock. Simple really. We had the layout of the houses, each the same as the other. One nice living room with big balcony on the seaward side. One master bedroom with sea views and one cupboard-sized second bedroom for a child. Bathroom and kitchen-diner below, and the walls paper-thin, which we knew from the estate agent's particulars. So if you don't hear anything apart from the sea, assume they're hiding or not there, employ extreme caution at all times, plus don't use your weapon except in self-defence and get the hell out in double-quick time. It didn't feel like an op, why should it? More a silly ghost walk. The boys go in, one house each. I'm outside keeping an eye on the open staircases down to the sea-shore. "Nothing there." That's Don in six. "Nothing there." That's Andy, house eight. "I've got something." That's Shorty, in seven. What have you got, Shorty? "Droppings." What the hell d'you mean, boy, droppings? "Come and see for yourself, man."

'Well, you can fake an empty house, I know that, but house seven was truly empty. Not a skid-mark on the parquet floor. Not a hair in the bathtub. Kitchen the same. Except for this one plastic bowl on the floor, pink plastic, with bits of pitta bread and chicken meat in it, torn up small like you would for' – he is searching for the right small creature – 'for a cat, a young cat.' But cat's not right: 'Or a puppy or something. And the bowl, the pink bowl, warm to touch. If it hadn't been on the floor, I suppose I would have thought different. Not cats and dogs but something else. I wish I had now. If I'd thought different, maybe it wouldn't have happened, would it? But I didn't. I thought cat or dog. And the food in the bowl warm too. I pulled my glove off to put my knuckles on it. Like a warm body, it was. There's a small frosted window overlooking the outside staircase. The latch is loose. You'd have to be a midget to squeeze through a space like that. But maybe it's a midget we're looking for. I call up to Don and Shorty: check the outside staircases, but no going down to the shore, mind, because if anyone's going to tangle with the boat party it'll be me.

'I'm talking slow motion because that's how I remember it,' Jeb explains apologetically, while Kit watches the sweat running down his face like tears. 'It's one thing then the next thing for me. Everything single, like. That's how I remember it. Don comes through. He's heard this scuffle. Thinks there's someone hiding down on the rocks underneath the outside staircase. "Don't go down there, Don," I tell him. "Stay right where you are, Don, I'm coming right up." The intercom's a proper madhouse, frankly. Everything's going through Elliot. "We've had a tentative, Elliot," I tell him. "Exterior staircase number seven. Underneath." Message received and out. Don's standing sentry at the top, pointing down with his thumb.'

Kit's own thumb, as if unknown to him, was making the same gesture as he told Jeb's story into the flames.

'So I'm going down the outside staircase. One step, pause. Another step, pause. It's concrete all the way, no gaps. There's a turn to the staircase, like a half-landing. And there's six armed men on the rocks below me, four flat on their bellies and two kneeling, plus two more back in the inflatable behind them. And they're all in their firing positions, every one of them, silenced semis at the ready. And underneath me – right under my feet here – there's this scrabbling noise like a big rat. And then a little shriek to go with it, like. Not a loud shriek. More pressed in, like it was too scared to speak. And I don't know – and never will, will I? – whether that shriek came from the mother or her child. Nor will they, I don't suppose. I couldn't count the bullets – who could? But I can hear them now, like the sound you get inside your head when they pull your teeth out. And there she is, dead. She's a young Muslim woman, brown-skinned, wearing a hijab, an illegal from Morocco, I suppose, hiding in the empty houses and living off her friends, shot to ribbons while she's holding her baby girl away from her to keep her out of the line of fire, the little girl she's been making the food for. The same food I thought was for a cat because it was on the floor, see. If I'd used my head better, I'd have known it was a child, wouldn't I? Then I could have saved her, I suppose. And her mother too. Curled up on the rocks like she's flying forward on her knees from the bullets they put into her, the mother is. And the baby girl lying out of her grasp in front of her. A couple of the sea party look a bit puzzled. One man stands with his fingers spread across his face like he's trying to tear it off. And there's this quiet moment, like, when you'd have thought they were going to have a good quarrel about who's responsible, until they decide there's no time for any of that. They're trained men – of a sort, anyway – they know what to do in an emergency, all right, even if they don't know anything else. Those two bodies were on the inflatable and back to the mother ship faster than ever *Punter* would have been. And Elliot's boys along with them, all eight, no stragglers.'

The two men are staring at one another across the bedside table, just as Toby is staring at Kit now, Kit's rigid face lit not by the glow of the London night but by the firelight in the stable.

'Did Elliot lead the sea party?' Kit asks Jeb.

Jeb shakes his head. 'Not American, see, Paul. Not immune. Not exceptional. Elliot stays home with the mother ship.'

'So why did the men fire?' Toby asked at last.

'You think I didn't bloody *ask* him?' Kit flared.

'I'm sure you did. What did he say?'

It took several deep breaths for Kit to come up with a version of Jeb's answer.

'Self-defence,' he snapped.

'You mean, she was *armed*?'

'No I bloody don't! Neither did Jeb. He's thought of nothing else for three years, can't you imagine? Telling himself he was to blame. Trying to work out why. She knew *somebody* was there, sussed them somehow – saw them or heard them – so she grabbed the child and wrapped it in her robe. I didn't presume to ask him why she ran down the steps instead of heading inland. He's been asking himself the same question day and night. Maybe inland scared her more than the sea. Her food bag had been picked up, but who by? Maybe she mistook the boat team for people smugglers, the same crowd that had brought her to the Rock in the first place – if they did – and they were bringing her man to her, and she was running down the steps to greet him. All Jeb knows is, she came down the steps. Bulked out by the child inside her robe. And what did the beach team think? Bloody suicide bomber, coming to blow them up. So they shot her. Shot her child while he watched. "I could have stopped them." That's all the poor bugger can say to himself when he can't sleep.'

*

Summoned by the lights of a passing car, Kit strode to the arched window and, standing on tiptoe, peered keenly out until the lights disappeared.

'Did Jeb tell you what happened to him and his men after the boat party had returned to the mother ship with the bodies?' Toby asked, of his back.

'Flown to Crete same night by charter. For a debriefing, so-called. The Americans have got a bloody great airbase there, apparently.'

'Debriefing by?'

'Men, plain-clothes chaps. Brainwashing, by the sound of it. Professionals, was all he could say. Two Americans, two Brits. No names, no introductions. Said one of the Americans was a little fat bastard with effeminate mannerisms. Pansy-boy, according to Jeb. The pansy-boy was the worst.'

But better known to the staff of the Private Office as Brad the Music Man, thought Toby.

'Soon as the British combat team touched down in Crete they were separated,' Kit went on. 'Jeb was leader so he got the heavy treatment. Said the pansy-boy ranted at him like Hitler. Tried to persuade him he hadn't seen what he saw. When that didn't work, he offered him a hundred thousand dollars not to bubble. Jeb told him to shove it up his arse. Thinks he was confined in a special compound for non-accountable prisoners in transit. Thinks it's where they would've put *Punter* if the story hadn't been a lot of bollocks from the start.'

'How about Jeb's comrades-in-arms?' Toby persisted. 'Shorty and the others. What became of them?'

'Thin air. Jeb's hunch is, Crispin made them an offer they couldn't refuse. Jeb didn't blame them. Not that sort of chap. Fair-minded to a fault.'

Kit had lapsed into silence, so Toby did the same. More headlights drifted across the rafters and vanished.

'And *now*?' Toby asked.

'Now? Now *nothing*! The big empty. Jeb was due here last Wednesday. Breakfast 9 a.m. sharp, and we'd go to work. Said he was a punctual chap. I didn't doubt him. Said he'd do the journey at night, safer. Asked me if he could hide his van in the barn. I said of course he bloody could. What did he want for breakfast? Scrambled egg. Couldn't get enough of scrambled egg. I'd get rid of the women, we'd scramble ourselves some eggs, then put the story down on paper: his part, my part. Chapter and verse all the way. I'd be amanuensis, editor, scribe, and we'd take as long as it took. He'd got this piece of evidence he was all excited about. Didn't say what it was. Cagey to a fault, so I didn't press. You don't press a chap like that. He'd bring it or he wouldn't. I accepted that. I'd make the written presentation for both of us, he'd vet it, sign off on it, and it would be my job to see it through the proper channels to the top. That was the deal. Shook hands on it. We were –' he broke off, scowled into the flames. 'Happy as fleas,' he said jerkily, colouring. 'Eager for the fray. Pumped up. Not just him. Both of us.'

'Because?' Toby ventured.

'Because we were going to tell the bloody truth at last, why d'you think?' Kit barked angrily, taking a pull of Scotch and subsiding into his chair. 'Last time I saw him, all right?'

'All right,' Toby agreed softly, and a long silence followed, until Kit grudgingly resumed.

'Gave me a cellphone number. Not his own. Hasn't got one. A friend's. Comrade's. Only chap he still trusted. Well, partly, anyway. My guess is it was Shorty, because they seemed to have a rapport in the hide. I didn't ask, wasn't my business. If I left a message, somebody would get it to him. That was all that mattered. Then he left. Left the club. Down the stairs and away, don't ask me how. I thought he'd leave by the fire escape, but he didn't. He just left.'

Another pull of Scotch.

'And you?' Toby enquired in the same quiet, respectful voice.

'I came home. What d'you think? To this place. To Suzanna, my wife. I'd promised her everything was all right, now I had to tell her it wasn't all right at all. You can't fake it with Suzanna. I didn't tell her the details. I told her Jeb was coming to stay, and between us we'd sort it out. Suzanna took it – the way she does. "Just as long as it means resolution, Kit." I said it did, and that was good enough for *her*,' he ended aggressively.

Another wait while Kit wrestled with his memory.

'Wednesday came. All right? Midday, Jeb still hadn't shown up. Two o'clock, three, still hadn't. I call the cellphone number he's given me, get an automated answer, leave a message. Nightfall, I leave another message: *hullo, it's me, Paul, here again. Just wondered what happened to our date.* Keeping Paul as my code name. For security. I'd given him our landline number here because we don't get a signal. Thursday I leave another bloody message, get the same answering service. Friday morning, ten, we get a phone call. *Jesus Christ!*'

He has clapped a bony hand over his lower jaw and is holding it there, muzzling the pain that refuses to be stilled, because the worst is evidently still to come.

★

Kit isn't sitting in his club bedroom listening to Jeb any more. He isn't shaking Jeb's hand by the light of a London dawn, or watching him slip away down the club stairs. He's not happy as a flea or pumped up, even if he's still eager for the fray. He's back home at the Manor and, having broken the bad news to Suzanna, he's worried sick and eating his heart out, praying with every hour that slips by for a belated sign of life from Jeb. In an effort to keep himself busy, he's sanding the floorboards next to the guest room and he can't hear a bloody thing, so when the phone rings in the kitchen, it's Suzanna who picks it up, and Suzanna who has to climb the stairs to the top floor and hammer on Kit's shoulder to get his attention.

'It's somebody wanting Paul,' she says, when he's turned off the sander. 'A woman.'

'What *sort* of woman, for God's sake?' – Kit, already heading downstairs.

'She won't say. She needs to speak to Paul personally' – Suzanna, hurrying down after him.

In the kitchen, Mrs Marlow, all agog, is doing flowers at the sink.

'Bit of privacy, if you don't mind, Mrs M,' Kit commands.

And waits till she has left the room before picking up the phone from the sideboard. Suzanna closes the door after her and stands rigid beside him, arms across her chest. The telephone has a loudspeaker mode for when Emily calls. Suzanna knows how to work it, and switches it on.

'Am I speaking to Paul, please?' – educated, middle-aged female in professional mode.

'Who's this?' Kit asks warily.

196

'My name is Dr Costello and I'm calling from the mental-health wing of Ruislip General Hospital, at the request of an inpatient who wishes to be known only as Jeb. Am I speaking to Paul, or to someone else?'

Fierce nod from Suzanna.

'I'm Paul. What's the matter with Jeb? Is he all right?'

'Jeb is receiving excellent professional care and is in good physical health. I understand you were expecting a visit from him.'

'Yes. I was. Still am. Why?'

'Jeb has asked me to speak to you frankly, in confidence. May I do that? And this really *is* Paul?'

Another nod from Suzanna.

'Of course it is. It's Paul. Absolutely. Go ahead.'

'I assume you know that Jeb has been mentally unwell for some years.'

'I was aware of that. So what?'

'Last night, Jeb volunteered himself as an inpatient here. We diagnosed chronic schizophrenia and acute depression. He has been sedated and is on suicide watch. In his lucid moments his greatest concern is for you. For Paul.'

'Why? Why should he be worried about *me*?' – eyes on Suzanna – 'I should be worrying about *him*, for Heaven's sake.'

'Jeb is suffering from severe guilt syndrome brought on in part by malicious stories that he fears he's been spreading among his friends. He asked that you treat them for what they are: symptoms of his schizophrenic condition, with no basis in reality.'

Suzanna thrusts a note at him: *Visit?*

'Yes, well look here, Dr Costello, the point is, when can I come and see him? I could hop in the car now, if that would help. I mean, d'you have *hours*? What goes on?'

'I'm very sorry, Paul. I'm afraid a visit by you at this time could cause serious damage to Jeb's mental health. You are his fear object and he is not ready for a confrontation.'

Fear object? Me? Kit would like to refute this outrageous allegation but tactic prevails.

'Well, who else has he got?' he demands, this time off his own bat, no prompting from Suzanna. 'Has he got other friends who visit him? Relatives? I know he's not exactly *gregarious*. How about his wife?'

'They're estranged.'

'Not exactly what he told me, but still.'

Brief silence while Dr Costello apparently checks the record:

'We are in touch with a *mother*,' she recites. 'Any developments, any decisions regarding Jeb's treatment and welfare, will be referred to his natural mother. She is also his empowered guardian.'

The phone pressed to his ear, Kit flings up an arm, and at the same time swings round to Suzanna in astonishment and blatant disbelief. But his voice stays steady. He's a diplomat, he's not about to give the game away.

'Well, many thanks for that, Dr Costello. Very kind of you indeed. At least he's got some family to look after him. Can you give me his mother's phone number? Maybe she and I could have a chat.'

But Dr Costello, kind though she may be, cites data protection and regrets that parting with Jeb's mother's number is not, in the circumstances, something she is able to do. She rings off.

Kit on fire.

With Suzanna looking on in approving silence, he dials 1471 and establishes that the caller withheld her number.

He calls Enquiries, gets himself put through to Ruislip General Hospital, asks for the mental-health wing, asks for Dr Costello.

The male nurse couldn't be more helpful:

'Dr Costello's attending a course, mate, back next week.'

'How long's she been away?'

'Also a week, mate. It's a he, actually. Joachim. Sounds more German to me, but he's Portuguese.'

Kit somehow keeps his head.

'And Dr Costello has not come into the hospital during all that time?'

'No, mate, sorry. Can anyone else help at all?'

'Well, yes, actually, I'd like to talk to one of your inpatients, a chap named Jeb. Just tell him it's Paul.'

'*Jeb?* Doesn't ring a bell, mate, hang on a jiffy –'

A different nurse comes to the phone, also male, but not so friendly:

'No Jeb here. Got a John, got a Jack. That's your lot.'

'But I thought he was a regular,' Kit protests.

'Not here. Not Jeb. Try Sutton.'

Now the same thought occurs simultaneously to both Kit and Suzanna: get on to Emily, fast.

Best if Suzanna rings her. With Kit, just at the moment, she tends to be a bit scratchy.

Suzanna calls Emily's cellphone, leaves a message.

By midday, Emily has called back twice. The sum of her enquiries is that a Dr Joachim Costello recently joined the mental-health unit at Ruislip as a temporary, but he's a Portuguese citizen and the course he's attending is to improve his English. Did their Costello sound Portuguese?

'No she bloody didn't!' Kit roars at Toby, repeating the answer he gave Emily on the phone as he paces the stable floor. 'And she was a bloody *woman*, and she sounded like an Essex schoolmistress with a plum up her arse, and Jeb hasn't got a bloody mother and never did have, as he was pleased to tell me. I'm not a big chap for intimate revelations as a rule, but he was talking his heart out for the first time in three bloody years. Never met his mother, only thing he knows about her is her name: Caron. He fled the coop when he was fifteen and joined the army as an apprentice. Now tell me he made it all up!'

*

It is Toby's turn to go to the window and, freed from Kit's accusing stare, abandon himself to his thoughts.

'By the time this Dr Costello rang off, had you given her any reason to think you didn't believe her?' he asks at last.

Equally long deliberation by Kit:

'No. I hadn't. I played her along.'

'Then as far as she's concerned, or *they* are: mission accomplished.'

'Probably.'

But Toby isn't about to be satisfied with 'probably':

'So far as *they're* concerned, whoever they are, you've been squared. Fobbed off. You're on *side*' – gathering conviction as he speaks. 'You believe the gospel according to Crispin, you believe Dr Costello even if she's the wrong sex, and you believe Jeb is schizoid and a compulsive liar and is sitting in the isolation ward of a mental hospital in Ruislip and can't be visited by his fear object.'

'No, I bloody don't,' Kit snaps. 'Jeb was telling me the literal truth. It shone out of him. It may be tearing him apart: that's another matter. Man's as sane as you or me.'

'I absolutely accept that, Kit. I really do,' Toby says at his most forbearing. 'However, for Suzanna's protection as well as your own, I suggest that the position you have *very cleverly* carved out for yourself in the eyes of the opposition is well worth preserving.'

'Until when?' Kit demands, unappeased.

'How about until I find Jeb? Isn't that why you asked me to come here? Or are you proposing to go and look for him yourself – thereby, incidentally, setting the whole howling mob on you?' Toby demands, no longer quite so diplomatically.

200

And to this, for a while at least, Kit can find no convincing answer, so instead chews at his lip, and grimaces, and gives himself a gulp of Scotch.

'Anyway, you've got that tape you stole,' he growls, by way of bitter consolation. 'That meeting in the Private Office with Quinn, Jeb and me. Stored away somewhere. That's proof, if it's ever needed. It would scupper *you*, all right. Might scupper me as well. Not sure I care too much about that either.'

'My stolen tape proves *intent*,' Toby replies. 'It doesn't prove the operation ever took place, and it certainly doesn't address the outcome.'

Kit grudgingly mulls this over.

'So what you're trying to tell me *is*' – as if Toby is somehow dodging the point – 'Jeb's the only witness to the shootings. Right?'

'Well, the only one willing to talk, so far as we know,' Toby agrees, not quite liking the sound of what he has just said.

*

If he slept he wasn't aware of it.

Sometime in the few short hours in bed he heard a woman's cry and supposed it was Suzanna's. And after the cry, a flurry of feet across the dust sheets in the corridor below him, and they must have been Emily's feet, hastening to her mother's side, a theory borne out by the murmurings that followed.

And after the murmurings, Emily's bedside light shining up through the cracks in the floorboards – is she reading, thinking, or listening for her mother? – until either he or Emily went to sleep, and he supposed he went first because he didn't remember her light going out.

And when he woke later than he meant to, and hurried downstairs to breakfast: no Emily and no Sheba, just Kit in his church tweeds and Suzanna in her hat.

'It was *honourable* of you, Toby,' Suzanna said, grasping his hand and keeping it. 'Wasn't it, Kit? Kit was worried sick, we both were, and you came straight away. And poor Jeb's honourable too. And Kit's not good at *sly*, are you, darling? Not that *you* are, Toby, I don't mean that at all. But you're young and you're clever, you're in the Office, and you can *delve* without, well' – little smile – 'losing your pension.'

Standing in the granite porch she fervently embraces him:

'We never had a son, you see, Toby. We tried to, but we lost him.'

Followed by a gruff 'be in touch then' from Kit.

★

Toby and Emily sat in the conservatory, Toby perched on an old sunlounger and Emily on a rush chair at the furthest end of the room. The distance between them was something they had tacitly agreed upon.

'Good talk with Dad last night?'

'If you can call it that.'

'Perhaps you'd like me to go first,' Emily suggested. 'Then you won't be tempted into some indiscretion you may regret.'

'Thank you,' Toby replied politely.

'Jeb and my father are planning to produce a document about their exploits together, nature unknown. Their document will have earth-shaking consequences in official quarters. In other words, they will be whistle-blowers. At issue are a dead woman and her child, according to my mother. Or *possibly* dead. Or *probably* dead. We don't know, but we fear the worst. Am I warm so far?'

Receiving only a straight stare from Toby, she drew in her breath and went on:

'Jeb fails to make the date. So no whistle. Instead, a woman doctor who is patently not a doctor and should have been a man calls Kit, alias Paul, and tells him that Jeb has been confined in a mental hospital. Investigations reveal this to be untrue. I feel I'm talking to myself.'

'I'm listening.'

'Jeb, meanwhile, is unfindable. He has no surname, and is not in the habit of leaving a forwarding address. Official avenues of enquiry, such as the police, are closed – not for us frail women to reason why. You're still listening, I hope?'

'Yes.'

'And Toby Bell is some kind of player in this scenario. My mother likes you. My father prefers not to, but sees you as a necessary evil. Is that because he doubts your allegiance to the cause?'

'You'd have to ask him that.'

'I thought I'd ask you. Is he expecting you to find Jeb for him?'

'Yes.'

'For both of you, then?'

'In a way.'

'*Can* you find him?'

'I don't know.'

'Do you know what you'll do when you *have* found him? I mean, if Jeb's about to blow the whistle on some great scandal, perhaps you might have a last-minute change of heart and feel bound to turn him over to the authorities. Might you?'

'No.'

'And I'm to believe that?'

'Yes.'

'And you're not settling some old score?'

'Why the hell should I be doing that?' Toby protested, but Emily graciously ignored this little display of temper.

'I've got his registration number,' she said.

She had lost him. 'You've what?'

'Jeb's.' She was fumbling in the thigh pocket of her tracksuit. 'I photographed his van while he was giving Dad grief at

Bailey's. I photographed the licence disc, too' – extracting an iPhone and fiddling with the icons – 'Valid twelve months and paid eight weeks ago.'

'Then why haven't you given the registration number to Kit?' Toby asked in bewilderment.

'Because Kit fucks up, and I don't want my mother living through a fucked-up manhunt.'

Unfolding herself from the rush chair, she strolled over to him and held the phone deliberately to his face.

'I'm not putting this into my own phone,' Toby said. 'Kit doesn't want electronic. I don't either.'

He had a pen but nothing to write on. She produced a piece of paper from a drawer. He wrote down the registration number of Jeb's van.

'If you give me your cellphone number, perhaps I can tell you how my enquiries are going,' he suggested, by now recovered.

She gave him her cellphone number. He wrote that down too.

'And you might as well have my surgery number and hospital roster,' she said, and watched him add it all to his collection.

'But we say absolutely nothing specific to each other over the phone, all right?' he warned her severely. 'No winks and nods or arch references' – remembering his security training – 'and if I text you or need to leave a message for you, I'll be Bailey, after the Fayre.'

She gave a shrug, as if to humour him.

'And will I be disturbing you if I have to call you late at night?' he enquired finally, doing his best to sound, if anything, even more practical and down-to-earth.

'I live alone, if that's what you're asking,' she said.

It was.

5.

On the slow train back to London, through the hours of half-sleep in his flat, and on the bus to work on the Monday morning, Toby Bell, not for the first time in his life, pondered his motives for putting his career and freedom at risk.

If his future had never looked rosier, which was what Human Resources were forever telling him, why go back to his past? Was this his *old* conscience he was dealing with – or a newly invented one? *And you're not settling some old score?* Emily had asked him: and what was *that* supposed to mean? Did she imagine he was on some kind of vengeance kick against the Fergus Quinns and Jay Crispins of this world, two men of such glaring mediocrity in his eyes as to be not worth a second thought? Or was she externalizing some hidden motive of her own? Was it *Emily* who was settling an old score – against the entire race of men, her father included? There had been moments when she'd given him that impression, just as there had been others, admittedly short-lived, when she had seemed to come over to his side, whatever that side was.

Yet for all this fruitless soul-searching – perhaps even because of it – Toby's performance on his first day at his new desk was exemplary. By eleven o'clock he had interviewed every member of his new staff, defined their areas of responsibility, cut potential overlap and streamlined consultation and control. By midday he was delivering a well-received mission statement to a meeting of managers. And by lunchtime he was sitting in his regional director's office, munching a sandwich with her. It was not till his day's work was well and truly done that, pleading an external appointment, he took a bus to Victoria station, and from there, at the height of the rush-hour bustle, telephoned his old friend Charlie Wilkins.

★

Every British Embassy should have its Charlie Wilkins, they used to say in Berlin, for how could they ever have managed without this genial, unflappable sixty-something English ex-copper with half a lifetime of diplomatic protection under his belt? A bollard jumped out at your car, did it, as you were leaving the Bastille Day bash at the French Embassy? Shame on it! An overzealous German policeman took it into his head to breathalyse you? The liberty! Charlie Wilkins will have a quiet word with his certain friends in the Bundespolizei and see what can be done.

But in Toby's case the boot, unusually, was on the other foot because he was one of the few people in the world who had actually managed to do a favour for Charlie and his German wife, Beatrix. Their daughter, a budding cellist, had lacked the academic qualifications for an audition at a grand music college in London. The principal of the college turned out to be a bosom friend of Toby's maternal aunt, herself a music teacher. Phone calls were hastily made, auditions arranged. No Christmas had gone by since but Toby, wherever he was stationed, had received a box of Beatrix's home-made *Zuckergebäck* and a gilded card proudly reporting their brilliant daughter's progress. And when Charlie and Beatrix retired gracefully to Brighton, the *Zuckergebäck* and the cards kept flowing, and Toby never failed to write his little note of thanks.

★

The Wilkins's bungalow in Brighton was set back from its fellows and might have been transported from the Black Forest.

Ranks of red-coated tulips lined the path to the Hansel and Gretel porch. Garden gnomes in Bavarian costume thrust out their buttoned chests, and cacti clawed at the enormous picture window. Beatrix had decked herself in her best finery. Over Baden wine and liver dumplings the three friends talked old times and celebrated the musical accomplishments of the Wilkins daughter. And after coffee and sweet liqueurs, Charlie and Toby retired to the den in the back garden.

'It's for a lady I know, Charlie,' Toby explained, imagining for convenience's sake that the lady was Emily.

Charlie Wilkins gave a contented smile. 'I said to Beatrix: if it's Toby, look for the lady.'

And this lady, Charlie – he explained, now blushing becomingly – was out shopping last Saturday and managed to go head to head with a parked van and do it serious damage, which was doubly unfortunate since she's already got a whole bunch of points on her licence.

'Witnesses?' Charlie Wilkins enquired sympathetically.

'She's sure not. It was in an empty corner of the car park.'

'Glad to hear it,' Charlie Wilkins commented, with a slight note of scepticism. 'And no CCTV footage at all?'

'Again not,' said Toby, avoiding Charlie's eye. 'So far as we know, obviously.'

'Obviously,' Charlie Wilkins echoed politely.

And since she's a good girl at heart, Toby forged on, and since her conscience won't let her sleep till she's paid her dues – but no way can she afford to lose her licence for six months, Charlie – and since she at least had the nous to write down the van's registration number, Toby was wondering – well, *she* was wondering whether there was any way – and delicately left the sentence for Charlie to finish for himself.

'And has our lady friend any idea what this exclusive service might cost us?' Charlie enquired, pulling on a pair of grandfatherly spectacles to scrutinize the piece of plain card Toby had passed him.

'Whatever it costs, Charlie, I'm paying for it,' Toby replied grandly, with renewed acknowledgements to Emily.

'Well, in that case, if you will kindly join Beatrix for a nightcap, and bear with me for ten minutes,' said Charlie, 'the charge will be two hundred pounds to the widows and orphans fund of the Metropolitan Police, cash please, no receipt, and for old times' sake, nothing for me.'

And ten minutes later, sure enough Charlie was handing back the card with a name and address written out in a policeman's careful hand, and Toby was saying, *Fantastic, Charlie, wonderful, she'll be over the moon, and can we please stop at a cash machine on the way to the station?*

But none of this quite removed the cloud of concern that had formed on Charlie Wilkins's normally untroubled face, and it was still there when they stopped at a hole in the wall and Toby duly handed Charlie his two hundred pounds.

'That gentleman you asked me to find out about just now,' Charlie said. 'I don't mean the car. I mean the gentleman who owns it. The *Welsh* gentleman, according to his address.'

'What about him?'

'My certain friend in the Met informs me that the said gentleman with the unpronounceable address has a rather large red ring round his name, in a metaphorical manner of speaking.'

'Meaning what?'

'Any sight or sound of said gentleman, and the force concerned will take no action but report immediately to the very top. I don't suppose you'd like to tell me the reason for that large red ring at all, would you?'

'Sorry, Charlie. I can't.'

'And that's it, is it?'

'I'm afraid it is.'

Parking in the station forecourt, Charlie turned off the engine but kept the doors locked.

'Well, I too am afraid, son,' he said severely. 'For your sake. And your lady's sake, if there is one. Because when I ask my certain friend in the Met for a favour like that, and loud bells start ringing in his ear, which in the case of your Welshman they did, he has his own official commitments to consider, doesn't he? Which is what he was good enough to tell me by way of a warning. He can't just push a button like that and run away, can he? He has to protect himself. So what I'm saying to you is, son: give her my love, if she exists, and take a lot of care because I have a bad feeling you're going to need it, now that our old friend Giles, alas, is no longer with us.'

'Not *with us*? You mean he's *dead*?' Toby exclaimed, ignoring in his concern the implication that Oakley was in some way his protector.

But Charlie was already chuckling away:

'Dear me, no! I thought you knew. Worse. Our friend Giles Oakley is a *banker*. And you thought he was dead. Oh dear, oh dear, wait till I tell Beatrix. Trust our Giles to make timely use of the revolving door, I say.' And lowering his voice to one of sympathy, 'He'd got as high as they'd let him go, mind you. Reached his ceiling, hadn't he? – as far as *they* were concerned. Nobody's going to give him the top billet, not after what happened in *Hamburg*, are they? You'd never know when it was coming home to roost – well, would you?'

But Toby, reeling from so many blows at once, had no words. After only a week back in London and a full tour in Beirut, during which Oakley had vanished into mandarin thin air, Toby had been curious to know when and how his erstwhile patron would surface, if at all.

Well, now he had his answer. The lifelong foe of speculative bankers and their works, the man who had branded them drones, parasites, socially useless and a blight on any decent economy had taken the enemy's shilling.

And why had Oakley done that, according to Charlie Wilkins?

Because the wise heads of Whitehall had decided he wasn't bankable.

And why wasn't Oakley bankable?

Lean your head back on the iron-hard cushions of the late train back to Victoria.

Close your eyes, say *Hamburg*, and tell yourself the story you swore you would never speak aloud.

★

Shortly after arriving at the Berlin Embassy, Toby happens to be on night duty when a call comes in from the superintendent of the Davidwache in Hamburg, the police station charged with monitoring the Reeperbahn's sex industry. The superintendent asks to speak to the most senior person available. Toby replies that he himself is that person, which at 3 a.m. he is. Knowing that Oakley is in Hamburg addressing an august body of ship-owners, he is immediately wary. There had been talk of Toby tagging along for the experience, but Oakley had scotched it.

'We have a *drunk Englishman* in our cells,' the superintendent explains, determined to air his excellent English. 'It is unfortunately necessary to *arrest* him for causing a serious disturbance at an extreme establishment. He also has many *wounds*,' he adds. 'On his torso, actually.'

Toby suggests the superintendent contact Consular Section in the morning. The superintendent replies that such a delay might not be in the best interests of the British Embassy. Toby asks why not.

'This Englishman has no papers and no money. All are stolen. Also no clothes. The owner of the establishment tells us he

210

was flagellated in the normal manner and regrettably became out of control. However, the prisoner is telling us he is an important official of your embassy, not your ambassador, maybe, but better.'

It takes Toby just three hours to reach the doorstep of the Davidwache, having driven at top speed down the autobahn through clouds of ground mist. Oakley is lolling half awake in the superintendent's office wearing a police dressing gown. His hands, bloodied at the fingertips, are bandaged to the arms of his chair. His mouth is swollen in a crooked pout. If he recognizes Toby, he gives no sign of it. Toby gives none in return.

'You *know* this man, Mr Bell?' the superintendent enquires, in a heavily suggestive tone. 'Maybe you decide you have never seen him before in your life, Mr Bell?'

'This man is a complete stranger to me,' Toby replies obediently.

'He is an imposter, perhaps?' the superintendent suggests, again too knowingly by half.

Toby concedes that the man may indeed be an imposter.

'Then maybe you should take this *imposter* back to Berlin and interrogate him sharply?'

'Thank you. I will.'

From the Reeperbahn, Toby drives Oakley, now in a police tracksuit, to a hospital on the other side of town. No broken bones but the body a mess of lacerations that could be whip marks. At a crowded superstore, he buys him a cheap suit, then calls Hermione to explain that her husband has had a minor car accident. Nothing grave, he says, Giles was sitting in the back of a limousine without his seat belt. On the return journey to Berlin, Oakley speaks not a word. Neither does Hermione, when she comes to unload him from Toby's car.

And from Toby, also not a word, and none from Giles Oakley either, beyond the three hundred euros in an envelope that

Toby found lying in his embassy mailbox in payment for the new suit.

★

'And that's the monument there, look!' the driver called Gwyneth exclaimed, pointing her ample arm out of the window and slowing down to give Toby a better view. 'Forty-five men, a thousand feet down, God help them.'

'What caused it, Gwyneth?'

'One falling stone, boy. One little spark was all it ever took. Brothers, fathers and sons. Think of the women, though.'

Toby did.

After another sleepless night, and in defiance of every principle he had held dear from the day he entered the Foreign Service, he had pleaded a raging toothache, taken a train to Cardiff and a taxi for the fifteen-mile journey to what Charlie Wilkins had called Jeb's unpronounceable address. The valley was a graveyard of abandoned collieries. Pillars of blue-black rain rose above the green hills. The driver was a voluble woman in her fifties. Toby sat beside her in the front seat. The hills drew together and the road narrowed. They passed a football field and a school, and behind the school an overgrown aerodrome, a collapsed control tower and the skeleton of a hangar.

'If you'd just put me down at the roundabout,' Toby said.

'Now I thought you said you was visiting a friend,' Gwyneth replied accusingly.

'So I am.'

'Well, why don't you want me to drop you at your friend's house then?'

'Because I want to surprise them, Gwyneth.'

'Not many surprises left in this place, I can tell you, boy,' she said, and handed him her card for when he wanted to go back.

The rain had eased to a fine drizzle. A red-haired boy of eight or

212

so was riding a brand-new bicycle up and down the road, honking an antiquated brass horn that had been screwed to the handlebars. Black-and-white cattle grazed amid a forest of pylons. To his left ran a row of prefabricated houses with hooped green roofs and the same shed in each front garden. He guessed they were once the quarters of married servicemen. Number ten was the last of the row. A whitewashed flagpole stood in the front garden, but no flag flew from it. He unlatched the gate. The boy on the bicycle came skidding to a halt beside him. The front door was of stippled glass. No doorbell. Watched by the boy, he tapped on the glass. A woman's shadow appeared. The door sprang open. Blonde, his own age, no make-up, curled fists, a set jaw and angry as all hell.

'If you're press, you can bugger off! I've had my fill of the lot of you!'

'I'm not press.'

'Then what the fuck d'you want?' – her voice not Welsh but old-fashioned fighting Irish.

'Are you Mrs Owens, by any chance?'

'What if I am?'

'My name's Bell. I wondered whether I could have a word with your husband, Jeb.'

Leaning his bicycle against the fence, the boy squeezed past him and stood at the woman's side, one hand clasped possessively round her thigh.

'And about *what the fuck* are you wishing to have a word with my husband, *Jeb*?'

'I'm actually here on behalf of a friend. *Paul*, his name is' – watching for a reaction but seeing none – 'Paul and Jeb had a date to meet last Wednesday. Jeb didn't show up. Paul's worried for him. Thinks he may have had an accident with his van or something. The cellphone number Jeb gave him doesn't answer. I was coming up this way, so he asked me to see if I could track him down,' he explained lightly, or as lightly as he could.

'*Last* Wednesday?'

'Yes.'

'Like a week ago?'

'Yes.'

'Six fucking days?'

'Yes.'

'Appointment where?'

'At his house.'

'Where the fuck's his house, for Christ's sake?'

'In Cornwall. North Cornwall.'

Her face rigid, the boy's also.

'Why didn't your friend come himself?'

'Paul's stuck at home. His wife's sick. He can't leave her,' Toby replied, beginning to wonder how much of this he could do.

A big, ungainly, grey-haired man in a buttoned woollen jacket and spectacles was looming at her shoulder, peering at him.

'What seems to be our problem, Brigid?' he enquired in an earnest voice that Toby arbitrarily awarded to the far north.

'The man wants Jeb. He's got a friend called Paul had a date with Jeb in Cornwall last Wednesday. Wants to know why the fuck Jeb didn't show for it, if you can believe him.'

The man laid an avuncular hand on the boy's red head.

'Danny, I think you should pop across to Jenny's for a play. And we mustn't keep the gentleman standing on the doorstep, must we, Mr –?'

'Toby.'

'And I'm Harry. How d'you do, Toby?'

Curved ceiling, iron trusses holding it up. The linoleum floor glistening with polish. In a kitchen alcove, artificial flowers on a white tablecloth. And in the centre of the room facing a television set, a two-piece sofa and matching armchairs. Brigid sat on an arm. Toby stood opposite her while Harry pulled open the drawer of a sideboard and extracted a buff army-style folder. Holding it in both hands like a hymnal, he placed himself in front of Toby and drew a breath as if he were about to sing.

'Now did you know Jeb *personally* at all, then, Toby?' he suggested, by way of a precautionary introduction.

'No. I didn't. Why?'

'So your friend Paul knew him but you didn't, is that correct, Toby?' – making doubly sure.

'Just my friend,' Toby confirmed.

'So you never met Jeb at all. Not even to set eyes on, as we may say.'

'No.'

'Well, this will come as a shock to you, Toby, all the same, and no doubt a much bigger shock to your friend Paul, who is sadly unable to be with us today. But poor Jeb very tragically passed away by his own hand last Tuesday, and we're still trying to come to terms with it, as you may suppose. Not to mention Danny, naturally, although sometimes you have to wonder whether children manage these things better than we adults do.'

'It was splashed enough over the papers, for fuck's sake,' Brigid said, speaking across Toby's mumbled protestations of condolence. 'Everyone in the fucking world knows about it except him and his friend Paul.'

'Well, only *local* papers now, Brigid,' Harry corrected her, passing Toby the folder. 'It's not everyone reads the *Argus*, is it?'

'*And* the fucking *Evening Standard*.'

'Yes, well, not everyone reads the *Evening Standard* either, do they? Not now it's free. People like to appreciate what they buy, not what's pressed on them for nothing. That's only human nature.'

'I really am deeply sorry,' Toby managed to get in, opening the folder and staring at the cuttings.

'Why? You didn't bloody know him,' Brigid said.

WARRIOR'S LAST BATTLE

Police are not looking for any other suspect in the death by shooting of ex-Special Forces David Jebediah (Jeb) Owens aged 34 who, in the words of the coroner, 'fought a losing battle against post-traumatic stress disorder and its associated forms of clinical depression . . .'

SPECIAL FORCES HERO ENDS OWN LIFE

. . . served gallantly in Northern Ireland, where he met his future wife, Brigid, of the Royal Ulster Constabulary. Later served in Bosnia, Iraq, Afghanistan . . .

'Would you like to telephone your friend, Toby?' said Harry hospitably. 'There's a conservatory at the back if you require the privacy, and we've a good signal, thanks to the radar station nearby, I shouldn't wonder. We had the cremation for him yesterday, didn't we, Brigid? Family only, no flowers. Your friend wouldn't have been missed, tell him, so no cause to reproach himself.'

'What else are you going to tell your friend, Mr Bell?' Brigid demanded.

'What I've read here. It's awful news.' He tried again: 'I'm dreadfully sorry, Mrs Owens.' And to Harry: 'Thanks, but I think I'd rather break it to him personally.'

'Quite understood, Toby. And respectful, if I may say so.'

'Jeb blew his fucking brains out, Mr Bell, if it's of interest to your friend at all. In his van. They didn't put that bit in the papers; they're considerate. Some time last Tuesday evening, they think he did it, between six and ten o'clock. He was parked in the corner of a flat field near Glastonbury, Somerset, what they call the Levels. Six hundred yards from the nearest human habitation – they paced it. He used a 9mm Smith & Wesson, his weapon of choice, short barrel. I never knew he had a fucking Smith & Wesson, and as a matter of fact he hated handguns, which is paradoxical, but there it was in his hand, they say, short barrel and all. "Can we trouble you for an official identification, Mrs Owens?" "No trouble at all, Officer. Any time. Lead me to him." Just as well I'd been in the constabulary. Straight through the fucking right temple. Small hole on the right side and not much of his face at all on the other. That's exit wounds for you. He didn't miss. He wouldn't, not Jeb. He was always a lovely shot. Won prizes, Jeb did.'

'Yes, well, reliving it doesn't bring him back, does it, Brigid?' said Harry. 'I think Toby here deserves a cup of tea, don't you, Toby? Coming all this way for his friend, that's what I call loyalty. And a piece of Danny's shortbread that you made with him, Brigid.'

'They couldn't wait to cremate him either. Suicides jump the queue, Mr Bell, in case you should ever have the problem.' She had flopped from the arm into the chair, and was thrusting her pelvis at him in some kind of sexual contempt. 'I had the pleasure of washing his fucking van out, didn't I? Soon as they'd had their way with it. "Here you are, Mrs Owens, it's all yours now." Nice polite people, mind you, in Somerset. Very courteous to a lady. Treated me like a colleague too. There was a couple from the Met there. Directing operations for their country brothers.'

'Brigid didn't phone me, not till dinner time, she wouldn't,' Harry explained. 'I'd lessons back to back. She knew that, which was very considerate on your part, wasn't it, Brigid? You can't let fifty children run wild for two hours, can you?'

'Lent me their fucking hose too, which was nice. You'd think cleaning it out would be part of the service, wouldn't you? But not with the austerity, not in Somerset. "Now are you quite sure you've done all your forensics?" I asked them, "because I don't want to be the one to wash away the clues, now." "We've all the clues we need, thank you, Mrs Owens, and here's a scrubbing brush for you, in case you need it."'

'You're just upsetting yourself, Brigid,' Harry warned from the kitchen alcove, filling a kettle and putting out pieces of shortbread.

'I'm not upsetting Mr Bell, though, am I? Look at him. He's a model of composure. I'm a woman playing catch-up on my dead husband, who is a dead stranger to me, you see, Mr Bell. Until three years ago I knew Jeb very well indeed, and so did Danny. The man we knew three years ago would not have killed himself with a fucking short-barrelled pistol, or a long-barrelled one for that matter. He'd never have left his son without a fucking father or his wife without a husband. Danny was the world to him. Even after Jeb turned bloody mad, it was Danny, Danny. Shall I tell you something about suicide that isn't generally known, Mr Bell?'

'Toby doesn't need this, Brigid. I'm sure he's a well-informed young gentleman who's familiar with the psychology and suchlike. Am I not right, Toby?'

'It's fucking murder is what suicide is, Mr Bell. Never mind you murder yourself along with it. It's other people you're after killing. Three years ago I'd a great marriage going to the man of my dreams. I wasn't bad myself, which he was good enough to comment on frequently. I'm a good fuck and he loved me full on, or so he said. Gave me every reason to believe him. I still do. I believe him. I love him. Always did. But I don't believe the bastard who shot himself to kill us, and I don't love him either. I hate him. Because if he did that, he *is* a bastard, I don't care what the fucking cause was.'

If he did that? Was the *if* delivered with greater force than she intended? Or was this merely Toby's imagination?

'And come to think of it, I don't know what it was drove him round the fucking bend in the first place. I never did. He'd had a bad mission. There'd been some wrong killing. That was my full ration. After that, I could sing for it. Maybe you and your friend Paul know. Maybe Jeb trusted your friend Paul the way he wouldn't trust me, his fucking wife. Maybe the police know too. Maybe the whole fucking street knows, and me and Danny and Harry here are the only odd ones out.'

'Going over it won't help, Brigid,' Harry said, unwrapping a packet of paper napkins. 'It won't help *you*, it won't help Danny. And I don't expect it will help Toby here. Will it, Toby?' – passing him a cup of tea with a piece of sugared shortbread on the saucer, and a paper napkin.

'I come out the fucking constabulary for Jeb, once we knew Danny was on his way. Lost my seniority pay and the promotion that was round the corner. We were both off the slag heap, what with Jeb's dad a useless layabout and no mother, and me never knowing who my dad was, and my mother not bloody knowing neither. But we was going to be straight, decent people if it killed us. Got myself a course in Physical Education, all so's we could make a home for Danny.'

'And she's the best PE teacher the school's ever had, or likely to, aren't you, Brigid?' Harry said. 'All our children love her, and Danny's proud of her you wouldn't believe. We all are.'

'What do *you* teach?' Toby asked Harry.

'Arithmetic, all the way up to A level, when I've got the pupils, don't I, Brigid?' – handing her a cup of tea as well.

'So is your friend Mr Paul down in Cornwall some kind of fucking psychiatrist Jeb was hooked on, or what?' Brigid demanded.

'No. Not a psychiatrist, I'm afraid.'

'And you're not a gentleman of the press? You're quite sure of that?'

'I'm sure I'm not press.'

'So if you don't mind me being inquisitive, Mr Bell: if you're not press and your pal Paul's not a shrink, what the fuck are you?'

'Now Brigid,' said Harry.

'I'm here purely privately,' said Toby.

'Then what the hell are you purely *publicly*, may I ask?'

'Publicly, I'm a member of the Foreign Office.'

But instead of the explosion he was expecting, all he got was a sustained critical examination.

'And your friend *Paul*? Would he be from the Foreign Office too at all?' – not releasing him from her gaze, which was wide and green-eyed.

'Paul's retired.'

'And would Paul be somebody Jeb knew, like, three years back?'

'Yes. He would.'

'Professionally then?'

'Yes.'

'And would that have been what their summit conference was going to be about, Jeb and Paul's, if Jeb hadn't blown his head off the day before? Something in the professional line, for example, from three years back?'

'Yes. It would,' Toby replied steadily. 'That was the connection between them. They didn't know each other well, but they were on the way to becoming friends.'

Her eyes had still not left his face, and they didn't now:

'Harry. I'm worried about Danny. Would you kindly go over to Jenny's a minute and make sure he hasn't fallen off his fucking bike. He's only had it a day.'

★

Toby and Brigid were alone, and some kind of guarded understanding was forming between them as each waited for the other to speak.

'So should I be calling up the Foreign Office in London to check you out, then?' Brigid asked in a noticeably less strident voice. 'Confirming that Mr Bell is who he says he is?'

'I don't think Jeb would have liked you to do that.'

'And your friend Paul? What about him? Would *he* like it?'

'No.'

'And *you* wouldn't either?'

'I'd lose my job.'

'This conversation they were proposing to have. Would it have been about a certain *Operation Wildlife* at all?'

'Why? Did Jeb tell you about it?'

'About the operation? You're joking. White-hot tongs wouldn't have dragged it out of him. It stank, but it was duty.'

'Stank how?'

'Jeb didn't like mercs, never did. In it for the ride and the money, they are. Think they're heroes when they're fucking psychos. "I fight for my country, Brigid. Not for the fucking multinationals with their offshore bank accounts." Except he didn't say *fucking*, if I'm honest. Jeb was Chapel. Didn't swear and couldn't drink above a couple of sips. God knows what I am. Fucking Prot, I'm told. I'd have to be, wouldn't I, for the fucking Royal Ulster Constabulary?'

'And it was the presence of mercenaries that he didn't like about *Wildlife*? He said that of this particular operation?'

'Just generally. Just mercs. Get them off his back, he hated the buggers. "It's another merc job, Brigid. Makes you wonder sometimes who starts the wars these days."'

'Did he have other reservations about the operation?'

'It sucked but what the hell?'

'And afterwards? When he came back from the operation?'

She closed her eyes, and when she opened them she seemed to become a different woman – inward, and appalled:

'He was a ghost. Washed out. Couldn't hold a knife and fork.

Kept showing me the letter from his beloved regiment: *thank you and goodnight and remember you're bound for life by the Official Secrets Act*. I thought he'd seen it all. I thought we both had. Northern Ireland. Blood and bone all over the street, the kneecappings, bombings, necklace killings. Holy God.'

She took a couple of deep breaths, collected herself and went on:

'Till he gets the one-too-many. The one they all talk about. The one that's got his name on and won't let him go. The one-too-many bomb in the marketplace. The lorryload of kids on their way to school that gets blown to kingdom come. Or maybe it's only a dead dog in a ditch, or he's cut his little finger and it's bleeding. Whatever it was, it was the straw that broke his back for him. He'd no defences. Couldn't look at what he loved best in the world without hating us for not being covered in blood.'

Again she stopped, her eyes this time opening wide in outrage at whatever she was seeing, and Toby wasn't:

'He fucking *haunted* us!' she blurted, then clapped her hand to her lips in reproach. 'Christmas, we'd set the bloody table for him. Danny, me, Harry. We'd sit there gawping at his empty place. Danny's birthday, the same. Presents on the doorstep in the middle of the fucking night. What the hell have we got that he's going to catch if he comes in? Fucking leprosy? It's his own house, for Christ's sake. Didn't we love him enough?'

'I'm sure you did,' Toby said.

'How the fuck would *you* know?' she demanded, and sat dead still with her fingers jammed between her teeth while she stared at something in her memory.

'And the leathercraft?' Toby asked. 'Where did Jeb get his leathercraft skills from?'

'His fucking father, who d'you think? A bespoke shoemaker, he was, when he wasn't drinking himself into oblivion. But that didn't stop Jeb loving him rotten, and laying out his fucking tools in the shed there like the Holy Grail when the bugger died. Then one night the shed's empty and the tools is all gone and Jeb with them. Same as now.'

She turned and stared at him, waiting for him to speak. Cautiously, he did:

'Jeb told Paul he had a piece of evidence. About *Wildlife*. He was going to bring it to their meeting in Cornwall. Paul didn't know what it was. I wondered if you did.'

She spread her palms and peered into them as if reading her own fortune, then sprang up, marched to the front door and pulled it open:

'Harry! Mr Bell wishes to pay his respects so's he can tell his friend Paul. And Danny, you stay over with Jenny till I call you, hear me?' And to Toby: 'Come back after without Harry.'

★

The rain had returned. On Harry's insistence Toby borrowed a raincoat and noticed that it was too small for him. The garden behind the house was narrow but long. Wet washing hung from a line. A man-gate led to a patch of wasteland. They passed a couple of wartime pillboxes covered in graffiti.

'I tell my pupils they're reminders of what their grandparents fought for,' Harry called over his shoulder.

They had reached a dilapidated barn. The doors were padlocked. Harry had the key.

'We don't let Danny know it's here, not at the moment,' said Harry earnestly. 'So I'll trouble you to bear that in mind on your return to the house. We plan to offer it on eBay once the hue and cry's died down. You don't want people put off by the association, do you?' – giving the doors a shove and releasing a squadron of jubilant small birds. 'Mind you, he did a good conversion, did Jeb, I'll give him that. Slightly obsessive, in my private opinion. Not for Brigid's ear, naturally.'

223

The tarpaulin was fastened to the ground with tent pegs. Toby looked on while Harry went from peg to peg, easing the cleat, then lifting the loop off the peg till one side of the tarpaulin hung loose; then sweeping the whole tarpaulin clear to reveal a green van, and the scrawled inscription, gold on green, JEB'S LEATHERCRAFT in capitals, and beneath it in smaller letters *Buy From Van*.

Ignoring Harry's extended arm, Toby mounted the tailgate. Wood panelling, some panels removed, others dangling open. A flap table, raised and scrubbed, one wooden chair, no cushion. A rope hammock taken down and neatly rolled. Bare, scrubbed shelves, craftsman-fitted. A smell of stale blood not quite overcome by the stink of Dettol.

'What happened to his reindeer hides?' Toby asked.

'Well now, they were best burned, weren't they?' Harry explained brightly. 'There wasn't that much *could* be saved, frankly, Toby, given the extent of the mess the poor man made of himself. No alcohol involved to help him on his way, which they say is unusual. But that's Jeb for you. Not a man to let his hair down. Never was.'

'And no farewell note?' Toby asked.

'Just the gun in his hand and eight bullets left in the magazine, which makes you wonder what he thought he would do with the others after he'd shot himself, I suppose,' Harry replied in the same informative tone. 'Same as him using his wrong hand. Why? you ask yourself. Well, of course there's no answer to that. There never will be. He was left-handed was Jeb. But he shot himself with his right, which could be described as an aberration. But Jeb was a shooter by trade, they tell me. Well, he'd have to be, wouldn't he? If Jeb had put his mind to it, he could have shot himself with his own foot, could Jeb, according to what I'm told by Brigid. Plus the fact that when you reach that point you're not accessible to rational argument, as we all know.

Which is what the police said, very rightly, in my opinion, me not being an expert by a long chalk.'

Toby had found a pockmark as wide as a tennis ball but not so deep halfway up the wood cladding and midway down one side, and was tracing its outline with his finger.

'Yes, well now,' Harry explained, 'a bullet like that has to go somewhere, which is common sense, though you wouldn't believe it watching some of the films they make these days. It can't just vanish into thin air, can it, not a bullet? So, what I say is, fill the hole with your Polyfilla, rub it down, paint it over, and with any luck it won't notice.'

'And his tools? For his leathercraft?'

'Yes, well that's an embarrassment to all concerned, his father's tools are, Toby, same as his ship's stove, which was worth a bob or two of anybody's money. First on the spot was the fire brigade, I'm not sure why, but clearly somebody summoned them. Then along come the police, then the ambulance. So you don't know whose light fingers were to blame, do you? Not the police, I'm sure. I've great respect for our guardians of the law, more than what Brigid's got, to be frank, her having been one. Still, that's Ireland for you, I suppose.'

Toby supposed it was.

'He never grudged me, mind. Not that he had the right. You can't expect a woman like Brigid to do without, can you? I'm good to her, which couldn't always be said for Jeb, not if we're honest.'

Together they closed the tailgate, then together hauled the tarpaulin back over the van and together tightened the guy ropes.

'I think Brigid wanted another quick word with me,' Toby said. And for a lame explanation: 'Something to do with Paul that she felt was private.'

'Well, she's a free soul, is Brigid, same as all of us,' Harry said heartily, patting Toby's arm in comradeship. 'Just don't listen too hard to her views on the police is my advice. There's always got to be somebody to blame in a case like this, it's human nature. Good to see you, Toby, and very thoughtful of you to come. And you don't mind my saying this, do you? I know it's cheeky. Only, should you happen, just by chance, but you never know, to bump into somebody who's looking for a well-maintained utility vehicle converted to a high standard – well, they know where to come, don't they?'

★

Brigid was curled into a corner of the sofa, clutching her knees.

'See anything?' she asked.

'Was I meant to?'

'The blood was never logical. There was splashes all over the rear bumper. They said it was *travelled* blood. "How the hell did it travel?" I asked them. "Through the fucking window and round the bloody back?" "You're overwrought, Mrs Owens. Leave the investigating to us and have a nice cup of tea." Then another fellow comes over to me, plain clothes from the Met, posh-spoken. "Just to put your mind at ease, Mrs Owens, that was never your husband's blood on the bumper. It's red lead. He must have been doing a repair job." They did the house over too, didn't they?'

'I'm sorry? Which house?'

'*This* fucking house. Where you're sitting now, looking at me, where d'you think? Every bloody drawer and cubbyhole. Even Danny's toy cupboard. Searched from top to fucking bottom by people who knew their business. Jeb's papers from the drawer there. Whatever he'd left behind. Took out and put back, in the right order except not quite. Our clothes the same. Harry thinks I'm paranoid. Seeing conspiracies under the bed, I am. Fuck that, Mr Bell. I've turned over more

226

houses than Harry's had bloody breakfasts. It takes one to know one.'

'When did they do this?'

'Fucking yesterday. When d'you think? While we was out cremating Jeb, when else? We're not talking fucking amateurs. Don't you want to know what they were looking for?'

Reaching under the sofa, she drew out a flat brown envelope, unsealed, and pushed it at him.

Two A4 photographs, matt finish. No borders. Black and white. Poor resolution. Night shots, much enhanced.

A format to remind Toby of all the fuzzy images he'd ever seen of suspects covertly photographed from across the street: except that these two suspects were dead and lying on a rock, and one of them was a woman in a shredded Arab dress and the other a much-shot child with one leg half off, and the men standing around them were bulked out in combat gear and holding semi-automatics.

In the first photograph, an unidentifiable standing man, also in combat gear, points his gun at the woman as if about to finish her off.

In the second, a different man, again in combat gear, kneels on one knee, his weapon beside him, and holds his hands to his face.

'From under where the ship's stove was, before the buggers stole it,' Brigid was explaining contemptuously, in answer to a question Toby hadn't asked. 'Jeb had fixed a slab of asbestos there. The stove was gone. But the asbestos was still there. The police thought they'd searched the van before they gave it me to clean. But I knew Jeb. They didn't. And Jeb knew concealment. Those photos had to be in there somewhere, not that he ever showed them to me. He wouldn't. "I've got the proof," he'd say. "It's there in black and white except that nobody wants to believe it." "Proof of what, for fuck's sake?" I'd say. "Photographs taken at the scene of the crime." But ask him what the crime was and all you'd get was a dead man's face.'

'Who was the photographer?' Toby asked.

'Shorty. His mate. The only one he had left after his mission. The only one as stuck by him after the others had the fear of God put into them. Don, Andy, Shorty – they was all good buddies until *Wildlife*. Never after. Only Shorty, till him and Jeb had their fight and broke it off.'

'What was the fight about?'

'The same bloody pictures you're holding in your hand. Jeb was still home then. Sick but managing, like. Then Shorty came to have a word with him, and they had this God-awful fight. Six foot four Shorty is. But Jeb come in from under him, buckled his knees for him, then broke his nose for him on the way down. Textbook it was, and Jeb half his size. You had to admire it.'

'What did he want to talk to Jeb about?'

'Give him back those pictures, that was first. Shorty had been all for showing them around the ministries till then. Even giving them to the press. Then changed his mind.'

'Why?'

'They'd bought him. The defence contractors had. Given him a job for life, provided he keeps his stupid mouth shut.'

'Do the defence contractors have a name?'

'There's a fellow Crispin. Started up this great new company with American money. Red-hot professionals. The shape of tomorrow, according to Shorty. The army could go fuck itself.'

'And according to Jeb?'

'Not professional at all. Carpetbaggers, he called them, and told Shorty he was another. Shorty wanted him to join up with them, if you can believe it. They'd tried to sign Jeb as soon as the mission was over. To shut him up. Now they'd sent Shorty to try again. Brought Jeb a fucking letter of agreement all typed up for him. All he had to do was sign it, give back the photos and join the company and the sky was the limit. I could have told Shorty to spare himself the journey and a broken nose, but he wouldn't have fucking listened. Actually, I hate the bloody man. Thinks he's God's gift to women. Had his hands all over me whenever Jeb wasn't looking. Plus he wrote me a smarmy letter of condolence, enough to vomit.'

From the drawer that had held the press cuttings she produced a handwritten letter and shoved it at him.

Dear Brigid,

I'm real Sorry to hear bad News regarding Jeb, same as I'm sorry it ended so Bad between us. Jeb was the Best of the Best, he always will be, never mind old squabbles, he'll always be in my Memory as I know he will in yours. Plus Brigid, if you're short of Cash in any way, call this mobile number attached and I will remit without fail. Plus Brigid, I will trouble you kindly to remit forthwith two Pics on loan which are Personal property of self. SAE attached.

As ever in Grief, Jeb's old Comrade, trust me,

Shorty.

Shouts of argument from outside the front door: Danny having a screaming fit, Harry vainly reasoning. Brigid makes to grab back the photographs.

'Can't I keep them?'

'Can you fuck!'

'Can I copy them?'

'All right. Go on. Copy them,' she replies, again without a moment's hesitation.

Beirut Man lays the full-plate photographs flat on the dining table and, ignoring the advice he gave to Emily only a couple of days ago, copies the photographs into his BlackBerry. Handing them back, he peers over Brigid's shoulder at Shorty's letter, then copies his cellphone number into his notebook.

'What's Shorty's other name?' he asks, while the din outside rises in a crescendo.

'Pike.'

He writes down *Pike* too, for safety's sake.

'He called me the day before,' she says.

'*Pike* did?'

'*Danny, shut the fuck up, for Christ's sake!* Jeb did, who d'you think? Tuesday, nine o'clock in the morning. Harry and Danny had just gone off on a school outing. I pick up the phone, it's Jeb, like I never heard him these last three years. "I've found my witness, Brigid, the best you could ever think of. Him and me are going to set the record straight once and for all. Get rid of Harry, and as soon as I'm done we'll start over again: you, me and Danny, same as old times." That's how depressed he was a few hours before he shot his fucking head off, Mr Bell.'

*

If a decade of diplomatic life had taught Toby one thing, it was to treat every crisis as normal and soluble. On the taxi ride back to Cardiff his mind might be a cauldron of unsorted fears for Kit, Suzanna and Emily; it might be in mourning for Jeb, and wrestling with the timing and method of his murder, and the complicity of the police in its cover-up, but outwardly he was the same chatty passenger and Gwyneth was the same chatty driver. Only on reaching Cardiff did he go about his dispositions exactly as if he'd spent the journey preparing them, which in truth he had.

Was he under scrutiny? Not yet, but Charlie Wilkins's warning words were not lost on him. At Paddington, he had bought his railway ticket with cash. He had paid Gwyneth cash and asked her to drop him off and pick him up at the roundabout. He had kept to himself the identity of the person he was visiting, although he knew it was a lost cause. More than likely, at least one of Brigid's neighbours had a watching brief to tip off the police, in which case a description of his personal appearance would have been reported, although, with any luck, police incompetence would ensure that word would take its time to travel.

Needing more cash than he'd reckoned on, he had no option but to draw some from a machine, thus advertising his presence in Cardiff. Some risks you just have to take. From an electronics shop a stone's throw from the station he bought a new hard drive for his desktop and two second-hand cellphones, one black, one silver, with pay-as-you-go SIM cards and guaranteed fully charged batteries. In the world of downmarket electronics, he had been taught on his security courses, such cellphones were known as 'burners' because of the tendency of their owners to dispose of them after a few hours.

In a café favoured by Cardiff's unemployed he bought a cup of coffee and a piece of slab cake and took them to a corner table. Satisfied that the background sound suited his purpose, he touched Shorty's number into the silver burner and pressed green. This was Matti's world, not his. But he had been at the edge of it, and he was not a stranger to dissembling.

The number rang and rang and he was reconciled to getting the messaging service when an aggressive male voice barked at him:

'Pike here. I'm at work. What d'you want?'

'Shorty?'

'All right, Shorty. Who is this?'

Toby's own voice, but without its Foreign Office polish:

'Shorty, this is Pete from the *South Wales Argus*. Hi. Look, the paper's putting together a spread on Jeb Owens, who sadly killed himself last week, as you probably know. *Death of our unsung hero* stuff. We understand you were quite a mate of his, that right? I mean, like, best mate? His winger, kind of thing. You must be pretty cut up.'

'How'd you get this number?'

'Ah well, we have our methods, don't we? Look, what we're wondering is – what my editor's wondering – can we do an interview, like what a fine soldier Jeb was, Jeb as his best mate knew him, kind of thing, a full-page splash? Shorty? You still there?'

'What's your other name?'

'Andrews.'

'This supposed to be off the record or on?'

'Well, we'd *like* it on the record, naturally. And face to face. We *can* do deep background, but that's always a pity. Obviously, if there are issues of confidentiality, we'd respect them.'

Another protracted silence, with Shorty's hand over the mouthpiece of his phone:

'Thursday any good?'

Thursday? The conscientious foreign servant mentally checks his appointments diary. Ten a.m., departmental meeting. Twelve thirty p.m., inter-services liaison officers' working lunch at Londonderry House.

'Thursday's fine,' he replied defiantly. 'Where've you got in mind? No chance of you coming up to Wales at all, I sup-pose?'

'London. Golden Calf Café, Mill Hill. Eleven a.m. Do you?'

'How do I recognize you?'

'I'm a midget, aren't I? Two foot six in my boots. And come alone, no photography. How old are you?'

'Thirty-one,' he replied too quickly, and wished he hadn't.

★

On the return train journey to Paddington, again using the silver burner, Toby sent his first text message to Emily: *need consultation asap please advise on this number as old number no longer operative, Bailey.*

Standing in the corridor, he rang her surgery as a back-up and got the out-of-hours answering service:

'Message for Dr Probyn, please. Dr Probyn, this is your patient Bailey asking for an appointment tonight. Please call me back on this number, as my old number no longer works. Thank you.'

For an hour after that it seemed to him that he thought of nothing but Emily: which was to say that he thought of everything from Giles Oakley's defection and back again, but wherever he went, Emily went too.

Her reply to his text, barren though it was, lifted his spirits beyond anything he could have imagined:

I'm on shift till midnight. Ask for urgent-care centre or triage unit.

No signature. Not even an E.

At Paddington it was gone eight when he alighted but by then he had a new wish list of operational supplies: a roll of packaging tape, wrapping paper, half a dozen A5 padded envelopes and a box of Kleenex tissues. The newsagent in the station concourse was closed, but in Praed Street he was able to buy everything he needed, and add a reinforced carrier bag, a handful of top-up vouchers for the burners and a plastic model of a London Beefeater to his collection.

The Beefeater himself was surplus to requirements. What Toby needed was the cardboard box he came in.

★

His flat in Islington was on the first floor of a row of joined eighteenth-century houses that were identical save for the colour of their front doors, the condition of their window frames and the quality of their curtains. The night was dry and unseasonably warm. Taking the opposing pavement to his house, Toby first strolled past it, keeping a casual eye out for the classic telltale signs: the parked car with occupants, the bystanders on street corners chatting into cellphones, the men in overalls kneeling insincerely at junction boxes. As usual, his street contained all of these and more.

Crossing to his own side, he let himself into the house and, having climbed the stairs and unlocked his front door as silently as he knew how, stood still in the hall. Surprised to find the heating on, he remembered it was Tuesday, and on Tuesdays Lula, the Portuguese cleaning woman, came from three till five, so perhaps she had been feeling the cold.

All the same, Brigid's calm announcement that her house had been professionally searched from top to bottom was still with him, and it was only natural that a sense of irregularity lingered in him as he went from room to room, sniffing the air for alien smells, poking at things, trying to remember how he'd left them and failing, pulling open cupboards and drawers to no effect. On his security training courses he had been told that professional searchers filmed their own progress in order to make sure they put everything back where they found it, and he imagined them doing that in his flat.

But it wasn't until he went to reclaim the back-up memory stick which, three years ago, he had pasted behind the framed photograph of his maternal grandparents on their wedding day, that he felt a real frisson. The picture was hanging where it had always hung: in a bit of dead corridor between the hall and the lavatory. Every time he had thought of moving it over the years, he had failed to come up with a darker or less conspicuous spot and in the end left it where it was.

And the memory stick was still there now, secured beneath layers of industrial masking tape: no outward sign that it had been tampered with. The trouble was, the picture-glass had been *dusted*, and by Lula's standards this was an all-time first. Not only its glass, but its frame. And not only its frame, if you please, but the *top* of the frame, which was situated well above the height of diminutive Lula's natural reach.

Had she stood on a chair? Lula? Had she, against all previous form, been seized by an urge to spring-clean? He was in the act of calling her – only to break out in derisive laughter at his own paranoia. Had he *really* forgotten that Lula had taken herself off on holiday at short notice, to be temporarily replaced by her infinitely more efficient and Junoesque friend Tina, all of five foot ten tall?

Still smiling to himself, he did what he'd set his mind on doing before it went chasing after wild geese. He removed the masking tape and took the memory stick to the living room.

*

His desktop computer was a source of worry to him. He knew – had had it religiously dinned into him – that no computer *ever* was a safe hiding place. However deep you may think you've buried your secret treasure, today's analyst with time on his side will dig it up. On the other hand, replacing the old hard drive with the new one that he had bought in Cardiff also had its risks: such as how to explain the presence of a brand-new drive with nothing on it? But any explanation, however implausible, was going to sound a lot better than the three-year-old voices of Fergus Quinn, Jeb Owens and Kit Probyn, as recorded days or even hours before the disastrous launch of *Operation Wildlife*.

First retrieve the secret recording from the depths of the desktop. Toby did. Then make two more copies of it on separate memory sticks. He did that too. Next, remove hard disk. Essential equipment for the operation: one fine screwdriver, rudimentary technical understanding and neat fingers. Under pressure, Toby possessed them all. Now for the disposal of the hard disk. For this he needed the Beefeater's box and the Kleenex tissues for padding. For an addressee, he selected his beloved

Aunt Ruby, a solicitor who practised in Derbyshire under her married name, and not therefore by his calculation toxic. A short covering note – Ruby would expect no more – urged her to guard the enclosed with her life, explanations to follow.

Seal box, inscribe to Ruby.

Next, for that rainy day he prayed would never dawn, address two of the padded envelopes to himself, poste restante, to the central post offices of Liverpool and Edinburgh respectively. Flash-forward to visions of Toby Bell on the run, arriving panting at the counter of Edinburgh main post office with the forces of darkness hot on his heels.

There remained the third, the original, the unconsigned memory stick. On his security courses there had always been a game of hide-and-seek:

So, ladies and gentlemen, you have this highly secret and compromising document in your hands and the secret police are at your door. You have precisely ninety seconds from now before they will begin ransacking your apartment.

Discount the places you first thought of: so NOT behind the cistern, NOT under the loose floorboard, NOT in the chandelier, the ice compartment of the fridge or the first-aid box, and absolutely NOT, thank you, dangling outside the kitchen window on a piece of string. So where? Answer: the most obvious place you can think of, among its most obvious companions. In the bottom drawer of the chest currently containing his unsorted junk from Beirut resided CDs, family snaps, letters from old girlfriends and – yes, even a handful of memory sticks with handwritten labels round their plastic cases. One caught his attention: UNI GRADUATION PARTY, BRISTOL. Removing the label, he wrapped it round the third memory stick and tossed it into the drawer with the rest of the junk.

He then took Kit's letter to the kitchen sink and set fire to it, broke the ash and washed it down the plughole. For good measure he did the same with the duplicate contract for his hire car from Bodmin Parkway railway station.

Satisfied with progress so far, he showered, changed into fresh clothes, put the two burners in his pocket, packed the envelopes and parcel into the carrier bag and, observing the Security Department's well-worn injunction never to accept the first cab on offer, hailed not the second cab but the third, and gave the driver the address of a mini-market in Swiss Cottage which he happened to know operated a late-night post-office counter.

And in Swiss Cottage, breaking the chain yet again, he took a second cab to Euston station and a third to the East End of London.

★

The hospital rose out of the darkness like the hulk of a warship, windows ablaze, bridges and stairways cleared for action. The upper forecourt was given over to a car park and a steel sculpture of interlocking swans. At ground level, ambulances unloaded casualties in red blankets on to trolleys while health workers in scrubs took a cigarette break. Aware that video cameras stared at him from every rooftop and lamp post, Toby cast himself as an outpatient and walked with an air of self-concern.

Following the stretcher trolleys, he entered a glistening hallway that served as some kind of collecting point. On one bench sat a group of veiled women; on another three very old men in skullcaps, bowed over their beads. Close by stood a minyan of Hasidic men in communal prayer.

A desk offered Patient Advice & Liaison, but it was unmanned. A signpost directed him to Human Resources, Workforce Planning, Sexual Health and Children's Day-stay, but none to where he needed to go. A notice screamed: STOP! ARE YOU HERE FOR

A&E? But if you were, there was nobody to tell you what to do next. Selecting the brightest, widest corridor, he walked boldly past curtained cubicles until he came to an elderly black man seated at a desk in front of a computer.

'I'm looking for Dr Probyn,' he said. And when the grizzled head didn't lift: 'Probably in the Urgent Care unit. Could be triage. She's on till midnight.'

The old man's face was slashed with tribal marks.

'We don't give out no names, son,' he said, after studying Toby for a while. 'Triage, that's turn left and two doors down. Urgent Care, you gotta go back to the lobby, take the Emergency corridor.' And seeing Toby produce his cellphone, 'No good callin', son. Mobiles just don't work in here. Outside's another story.'

In the triage waiting room, thirty people sat staring at the same blank wall. A stern white woman in a green overall with an electronic key round her neck was studying a clipboard.

'I've been informed that Dr Probyn needs to see me.'

'Urgent Care,' she replied to her clipboard.

Under strips of sad white lighting, more rows of patients stared at a closed door marked ASSESSMENT. Toby tore off a ticket and sat with them. A lighted box gave the number of the patient being assessed. Some took five minutes, others barely one. Suddenly he was next, and Emily, with her brown hair bundled into a ponytail and no make-up, was looking at him from behind a table.

She's a doctor, he had been telling himself consolingly since early afternoon. Hardened to it. Does death every day.

'Jeb committed suicide the day before he was due at your parents' house,' he begins without preamble. 'He shot himself through the head with a handgun.' And when she says nothing: 'Where can we talk?'

Her expression doesn't change but it freezes. Her clasped

hands rise to her face until the knuckles of her thumbs are jammed against her teeth. Only after recovering herself does she speak:

'In that case I got him all wrong, didn't I?' she says. 'I thought he was a threat to my father. He wasn't. He was a threat to himself.'

But Toby's thinking: I got *you* all wrong, too.

'Does anyone have any idea *why* he killed himself?' she enquires, hunting for detachment and not finding it.

'There was no note, no last phone call,' Toby replies, hunting for his own. 'And nobody he confided in, so far as his wife knows.'

'He was married then. Poor woman' – the self-possessed doctor at last.

'A widow and a small son. For the last three years he couldn't live with them and couldn't live without them. According to her.'

'And no suicide note, you say?'

'Apparently not.'

'Nobody blamed? Not the cruel world? Not anyone? Just shot himself. Like that?'

'It seems so.'

'And he did it just before he was due to sit down with my father and prepare to blow the whistle on whatever they had both got up to?'

'It seems so.'

'Which is hardly logical.'

'No.'

'Does my father know yet?'

'Not from me.'

'Will you wait for me outside, please?'

She presses a button on her desk for the next patient.

★

239

As they walked, they kept consciously apart, like two people who have quarrelled and are waiting to make up. When she needed to speak, she did so angrily:

'Is his death *national* news? In the press, on TV, and so on?'

'Only the local paper and the *Evening Standard*, as far as I know.'

'But it could go wider at any moment?'

'I assume so.'

'Kit takes *The Times*.' And as an abrupt afterthought: 'And Mum listens to the radio.'

A gateway that should have been locked but wasn't led across a scruffy patch of public park. A group of kids with dogs sat under a tree smoking marijuana. On a traffic island stood a long, single-storey complex. A sign said HEALTH CENTRE. Emily needed to walk the length of it, checking for broken windows while Toby trailed after her.

'The kids think we keep drugs here,' she said. 'We tell them we don't, but they won't believe us.'

They had entered the brick lowlands of Victorian London. Under a starry, unobstructed sky ran rows of cottages in pairs, each with its oversized chimney pot, each with a front garden split down the middle. She opened a front gate. An outside staircase led up to a first-floor porch. She climbed. He followed her. By the porch light he saw an ugly grey cat with one forepaw missing rubbing itself against her foot. She unlocked the door and the cat shot past her. She stepped in after it, then waited for him.

'Food in the fridge if you're hungry,' she said, disappearing into what he took to be her bedroom. And as the door closed: 'The bloody cat thinks I'm a vet.'

★

She is sitting, head in hands, staring at the uneaten food on the table before her. The living room is sparse to the point of self-

240

denial: minimal kitchen one end, a couple of old pine chairs, a lumpy sofa and the pine table that is also her workspace. A few medical books, a stack of African magazines. And on the wall, a photograph of Kit in full diplomatic rig presenting his letter of credentials to an abundant female Caribbean head of state while Suzanna in a big white hat looks on.

'Did you take that?' he asked.

'God, no. There was a court photographer.'

From the refrigerator he has rustled up a piece of Dutch cheese, a few tomatoes, and from the freezer sliced bread which he has toasted. And three quarters of a bottle of stale Rioja which with her permission he has poured into two green tumblers. She has put on a shapeless housecoat and flat slippers, but kept her hair bundled. The housecoat is buttoned to her ankles. He's surprised by how tall she is despite the flat shoes. And how stately her walk is. And how her gestures appear at first glance gauche, when actually, when you think about them, they're elegant.

'And that woman doctor who isn't one?' she asks. 'Calling Kit to say Jeb's alive when he isn't? That wouldn't impress the police?'

'Not in their present mood. No.'

'Is Kit at risk of suicide too?'

'Absolutely not,' he retorts firmly, having asked himself the same question ever since leaving Brigid's house.

'*Why* not?'

'Because as long as he believes the fake doctor's story he doesn't present any threat. That was the purpose of the phoney doctor's call. So for God's sake let them think they've achieved it, *they*, whoever they are.'

'But Kit *doesn't* believe it.'

This is old ground, but he goes over it nonetheless, for her sake:

'And has said so very loudly, mercifully only to his nearest and

241

dearest, and me. But he pretended to believe it on the phone, and he must keep pretending now. It's only about buying time. Keeping his head down for a few days.'

'Until what?'

'I'm putting together a case,' Toby says, more boldly than he feels. 'I've got bits of the puzzle, I need more. Jeb's widow has photographs that may be useful. I've taken copies. She also gave me the name of someone who may be able to help. I've arranged to see him. Someone who was part of the original problem.'

'Are *you* part of the original problem?'

'No. Just a guilty bystander.'

'And when you've put your case together, what will you be then?'

'Out of a job, most likely,' he says, and in an effort at light relief reaches out for the cat, which has been sitting all this while at her feet, but it ignores him.

'What time does your father get up in the morning?' he asks.

'Kit does early. Mum lies in.'

'Early being what?'

'Sixish.'

'And the Marlows, how about them?'

'Oh, they're up at crack of dawn. Jack milks for Farmer Phillips.'

'And how far from the Manor is the Marlows' house?'

'No distance. It's the old Manor cottage. Why?'

'I think Kit should be told about Jeb's death as soon as possible.'

'Before he gets it from anyone else and blows a gasket?'

'If you put it like that.'

'I do.'

'The problem is, we can't use the landline to the Manor. Or his cellphone. And certainly not email. That's very much Kit's opinion too. He made a point of it when he wrote to me.'

He paused, expecting her to speak, but her gaze remained on him, challenging him to go on.

'So I'm suggesting you call Mrs Marlow first thing in the morning and ask her to pop over to the Manor and bring Kit to the phone in the cottage. That's assuming you'd like to break the news to him yourself rather than have me do it.'

'What lie do I tell her?'

'There's a fault on the Manor line. You can't get through direct. No panic, but there's something special you need to talk to Kit about. I thought you could use one of these. They're safer.'

She picks up the black burner and, like someone who's never seen a cellphone before, turns it speculatively in her long fingers.

'If it makes it any easier, I can hang around,' he says, careful to indicate the meagre sofa.

She looks at him, looks at her watch: 2 a.m. She fetches an eiderdown and a pillow from her bedroom.

'Now you'll be too cold,' he objects.

'I'll be fine,' she replies.

6.

A stubborn Cornish mist had settled itself in the valley. For two days now no westerly had managed to drive it away. The arched brick windows of the stable that Kit had made his office should by rights have been full of budding leaves. Instead they were blanked out with the deadly whiteness of a shroud: or so it seemed to him as he quartered the harness room in his agitation, much as three years ago he had pounded his hated prison bedroom in Gibraltar waiting for the call to arms.

It was half past six in the morning and he was still wearing the wellingtons he'd put on to hurry across the orchard at Mrs Marlow's urging to take the phone call from Emily on the spurious grounds that she couldn't get through on the Manor line. Their conversation, if you could call it that, was with him now, albeit out of sequence: part information, part exhortation, and all of it a knife thrust through the gut.

And just as in Gibraltar, so here in the stables he was muttering and cursing at himself, half aloud: *Jeb. Jesus Christ, man. Utter bloody nonsense . . . We were on a roll . . . Everything to go for* – all of this interspersed by imprecations of *bastards, bloody murderous bastards* and the like.

'You've got to lie low, Dad, for Mum's sake, not just for yours. And for Jeb's widow. It's only for a few days, Dad. Just believe whatever Jeb's psychiatrist said to you, even if she wasn't Jeb's psychiatrist. Dad, I'm going to hand you over to Toby. He can say it better than me.'

Toby? What the hell's she doing with that sneaky bugger Bell at six in the morning?

'Kit? It's me. Toby.'

'Who shot him, Bell?'

'Nobody. It was suicide. Official. The coroner's signed off on it, the police aren't interested.'

Well, they ought to be bloody interested! But he hadn't said that. Not at the time. Didn't feel he'd said *anything* much at the time, apart from *yes*, and *no*, and *oh well, yes, right, I see*.

'Kit?' – Toby again.

'Yes. What is it?'

'You told me you'd been putting together a draft document in anticipation of Jeb's visit to the Manor. Your own account of what happened from your perspective three years back, plus a memorandum of your conversation with him at your club, for him to sign off on. Kit?'

'What's wrong with that? Gospel truth, the whole bloody thing,' Kit retorts.

'Nothing's wrong with it, Kit. I'm sure it will be extremely useful when the time comes for a démarche. It's just: could you please find somewhere clever to put it for a few days? Out of harm's way. Not in a safe or anywhere obvious. Maybe in the attic of one of the outhouses. Or perhaps Suzanna would have a brainwave. Kit?'

'Have they buried him?'

'Cremated.'

'That's a bit bloody quick, isn't it? Who put them up to that? More jiggery-pokery, by the sound of it. *Christ Almighty*.'

'Dad?'

'Yes, Em. Still here. What is it?'

'Dad? Just do what Toby says. Please. Don't ask any more questions. Just do nothing, find somewhere safe for your opus, and take care of Mum. And leave Toby to do whatever he's got to do up here, because he's really working on this from every angle.'

I'll bet he is, sneaky bastard – but he manages not to say that, which is surprising given that, with the devious Bell telling him what he should or shouldn't be doing, and Emily backing him to the hilt, and Mrs Marlow with her ear to the parlour door, and poor Jeb dead with a bullet through his head, he might have said any bloody thing.

*

Wrestling for sanity, he goes back to the beginning yet again.

He's standing in Mrs Marlow's kitchen in his wellingtons and the washing machine's going, and he's told her to switch the bloody thing off or he won't be able to hear a word.

Dad, this is Emily.

I know it's Emily, for God's sake! Are you all right? What's going on? Where are you?

Dad, I've got really sad news for you. Jeb's dead. Are you listening, Dad? Dad?

Holy God.

Dad? It was suicide, Dad. Jeb shot himself. With his own handgun. In his van.

No, he didn't. Bloody nonsense. He was on his way here. When?

On Tuesday night. A week ago.

Where?

In Somerset.

He can't have done. Are you telling me he killed himself that night? That bogus doctor woman called me on Friday.

Afraid so, Dad.

Has he been identified?

Yes.

Who by? Not that bogus bloody doctor, I trust?

His wife.
Christ Almighty.

★

Sheba was whimpering. Stooping to her, Kit gave her a consoling pat then glowered into the distance while he listened to Jeb's parting words murmured to him on the club landing at first light:

You get to think you're abandoned, sometimes. Cast out, like. Plus the child and her mother, lying there in your head. You feel responsible, like. Well, I don't feel that any more, do I? So if you don't mind, Sir Christopher, I'll give your hand a shake.

Offering me the hand he's supposed to have shot himself with. A good firm shake, along with a *See you first thing Wednesday at the Manor then,* and me promising to be short-order chef and run him up scrambled eggs for his breakfast, which he said was his favourite.

And wouldn't call me Kit although I told him to. Didn't think it was respectful, not to Sir Christopher. And me saying I never deserved a bloody knighthood in the first place. And him blaming himself for horrors he never committed. And now he's being blamed for another horror he didn't bloody commit: to wit, killing himself.

And what am I being asked to do about it? Sweet Fanny Adams. Go and hide the draft document in some hayloft, leave everything to the devious Bell and keep my stupid mouth shut.

Well, maybe I've kept it shut a bit too bloody much.

Maybe that's what was wrong with me. Too willing to blast off about things that don't matter a fart, and not quite willing enough to ask a few awkward questions like: *what actually happened down there on the rocks behind the houses?* Or: *why am I being handed a cushy retirement posting in the Caribbean when there are half a dozen chaps above me who deserve it a bloody sight more than I do?*

Worst of all, it was his own daughter telling him to keep his mouth shut, led on by young Bell, who seemed to have a knack of wearing two hats at once and getting away with it and – the rage rising in him again – getting away with old Em too, and *persuading* her, *totally against her better judgement by the sound of her*, to poke her nose into matters she doesn't know the first bloody thing about, except what she's overheard or picked up from her mother and shouldn't have done.

And just for the record: if *anybody* was going to dish old Em the dirt about *Operation Wildlife* and related matters, it wasn't going to be the devious Bell, whose sole qualification appeared to be spying on his minister, and it wasn't going to be Suzanna. *It was going to be her own bloody father, in his own time and in his own way.*

And with these uncoordinated thoughts resounding furiously in his head he strode back across the fog-ridden courtyard to the house.

*

Deploying all available stealth lest he rouse Suzanna from her morning sleep, Kit shaved and put on a dark town suit, as opposed to the country effort he had mistakenly worn for that shit Crispin, whose role in this affair he would drag into the daylight if it cost him his pension and his knighthood.

Surveying himself in the wardrobe mirror, he pondered whether to add a black tie out of respect for Jeb and decided: too demonstrative, sends the wrong message. With an antique key that he had recently added to his key-ring, he unlocked a drawer of the commander's desk and extracted the envelope to which he had consigned Jeb's flimsy receipt and, from beneath it, a folder marked DRAFT containing his handwritten document.

Pausing for a moment, he discovered almost to his relief that he was weeping hot tears of grief and anger. A quick glance at the title of his document, however, restored his spirits and determination:

'*Operation Wildlife*, Part I: Eyewitness account by HM Minister's Acting Representative in Gibraltar, in the light of additional information supplied by Field Commander, UK Special Force'.

Part II, subtitled 'Field Commander's Eyewitness Account' would remain forever pending, so Part I would have to do double duty.

Progressing softly over dust sheets to the bedroom, he gazed in shame and marvel at his sleeping wife, but took good care not to wake her. Gaining the kitchen – and the one telephone in the house from which it was possible to speak without being overheard in the bedroom – he went to work with a precision worthy of the devious Bell.

Call Mrs Marlow.

He does, keeping his voice down; and yes, of course, she will be more than happy to spend the night at the Manor, just as long as it's what Suzanna wants, because that's the main thing, isn't it? – and is the Manor telephone working again, because it sounds perfectly all right to *her*?

Call Walter and Anna, dull but sweet friends.

He does, and wakes Walter up, but nothing's too much trouble for Walter. Yes, of course he and Anna will be happy to drop by this evening and make sure Suzanna isn't feeling neglected if Kit can't make it back from his business appointment till tomorrow, and is Suzanna watching *Sneakers* on Sky, because they are?

Take deep breath, sit down at kitchen table, write non-stop as follows, no self-editing, crossings-out, marginal notes, et cetera:

Darling Suki,
A lot has come up regarding our soldier friend while you were asleep, and the net result is, I've got to trolley up to London as a

matter of urgency. With luck the whole thing will be thrashed out in
time for me to catch the five o'clock back, but if not I'll take the night
sleeper even if I can't get a berth.

Then his pen started running away with him, and he let it:

Dearest You, I love you terribly, but the time has come for me to stand
up and be counted, and if you were able to know the circumstances
you would agree wholeheartedly. In fact you'd do the job a sight
better than I ever could, but it's time I rose to your standards of
courage instead of dodging bullets.

And if the last line on inspection read more starkly to him than
the rest, there was no time for a second draft if he was going to
make the eight forty-two.

Taking the letter upstairs, he laid it on the dust sheets in front
of their bedroom door and weighted it with a chisel from his
faded canvas tool-bag.

Delving in the library, he found an unused A4 On Her Majesty's Service envelope from his last posting, inserted his draft
document and sealed it with liberal quantities of Sellotape, much
in the manner that he had sealed his letter to young Bell last week.

Driving over the windswept moonscape of Bodmin Moor, he
enjoyed symptoms of release and levitation. Alone on the
station platform among unfamiliar faces, however, he was
seized with an impulse to hurry home while there was time,
grab back the letter, get into his old clothes and tell Walter,
Anna and Mrs Marlow not to bother after all. But with the
arrival of the express train to Paddington, this mood, too,
passed, and soon he was treating himself to the full English
breakfast 'at seat', but tea not coffee, because Suzanna worried
about his heart.

★

While Kit was speeding on his way to London, Toby Bell sat rigidly at his desk in his new office, addressing the latest crisis in Libya. His lower back was in near-terminal spasm, for which he had to thank Emily's sofa, and he was keeping himself going on a diet of Nurofen, the remains of a bottle of sparkling water, and disjointed memories of their last couple of hours together in her flat.

At first, having supplied him with pillow and eiderdown, she had withdrawn to her bedroom. But quite soon she was back, dressed as before, and he was more awake and even less comfortable than he had been when she left him.

Seating herself out of striking distance, she invited him to describe his journey to Wales in greater detail. All too willingly, he obliged. She needed the grim details, and he provided them: the travelled blood that couldn't possibly have travelled there and turned out to be red lead, or didn't; Harry's concern to get the highest price for Jeb's van; Brigid's unsparing adjectival use of 'fucking' and her cryptic account of Jeb's last joyful phone call to her following his encounter with Kit at the club, urging her to dump Harry and prepare for his return.

Emily listened patiently, mostly with her large brown eyes, which in the half-light of early morning had acquired a disconcerting immobility.

He then told her about Jeb's fight with Shorty over the photographs, and how Jeb had afterwards hidden them, and how Brigid had discovered them, and how she had let Toby copy them into his BlackBerry.

On her insistence, he showed them to her, and watched her face freeze the way it had frozen in the hospital.

'Why do you think Brigid trusted you?' she asked, to which he could only reply that Brigid was desperate and had presumably come to the conclusion that he was trustworthy, but this didn't seem to satisfy her.

Next she needed to know how he had wangled Jeb's name and address out of the authorities, to which Toby, while not identifying Charlie by name, beyond saying that he and his wife were old friends, explained that he had once done a favour for their musical daughter.

'And apparently she really *is* a very promising cellist,' he added inconsequentially.

Emily's next question therefore struck him as totally unreasonable:

'Did you sleep with her?'

'God, no! That's bloody outrageous!' he said, genuinely shocked. 'What the hell made you think that?'

'My mother says you've had masses of women. She checked you out with her Foreign Office wives.'

'Your *mother*?' Toby protested indignantly. 'Well, what do the wives say about *you*, for Christ's sake?'

At which they both laughed, if awkwardly, and the moment passed. And after that, all Emily wanted to know was who had murdered Jeb, assuming he *was* murdered, which in turn led Toby into a rather inarticulate condemnation of the Deep State, and thence into a denunciation of the ever-expanding circle of non-governmental insiders from banking, industry and commerce who were cleared for highly classified information denied to large swathes of Whitehall and Westminster.

And as he concluded this cumbersome monologue, he heard six striking, and was by now sitting on the sofa and no longer lying on it, which allowed Emily to sit primly beside him with the burners on the table in front of them.

Her next question has a schoolmistressy ring:

'So what do you hope to get out of Shorty when you meet him?' she demands, and waits while he thinks of an answer, which is the more difficult since he hasn't got one; and anyway he hasn't told her, for fear of alarming her, that he will be meeting Shorty in the first instance under the slender guise of a journalist, before declaring himself in his true colours.

'I'll just have to see which way he jumps,' he says nonchalantly. 'If Shorty's as cut up about Jeb's death as he says he is, maybe he'll be willing to step into Jeb's shoes and testify for us.'

'And if he isn't willing?'

'Well, I suppose we just shake hands and part.'

'That doesn't sound like Shorty, from what you've told me,' she replies severely.

And at this point, a drought overcomes their conversation, during which Emily lowers her eyes and lays her fingertips together beneath her chin in contemplation, and he supposes she is preparing herself for the phone call she is about to make to her father, by way of Mrs Marlow.

And when she reaches out her hand, he assumes that it's to pick up the black burner. But instead, it's his own hand she picks up, and holds gravely in both of hers as if she's taking his pulse, but not quite; then without comment or explanation lays it carefully back on his lap.

'Actually, never mind,' she mutters impatiently to herself – or to him; he's not quite sure.

Does she want his comfort in this moment of crisis, and is too proud to ask for it?

Is she telling him she has thought about him and decided she isn't interested, so have his hand back?

Or was it the imaginary hand of a present or former lover that she was reaching for in her anxiety? – which was the interpretation he was still favouring as he sat diligently at his new desk on the first floor of the Foreign Office, and the silver burner in his jacket pocket announced in a raucous burp that it had a text message for him.

Toby was not at this point wearing his jacket. It was slung over the back of his chair. So he had to swing round and fish for the burner with rather more enthusiasm than he would have deployed had he known that Hilary, his formidable second-in-command, was standing in the doorway needing his urgent attention. Nevertheless he persisted in the movement and, with a smile that asked her forbearance, extracted the burner from his pocket, searched for the unfamiliar button to press, pressed it and, still smiling, read the message:

Dad has written a mad letter to Mum and is on the train to London.

★

The Foreign Office waiting room was a windowless dungeon of prickly chairs, glass tables and unreadable magazines about Britain's industrial skills. At the door lurked a burly black man in a brown uniform with yellow epaulettes, and at a desk an expressionless Asian matron in the same uniform. Kit's fellow detainees included a bearded Greek prelate and two indignant ladies of an age who had come to complain about their treatment at the hands of the British Consulate in Naples. It was of course a crying outrage that a ranking former member of the Service – and a Head of Mission at that – should be required to wait here, and in due season he would make his feelings known in the right quarter. However, alighting at Paddington, he had vowed to remain courteous but purposeful, keep his wits about him at all times and, in the interests of the greater cause, ignore whatever slings and arrows came his way.

'My name's *Probyn*,' he had told them cheerfully at the front gate, volunteering his driving licence in case they needed verification. '*Sir Christopher Probyn*, former High Commissioner. Do I still regard myself as staff? Apparently, I don't. Well, never mind. How are you?'

'To see?'

'The Permanent Under-Secretary – better known these days, I understand, as the Executive Director,' he added indulgently, careful to conceal his visceral distaste at the Office's rush towards corporatization. 'I know it's a big call and I'm afraid I haven't a date. But I do have a very sensitive document for him. Failing that, his Private Secretary. Rather confidential, I'm afraid, and rather urgent' – all delivered merrily through a six-inch hole in a wall of armoured glass, while on the other side of it an unsmiling youth in a blue shirt and chevrons tapped details into a computer.

'*Kit*, they'll probably know me as in his Private Office. Kit *Probyn*. You're quite *sure* I'm not staff? Probyn with a Y.'

Even when they patted him down with an electric ping-pong bat, took his cellphone off him and fed it into a cabinet of glass-fronted lockers with numbered keys, he had continued to remain totally calm.

'You chaps full time here, or do you look after other government buildings as well?'

No answer, but still he hadn't bridled. Even when they tried to get their hands on his precious draft document, he had remained courteous, if implacable.

'No go, I'm afraid, old boy, with all due respect. You have your duty to do, I have mine. I came here all the way from Cornwall to hand-deliver this envelope, and hand-deliver it I shall.'

'We only want to run it through X-ray, sir,' the man said, after a glance at his colleague. So Kit looked on benignly while they operated their laborious machine, then grabbed back the envelope.

'And it *was* the Executive Director in person you were wishing to see, was it, sir?' the colleague enquired, with what Kit might easily have mistaken for irony.

'Indeed it was,' he replied jauntily. 'And still is. The big chief himself. And if you'd pass that message upstairs rather sharply, I'd be obliged.'

One of the men left the cubicle. The other stayed and smiled.

'Come by train then, did you?'

'I did.'

'Nice trip, was it?'

'Very, thank you. Most enjoyable.'

'That's the way then. My wife comes from Lostwithiel, actually.'

'Splendid. A proper Cornish girl. What a coincidence.'

The first man had returned: but only to escort Kit to the featureless room where he now sat, and had sat for the last half-hour, inwardly fulminating but resolved not to show it.

And now at last his patience was rewarded, for who should come bustling up to him grinning like a schoolgirl but Molly Cranmore herself, his long-time buddy from Logistical Contingencies, wearing a name tag and a bunch of electronic keys round her neck and holding out her hands and saying, 'Kit Probyn, what a lovely, lovely surprise!' while Kit in return was saying, 'Molly, my God, of *all* people, I thought you'd retired *aeons* ago, what on earth are *you* doing here?'

'Alumni, darling,' she confided in a happy voice. 'I get to meet all our old boys and girls whenever they need a helping hand or fall by the wayside, which isn't you *at all*, you lucky man, you're here on business, I know. *Now* then. What *kind* of business? You've got a document and you want to hand it personally to God. But you can't because he's on a swan to Africa – *well deserved*, I may add. A *great* pity because I'm sure he'll be furious when he hears he missed you. What's it about?'

'I'm afraid that's something I can't tell even you, Molly.'

'So can I take your document up to his Private Office and find the right minion for it? – I can't? – not even if I promise not to let it out of my sight in the meantime? – not even then. Oh dear,' she confirmed, as Kit continued to shake his head. 'So does it have a name, your envelope? Something that will set bells ringing on the first floor?'

Kit debated the question with himself. A cover name, after all, was what it said it was. It was there to cover things up. Ah, but was a cover name *of itself* something to be covered up? If so, then there would have to be cover names for cover names, ad infinitum. All the same, the idea of blurting out the hallowed word *Wildlife* in the presence of a Greek prelate and two irate ladies was more than he could stomach.

'Then kindly tell them that I need to speak to his highest authorized representative,' he said, hugging the envelope to his chest.

Getting there, he thought.

★

Toby, meanwhile, has sought instinctive refuge in St James's Park. With the silver burner pressed to his ear, he is hunched under the very same plane tree from which, just three years earlier, he dispatched his futile appeal to Giles Oakley, informing him that a fictitious Louisa had walked out on him and begging his advice. Now he is listening to Emily, and noting that her voice is as calm as his own.

'How was he dressed?' he asks.

'The full monty. Dark suit, best black shoes, favourite tie and a navy raincoat. And no walking stick, which Mother takes as an omen.'

'Has Kit told your mother that Jeb's dead?'

'No, but I did. She's distraught and very scared. Not for herself, for Kit. And, as always, practical. She's checked with Bodmin station. The Land Rover's in the car park and they think he bought a senior citizen's day return, first class. The train was on time out of Bodmin, and arrived on time in Paddington. And she's rung his club. If he shows up, would they please get him to ring her? I told her that wasn't good enough. If he shows up, *they* should ring her. She said she'd call them again. Then she'll call me.'

'And Kit hasn't been in touch since he left the house?'

'No, and he's not answering his cellphone.'

'Has he done this kind of thing before?'

'Refused to speak to us?'

'Thrown a tantrum – gone AWOL – taken matters into his own hands – whatever.'

'When my beloved ex-partner waltzed off with a new girl-friend and half my mortgage, Dad went and laid siege to their flat.'

'Then what did he do?'

'It was the wrong flat.'

Resigned to returning to his desk, Toby glances up with apprehension at the great bowed windows of his own Foreign Office. Joining the unsmiling throng of black-suited civil servants passing up and down Clive Steps, he succumbs to the same wave of nervous nausea that afflicted him on that gorgeous spring Sunday morning three years ago when he came here to filch his illicit tape recording.

At the front gate, he takes a calculated risk:

'Tell me, please' – displaying his pass to the security guard – 'has a retired member called *Sir Christopher Probyn* checked in today, by any chance?' And to be helpful: 'P–R–O–B–Y–N.'

Wait while guard consults computer.

'Not here. Could have checked in elsewhere. Did he have an appointment, at all?'

'I don't know,' says Toby and, back at his post, resumes his department's deliberations about which way to look in Libya.

*

'Sir Christopher?'

'The same.'

'I'm Asif Lancaster from the Executive Director's depart-ment. How d'you do, sir?'

258

Lancaster was a black man, spoke with a Mancunian accent and looked about eighteen years old, but to Kit's eye most people seemed to these days. Nevertheless he warmed to the fellow at once. If the Office had finally opened its gates to the Lancasters of the world, he reasoned vaguely, then surely he could expect a more receptive ear when he told them a few home truths about their handling of *Operation Wildlife* and its aftermath.

They had reached a conference room. Easy chairs. A long table. Watercolours of the Lake District. Lancaster holding out his hand.

'Look here, there's one thing I have to ask you,' said Kit, even now not quite willing to part with his document. 'Are you and your people cleared for *Wildlife?*'

Lancaster looked at him, then at the envelope, then allowed himself a wry smile.

'I think I can safely say we are,' he replied and, gently removing it from Kit's unresisting grasp, disappeared to an adjoining room.

★

It was another ninety minutes by the gold Cartier watch presented to him by Suzanna on their twenty-fifth before Lancaster opened the door to admit the promised senior legal advisor and his sidekick. In that period, Lancaster had appeared no fewer than four times, once to offer Kit coffee, once to bring it, and twice to assure him that Lionel was on the case and would be heading this way 'just as soon as he and Frances have got their heads round the paperwork'.

'Lionel?'

'Our deputy legal advisor. Spends half his week in the Cabinet Office, and the other half with us. He tells me he was assistant legal attaché in Paris when you were commercial counsellor there.'

'Well, well, *Lionel*,' Kit says, brightening as he recalls a worthy, rather tongue-tied young man with fair hair and freckles who made it a point of honour to dance with the plainest women in the room.

'And Frances?' he enquires hopefully.

'Frances is our new Director in Charge of Security, which comes under the Executive Director's umbrella. Also a lawyer, I'm afraid.' Smile. 'Used to be in private practice, till she saw the light, and is now happily with us.'

Kit was glad of this information since it would not otherwise have occurred to him that Frances was happy. Her demeanour on sitting herself opposite him across the table struck him as positively mournful: thanks not least to her black business suit, short-cropped hair and apparent refusal to look him in the eye.

Lionel, on the other hand, though it was twenty years on, had remained his decent, rather prissy self. True, the freckles had given way to liver spots, and the fair hair had faded to an uneasy grey. But the blameless smile was undimmed and the handshake as vigorous as ever. Kit remembered that Lionel used to smoke a pipe and supposed he'd given it up.

'Kit, super to see you,' he declared, bringing his face a little closer than Kit had bargained for in his enthusiasm. 'How's well-earned retirement? God knows, I'm looking forward to mine! And marvellous things we hear about your Caribbean tour, by the way.' Drop of the voice: 'And Suzanna? How's all *that* going? Things looking up a bit?'

'Very much so. Yes, fine, thank you, *great* improvement,' Kit replied. And gruffly, as an afterthought: 'A bit keen to get this over, frankly, Lionel. We both are. Been a bit of an ordeal. 'Specially for Suki.'

'Yes, well, of course we're *absolutely* aware of that, and *more* than grateful to you for your extremely helpful, not to say *timely*, document, and for bringing the whole thing to our attention without – well – rocking the boat,' said Lionel, no longer so tongue-tied, settling himself at the table. 'Aren't we, Frances? And of course' – briskly opening a file and revealing a photocopy of Kit's handwritten draft – 'we're *immensely* sympathetic. I mean, one can only *imagine* what you've been through. And Suzanna too, poor girl. Frances, I think I'm speaking for both of us?'

If he was, Frances, our Director in Charge of Security, gave no sign of it. She too was leafing through a photocopy of Kit's document, but so intently and slowly that he began to wonder whether she was learning it by heart.

'Did Suzanna ever sign a declaration, Sir Christopher?' she enquired, without raising her head.

'Declaration of *what?*' Kit demanded, for once not appreciating the *Sir Christopher*. 'Sign *what?*'

'An Official Secrets Act declaration' – her head still buried in his document – 'stating that she's aware of its terms and penalties.' And to Lionel, before Kit could answer: 'Or didn't we do that for partners and significant others in his day? I forget when that came in, precisely.'

'Well now, I don't think I'm totally sure either,' Lionel replied keenly. 'Kit, what's *your* take on this?'

'No idea,' Kit growled. 'Never saw her sign *any* document of that sort. She certainly never *told* me she'd signed one.' And as the sick fury he had been suppressing for too long came to the surface: 'Hell does it matter what she signed or didn't sign? Not *my* fault she knows what she knows. Not hers either. The girl's desperate. *I'm* desperate. She wants answers. We all do.'

'All?' Frances repeated, lifting her pallid face to him in a kind of frigid alarm. 'Who is *all* in this equation? Are you telling us there are other people who are aware of the content of this paper?'

'If they are, it's none of *my* doing,' Kit retorted angrily, turning to Lionel for the male relief. 'And not Jeb's either. Jeb wasn't gabby, Jeb stuck to the rules. Didn't go to the press or any of that stuff. Stayed strictly inside the camp. Wrote to his MP, his regiment – and probably to you people, for all *I* know,' he ended accusingly.

'Yes, well, it's all *very* painful and *very* unfair,' Lionel agreed, delicately touching the top of his frizzy grey hair with his open palm as if to console it. 'And I think I may say that we have gone to very serious lengths over the last years to get to the bottom of what was obviously a *very* controversial, *very* complex, many-faceted – what can we say, Frances? – episode.'

'*We* being who?' Kit grunted, but the question seemed to go unheard.

'And everyone's been very helpful and forthcoming – wouldn't you agree, Frances?' Lionel continued, and transferring his hand to his lower lip gave it too a consoling tweak. 'I mean, even the *Americans*, who are normally very tight *indeed* about these things – and of course had no official locus at *all*, let alone *unofficial* – came through with a *very* clear statement distancing themselves from any *hint* that the Agency might have provided support-in-aid – for which we were duly grateful, weren't we, Frances?'

And turning to Kit again:

'And of course we *did* hold an inquiry. Internally, obviously. But with due diligence. And as a result, poor Fergus Quinn fell on his sword, which – and I think, Frances, you would share this view – *was absolutely* the decent thing to do at the time. But these days, who *does* the decent thing? I mean, when one *thinks* of the politicians who *haven't* resigned and should have done, poor Fergus comes over like a shining knight. Frances, I believe you had a point?'

Frances had:

'What I don't understand, Sir Christopher, is what this

262

document is supposed to *be*? Is it an accusation? A witness statement? Or simply a minute of what somebody said to you, and you have reported it on a take-it-or-leave-it basis, with no commitment on your own part either way?'

'It's what it *is*, for Christ's sake!' Kit retorted, his flame now fully lit. '*Operation Wildlife* was an utter cock-up. Total. The intelligence that prompted it was a lot of balls, two innocent people were shot dead, and there's been a three-year cover-up by all parties involved – including, I strongly suspect, *this* place. And the one man who *was* willing to speak up has met an untimely death, which needs some very serious looking into. *Bloody* serious,' he ended, on a bark.

'Yes, well, I think we could just settle for *unsolicited document of record*, actually,' Lionel murmured to Frances helpfully.

Frances was not to be appeased:

'Would I be overstating the case, Sir Christopher, if I suggested that the whole burden of your testimony against Mr Crispin and others is derived from what Jeb Owens said to you between the hours of 11 p.m. and 5 a.m. on that one night in your club? I am excluding for the moment the so-called *receipt* that Jeb passed to your wife, and which I see you have added as an annexe of some sort.'

For a moment Kit appeared too stunned to speak.

'What about *my* bloody testimony? I was *there*, wasn't I? *On* the hillside! *In* Gibraltar. The minister's man on the spot. He wanted my advice. I gave it to him. Don't tell me nobody was recording what was being said back and forth. *There's no case for going in.* My words, loud and clear. And Jeb agreed with me. They all did. Shorty, every man jack of them. But they'd got the order to go, so they went. Not because they're sheep. But because that's what decent soldiers do! However bloody silly the orders are. Which they were. *Bloody* silly. No rational grounds? Never mind. Orders are orders,' he added, for emphasis.

Frances was scrutinizing another page of Kit's document:

'But surely everything you *saw* and *heard* in Gibraltar tallied precisely with the account you were *afterwards* given by those who had planned the operation, and were in a position to assess the outcome? Which *you* were patently not, were you? You had absolutely no idea of the outcome. You simply take your tune from other people. First you believe what the planners tell you. Then you believe what Jeb Owens tells you. On no more substantial evidence than your own preferences. Am I not right?'

And providing Kit with no opportunity to answer that question, she asked another:

'Can you tell me, please, how much alcohol you had consumed before you went upstairs that night?'

Kit faltered, then blinked several times, like a man who has lost his sense of time and place, and is trying to recover them.

'Not a lot,' he said. 'Soon wore off. I'm used to drink. You get a shock like that, you sober up bloody fast.'

'Did you sleep at all?'

'Where?'

'In your club. In your club bedroom. During the passage of that night and early morning. Did you sleep or not?'

'How the hell could I sleep? We were *talking* all the time!'

'Your document suggests Jeb abandoned you at first light and spirited himself out of the club, we know not how. Did you go back to sleep after Jeb had disappeared so miraculously?'

'I hadn't slept in the first place, so how could I go back to sleep? And his departure wasn't *miraculous*. It was professional. He's a pro. Was. Knew all the tricks of the trade.'

'And when you woke up – abracadabra, he wasn't there any more.'

'He'd gone already, I told you! There was no bloody *abracadabra* about it! It was *stealth*. The chap was a master of *stealth*' – as if propounding a concept that was new to him.

Lionel chipped in, decent Lionel:

'Kit – man to man – just tell us how much you and Jeb put away that night – give us a rough idea. Everybody balks about how much they actually drink, but if we're going to get to the bottom of this, we need the whole story, warts and all.'

'We drank *warm beer*,' Kit retorted contemptuously. 'Jeb sipped his and left most of it. That satisfy you?'

'But in *fact*' – Lionel looking at his gingery-haired fingers now, rather than at Kit – 'when you really get down to it, we *are* talking two pints of beer, aren't we? And Jeb, as you say, is no sort of drinker – or wasn't, poor chap – so presumably you mopped up the rest. True?'

'Probably.'

Frances was once more talking to her notes.

'So, effectively, two pints of beer on top of the very considerable quantity of alcohol you'd already drunk during and after dinner, not to mention two double eighteen-year-old Macallan whiskies consumed with Crispin at the Connaught before you ever reached your club. Calculated together, let us say eighteen to twenty units. One might also draw conclusions from the fact that, when you suborned the night porter, you specified one beer glass only. In effect, therefore, you were ordering for yourself. Alone.'

'Have you been sniffing around my *club*? That's bloody disgraceful! Of *course* it was only one beer glass! D'you think I wanted to tell the night porter I'd got a *man* in my room? Who did you talk to anyway? The secretary? Christ Almighty!'

He was appealing to Lionel, but Lionel was back to patting his hair, and Frances had more to say:

'We are also reliably informed that it would be impossible for any individual, master of stealth though he may be, to infiltrate himself into your club's premises, *either* through the service entrance at the rear, *or* through the front door, which is kept under surveillance at all times, *both* by the porter *and* by CCTV. Added to which, all club personnel are police vetted and security-aware.'

Kit was fumbling, choking, fighting for lucidity, for moderation, for sweet reason:

'Look here, both of you. Don't grill *me*. Grill Crispin. Grill Elliot. Go back to the Americans. Find that fake doctor woman who told me Jeb had gone mad when he was already dead.' Stumble. Breathe. Swallow. 'And find Quinn, wherever he is. Get him to tell you what really happened down there on the rocks behind the houses.'

He thought he'd finished, but discovered he hadn't:

'And hold yourselves a proper public inquiry. Trace that poor bloody woman and her child and get some compensation for her relatives! And when you've done that, find out who killed Jeb the day before he was going to sign up to my document and put in his own word.' And somewhat erratically: 'And don't for God's sake believe anything that charlatan Crispin tells you. Man's a liar to his boots.'

Lionel had finished patting his hair:

'Yes, well, Kit, I don't want to make a big matter of this but, if push ever came to shove, you'd be in a pretty unhealthy position, frankly. A *public* inquiry of the sort you're hankering after – which could result from, well, from your document – is light years away from the sort of hearing that Frances and I envisage. Anything deemed in the *smallest* way to go against national security – secret operations successful or otherwise, extraordinary rendition whether merely planned or actually achieved, robust interrogation methods, ours or more particularly the Americans' – goes straight into the Official Secrets box, I'm afraid, and the witnesses with it' – raising his eyes respectfully to Frances, which is the cue for her to square her shoulders and place her hands flat on the open folder before her as if she is about to levitate.

'It is my duty to advise you, Sir Christopher,' she announces, 'that you are in a most serious position. Yes, acknowledged, you took part in a certain very secret operation. Its authors are scattered. The documentation, other than your own, is patchy. In the few files that *are* available to this Office, no names of participants are mentioned – save one. Yours. Which does rather mean that in any *criminal* investigation that resulted from this document, *your* name would predominate as senior British representative on the ground, and you would have to answer accordingly. Lionel?' – turning hospitably to him.

'Yes, well, that's the bad news, Kit, I'm afraid. And the good news is, frankly, pretty hard to come by. We have a new set of rules since your day for cases where sensitive issues are involved. Some already in place; others, we trust, imminent. And, very unfortunately, *Wildlife* does tick a lot of those boxes. Which would mean, I'm afraid, that any inquiry would have to take place behind closed doors. Should it find against you – and should you elect to bring a suit – which would naturally be your good right – then the resultant hearing would be conducted by a hand-picked and very carefully briefed group of approved lawyers, some of whom would obviously do their best to speak *for* you and others *not* so for you. And *you* – the *claimant*, as he or she is rather whimsically called – would I'm afraid be banished from the court while the government presented its case to the judge without the inconvenience of a direct challenge by you or your representatives. And under the rules currently being discussed, the very *fact* that a hearing is being conducted might of itself be kept secret. As of course, in that case, would the judgement.'

After a rueful smile to harbinger a further spot of bad news, and a pat for his hair, he resumed:

'And then, as Frances so *rightly* says, if there *were* ever a criminal case against you, any prosecution would take place in *total* secrecy until a sentence was handed down. Which is to say, I'm afraid, Kit' – allowing himself another sympathetic smile, though whether for the law or its victim was unclear – '*draconian* though it may sound, Suzanna wouldn't *necessarily* know you were on trial, assuming for the moment that you *were*. Or at least not until you'd been found guilty – assuming, once more, that you had been. There *would* be a jury of sorts – but of course its members would have to be very heavily vetted by the security services prior to selection, which obviously does *rather* stack the odds against one. And *you*, for *your* part, *would* be allowed to see the evidence against you – at least, let us say, in broad brush – but I'm afraid *not* share it with your nearest and dearest. Oh and whistle-blowing *per se* would absolutely not be a defence, whistle-blowing being – and may it forever remain so in my personal view – by definition a risk business. I'm deliberately *not* pulling my punches here, Kit. I think Frances and I both feel we owe you that. Don't we, Frances?'

'He's dead,' Kit whispered incoherently. And then again, fearing he might not have spoken aloud: 'Jeb's *dead*.'

'Most unhappily, yes, he is,' Frances agreed, for the first time accepting a point of Kit's argument. 'Though not perhaps in the circumstances you seek to imply. A sick soldier killed himself with his own weapon. Regrettably, that is a practice that is on the increase. The police have no grounds for suspicion, and who are we to dispute their judgement? Meanwhile, your document will be kept on record in the hope that it will never have to be used against you. I trust you share that hope.'

★

Reaching the foot of the great staircase, Kit appears to forget which way to turn, but fortunately Lancaster is on hand to guide him to the front gates.

'What did you say your name was, my dear fellow?' Kit asks him as they shake hands.

'Lancaster, sir.'

'You've been very kind,' says Kit.

*

The news that Kit Probyn had been positively sighted in the smoking room of his club in Pall Mall – transmitted yet again by text over Emily's black burner, thanks to a tip-off from her mother – had reached Toby just as he was settling down at the long table in the third-floor conference room to discuss the desirability of engaging in talks with a Libyan rebel group. What excuses he had pleaded for leaping from his seat and stalking out of the room now escaped him. He remembered pulling the silver burner from his pocket in full view of everyone – he had no alternative – and reading the text and saying, 'Oh my God, I'm terribly sorry,' then probably something about somebody dying, given that the news of Jeb's death still occupied his mind.

He remembered pelting down the stairs past a Chinese delegation coming up, then running and walking the thousand-odd yards from the Office to Pall Mall, all the while talking feverishly to Emily, who had summarily abandoned her evening surgery and got herself on to a tube headed for St James's Park. The club secretary, she had reported before she descended, had at least honoured his promise to inform Suzanna the moment Kit appeared, if not with the good grace that might have been expected of him:

'Mum said he made Dad sound like some sort of criminal on the loose. Apparently the police went round there this afternoon, asking a lot of questions about him. Said it was to do with something called *enhanced vetting*. How much he drank and whether he'd had a man in his room when he stayed in the club recently, if you can believe it. And had he bribed the night

269

porter to serve them food and drink – what on earth was *that* about?'

Panting from his exertions and clutching the silver burner to his ear, Toby took up his agreed position next to the flight of eight stone steps that led up to the imposing portals of Kit's club. And suddenly Emily was flying towards him – Emily as he'd never seen her – Emily the runner, the freed wild child, her raincoat billowing, dark hair streaming behind her against a slate-grey sky.

They climbed the steps, Toby leading. The lobby was dark and smelt of cabbage. The Secretary was tall and desiccated.

'Your father has removed himself to the Long Library,' he informed Emily in a dispirited nasal twang. 'Ladies can't go in, I'm afraid. You're allowed downstairs, but only after 6.30.' And to Toby, having looked him over: tie, jacket, matching trousers. 'You're all right to go in as long as you're his guest. Will he vouch for you as his guest?'

Ignoring the question, Toby turned to Emily:

'No need for you to hang around in here. Why don't you hail a cab and sit in it till we come?'

At low-lit tables, amid cages of ancient books, greying men drank and murmured head to head. Beyond them, in an alcove given over to marble busts, sat Kit, alone, bowed over a glass of whisky, his shoulders shaking to the uneasy rhythm of his breathing.

'It's Bell,' Toby said into his ear.

'Didn't know you were a member,' Kit replied, without lifting his head.

'I'm not. I'm your guest. So I'd like you to buy me a drink. Vodka, if that's all right. A large one,' he told a waiter. 'On Sir Christopher's tab, please. Tonic, ice, lemon.' He sat down. 'Who've you been talking to at the Office?'

'None of your business.'

'Well, I'm not sure about that. You made your démarche. Is that right?'

Kit, head down. Long pull of Scotch:

'Some bloody démarche,' he muttered.

'You showed them your document. The one you'd drafted while you were waiting for Jeb.'

With improbable alacrity, the waiter set Toby's vodka on the table, together with Kit's bill and a ballpoint pen.

'In a minute,' Toby told him sharply, and waited till he'd left. 'Just please tell me this. Did your document – *does* your document – make any mention of *me*? Maybe you found it necessary to refer to a certain illegal tape recording? Or Quinn's erstwhile Private Secretary. Did you, Kit?'

Kit's head still down, but rolling from side to side.

'So you didn't refer to me at all? Is that right? Or are you just refusing to answer? No Toby Bell? *Anywhere?* Not in writing, not in your conversations with them?'

'*Conversations!*' Kit retorted with a rasping laugh.

'Did you or didn't you mention my involvement in this? Yes or no?'

'No! I didn't! What d'you think I am? A snitch, as well as a bloody fool?'

'I saw Jeb's widow yesterday. In Wales. I had a long talk with her. She gave me some promising leads.'

Kit's head rose at last, and Toby to his embarrassment saw tears lying in the rims of his reddened eyes.

'You saw *Brigid?*'

'Yes. That's right. I saw Brigid.'

'What's she like, poor girl? Christ Almighty.'

'As brave as her husband. The boy's great too. She put me on to Shorty. I've arranged to meet him. Tell me again. You really didn't mention me? If you did, I'll understand. I just need to know for sure.'

'*No*, repeat *no*. Holy God, how many times do I have to say it?'

Kit signed the bill and, refusing Toby's proffered arm, clambered uncertainly to his feet.

'Hell are you doing with my daughter anyway?' he demanded, as they came unexpectedly face to face.

'We're getting along fine.'

'Well, don't do what that shit Bernard did.'

'She's waiting for us now.'

'Where?'

Keeping a hand at the ready, Toby escorted Kit on the journey across the Long Library into the lobby, past the Secretary and down the steps to where Emily was waiting with the cab: not inside it, as instructed, but standing in the rain, stoically holding the door open for her father.

'We're going straight off to Paddington,' she said, when she had settled Kit firmly into the cab. 'Kit needs some solids before the night sleeper. What about you?'

'There's a lecture at Chatham House,' he replied. 'I'm expected to put in an appearance.'

'Talk later in the evening then.'

'Sure. See how the land lies. Good idea,' he agreed, conscious of Kit's befuddled gaze glowering at them from inside the cab.

Had he lied to her? Not quite. There was a lecture at Chatham House and he was indeed expected, but he did not propose to attend. Lodged behind the silver burner in his jacket pocket – he could feel it pricking at his collarbone – was a letter on stiff paper from an illustrious-sounding banking house, hand-delivered and signed for at the main entrance of the Foreign Office at three that afternoon. In bold electronic type, it requested Toby's presence at any time between now and midnight at the company's headquarters in Canary Wharf.

It was signed G. Oakley, Senior Vice-President.

★

A chill night air whipped off the Thames, almost clearing away the stink of stale cigarette smoke that lingered in every fake Roman arcade and Nazi-style doorway. By the sodium glare of Tudor lanterns, joggers in red shirts, secretaries in top-to-toe black livery, striding men with crew cuts and paper-thin black briefcases glided past each other like mummers in a macabre dance. Before every lighted tower and at every street corner, bulked-out security guards in anoraks looked him over. Selecting one at random, Toby showed him the letter heading.

'Must be Canada Square, mate. Well, I *think* it is, I've only been here a year' – to a loud peal of laughter that followed him down the street.

He passed under a walkway and entered an all-night shopping mall offering gold watches, caviar and villas on Lake Como. At a cosmetics counter a beautiful girl with bare shoulders invited him to sniff her perfume.

'You don't by *any* chance know where I can find Atlantis House, do you?'

'You wanna buy?' she asked sweetly, with an uncomprehending Polish smile.

A tower block rose before him, all its lights blazing. At its base a pillared cupola. On its floor a Masonic starburst of gold mosaic. And round its blue dome, the word *Atlantis*. And at the back of the cupola, a pair of glass doors with whales engraved on them that sighed and opened at his approach. From behind a counter of hewn rock, a burly white man handed him a chrome clip and plastic card with his name on it:

'Centre lift and no need for you to press anything. Have a nice evening, Mr Bell.'

'You too.'

The lift rose, stopped, and opened into a starlit amphitheatre of white archways and celestial nymphs in white plaster. From the middle of the domed firmament hung a cluster of illuminated seashells. From beneath them – or as it seemed to Toby from among them – a man was striding vigorously towards him. Back-lit, he was tall, even menacing, but then as he advanced he diminished, until Giles Oakley in his new-found executive glory stood before him: the achiever's rugged smile, the honed body of perpetual youth, the fine new head of darkened hair and perfect teeth.

'Toby, dear man, *what* a pleasure! And at *such* short notice. I'm touched and honoured.'

'Nice to see you, Giles.'

*

An air-conditioned room that was all rosewood. No windows, no fresh air, no day or night. When we buried my grandmother, this is where we sat and talked to the undertaker. A rosewood desk and throne. Below it, for lesser mortals, a rosewood coffee table and two leather chairs with rosewood arms. On the table, a rosewood tray for the very old Calvados, the bottle not quite full. Until now, they had barely looked each other in the eye. In negotiation, Giles doesn't do that.

'So, Toby. How's love?' he asked brightly when Toby had declined the Calvados and watched Oakley pour himself a shot.

'Fair, thank you. How's Hermione?'

'And the great novel? Done and dusted?'

'Why am I here, Giles?'

'For the same reason that you came, surely' – Oakley, putting on a little pout of dissatisfaction at the unseemly pace of things.

'And what reason is that?'

'A certain covert operation, dreamed up three years ago but mercifully – as we both know – never executed. Might *that* be the reason?' Oakley enquired with false jocularity.

But the impish light had gone out. The once-lively wrinkles

round the mouth and eyes were turned downward in permanent rejection.

'You mean *Wildlife*,' Toby suggested.

'If you want to bandy state secrets about, yes. *Wildlife*.'

'*Wildlife* was executed all right. So were a couple of innocent
people. You know that as well as I do.'

'Whether *I* know it or *you* know it is neither here nor there.
What is at issue is whether the world knows it, and whether it
should. And the answer to those two questions, dear man –
as must be evident to a blind hedgehog, let alone a trained
diplomat such as yourself – is very clearly: no, thank you, never.
Time does not heal in such cases. It festers. For every year of
official British denial, count hundreds of decibels of popular
moral outrage.'

Pleased with this rhetorical flourish, he smiled mirthlessly, sat
back and waited for the applause. And when none came, treated
himself to a nip of Calvados and airily resumed:

'Think on it, Toby: a rabble of American mercenaries, aided
by British Special Forces in disguise and funded by the Republican evangelical right. And for good measure, the whole thing
masterminded by a shady defence contractor in cahoots with a
leftover group of fire-breathing neocons from our fast-dissolving
New Labour leadership. And the dividend? The mangled corpses
of an innocent Muslim woman and her baby daughter. Watch
that play out in the media marketplace! As to gallant little
Gibraltar with her long-suffering multi-ethnic population: the
cries to give her back to Spain would deafen us for decades to
come. If they don't already.'

'So?'

'I beg your pardon?'

'What d'you want me to do?'

Suddenly Oakley's gaze, so often elusive, was fixed on Toby
in fiery exhortation:

'Not *do*, dear man! *Cease* to do. Desist forthwith and for ever! Before it's too late.'

'Too late for *what*?'

'For your career – what else? Give up this self-righteous pursuit of the unfindable. It will destroy you. Become again what you were before. All will be forgiven.'

'Who says it will?'

'I do.'

'And who else? Jay Crispin? Who?'

'What does it matter *who else*? An informal consortium of wise men and women with their country's interests at heart, will that do you? Don't be a *child*, Toby.'

'Who killed Jeb Owens?'

'Killed him? Nobody. *He* did. He shot himself, the poor man. He was deranged for years. Has nobody told you that? Or is the truth too inconvenient for you?'

'Jeb Owens was murdered.'

'Nonsense. Sensational nonsense. Whatever makes you say that?' – Oakley's chin coming up in challenge, but his voice no longer quite so sure of itself.

'Jeb Owens was shot through the head by a gun that wasn't his own, with the wrong hand, just one day before he was due to join up with Probyn. He was bubbling over with hope. He was so full of hope he rang his estranged wife on the morning of the day he was killed to tell her just how full of hope he was and how they could start their lives all over again. Whoever had him murdered got some B-list actress to pretend she was a doctor – a male doctor, actually, but she didn't know that, unfortunately – and make a cold call to Probyn's house *after* Jeb's death with the happy message that Jeb was alive and languishing in a mental hospital and didn't want to talk to anyone.'

'Whoever told you such drivel?' – but Oakley's face was a lot less certain than his tone.

'The police investigation was led by diligent plain-clothes officers from Scotland Yard. Thanks to their diligence, not a single clue was followed up. There was no forensic examination, a whole raft of formalities were waived, and the cremation went through with unnatural speed. Case closed.'

'Toby.'

'What?'

'Assuming this is the truth, it's all news to me. I had no idea of it, I swear. They told me –'

'*They? Who's they?* Who the fuck is *they? They* told you *what?* That Jeb's murder had been covered up and everybody could go home?'

'My understanding was and is that Owens shot himself in a fit of depression, or frustration, or whatever the poor man was suffering from – *wait!* What are you doing? *Wait!*'

Toby was standing at the door.

'Come back. I insist. Sit down' – Oakley's voice close to breaking. 'Perhaps I've been misled. It's possible. Assume it. Assume you're right in everything you say. For argument's sake. Tell me what you know. There are bound to be contrary arguments. There always are. Nothing is set in stone. Not in the real world. It can't be. Sit down here. We haven't finished.'

Under Oakley's imploring gaze, Toby came away from the door but ignored the invitation to sit.

'Tell it to me again,' Oakley ordered, for a moment recovering something of his old authority. 'I need chapter and verse. What are your sources? All hearsay, I've no doubt. Never mind. They killed him. The *they* you are so exercised about. We assume it. And having assumed it, what do we then conclude from that assumption? Allow me to tell you' – the words coming in breathless gasps – 'we conclude decisively that the time has come for you to withdraw your cavalry from the charge – a temporary, tactical, orderly, dignified withdrawal while there's time. A détente.

277

A truce, enabling both sides to consider their positions and let tempers cool. You won't be walking away from a fight – I know that isn't your style. You'll be saving your ammunition for another day – for when you're stronger and you've got more power, more traction. Press your case now, you'll be a pariah for the rest of your life. *You*, Toby! Of all people! That's what you'll be. An outcast who played his cards too early. It's not what you were put on earth for – I know that, better than anyone. The whole country's crying out for a new elite. Begging for one. For people like you – real men – the real men of England, unspoiled – all right, dreamers too – but with their feet on the ground. Bell's the real thing, I told them. Uncluttered mind, and the heart and body to go with it. You don't even know the meaning of real love. Not love like mine. You're blind to it. Innocent. You always were. I knew that. I understood. I loved you for it. One day, I thought, he'll come to me. But I knew you never would.'

But by then, Giles Oakley was talking to an empty room.

*

Lying on his bed in the darkness, the silver burner at his right hand, Toby listens to the night shouts from the street. Wait till she's home. The sleeper leaves Paddington at 11.45. I've checked and it left on time. She hates taking taxis. She hates doing anything the poor can't afford. So wait.

He presses green anyway.

'How was Chatham House?' she asked drowsily.

'I didn't go.'

'So what did you do?'

'Called on an old friend. Had a chat.'

'About anything in particular?'

'Just this and that. How was your father?'

'I handed him over to the attendant. Mum will scrape him off the train at the other end.'

A scuffle, quickly suppressed. A smothered murmur of 'Get off!'

'That bloody cat,' she explained. 'Every night she tries to get on my bed, and I shove her off. Who did you think it was?'

'I didn't dare wonder.'

'Dad's convinced you have designs on me. Is he right?'

'Probably.'

Long silence.

'What's tomorrow?' she asked.

'Thursday.'

'You're meeting your man. Yes?'

'Yes.'

'I have a clinic. It finishes around midday. Then a couple of house calls.'

'Maybe the evening then,' he said.

'Maybe.' Long silence. 'Did something go wrong tonight?'

'Just my friend. He thought I was gay.'

'And you're not?'

'No. I don't think so.'

'And you didn't succumb out of politeness?'

'Not that I recall.'

'Well, that's all right then, isn't it?'

Keep talking, he wanted to tell her. It doesn't have to be your hopes and dreams. Any old thing will do. Just keep talking till I've got Giles out of my head.

7.

He had woken badly, with feelings he needed to disown and others he needed urgently to revive. Despite Emily's consoling words to him it was Oakley's anguished face and supplicating voice that stayed with him when he woke.

I'm a whore.

I didn't know.

I knew, and led him on.

I didn't know, and should have done.

Everybody knew but me.

And most frequently: after Hamburg, how could I be such a bloody fool – telling myself every man's entitled to his appetites, and after all nobody got hurt but Giles?

Concurrently, he had undertaken a damage assessment of the information Oakley had, or had not, revealed about the extent to which his extramural journeyings were compromised. If Charlie Wilkins, or his certain friend in the Met, was Oakley's source, which he took pretty much for granted, then the trip to Wales and his meeting with Brigid were blown.

But the photographs weren't blown. The path to Shorty wasn't blown. Was his visit to Cornwall blown? Possibly, since the police, or versions of them, had trampled all over Kit's club and were by now presumably aware that Emily had come to rescue him in the company of a friend of the family.

In which case, *what*?

In which case, presenting himself to Shorty in the guise of a Welsh journalist and asking him to turn whistle-blower might not be the wisest course of action to pursue. It might in fact be an act of suicidal folly.

So why not abandon the whole thing, and pull the sheets over our heads, follow Oakley's advice and pretend none of it ever happened?

Or in plain language, stop flailing yourself with unanswerable questions, and get down to Mill Hill for your date with Shorty, because one eyewitness who is prepared to stay alive and speak is all you're ever going to need. Either Shorty will say yes, and we'll do together what Kit and Jeb had planned to do, or Shorty will say no and scuttle off to tell Jay Crispin what a good boy he is, and the roof will fall in.

But whichever of these things happens, Toby will finally be taking the battle to the enemy.

*

Ring Sally, his assistant. Get her voicemail. Good. Affect a tone of suffering bravely borne:

'Sally. Toby here. Bloody wisdom tooth acting up, I'm afraid. I'm booked in at the tooth fairy in an hour. So listen. They'll have to count me out of this morning's meeting. And maybe Gregory can stand in for me at the NATO bash. Apologies all round, okay? I'll keep you posted. Sorry again.'

Next, the sartorial question: what does your enterprising provincial journalist wear on his visit to London? He settled for jeans, trainers and a light anorak, and – a neat touch in his opinion – a brace of ballpoints to go with the reporter's notebook from his desk.

But reaching for his BlackBerry, he checked himself, remembering that it contained Jeb's photographs that were also Shorty's.

He decided he was better off without it.

*

The Golden Calf Café & Patisserie lay halfway along the high street, squeezed between a halal butcher and a kosher delicatessen. In its pink-lit windows, birthday cakes and wedding cakes jostled with meringues the size of ostrich eggs. A brass handrail divided the café from the shop. This much Toby saw from across the road before turning into a side street to complete his survey of parked cars, vans and the crowds of morning shoppers who packed the pavements.

Approaching the café a second time, now on the same side, Toby confirmed what he had observed on his first pass: that the café section at this hour was empty of customers. Selecting what the instructors called the bodyguard's table – in a corner, facing the entrance – he ordered a cappuccino and waited.

In the shop section on the other side of the brass handrail, customers armed with plastic tongs were loading up their paper boxes with patisserie, sidling along the counter and paying their dues at the cash desk. But none qualified as Shorty Pike, six foot four – *but Jeb come in from under him, buckled his knees for him, then broke his nose for him on the way down.*

Eleven o'clock turned to ten past. He's got cold feet, Toby decided. They reckon he's a health risk, and he's sitting in a van with his head blown off with the wrong hand.

A bald, heavy-set man with a pockmarked olive complexion and small round eyes was peering covetously through the window: first at the cakes and pastries, now at Toby, now at the cakes again. No blink-rate, weightlifter's shoulders. Snappy dark suit, no tie. Now he's walked away. Was he scouting? Or was he thinking he would treat himself to a cream bun, then changed his mind for his figure's sake? Then Toby realized that Shorty was sitting beside him. And that Shorty must have been hovering all the time in the toilet at the back of the café, which was something Toby hadn't thought of and should have done, but clearly Shorty had.

He seemed taller than his six foot four, probably because he was sitting upright, with both very large hands on the table in the half-curled position. He had oily black hair, close cropped at the back and sides, and high film-star cheekbones with a built-in grin. His dark complexion was so shiny it looked as though it had been scrubbed with a soapy nail-brush after shaving. There was a small dent at the centre of his nose, so perhaps Jeb had left his mark. He was wearing a sharply ironed blue denim shirt with buttoned-up regulation patch pockets, one for his cigarettes, the other for a protruding comb.

'You're Pete then, right?' he asked out of the corner of his mouth.

'And you're Shorty. What can I get you, Shorty? Coffee? Tea?'

Shorty raised his eyebrows and looked slowly round the café. Toby wondered whether he was always this theatrical, or whether being tall and narcissistic made you behave like this.

And wondering this, he caught another glimpse, or thought he did, of the same bald, heavy-set man who had debated with himself about buying a cream bun, hurrying past the shop window with an air of conspicuous unconcern.

'Tell you what, Pete,' said Shorty.

'What?'

'I'm not all that comfortable being here, frankly, if it's all the same to you. I'd like it a bit more private, like. Far from the maddening crowd, as they say.'

'Wherever you like, Shorty. It's your call.'

'And you're not being clever, are you? Like, you haven't got a photographer tucked round the corner, or similar?'

'I'm clean as a whistle and all alone, Shorty. Just lead the way' – watching how the beads of sweat were forming on Shorty's brow, and how his hand shook as it plucked at the pocket of his denim shirt for a cigarette before returning to the table without one. Withdrawal symptoms? Or just a heavy night on the tiles?

'Only I've got my new wagon round the corner, see, an Audi. I parked it early, for in case. So I mean, what we could do, we could go somewhere like the recreation park, or somewhere, and have a talk there, where we're not noticeable, me being somewhat conspicuous. A full and frank exchange, as they say. For your paper. The *Argus*, right?'

'Right.'

'That a big paper, is it, or what – just local – or is it, like, more national, your paper?'

'Local, but we're online too,' Toby replied. 'So it all adds up to quite a decent number.'

'Well, that's good, isn't it? You don't mind then?' – huge sniff.

'Mind what?'

'Us not sitting here?'

'Of course not.'

Toby went to the counter to pay for his cappuccino, which took a moment, and Shorty stood behind him like the next person in line, with the sweat running freely from his face.

But when Toby had done his paying, Shorty walked ahead of him to the entrance, playing the minder, his long arms lifted from his sides to make way.

And when Toby stepped on to the pavement, there was Shorty, waiting, all ready to steer him through the teeming shoppers: but not before Toby, glancing to his left, had again spotted the bald, heavy-set man with a weakness for pastries and cakes, this time standing on the pavement with his back to him, speaking to two other men who seemed equally determined to avoid his eye.

And if there was a moment when Toby contemplated making a dash for it, it was now, because all his training told him: don't dither, you've seen the classic set-up, trust your instincts and go now, because an hour from now or less you'll be chained to a radiator with your shoes off.

But his desire to see things through must have outweighed these reservations because he was already letting Shorty shepherd him round the corner and into a one-way street, where a shiny blue Audi was indeed parked on the left side, with a black Mercedes saloon parked directly behind it.

And once again his trainers would have argued that this was another classic set-up: one kidnap car and one chase car. And when Shorty pressed his remote from a yard away, and opened the *back* door of the Audi for him instead of the passenger door, while at the same moment his grasp on Toby's arm tightened and the heavy-set man and his two chums came round the corner, any residual doubts in Toby's mind must have died on the spot.

All the same, his self-respect obliged him to protest, if only lightly:

'You want me in the *back*, Shorty?'

'I've got another half-hour on the meter, haven't I? Pity to waste it. Might as well sit here and talk. Why not?'

Toby still hesitated, as well he might, for surely the normal thing to do, for any two men who want to talk privately in a car, far from what Shorty insisted on calling the maddening crowd, was to sit in the front.

But he got in anyway, and Shorty climbed in beside him, at which moment the bald, heavy-set man slid into the driving seat from the street side and locked all four doors, while in the off-side wing mirror his two male friends settled themselves comfortably into the Mercedes.

The bald man hasn't switched on the engine, but neither has he turned his head to look at Toby, preferring to study him in the driving mirror in darting flicks of his little round eyes, while Shorty stares ostentatiously out of the window at the passers-by.

★

The bald man has put his hands on the steering wheel, but with the engine not running and the car not moving, this seems odd. They're powerful hands, very clean and fitted with encrusted rings. Like Shorty, the bald man gives an impression of regimental hygiene. His lips in the driving mirror are very pink, and he has to moisten them with his tongue before speaking, which suggests to Toby that, like Shorty, he's nervous.

'Sir, I believe I have the singular honour of welcoming Mr Toby Bell of Her Majesty's Foreign Office. Is that correct, sir?' he enquires in a pedantic South African accent.

'I believe you do,' Toby agrees.

'Sir, my name is Elliot, I am a colleague of Shorty here.' He is reciting: 'Sir – or Toby if I may make so bold – I am instructed to present the compliments of Mr Jay Crispin, whom it is our privilege to serve. He wishes us to apologize in advance for any discomfort you will have sustained thus far, and he assures you of his goodwill. He advises you to relax, and he looks forward to a constructive and amicable dialogue immediately upon arrival at our destination. Do you wish to speak personally to Mr Crispin at this moment in time?'

'No, thank you, Elliot. I think I'm fine as I am,' Toby replies, equally courteously.

Albanian-Greek renegade, used to call himself Eglesias, ex-South African Special Forces, killed some chap in a bar in Jo'burg and came to Europe for his health? That sort of Elliot? Oakley is asking, as they sip their after-dinner Calvados.

'Passenger on board,' Elliot reports into his mouthpiece, and raises a thumb in his side mirror for the benefit of the black Mercedes behind them.

'Sad about poor Jeb, then,' Toby remarks conversationally to Shorty, whose interest in the passers-by only intensifies.

But Elliot is instantly forthcoming:

'Mr Bell, sir, every man has his destiny, every man has his

allotted time span, I say. What is written in the stars is written. No man can beat the rap. Are you comfortable there in the back seat, sir? We drivers sometimes have it too easy, in my opinion.'

'Very comfortable indeed,' says Toby. 'How about you, Shorty?'

★

They were heading south, and Toby had refrained from further conversation, which was probably wise of him because the only questions he could think of came out of a bad dream, like: 'Did you personally have a hand in Jeb's murder, Shorty?' Or: 'Tell us, Elliot, what did you actually *do* with the bodies of that woman and her child?' They had descended Fitzjohn's Avenue and were approaching the exclusive marches of St John's Wood. Was this by chance 'the wood' that Fergus Quinn had referred to in his obsequious conversation with Crispin on the stolen tape recording?

'. . . all right, yes, fourish . . . the wood suits me a lot better . . . more private.'

In quick order, he glimpsed an army barracks guarded by British sentries with automatic rifles, then an anonymous brick house guarded by United States marines. A sign said CUL-DE-SAC. Green-roofed villas at five million and rising. High brick walls. Magnolia trees in full bloom. Fallen cherry blossom lying like confetti across the road. Two green gates, already opening. And in the offside wing mirror, the black Mercedes nosing close enough to touch.

★

He had not expected so much whiteness. They have negotiated a gravel circle edged in white-painted stones. They are pulling up before a low white house surrounded by ornamental lawns.

The white Palladian-style porch is too grand for the house. Video cameras peer at them from the branches of the trees. Fake orangeries of blackened glass stretch to either side. A man in an anorak and tie is holding the car door open. Shorty and Elliot get out, but Toby out of cussedness has decided to wait till he's fetched. Now at his own choice he gets out of the car, and as casually stretches.

'Welcome to Castle Keep, sir,' says the man in the anorak and tie, which Toby is inclined to take as some kind of joke until he spots a brass shield mounted beside the front door portraying a castle like a chess piece surmounted by a pair of crossed swords.

He climbs the steps. Two apologetic men pat him down, take possession of his ballpoint pens, reporter's notebook and wristwatch, then pass him through an electronic archway and say, 'We'll have it all waiting for you after you've seen the Chief, sir.' Toby decides to enter an altered state. He is nobody's prisoner, he is a free man walking down a shiny corridor paved with Spanish tiles and hung with Georgia O'Keeffe flower prints. Doors lead from either side of it. Some are open. Cheery voices issue from them. True, Elliot is strolling beside him, but he has his hands stored piously behind his back as if he's on his way to church. Shorty has disappeared. A pretty secretary in long black skirt and white blouse flits across the corridor. She gives Elliot a casual 'Hi', but her smile is for Toby, and, free man that he is determined to be, he smiles back. In a white office with a sloped ceiling of white glass, a demure, grey-haired lady in her fifties sits behind a desk.

'Ah, Mr Bell. Well done you. Mr Crispin *is* expecting you. Thank you, Elliot, I think the Chief is looking forward to a one-to-one with Mr Bell.'

And Toby, he decides, is looking forward to a one-to-one with the Chief. But alas, on entering Crispin's grand office, he feels only a sense of anticlimax, reminiscent of the anticlimactic feelings he experienced that evening three years ago, when the shadowy ogre who had haunted him in Brussels and Prague marched into Quinn's Private Office with Miss Maisie hanging from his arm and revealed himself as the same blankly handsome, forty-something television version of the officer-class business executive who was this minute rising from his chair with an orchestrated display of pleasurable surprise, naughty-boy chagrin and mannish good fellowship.

'Toby! Well, what a way to meet. Pretty damned odd, I must say, posing as a provincial hack writing up poor Jeb's obituary. Still, I suppose you couldn't tell Shorty you were Foreign Office. You'd have frightened the pants off him.'

'I was hoping Shorty would tell me about *Operation Wildlife*.'

'Yes, well, so I gather. Shorty's a bit cut up about Jeb, understandably. Not quite himself, 'twixt thee and me. Not that he'd have talked much to you. Not in his interests. Not in anyone's. Coffee? Decaf? Mint tea? Something stronger? Not every day I hijack one of Her Majesty's best. How far have you got?'

'With what?'

'Your investigations. I thought that's what we were talking about. You've seen Probyn, seen the widow. The widow gave you Shorty. You've met Elliot. How many cards does that leave you with? Just trying to look over your shoulder,' he explained pleasantly. 'Probyn? Spent force. Didn't see a sausage. All the rest is pure hearsay. A court would chuck it out. The widow? Bereaved, paranoid, hysterical: discount. What else have you got?'

'You lied to Probyn.'

'So would you have done. It was expedient. Or hasn't the dear old FO heard of lies of expediency? Your problem is, you're going to be out of a job pretty soon, with worse to come. I thought I might be able to help out.'

'How?'

'Well, just for openers, how about a bit of protection and a job?'

'With Ethical Outcomes?'

'Oh Christ, *those* dinosaurs,' said Crispin, with a laugh to suggest he'd forgotten all about Ethical Outcomes until Toby happened to remind him of them. 'Nothing to do with this shop, thank God. We got out early. Ethical put the chairs on the tables and went all offshore. Whoever owns the stock owns the liability. Absolutely no connection visible or otherwise with Castle Keep.'

'And no Miss Maisie?'

'Long gone, bless her. Showering Bibles on the heathens of Somalia when last heard of.'

'And your friend Quinn?'

'Yeah, well, alas for poor Fergus. Still, I'm told his party's busting to have him back, now it's been slung out of power, past ministerial experience being worth its weight in gold, and so on. Provided he forswears New Labour and all its works, of course, which he's only too happy to do. Wanted to sign up with us, between you and me. On his knees, practically. But I'm afraid, unlike you, he didn't cut the mustard.' A nostalgic smile for old times. 'There's always the defining moment when you start out in this game: do we risk the operation and go in, or do we chicken? You've got paid men standing by, trained up and rarin' to go. You've got half a million dollars' worth of intelligence, your finance in place, crock of gold from the backers if you bring it off, and just enough of a green light from the powers that be to cover your backside, but no more. Okay, there were rumbles about our intelligence sources. When aren't there?'

'And that was *Wildlife*?'

'Pretty much.'

'And the collateral damage?'

'Heartbreaking. Always is. The absolute worst thing about our business. Every time I go to bed, I think about it. But what's the alternative? Give me a Predator drone and a couple of Hellfire missiles and I'll show you what *real* collateral damage looks like. Want to take a stroll in the garden? Day like this, seems a pity to waste the sunshine.'

The room they were standing in was part office, part conservatory. Crispin stepped outside. Toby had no choice but to follow him. The garden was walled and long and laid out in the oriental style, with pebble paths and water trickling down a slate conduit into a pond. A bronze Chinese woman in a Hakka hat was catching fish for her basket.

'Ever heard of a little outfit called Rosethorne Protection Services?' Crispin asked over his shoulder. 'Worth about three billion US at last count?'

'No.'

'Well, bone up on them, I should, because they own us – for the time being. At our present rate of growth, we'll be buying ourselves out in a couple of years. Four, max. Know how many warm bodies we employ worldwide?'

'No. I'm afraid not.'

'Full time, six hundred. Offices in Zurich, Bucharest, Paris. Everything from personal protection to home security to counter-insurgency to who's spying on your firm to who's screwing your wife. Any notion of the sort of people we keep on our payroll?'

'No. Tell me.'

He swung round and, evoking memories of Fergus Quinn, began counting off his fingers in Toby's face.

'Five heads of foreign intelligence services. Four still serving. Five ex-directors of British intelligence, all with contracts in place with the Old Firm. More police chiefs and their deputies than you can shake a stick at. Throw in any odd Whitehall flunky who wants to make a buck on the side, plus a couple of dozen peers and MPs, and it's a pretty strong hand.'

'I'm sure it is,' said Toby politely, noticing how some kind of emotion had entered Crispin's voice, even if it was more the triumphalism of a child than of a grown man.

'And in case you have any remaining doubts that your beautiful Foreign Office career is finished, be so kind as to follow me,' he continued affably. 'Mind?'

*

They are standing in a windowless room like a recording studio with cushioned hessian walls and flat screens. Crispin is playing an extract from Toby's stolen recording to him at high volume, the bit where Quinn is putting the pressure on Jeb:

'. . . *so what I'm saying, Jeb, is, here we are, with the countdown to D-Day already ringing in our ears,* you *as the Queen's soldier,* me *as the Queen's minister . . .'*

'Enough, or more?' Crispin enquires and, receiving no answer, switches it off anyway, and sits himself down in a very modern rocking chair by the console while Toby remembers Tina: Tina, the temporary Portuguese cleaning woman who stood in for Lula while she went on holiday at short notice; Tina who was so tall and conscientious that she polished my grandparents' wedding photograph. If I'd been stationed abroad, it would never have occurred to me that she *wasn't* working for the secret police.

Crispin is rocking himself like someone on a swing, now leaning back, now gently landing with both shoes together on the thick carpet.

'How's about I spell it out?' he asks, and spells it out anyway. 'As far as the dear old FO is concerned, you're fucked. Any time I choose to send them that recording, they'll blow you out of the water. Say *Wildlife* loud enough to them, the poor dears will go wobbly at the knees. Look at what that idiot Probyn got for his trouble.'

Abandoning levity, Crispin braked his rocking chair and frowned theatrically into the middle distance:

'So let's move to part two of our conversation, the constructive part. Here's a package for you, take it or leave it. We have our own in-house lawyers, we do a standard contract. But we're flexible, we're not stupid, we take every case on its merits. Am I reaching you? Hard to tell. We also know all about you, obviously. You own your flat, got a bit from your grandfather, not a lot, not exactly fuck-you money, but you won't starve. The FO currently pays you fifty-eight grand rising to seventy-five next year if you keep your nose clean; no major outstanding debts. You're straight, you screw around where you can, but no wife and veg to tie you down. Long may it last. What else have you got that we like? A good health record, you enjoy outdoors, you're fit, you're solid Anglo-Saxon stock, low-born but you made it through the social lines. You've got three languages and a Class A Rolodex from every country where you've served Her Maj, and we can start you off at twice what she's paying you. There's a golden hullo of ten grand waiting for you on the day you join as an executive vice-president, car of your choice, all the trimmings, health insurance, business-class travel, entertainment expenses. Have I missed anything out?'

'Yes, actually. You have.'

Perhaps in order to avoid Toby's gaze, Crispin treats himself to a 360° turn on the runners of his very modern rocking chair. But when he comes back, Toby is there, still staring at him.

'You still haven't told me why you're frightened of me,' he complains, in a tone of mystification rather than challenge. 'Elliot presides over a fiasco in Gibraltar, but you don't fire him, you keep him where you can see him. Shorty thinks he may want to go public, so you hire him too, although he's a coke-head. Jeb wanted to go *very* public, and wouldn't come aboard, so he had to be suicided. But what have *I* got to threaten you with? Fuck all. So why am I getting an offer I can't refuse? It makes no sense to me. Maybe it does to you?'

Establishing that Crispin prefers to keep his counsel, he rolls on:

'So my reading of your situation would be this: Jeb's death was a bridge too far, and whoever has been protecting you up till now is getting cold feet about protecting you in the future. You want me off the case because, for as long as I'm on it, I'm a danger to your comfort and safety. And actually that's a good enough reason for me to stick with it. So do what you like with the recording. But my guess is you won't do anything with it because you're running scared.'

*

The world has gone into slow motion. For Crispin too? Or only for Toby? Rising to his feet, Crispin sadly assures Toby he's got it all so, so wrong. But no hard feelings, and perhaps when Toby's a few years older, he'll understand the way the real world works. They avoid the embarrassment of shaking hands. And would Toby like a car home? No thank you. Toby would rather walk. And walk he does. Back down the O'Keeffe corridor with its terrazzo tiles, past the half-open doors with young men and women like himself sitting before their computers or bowed into their telephones. He receives his wristwatch, ballpoint pens and notebook from the polite men at the door, then strolls across the gravel circle and past the gatehouse through the open gates, with no sight of Elliot or Shorty or the Audi that brought him here, or of the chase car that followed it. He keeps walking. Somehow it is later than he thought. The afternoon sun is warm and kind, and the magnolias, as ever in St John's Wood at this time of the year, are a perfect treat.

*

Toby never knew in any detail, then or afterwards, how he spent the next few hours, or how many of them there were. That he passed his life in review goes without saying. What else does a man do while he walks from St John's Wood to Islington contemplating love, life and death and the probable end of his career, not to mention gaol?

Emily would still be in surgery, by his calculation, and it was therefore too early to call her, and he didn't know what he was going to say to her if he did, and anyway he had taken the precaution of leaving the silver burner at home, and he absolutely didn't trust phone boxes, even if they worked.

So he didn't call Emily, and Emily later confirmed that he hadn't.

There is no doubt that he stopped at a couple of pubs, but only for the company of ordinary people, since in crisis or despair he refused to drink, and he had a sense of being in the grip of both conditions. A cash ticket later turned up in the pocket of his anorak, indicating that he had bought a pizza with extra cheese. But when and where he had bought it was not given, and he had no recollection of eating it.

And for sure, wrestling with his disgust and anger, and determined as usual to reduce them to a manageable level, he gave due thought to Hannah Arendt's concept of the banality of evil, and launched into a debate with himself about where Crispin fitted into her scheme of things. Was Crispin, in his own perception, merely one of society's faithful servants, obeying market pressures? Maybe that was how he saw himself, but Toby didn't. As far as Toby was concerned, Jay Crispin was your normal, rootless, amoral, plausible, half-educated, nicely spoken frozen adolescent in a bespoke suit, with an unappeasable craving for money, power and respect, regardless of where he got them from. So far, so good. He had met embryonic Crispins in every walk of life and every country where he

295

had served: just never until now one who had made his mark as a trader in small wars.

In a half-hearted effort to find excuses for Crispin, Toby even wondered whether, deep down, the man was just plain stupid. How else to explain the cock-up that was *Operation Wildlife*? And from there, he wandered off into an argument with Friedrich Schiller's grandiose statement that human stupidity was what the gods fought in vain. Not so, in Toby's opinion, and no excuse for anybody, whether god or man. What the gods and all reasonable humans fought in vain wasn't stupidity at all. It was sheer, wanton, bloody indifference to anybody's interests but their own.

And that, so far as will ever be known, was where his mind was drifting as he entered his house, climbed the stairs to his flat, unlocked the door and reached for the light switch, only to have a bundle of wet rag shoved down his throat and his hands wrenched behind his back and bound with plastic strip, and possibly – though he could never be sure, he never saw or afterwards found it, and only remembered it, if at all, by its gluey smell – a piece of prisoner-quality sacking pulled over his head, as a prelude to the worst beating he could have imagined.

Or perhaps – only an afterthought – the sacking was there to mark some sort of no-go area for his assailants, because the one part of his body they left intact turned out to be his face. And if there was any clue, then or later, as to who was administering the beating, it was the unfamiliar male voice with no identifiable regional accent saying 'Don't mark the cunt' in a tone of self-assured, military command.

The first blows were undoubtedly the most painful and the most surprising. When his assailants held him in the lock-grip, he thought his spine was going to snap, then that his neck was. And there was a period when they decided to strangle him, then changed their minds at the last moment.

But it was the hail of blows to his stomach, kidneys, groin and then his groin again that seemed never to end, and for all he knew it continued after he had lost consciousness. But not before the same unidentified voice had breathed into his ear in the same tone of command:

'Don't think this is over, son. This is for appetizers. Remember that.'

*

They could have dumped him on the hall carpet or tossed him on the kitchen floor and left him there but, whoever they were, they had their standards. They needed to lay him out with the respectful care of morticians, pull off his trainers and help him out of his anorak, and make sure there was a jug of water and a tumbler beside him on the bedside locker.

His wristwatch said five o'clock but it had been saying it for some while, so he supposed it had suffered collateral damage during the skirmish. The date was stuck between two numbers, and certainly Thursday was the day he'd fixed to meet Shorty, and therefore the day on which he'd been hijacked and driven to St John's Wood, and perhaps – but who could be sure? – today was Friday, in which case Sally, his assistant, was going to wonder how long his wisdom tooth was going to be acting up. The darkness in the uncurtained window suggested night-time, but whether it was night-time just for him or everybody else as well seemed to be in the balance. His bed was coated with vomit and there was vomit on the floor, both old and recent. He also had a memory of half rolling, half crawling to the bathroom in order to vomit into the lavatory, only to discover, like so many intrepid mountaineers before him, that the journey down was worse than the journey up.

The human and traffic sounds in the street below his window were turned low, but again he needed to know whether this was a general truth or one confined to him alone. Certainly the sounds he was getting were muted sounds, rather than the raucous evening variety – assuming that it was indeed evening. So the more rational solution might be: it was a grey dawn and he had been lying here for anything between, say, twelve to fourteen hours, dozing and vomiting or simply dealing with the pain, which was an activity in itself, unrelated to the passage of time.

It was also the reason why he was only now, by stages, identifying and gradually locating the caterwauling that was issuing from beneath his bed. It was the silver burner howling at him. He had secreted it between the springs and the mattress before setting out to meet Shorty, and why on earth he'd left it switched on was another mystery to him, as it was apparently to the burner, because its howl was losing conviction and quite soon it wouldn't have a howl at all.

Which was why he found it necessary to rally all his remaining strength and roll himself off the bed and crash to the floor where, if in his mind only, he lay dying for a while before making a grab for the springs, then hooking a finger round them and pulling himself up with his left hand, while his right hand – which was numb and probably broken – raked around for the burner, found it and clutched it against his chest, at the same moment as his left hand let go and he thumped back on to the floor.

After that it was only a matter of pressing green and saying 'Hi' with all the brightness he could muster. And when nothing came back and his patience ran out, or his energy did, he said:

'I'm fine, Emily. A bit knackered, that's all. Just don't come round. Please. I'm toxic' – by which he meant broadly that he was ashamed of himself; Shorty had been a washout; he had achieved nothing except the beating of a lifetime; he'd fucked up just like her father; and for all he knew the house was under

298

surveillance and he was the last person on earth that she should be visiting, whether in her capacity as a doctor or anything else.

Then as he rang off he realized that she couldn't come anyway, because she didn't know where he lived, he'd never mentioned it apart from saying Islington, and Islington covered quite a few square miles of dense real estate, so he was safe. And so was she, whether she liked it or not. He could switch the bloody thing off and doze, which he did, only to be woken again, not by the burner but by a thunderous hammering on the front door – done, he suspected, not by human hand but a heavy instrument – which stopped only to allow for Emily's raised voice, sounding very like her mother's.

'I'm standing at your front door, Toby,' she was saying, quite unnecessarily, for the second or third time now. 'And if you don't open it soon, I'm going to ask your downstairs neighbour to help me break into your flat. He knows I'm a doctor and he heard heavy thuds coming through the ceiling. Are you hearing me, Toby? I'm pressing the bell, but it's not ringing so far as I can hear.'

She was right. All the bell was emitting was a graceless burp.

'Toby, can you please come to the door? Just answer, Toby. I really don't want to break in.' Pause. 'Or have you got somebody with you?'

It was the last of these questions that was too much for him, so he said 'Coming' and made sure the zip of his fly was closed before rolling off the bed again and half shuffling, half crawling down the passage on his left side, which was the relatively comfortable one.

Reaching the door, he pulled himself into a semi-kneeling position long enough to get his key out of his pocket and into the lock and double-turn it with his left hand.

*

In the kitchen, a stern silence reigned. The bed sheets were turning quietly in the washing machine. Toby was sitting nearly upright in his dressing gown and Emily with her back to him was heating a tin of chicken soup she had fetched, along with her own prescriptions from the chemist.

She had stripped him and bathed his naked body with professional detachment, noting without comment his grossly swollen genitals. She had listened to his heart, taken his pulse, run her hands over his abdomen, checked him for fractures and damaged ligaments, paused at the chequered lacerations round his neck where they had thought to strangle him and then thought better of it, put ice packs on his bruises and given him Paracetamol for his pain, and helped him limp along the corridor while she held his left arm round her neck and over her shoulder and with her right arm clutched his right hip.

But until now, the only words they'd exchanged had been in the order of 'Do please try to keep still, Toby' or 'This may hurt a bit' and, more recently, 'Give me your door key and stay exactly where you are till I come back.'

Now she was asking the tough questions.

'Who did this to you?'

'I don't know.'

'Do you know *why* they did it to you?'

For appetizers, he thought. To warn me off. To punish me for being nosy and stop me being nosy in future. But it was all too woolly, and too much to say, so he said nothing.

'Well, whoever did it must have used a knuckleduster,' she pronounced, when she had got tired of waiting.

'Maybe just rings on his fingers,' he suggested, remembering Elliot's hands on the steering wheel.

'I shall need your permission before I call the police. Can I call them?'

'No point.'

'Why no point?'

Because the police aren't the solution, they're part of the problem. But again that's something you can't easily put across, so best just let it go.

'It's very possible that you're suffering internal bleeding of the spleen, which can be life-threatening,' Emily continued. 'I need to get you to a hospital for a scan.'

'I'm fine. I'm in one piece. You should go home. Please. They may come back. Honestly.'

'You are *not* in one piece, and you need treatment, Toby,' she replied tartly, and the conversation might have continued along these unproductive lines had not the front doorbell chosen that moment to emit its croak from the rusted tin box above Emily's head.

She stopped stirring the soup and glanced up at the box, then enquiringly at Toby, who started to shrug, thought better of it.

'Don't answer it,' he said.

'Why not? Who is it?'

'No one. Nobody good. Please.'

And seeing her pick up his house keys from the draining board and start towards the kitchen door:

'Emily. It's my house. Just let it ring!'

But it was ringing anyway: a second croak, longer than the first.

'Is it a woman?' she asked, still at the kitchen door.

'There is no *woman*!'

'I can't hide, Toby. And I can't be this afraid. Would you answer it if you were fit and I wasn't here?'

'You don't know these people! Look at me!'

But she refused to be impressed. 'Your neighbour from downstairs probably wants to ask how you are.'

'Emily, for Christ's sake! This isn't about good neighbours.'

But she had gone.

Eyes closed, he held his breath and listened.

He heard his key turn, he heard her voice, then a much softer male voice, like a hushed voice in church, but not one that in his over-attentive state he recognized, although he felt he should.

He heard the front door close.

She's stepped outside to talk to him.

But who the hell is he? Has he *pulled* her outside? Are they coming back to apologize, or to finish the job? Or did they think they might have killed me by mistake, and Crispin has sent them to find out? In the rush of terror that has taken hold of him, all of it is possible.

Still out there.

What's she doing?

Does she think she's fireproof?

What have they done to her? Minutes like hours. *Jesus Christ!*

The front door opening. Closing again. Slow, deliberate foot-steps approaching down the corridor. Not hers. Definitely not Emily's. Too heavy by half.

They've grabbed her and now they're coming for me!

But they were Emily's footsteps after all: Emily being all hospital and purposeful. By the time she reappeared, he had got up from his chair and was using the table to punt himself towards the kitchen drawer to find a carving knife. Then he saw her standing in the doorway, looking puzzled and holding a brown-paper parcel bound in string.

'Who was it?'

'I don't know. He said you'll know what it's about.'

'For fuck's sake!'

Grabbing the parcel, he turned his back on her – actually with the futile intention of protecting her in the event of an explosion – and set to work feverishly feeling the packet for det-onators, timers, nails or whatever else they might have thought to add for maximum effect, very much in the manner in which he had approached Kit's nocturnal letter, but with a greater sense of peril.

But all he could feel, after a lengthy exploration, was a wad of paper and a bulldog clip.

'What did he look like?' he demanded breathlessly.

'Small. Well dressed.'

'Age?'

'Sixtyish.'

'Tell me what he said: his words.'

'"I have a parcel here for my friend and former colleague, Toby Bell." Then something about had he come to the right address –'

'I need a knife.'

She handed him the knife he had been reaching for and he slit the parcel open exactly as he had slit open Kit's, down the side, and took from it a smeared photocopy of a Foreign Office file emblazoned with security caveats in black, white and red. He lifted the cover and found himself gazing incredulously at a clutch of pages held together by a bulldog clip, and written in the neat, unmistakeable handwriting that had followed him from post to post for the last eight years. And on top of them, by way of a covering letter, a single sheet of unheaded notepaper, again in the same familiar hand:

My dear Toby,

It is my understanding that you already have the prelude but not the epilogue. Here, somewhat to my shame . . .

He read no further. Jamming the note to the back of the document, he avidly scanned the top page:

OPERATION WILDLIFE – AFTERMATH AND RECOMMENDATIONS

By now his heart was racing so fast, his breathing so uneven, he wondered whether, after all, he was about to die. Perhaps Emily was wondering too, because she had dropped on her knees beside him.

'You opened the door. *Then* what?' he stammered out, frantically leafing through the pages.

'I opened the door' – gently now, to humour him – 'he stood there. He seemed surprised to see me and asked if you were in. He said he was a former colleague and friend of yours, and he had this parcel for you.'

'And *you* said?'

'I said yes, you *were* in. But you were unwell, and I was your doctor attending you. And I didn't think you should be disturbed, and could I help?'

'And *he* said? – go on!'

'He asked what you were suffering from. I said I was sorry, I wasn't allowed to tell him that without your permission but you were as comfortable as could be expected pending further examination. And I was about to call an ambulance, which I am. Are you hearing me, Toby?'

He was hearing her, but he was also churning his way through the photocopied pages.

'*Then* what?'

'He seemed a bit thrown, started to say something, looked at me again – a bit beadily, I thought – and then he said might he know my name?'

'Give me his words. His actual words.'

'*Jesus*, Toby.' But she gave them anyway: '"Would I be impertinent if I were to ask you your name?" How's that?'

'And you told him your name. You said Probyn?'

'Doctor Probyn. What do you expect me to say?' – catching Toby's stare. 'Doctors are *open*, Toby. Real doctors give their names. Their *real* names.'

'How did he take it?'

'"Then kindly tell him that I admire his taste in medical advisors," which I thought was a bit fresh of him. Then he handed me the package. For you.'

'*Me?* How did he describe me?'

'"For *Toby!*" How the fuck d'you think he described you?'

Fumbling for the note that he had shoved to the back of the photocopied pages, he read the rest of its message:

> . . . *you will not be surprised to learn that I have decided that a corporate life does not, after all, agree with me, and I have accordingly awarded myself a lengthy posting to distant parts.*
>
> > *Yours as ever,*
> > *Giles Oakley.*

> *PS. I enclose a memory stick containing the same material. Perhaps you will add it to the one I suspect you already have. G.O.*
> *PPS. May I also suggest that whatever you propose to do, it is done swiftly since there is every sign that others may act before you? G.O.*
> *PPPS. I shall refrain from our cherished diplomatic custom of renewing my assurances of the highest esteem, since I know they would fall on deaf ears. G.O.*

And in a transparent plastic capsule pasted to the top of the page, sure enough: a memory stick neatly marked SAME DOCUMENT.

*

He was standing at the kitchen window, uncertain how he had got there, craning his neck to look down into the street. Emily stood at his side, one hand to his arm to hold him steady. But of Giles Oakley, the diplomat who does everything by halves and had finally gone the whole hog, there was no sign. But what was the Kwik-Fit van doing, parked just thirty yards away on the opposite side of the street? And why did it take three burly men to change the front wheel of a Peugeot car?

'Emily, please. Do something for me.'

'After I've taken you to hospital.'

'Rummage in the bottom drawer of that chest over there, and find the memory stick of my graduation party at Bristol University. Please.'

While she rummaged, he punted himself along the wall until he came to his desk. With his undamaged hand he switched on the computer and nothing happened. He checked the cable, the mains switch, tried to reboot. Still nothing.

Meanwhile, Emily's rummaging was rewarded. She had found the memory stick, and was holding it aloft.

'I've got to go out,' he said, ungraciously seizing it from her.

His heart was racing again. He felt nauseous, but clear-headed and precise.

'Listen to me, please. There's a shop called Mimi's in the Caledonian Road. Opposite a tattoo parlour called Divine Canvas and an Ethiopian restaurant.' Why was everything so clear to him? Was he dying? From the way she was staring at him, he might as well be.

'What if there is?' she asked him. But his eyes had gone back to the street.

'Tell me first if they're still out there. Three workers talking to each other about bugger all.'

'People in the street talk about nothing all the time. What about Mimi's? Who's Mimi?'

'An Internet café. I need shoes. They've crashed my computer. And my BlackBerry for the addresses. Top-left drawer of my desk. And socks. I'll need socks. Then see if the men are still there.'

She had found his anorak, which was crumpled but otherwise intact, and put his BlackBerry into the left side pocket. She had helped him put on his socks and shoes, and she had checked to see whether the men were still there. They were. She had given up saying 'You can't do this, Toby' and was helping him to shuffle along the corridor.

'Are you sure Mimi will be receiving at this hour?' she asked, in an effort to be light-hearted.

'Just get me down the stairs. Then go. You've done everything. You've been great. Sorry about the mess.'

*

The staircase might have been less of a nightmare if they could have agreed where Emily should place herself: above him to help guide his footsteps, or below to catch him if he plunged? Toby's view was that below him was just bloody silly, she could never support his weight and they'd finish up in the hall on top of each other. Emily riposted that, if he started to fall, yelling in his ear from behind wasn't going to stop him.

But these exchanges came and went in flashes amid the business of manhandling him downstairs and into the street, then speculating – both of them now – why there was a uniformed policeman loitering at the corner of Cloudesley Road, because, these days, whoever saw a lone copper standing on a street corner, looking benign? And – Toby this time – why had the supposed Kwik-Fit team *still* not changed that bloody wheel? But whatever the explanation, he needed Emily out of sight and sound, clear of it all, for her own sake, please, because the last thing on earth he wanted to do was make her into an accomplice, which he explained to her very clearly and at length.

So it surprised him to discover, as he prepared to launch himself into Copenhagen Street for the downhill sprint, that she had not only remained at his side but was actually steering him, and probably holding him up as well, with one hand gripping his forearm with unladylike strength, and her other arm fastened like iron around his upper back, but somehow avoiding the bruising, which reminded him that by now she knew the geography of his body pretty well.

They were at the junction when he stopped dead.

'*Shit.*'

'What's shit?'

'I can't remember.'

'Can't remember *what*, for goodness' sake?'

'Whether Mimi's is left or right.'

'Wait here for me.'

She propped him on a bench and he waited dizzily for her while she made a hasty reconnaissance and returned with the news that Mimi's was a stone's throw away to the left.

But she needed his promise first:

'We get you to hospital as soon as this is done. Deal? *Now* what's the matter?'

'I've got no bloody money.'

'Well, I have. Plenty.'

We're arguing like an old married couple, he thought, and we haven't even kissed each other on the cheek. Perhaps he said it aloud, because she was smiling as she pushed open the door to a minuscule but scrupulously clean shop with a big plywood counter as you entered and nobody behind it and a bar at the far end selling coffee and refreshments and, on the wall, a poster offering to upgrade your PC, health-check it, recover lost data and remove any unfriendly virus. And beneath this poster, six computer booths and six customers perched upright before them, four black men and two blonde women. No booth free, so find somewhere to sit and wait.

So he sat at a table and waited while Emily fetched two teas and spoke to the manager. Then she came and sat down opposite Toby, holding both his hands across the table – not entirely, he wanted to believe, for medical reasons – until one of the men dismounted from his bar stool, leaving a booth free.

Toby's head was reeling and the fingers of his right hand were in bad shape, so it was Emily in the end who was pushing home the memory sticks while he called up the addresses for her from his BlackBerry: *Guardian*, *The New York Times*, *Private Eye*, Reprieve, Channel 4 News, BBC News, ITN, and finally – not quite as a joke – the Press and Information Department of Her Majesty's Foreign and Commonwealth Office.

'And one for my father,' she said, and typed in Kit's email address from memory, and pressed 'send', and included a copy to her mother in case Kit was still sulking in his tent and not opening his emails. Then, belatedly, Toby remembered the photographs that Brigid had let him copy into his BlackBerry, so he insisted Emily send them too.

And Emily was still doing this when Toby heard a siren wailing and thought at first it was the ambulance coming for him, and that Emily must somehow have managed to call for one when he wasn't listening, maybe back at the flat when she was outside his door talking to Oakley.

Then he decided that she couldn't possibly have done that without telling him, because if one thing was certain about Emily, it was that she didn't have an ounce of guile in her bones. If Emily said, 'I'll call for an ambulance when we've done our work at Mimi's,' then that's when she'd be calling for an ambulance and not a second before.

Next he thought: it's Giles they're coming for, Giles has thrown himself under a bus; because when a man like Giles, in his fractured state of mind, tells you he's about to award himself a posting to distant parts, you're entitled to take it any way you want.

Then it began to cross his mind that, by activating his Black-Berry in order to obtain the email addresses and dispatch

Brigid's photographs, he had sent up a signal that anyone with the necessary equipment could home on – he is briefly Beirut Man again – and if the spirit takes them, direct a rocket down the beam and blow the head off the unlucky user.

The sirens multiplied and acquired a more emphatic, bullying tone. At first, they seemed to be approaching from one direction only. But as the chorus grew to a howl, and the car brakes screamed in the street outside, Toby couldn't be certain any more – nobody could be certain, even Emily – which direction they were coming from.

Acknowledgements

My thanks to Danny, Jessica and Callum for enlivening my researches in Gibraltar; to Drs Jane Crispin, Amy Frost and John Eustace for advice on medical matters; to the journalist and writer Mark Urban for giving so freely of his military expertise; to writer, activist and founder of openDemocracy, Anthony Barnett, for educating me in the manners of New Labour in its dying days; and to Clare Algar and her colleagues at the legal charity Reprieve, for instructing me in the British Government's latest assaults on our liberty, whether implemented or planned.

Most of all I must thank Carne Ross, former British foreign servant and founder and director of the not-for-profit Independent Diplomat, who by his example demonstrated the perils of speaking a delicate truth to power. Without Carne's example before me, and his pithy advice in my ear, this book would have been the poorer.